T0243483

PAST CRIMES

PAST CRIMES

Jason Pinter

**SEVERN
HOUSE**

First world edition published in Great Britain and the USA in 2024
by Severn House, an imprint of Canongate Books Ltd,
14 High Street, Edinburgh EH1 1TE.

severnhouse.com

British Library Cataloguing-in-Publication Data
A CIP catalogue record for this title is available from the British Library.

ISBN-13: 978-1-4483-1212-2 (cased)
ISBN-13: 978-1-4483-1213-9 (e-book)

All Severn House titles are printed on acid-free paper.

MIX
Paper from
responsible sources
FSC
www.fsc.org   FSC® C013056

Typeset by Palimpsest Book Production Ltd.,
Falkirk, Stirlingshire, Scotland.
Printed and bound in Great Britain by
TJ Books, Padstow, Cornwall.

Praise for Jason Pinter

"Full-bodied characters in a compelling plot"
Booklist Starred Review of *A Stranger at the Door*

"Pinter's strong depictions of diverse types of love, respect, and
loyalty resonate loudly in this nail-biter novel"
Library Journal on *A Stranger at the Door*

"Pinter does a masterful job of ramping up suspense . . . spinning
an absolutely riveting plot with a cast of
full-bodied, fallible characters"
Booklist Starred Review of *Hide Away*

"Outstanding . . . recalls the works of Harlan Coben and
Linwood Barclay"
Library Journal Starred Review of *Hide Away*

"Pinter has crafted a wonderful mix of a domestic family saga, a
suburban thriller, and a crime novel. It's a blend
of Michael Connelly and Harlan Coben"
Associated Press on *Hide Away*

"Wow – I knew Pinter was good, but not this good"
Lee Child, #1 *New York Times* bestselling author, on *Hide Away*

About the author

Jason Pinter is the internationally bestselling author of the Rachel Marin series, the Henry Parker series, the standalone thriller *The Castle*, and the monster romcom *Dating & Dismemberment* (as A.L. Brody), as well as the children's books *Zeke Bartholomew: Superspy!* and *Miracle*. He has been nominated for numerous awards, including the Thriller, Strand Critics, Barry, Shamus, and more. His books have over 1.5 million copies in print and have been published in over a dozen languages. He has written for numerous outlets including *The New Republic*, *Esquire*, *Spy*, *Entrepreneur*, *The Daily Beast*, and more.

He is the Founder and Publisher of Polis Books, an independent press, as well as its imprint Agora, which is dedicated to under-represented voices. He was named an inaugural Publishers Weekly Star Watch honoree, which recognizes "young publishing professionals who have distinguished themselves as future leaders of the industry." He lives in New Jersey with his wife and two daughters.

www.JasonPinter.com
Twitter/Instagram: @JasonPinter
TikTok: @JerseyBookGuy

'Crime is my passion. My obsession. My vocation. Crime brings us together, giving us a common goal to unite behind the victims and against their aggressors. Crimes thrill us, chill us and mystify us. I want to know how they happened. Why they happened. I want to feel my pulse quicken as I attempt to unravel their mysteries. In a time when our world is fractured and isolated, it is crime that binds us together, that provides a touchstone where we can, once again, feel like a community. By the grace of God, I was born with gifts that allow me to use the future to bring the past to the present. It is my purpose to educate and entertain the world, and if I accomplish that, I will consider mine a life well lived.'

From *Ferryman*: *Life, Death, and
Everything In Between*
the autobiography of Crispin Lake,
Founder of Past Crimes

ONE

On May 13th, 2034, twenty-three-year-old Joy Ruiz disappeared. On July 19th, 2037, Cassie West sat at a table inside an encrypted Lockbox in front of the young woman's grieving family, preparing to tell them how much their daughter's life was worth.

Cassie was not responsible for Joy Ruiz's disappearance, and, in fact, had known nothing about the crime until it gained notoriety as amateur detectives recreated the crime within Earth+, the three-dimensional virtual world previously known as the Metaverse, in order to locate either the girl or her killer. So far, neither had been found.

Over the past decade, the virtual world had replaced the disintegrating physical one, which had come to be known mockingly as Earth−. The growing interest in Joy Ruiz's disappearance convinced Cassie and her superiors at Virtual Criminal Entertainment, or V.I.C.E., that the crime had tremendous licensing potential. Missing girls were, to put it bluntly, worth a hell of a lot of money. The revenue streams from unsolved disappearances could last for decades, and so the competition to license their crimes was fierce. Especially given the strange, riveting circumstances surrounding the disappearance of young Joy Ruiz.

In late 2033, Joy had hit it off with a young man named Jackson Rome at a Skatterbox concert at Virtual Madison Square Garden, or VMSG. Their early communications, which had been subpoenaed by the EPP, or Earth Plus Police, were flirty but chaste. At least in the beginning. In February 2034, Rome rented a Lockbox, a private, encrypted, hack-proof, virtual room within Earth+. Per testimony from Joy's friends, once Joy and Jackson met inside that Lockbox, any pretense of chastity evaporated.

After seventeen Lockbox rendezvous, Joy Ruiz took a bus to Albuquerque to meet Jackson in Earth−. She told her parents she was going hiking with friends to get away from their virtual tethers for a weekend. She confided in several friends, and her brother Hector, that she'd met someone. Jackson was the love of her life,

Joy said, and asked her confidantes to keep it a secret from her parents. They agreed.

Video footage from a ReVolt driverless taxi showed Joy Ruiz in the backseat, and then entering a bar called Carafe for her first 'official' date with Jackson Rome. At seven forty-nine p.m., Joy texted her friend Deondra Watkins: **Here waiting for Jackson. I'm going to explode!**

Deondra texted back: **You have to tell me EVERYTHING.**

Later, Joy replied. **Or maybe tomorrow, depending on how it goes. ;-)**

It was the last text Joy Ruiz ever sent. And it was the last day anyone saw her alive.

It turned out that Jackson Rome was not, in fact, a twenty-four-year-old graduate student at the Virtual University of Austin, but rather a forty-four-year-old divorced father of three named Harold Waltermeyer who had illegally duplicated the Wrap, or avatar, of a Swedish fitness model named Anders Viklund, which he'd worn during his meetings with Joy inside Earth+.

Waltermeyer's attorney successfully argued, in what turned out to be a landmark, precedent-setting case, that encounters between Waltermeyer and Ruiz were digital rather than physical. Ruiz's Wrap was not, in fact, Ruiz herself. And while Wrap Fraud was a Class D felony, Waltermeyer did not face any charges of sexual misconduct.

Security footage from Carafe showed Waltermeyer entering Carafe at seven fifty-five and introducing himself to Ruiz. Within moments, Ruiz and Waltermeyer were having a heated argument, Ruiz clearly expecting Waltermeyer to look like a chiseled twenty-four-year-old and not a paunchy, balding, middle-aged man. Five minutes and forty seconds after arriving at Carafe, Ruiz wiped tears from her eyes, slapped Waltermeyer across the left cheek and left. Ruiz had been wearing an onyx ring, which left a slight laceration just below Waltermeyer's cheekbone. Waltermeyer remained at Carafe for eight minutes after Ruiz left. In that time, he finished a glass of bourbon and dabbed at the cut on his face with a wet napkin. He then paid his tab and left the bar. Joy never made it home.

Harold Waltermeyer had been the primary suspect in Joy's disappearance from the start. He was convicted of Wrap Fraud and given a three-month suspended sentence, barred from altering his

Wrap inside Earth+ and fined $10,000. In the end, Waltermeyer, who had conned Joy Ruiz into both a sexual and emotional relationship, was fined 2.8 percent of his annual salary, spent no time in prison and kept his job.

Joy's body was never found.

As the investigation into Joy's disappearance stalled, the public, believing Waltermeyer's guilt, grew restless. But there was one large problem: despite being a world-class scumbag, Harold Waltermeyer was innocent of Joy's murder.

Security cameras showed that upon leaving Carafe, Waltermeyer went directly to his car. The GPS confirmed that Waltermeyer made no stops prior to arriving home. The EPP subpoenaed Waltermeyer's Earth+ activity log, which confirmed Waltermeyer's testimony that nine minutes after arriving home, he rented a Lockbox where he engaged in virtual sex with an Augmented Persona prostitute named Laffy Taffy, for which he paid $500. Waltermeyer's neighbor, Bernice Hopkins, testified to seeing Waltermeyer through a partially drawn window shade, wearing his Earth+ visor and nothing else.

And so, three years later, with no suspects and no leads, Cassie West sat inside a Lockbox with Joy's mother, father and brother, all of whom had endured unimaginable pain not only to have lost their daughter but still to be waiting for closure that might never come. Having exhausted all their legal options and drained their savings, the Ruiz family was depending on Cassie both to keep the memory of their daughter alive and to throw their family a financial lifeline.

For the past nine years, Cassie had worked as a licensing agent for V.I.C.E., the preeminent licensor of true crimes for entertainment and multimedia within both Earth+ and Earth−. Billions of dollars were spent on true crime licensing every year. Nearly every murder, every disappearance, every notorious grift or tawdry swindle could be monetized, with revenues from the thousands to hundreds of millions, depending on earning potential and the cultural relevance of the case. Cassie believed Joy's disappearance could spark multiple bidders across the crime entertainment spectrum. And both the Ruiz *and* the West families needed that money – badly.

All V.I.C.E. Lockboxes were coded to be soothing: neutral gray walls, white moldings, a crackling fireplace, windows overlooking a realistic stream. Angel and Carmen Ruiz held hands. Their son, Hector, seventeen, hadn't said a word since they entered the Lockbox. Angel and Carmen looked hopeful. Hector looked angry.

'So how exactly does it work?' Carmen asked, gesturing at the tablet in front of Cassie. 'Your company just . . . decides how much our family is worth?'

Cassie offered a sympathetic smile.

'Life is priceless,' Cassie said, with practiced sympathy. 'But your NTPs all have a dollar value. The NTP – or Non-Transferable Persona – Act of 2029 gave every person exclusive rights to their life, likeness and biometrics for media and entertainment purposes. At V.I.C.E., we would like to be the exclusive brokers in charge of licensing everything covered in the NTP Act for your family. We want to license Joy's story – your story. Our proprietary algorithm calculates what we might expect to earn in licensing fees over the first five years of our deal. Please keep in mind that this number is just an estimate. But we've licensed thousands of crimes, and our margin of error when estimating potential revenue is just five-point-eight percent. So the number we give you will be pretty much on the nose.'

Carmen nodded. Angel was staring off somewhere to the right of Cassie's head. His eyes were unfocused. Cassie had been working the Ruiz family for months. Their credit scores were abysmal. When Joy went missing, they could barely afford the $11,500 mortgage on their eighteen-hundred-square-foot colonial. Now, after three years of legal fees and spending hundreds of thousands of dollars plastering Earth+ with interactive 'MISSING' billboards featuring photos and videos of Joy, they were on the precipice of bankruptcy. Angel and Carmen were ready to sign. But their son could throw a wrench in the whole deal.

Hector had refused to speak to Cassie during their preliminary Lockbox discussions and barely hid his anger towards his parents for even entertaining V.I.C.E. Cassie had spent enough time around grieving teenagers to know that Hector's angry façade hid a vulner-able, anguished young man. Unlike his parents, Hector didn't act towards Cassie like she was on their side. He acted like she was there to steal his dog.

Hector Ruiz was a handsome young man, with striking azure eyes, unruly hair and sharp cheekbones. Hector and Joy had been close. She had looked out for her younger brother, had helped him

acclimate to the isolation of virtual learning in Earth+ after Earth−
schools had closed their doors. In turn, Hector had worshipped his
older sister. When Joy went missing, Hector likely blamed himself
for keeping her plans from his parents. For the rest of his life, Hector
would have to live with not just the grief but the guilt. And that
guilt was clearly manifesting itself in rage.

'So?' Carmen said. 'What's the number?'

'One million, five-hundred and forty-seven thousand dollars,'
Cassie said. 'If you agree to let V.I.C.E. license Joy's story, that's
your estimated earning potential from all revenue streams, in both
Earth+ and Earth−, over the next five years.'

She heard Angel take a sharp intake of breath. He looked at his
wife, cocked his head slightly and upturned his lip as if to say,
That's not bad.

'Is that . . . all?' Carmen asked Cassie, slightly disappointed. 'I
just thought it might be more. I'm not saying that amount is nothing,
but this is Joy's life. Her *life*. That figure would barely cover our
outstanding legal bills.'

'But it *would* cover them,' Angel replied. Then he turned to
Cassie. 'Isn't there a chance for more?'

'The hard truth is that the middle ground for crime licensing has
fallen off,' Cassie said. 'Companies will open their pockets for the
most infamous crimes, the home runs, the blockbusters. It's a buyer's
market for the rest. And Joy's story is—'

'One of the rest,' Hector said. Cassie said nothing.

'How exactly did your algorithm come to that figure?' Angel
asked.

'Our estimate factors in the current true crime marketplace and
the circumstances of Joy's disappearance, then compares it to
revenue earned from comparable crimes. Think of it like real estate.
You're seeing what other crimes in that neighborhood have sold for.
I could definitely see one of the ninety-seven streaming services
producing a series, scripted or unscripted.'

'So they hire actors to play us,' Hector said. 'How much money
will the suits who own those companies make? A lot more than
Joy's family makes, I'll bet.'

'Hector,' Carmen said. 'Please.'

'So we pay off lawyers while other people buy homes made from
real wood. Not the tissue paper our house is made with.'

'Hector,' Angel said.

'Even if it does just cover your bills,' Cassie said, 'wouldn't it be nice for your family to have a clean slate?'

'We have been struggling,' Angel said, both to Cassie and his son. 'Clearing our debts would be a weight off our shoulders.'

'Yes, it would,' Cassie said, thinking about her family's own mountainous debts. On the outside, Cassie was portraying effortless confidence. On the inside, she was terrified. She couldn't afford to lose a commission. Not now. Not with—

'How far along are you?'

The question from Carmen snapped Cassie to attention. She hadn't even realized it, but she had been absently rubbing her stomach.

'Twelve weeks,' she replied with a smile.

'Boy or girl?'

'We want to be surprised,' Cassie said. 'I turned off the Gender Reveal settings on my OvuWatch.'

'So what color are you going to decorate the nursery?' Angel asked.

'Right now, the living room is her nursery,' Cassie said with a laugh. 'Our house is barely big enough for my husband and me.'

'I thought you crime agents all raked it in,' Hector said, surprised.

'Some do,' Cassie said. 'But it's like the crimes we license. A blockbuster could set you up for life. Most of us are just trying to make ends meet.'

'Well,' Carmen said, 'I hope your baby brings you a lifetime of joy.'

'Thank you, Mrs. Ruiz.'

'This is all such bullshit,' Hector said.

'Take it easy,' Angel said. 'Mrs. West is here to help us.'

'No, she's here to make money off of Joy. Off our pain. A million and a half dollars. That's, what, like sixty grand for every year Joy was alive? And how much do *you* make? How much do your *bosses* make?' Hector's eyes bored holes into Cassie, venom dripping from his words.

'It's a way to keep Joy alive,' Angel said.

'You're such a hypocrite,' Hector snarled at his father. 'If you'd shown the slightest bit of interest in Joy's life, she would have told you about Waltermeyer. You could have found out who he really was before she met him and you could have stopped her. *That's* how you could have kept Joy alive.'

'Harold Waltermeyer didn't kill your sister,' Carmen said.

'If Joy hadn't gone to meet him, we wouldn't be here talking to this vampire.'

'I'm sorry, Mrs. West,' Angel said. 'Hector doesn't speak for all of us.'

'Speaking of Harold Waltermeyer,' Carmen said to Cassie, 'I know if we sign this, it gives you rights to use our likenesses and biometrics. But what about Waltermeyer? He surely hasn't agreed to all this, has he?'

'He doesn't need to,' Cassie said. 'Statute 486-16 states that upon being convicted of a felony, even posthumously, the subject's likeness and biometrics enter into the public domain. In short, we can use Waltermeyer however we want. And he'll never see a dime.'

Angel looked at Cassie and said, 'Look, we appreciate all of this. But other agencies have suggested we could get more.'

'If other people have made you guarantees, they're lying,' Cassie said, trying not to let desperation seep into her voice. 'Nobody has the connections or resources like we do.'

'What about Past Crimes?' Carmen said. 'Wouldn't it mean a lot more money if Past Crimes produced an Earth+ sim based on Joy's disappearance? You say V.I.C.E. has all these connections, what about Crispin Lake at Past Crimes?'

'Now that *would* change our lives,' Angel said. 'I've been a subscriber for ten years. I must have spent a hundred hours in the DeFeo house when Past Crimes launched their *Amityville Murders* sim. Having the chance to be *inside* that house, to find the bodies just like the police did. It was like I was trying to solve the crime myself. What if Past Crimes created a sim based on Joy's disappearance? Can you make that happen?'

Every potential client asked this question. Cassie knew she had to respond delicately.

'Past Crimes is the absolute gold standard when it comes to criminal entertainment. Everyone who thinks they have the next blockbuster crime wants to work with them.'

'Have *you* ever worked with them?' Angel asked.

'I was actually part of the team at V.I.C.E. that put together the deal for the Gerald Boone murders sim.'

'*You* licensed the Gerald Boone murders?' Angel asked, awed.

'Me and half a dozen colleagues,' Cassie said. 'But the fact is Past Crimes gets pitched a thousand crimes a day. And yes, if Crispin

Lake decided to license a Past Crimes sim based on Joy's disappearance, we'd be looking at eight figures easy, plus royalties. We'll pitch them, as we do with most crimes. But I don't want to get your hopes up, given how selective they are about the material they pursue.'

'Material,' Hector said. 'You mean my sister.'

'You really don't think Crispin Lake would be interested in Joy's story?' Carmen said. 'I mean, that would change everything. They have, what, a hundred million subscribers?'

'A hundred and twenty, give or take,' Cassie said. 'Look, Past Crimes is the Harry Winston of interactive criminal entertainment. The Gerald Boone killings were national news for months. Past Crimes only produces sims for crimes that have achieved global notoriety. Cultural impact. Crimes that will be talked about for years. Think Bundy. Dahmer. Mills and Hall. With all due respect, I just don't think Crispin Lake would consider Joy's disappearance *big* enough.'

'Fuck you,' Hector said, bolting up and knocking his chair over. 'You're saying my sister doesn't matter?'

'That is not what I'm saying, and I apologize if that's how it came across,' Cassie said calmly. She had to be careful. She had so much riding on this . . . 'My job will be to work for your family. But I will never lie to you. We pitch Past Crimes twenty times a day. We have a good sense of what crimes attract Crispin Lake. Hector, I know how much you love your sister.' Cassie made sure to say *love* and not *loved*. She'd made that mistake before and it had nearly cost her a lucrative contract. 'I can't change what's happened. But I can change the future for your family.'

Carmen smiled and put her hand on Angel's arm. They looked at each other. Cassie knew they were sold.

'So what do we do now?' Angel asked.

'If sign this agreement, I will dedicate myself to your family and put all of V.I.C.E.'s considerable resources to maximize the revenue of this crime.'

'Maximize the revenue of this crime,' Hector said acidly. 'Fuck you, blood banker.'

Hector stood up and spat on the floor, and his Wrap disappeared from the Lockbox, leaving Cassie alone with Carmen and Angel.

'I'm sorry,' Carmen said. 'Hector is in a lot of pain.'

'I understand,' Cassie said. 'I can't make his pain go away. But

I can take some weight off your shoulders to help your son get the help he needs.'

Angel thought for a moment, then said, 'Because Hector is a minor, don't we have the legal authority to license his likeness and biometrics?'

'You do,' Cassie said.

Angel turned to Carmen. She nodded and said, 'Where do we sign?'

Cassie took off her visor, exhaled and smiled. The Ruiz family was signed, sealed and delivered. On Monday she would put together her interactive sales packet and start pitching. She would send a copy over to Past Crimes, but she knew the chances of them licensing Joy's story were slim to none.

She was no longer inside the soothing confines of the Lockbox but seated at her narrow desk at the regional V.I.C.E. headquarters. Cassie sat in Row R, Seat 12. There were 350 agents working out of this location, all trying to sign and sell crimes every day, all day.

All around her, agents sat at their desks wearing Earth+ visors and contained within plastic IMPUs, or Individual Microbe Prevention Units. IMPUs were mandatory in most office settings, preventing employees from sharing oxygen and germs, even if it did make them look as though they were sitting inside a giant, clear umbrella.

Most of the agents had on Earth+ visors and were either meeting with clients inside company Lockboxes or pitching crimes to one of the thousands of entertainment outlets that were starving for content. While ninety percent of the populace worked remotely due to the accessibility of Earth+, V.I.C.E. mandated in-person attendance. This way, they could track their employees' efficiency. There was too much money at stake to allow for complacency, and working remotely increased the chances of a security breach. V.I.C.E. had a 97/3 rule: ninety-seven percent of your day had to be spent actively working. The other three percent could be spent on bathroom breaks, chatting about non-work-related issues with coworkers, or the nebulous 'thinking'. If your rolling average slipped below ninety-seven percent, well, V.I.C.E. had no shortage of applicants.

The walls of the V.I.C.E. licensing floor were covered in screens: news broadcasts, police channels, court cases being tried in both Earth+ and Earth−. As Cassie surveyed the onslaught of information,

something ate at her. The two words Hector Ruiz spat before
he left.

Blood banker.

She'd been called that before, and it stung every time. Cassie
took a deep breath and composed herself. Hector was just an angry
kid. She couldn't let it get to her.

Lenny Ames at the adjacent desk removed his visor and turned
to Cassie.

'So?' he said. 'Did you get the Ruiz family?'

'Signed, sealed and delivered.'

'Way to go,' Lenny said. 'I know you've been working them for
a while.'

'Six months. For a while, I was worried Murder, Incorporated
would land them.'

'Those amateurs have nothing on you,' Lenny said. 'Better put
aside some of that Ruiz commission for the baby-to-be. Hey, did
you hear Simone has a meeting with Past Crimes about the Drayden
Downs murders?'

'No,' Cassie said through gritted teeth, 'I hadn't heard.'

'Yeah. It hasn't made it all the way up to Crispin Lake yet, but
it's the first step. 'You ever meet him? Crispin Lake?'

'Only in Earth+,' Cassie replied. 'When the Gerald Boone simulation launched, Past Crimes held a virtual reception in a Lockbox
designed to look like the ranch where Boone embalmed his victims.
Lake was there. Our Wraps made small talk.'

'I heard Lake doesn't leave the Past Crimes complex. He talks
to maybe three people in Earth–, but otherwise doesn't deal with
anybody in person. Like a mob boss or something. Keeps himself
insulated.'

'Not many mob bosses run multi-billion-dollar entertainment
companies.'

'True,' Lenny said. 'Imagine the commission Simone is looking
at on the Drayden Downs license if Past Crimes picks it up.
Life-changing.'

Cassie felt no small amount of jealousy. The Drayden Downs
case was national news. The license would be rich, and the commission would be life-changing. It could wipe out Cassie's debt in one
fell swoop. Give her and Harris their own clean slate.

Just then, Cassie saw a red light appear above a workstation in
the P section. A woman wearing a V.I.C.E. uniform hustled down

the aisle pushing a beverage cart, made a sharp left and stopped in front of the desk. She poured a cup of brown liquid into a cup and handed it to the agent through a slot in her IMPU. The agent drank it greedily.

'You ever drink that stuff?' Lenny asked her.

'Nope. Knock wood, I've never had a Neural Flare. You?'

'Had a minor one a couple of years back,' Lenny said. 'Stuff tastes like salty syrup mixed with motor oil.'

'What did the flare feel like?'

'Like my brain suddenly caught fire. I was pulling eighteen-hour days before my twins were born. Trying to close as many deals as possible before my expenses skyrocketed.'

'I know what you mean,' Cassie said. She'd been pulling fourteen-hour days since getting pregnant. And she would likely have to ramp it up.

Hyponatremia was a common occurrence among V.I.C.E. employees. The more time you spent inside Earth+, the more suscept-ible you were to Hyponatremia, and if Hyponatremia went untreated it could lead to a Neural Flare. A bad Neural Flare could leave you . . . Cassie didn't want to think about it.

When the concept of the Metaverse first gained steam, many laughed it off. Others jumped in with both feet (and boatloads of cash). Optimists saw it as the next digital frontier, a video game with no boundaries or limits. Pessimists considered the Metaverse nothing more than *The Sims* meets *Dilbert*. The truth was somewhere in the middle.

Investors quickly realized the problem with the Metaverse wasn't one of functionality or potential, but of branding. Once they began referring to the virtual space as Earth+, everything kicked into gear.

Companies spent trillions of dollars buying space within Earth+, curating virtual stores, building virtual neighborhoods, and creating new, immersive forms of entertainment that put the first few itera-tions of virtual reality to shame. Many companies closed down their physical spaces entirely, migrating entire workforces into the virtual world.

As Earth+ expanded – and entertainment venues in the real world shuttered – the demand for a constant, fresh flow of virtual enter-tainment had skyrocketed. There were no more movie theaters. No more concert venues or sporting events. There were, however,

ninety-seven streaming networks and hundreds of Earth+ entertainment companies. Entertainment companies needed a constant
influx of content to keep subscribers happy and paying, and they
needed all of it *yesterday*. Every day was another battle in the multi-
trillion-dollar war for entertainment. And no entertainment sector
had grown with such ferocity, and revenue growth, as crime.

For years, the criminal entertainment sector had been dependent
on books, movies, podcasts and television shows. And while those
remained popular, people wanted *more*. It was no longer enough to
just watch or listen. People wanted to *experience*.

In her nine years with V.I.C.E., Cassie had licensed seventy-two
crimes for a shade over $119 million. The Ruiz deal would most
likely put her over one-twenty. Her commission was one percent of
revenue, which meant if she hit her goals on the Ruiz deal, she'd
stand to make fifteen grand. It wasn't much. Wouldn't pay the
mortgage for a month on their two-bedroom house. And their debts
were mounting. One thing a criminal licensing agent could *not* do
was rest. There were only so many blockbuster crimes to go around,
and Cassie had many, many competitors – many of whom worked
for the same company.

She thought about the child growing inside of her. It had taken so
much to get to this point. She wanted everything to be perfect. She
wanted to build a life for her baby, but fifteen grand in 2047 couldn't
even furnish a room.

Cassie checked her watch. It was nearly eight. Ordinarily, she'd
stay another hour, hour and a half, but she'd end the week on a
high note. She stood up, released her IMPU and stretched.

Then on one fifteen-foot-high screen, a red **Breaking News**
banner flashed with the headline: **Babysitter questioned for murder
of parents, kidnapping of children under her care.** Immediately
twenty agents put on their visors.

'Gotta chase the crime,' Lenny said. 'You?'

'Don't think so. Want to end the day on a high note.'

'Slacker,' Lenny said. His watch vibrated, and Lenny's eyes
widened in fear. 'Crap. I'm at ninety-eight percent for the day and
I need to save up for a bathroom break later.' He put his visor on.
'Say hi to Harris for me.'

'I will. See you Monday.'

Cassie got up to leave but felt something in her abdomen that
made her stop in her tracks.

Was that . . . could it be?

No. It was too early. But then she felt it again. Her hand went to her mouth. She took out her phone and texted Harris.

I think I felt the baby kick.

She'd waited what felt like a lifetime to experience that sensation. Now, all she wanted to do was get home and place Harris's hand on her belly. Even if she could feel the kicks, it was probably too early for him to feel anything on the outside. But she didn't care. Cassie's heart was so full she could barely take it.

She looked at Lenny, going into Earth+ in the hopes of landing licensing rights for the evil babysitter. That story was worth money. Maybe a lot more than fifteen grand. Her baby was worth the time. So Cassie went back to her desk, sat down and texted Harris.

Home late. Sorry, babe.

He didn't respond. Didn't matter. Cassie was chasing the crime.

She left work at nine. Harris hadn't responded to her text. Cassie felt a twinge of disappointment and impatience. She checked her biometric watch. Based on her hCG levels, the baby was due in mid-January. That wasn't much time. V.I.C.E. offered three weeks of paid maternity leave, more generous than most employers.

Cassie and Harris had been trying to conceive for three years. After exhausting all natural options and nearly exhausting their marriage, they had made the difficult decision to take out a loan from the Replenish program. The country's birth rates had been in steep decline for a decade, with four percent of the population leaving the United States and the number of families on welfare doubling following the Forced Birth Act of 2028. In a twist that surprised only the government, the act merely succeeded in lowering the birth rate further.

In order to both halt the slide and increase revenue, the government began offering high-interest loans on fertility treatments, medications, supplements, fertility-related surgeries, surrogacy, vitamins of questionable effectiveness and even dating app subscriptions for low-income singles. Cassie and Harris had borrowed nearly a quarter of a million dollars from Replenish. Their current interest payments were higher than their mortgage. And while they knew taking the loan meant they'd be digging themselves out of a financial hole for the rest of their lives, the incalculable joy of having the family they'd prayed for was worth the debt.

The Replenish agreement stated that if the loans were not paid off by the time the borrower expired (i.e. kicked the bucket), all remaining debts would transfer to the borrower's next of kin, a sword of Damocles hanging over them not only for the rest of their lives, but beyond. Cassie couldn't help but wonder if someone in the government was secretly proud of themselves for finally figuring out a way to get children into debt before they'd even been born.

Cassie would not let that happen to her child.

Now more than ever, every dollar counted. They needed more space. They needed a nursery. And they needed money for all of it.

Cassie stopped at an intersection and eyed her wedding ring. Harris had spent $1,500 on the platinum band, within which was embedded a 0.2-carat diamond. It wasn't a big stone, but it still sparkled in the right light. The market for physical diamond rings had all but evaporated, but the market for rings within Earth+ was robust. A one-carat, non-fungible Harry Winston virtual diamond ring ran upwards of fifty grand. Celebrities and influencers made millions wearing custom virtual rings in Earth+. But there was something about feeling the infinitesimal weight on her finger that meant more to Cassie. Her ring was much more than a status symbol.

Cassie texted Harris again. No response. Harris had been acting strange the last few weeks. He'd seemed distant. Distracted. Almost sad, sometimes. Two years ago, Harris had taken on a new job as a UI, or User Interface, freelancer for Earth+-based companies. With the ever-expanding virtual playground, good people like Harris were always in demand. His clients were always ultra-secretive, bordering on paranoid, and their draconian NDAs prevented Harris from even telling his wife exactly who he was working for. Many required Harris to use a thumb-sized Skin Reader before beginning work, a small device Harris kept on his desk that essentially functioned as a remote biometric lie detector test. *Have you spoken about your work with any third parties? Have you kept the details of your work confidential?* Etc., etc., etc. If he failed, he'd be out of a job before he took his next breath. It was a brave new world, but with billions of dollars at stake and companies fighting tooth and nail for every piece of the virtual pie, trust was in high demand and short supply.

She worried Harris was working too much. He spent fifteen hours a day inside Earth+. His eyes were constantly bloodshot, his skin pale, and she could tell he'd lost a few pounds. She couldn't remember the last time he'd been outside. She worried he could be suffering from Hyponatremia, but he claimed it was just a busy stretch at work. God, they needed a break. But with a baby on the way and debt accumulating, she had no idea when – or if – they would ever get one.

Half an hour into her commute, Cassie's irritation had turned into worry. Harris never took this long to respond. She called his cell. No answer. She texted him again.

Everything OK? Please just respond.

Still nothing. She turned the radio on. Something to distract her. *Nebraska* by Bruce Springsteen was playing. She smiled. Her grandfather had loved the oldies and knew every Springsteen song by heart. Cassie used to roll her eyes as he sang along, but as she got older, she began to appreciate it, even watching old concerts from back when people still went in person. She had a soft spot for this song and found herself entranced by the darkly beautiful, doomed romance between Caril Ann Fugate and Charles Starkweather, who killed eleven people back in the 1950s.

Cassie merged on to the highway. Half the road was occupied by cars, the other by people riding high-density steel commuter bicycles. The energy crisis had led to bikes becoming more popular than ever, with many people forced to pedal twenty or more miles each way to work. Cassie had biked ten miles to the V.I.C.E. offices every day for nine years until she got pregnant. The first trimester had been rough. Her iron levels were low, her doctor forbidding her from riding more than five minutes a day. So they bought the cheapest used ReVolt they could find at $84,000 – adding even more to their insurmountable debt.

The streets were full of abandoned buildings too expensive to raze, overgrown trees, and sidewalks with grass and weeds poking through cracks in the cement. Cranes hovered like rusted-out sentries over half-finished buildings. When materials and fuel became too expensive, builders simply abandoned sites already in progress. When she was a girl, Cassie used to marvel at the beauty of the world around her. But as the economy of the virtual world superseded that of the physical one, the real world fell into disrepair, the streets darkening as more and more businesses shuttered.

Parks that were once carpeted with freshly mowed grass, full of yapping dogs and laughing children, with shady trees perfect for a good book and a cold drink, became mangy and unkempt. The lawns in Earth+ were cheap to mow, virtual dogs were cheaper than real ones (not to mention the cost of carpet cleaning), and as cities and towns became isolated, it didn't matter what condition the highways were in. Having a pizza dropped down your chute by a delivery drone was faster, cheaper and safer than eating in a restaurant. Cassie and Harris both remembered the way things used to be, but their child would be born into a world that almost didn't exist on the surface.

Cassie heard the sound of drone rotors overhead, drowning out Bruce Springsteen's voice. She looked up and saw an ACM flying through the sky, its water bladder slowly expanding. ACMs, or Atmospheric Condensation Machines, had been used by local fire departments for the last fifteen years. ACMs took in ambient air and, using technology that was similar to dehumidifiers, cooled it over coils in order to produce moisture that filled their expandable bladders.

At first, ACM technology had been developed to provide drinking water to developing countries. However, making the water potable required distillation, which was too expensive, and so the initiative was scrapped. But some genius realized that the water ACMs created could be used to fight fires from the sky. Plus, ACMs didn't require pensions or medical insurance, and they never sued over injuries sustained on the job.

Then Cassie saw another ACM whizz by. Both ACMs seemed to be heading in the same general direction as Cassie. *Just a coincidence*, she thought. Still, a bad feeling gnawed at her insides. It was a humid day, which meant there was a lot of moisture in the air for the ACMs to draw from. Hopefully, the fire could be put out before anybody got hurt.

When Cassie saw the third ACM following the path of the first two, the gnawing in her stomach turned into a buzzsaw. Then a fourth ACM appeared. And a fifth. Suddenly, Cassie felt nauseous. Sweat began to trickle down her back. She pressed down on the accelerator.

'Call Harris,' Cassie said. The dashboard showed Harris's face as it dialed.

On the second ring, the phone picked up. Harris's image appeared on the Dashboard Holographic Projector, blurry and with a strange green tint. The DHPs on newer cars projected a near-perfect hologram on to the dashboard. In their 2032 ReVolt, images looked like puke-colored gummy bears. Cassie breathed a sigh of relief. Harris was OK.

'Hey, babe,' she said. 'I've been trying to reach you. Is everything—'

Then she noticed that the image was flickering all around Harris. She knew the DHP was a piece of crap, but she'd never seen it do that before. There had to be something wrong with the reception. The flickering was yellow and orange. In fact, it looked like . . .

Cassie's breath caught in her throat.

Were those . . . flames?

They were. Cassie cried out. Fire raged all around Harris, licking at the walls and climbing the ceiling.

The ACMs. Jesus Christ. They were heading towards their home. Their house was on fire. And Harris was inside.

'Oh my God, Harris! What's going on? Get out of there!'

'Cassie,' Harris said. His voice crackled but was scarily even. 'Cassie, I just want you to know that I love you. I'm sorry. This is what's best for you and our baby.'

'What are you talking about? Harris, just get out of there! *Harris!*'

Harris said, 'Forgive me. I . . .' He seemed to stumble over the words, like he was repeating something off a teleprompter. 'I am a beacon.'

'A beacon? Harris, what's going on? Please just talk to me.'

'Goodbye, Cassie.'

'Please, Harris. Whatever is happening, we can get through it together. As a family. *Just get out.*'

He shook his head. 'I can't. It's too late. I love you. Both of you. Forever. Remember me like it was yesterday. Promise me that.'

'Why? *Harris!* Talk to me!'

The DHP ended its transmission. Harris's image disappeared.

'Call nine-one-one,' Cassie shouted, tears streaming down her face. The second the operator picked up, Cassie shouted, 'My name is Cassandra West. My husband, Harris, is at home and there's a fire . . . oh God, just please send someone *now*!'

'Mrs. West?' the dispatcher said. 'Cassandra Ann West of Forty-four Otter Creek Drive?'

'Yes, that's me.'

'Mrs. West, we're already there. Forty-four Otter Creek Drive, correct?'

The ACMs. She was right. They were heading to her home.

'That's right.'

'We have multiple ACMs and trucks at your home. Mrs. West, I can see by your GPS that you're one mile south of Exit 37. I'd like you to pull off and park at the ReVolt charging station. It'll be on your right as you exit the highway. I'll send a unit there to meet you.'

'I don't want to pull over. I want to get home. Please get my husband out of the house!'

'Mrs. West, I'm asking you to pull off the road. You shouldn't go home. You need to—'

'The hell with you,' Cassie said. 'End call.'

Two more ACMs flew overhead. She veered on to the shoulder, nearly clipping a pair of cyclists. She swerved through two lanes of traffic, cutting off cars and bikes, ignoring the horns and bells. She was just over three miles from their house. Every second on the road felt like a lifetime. She tasted salt as tears slid into her mouth. She didn't have time to wipe them away.

Move, goddamnit, she thought, as the SUV in front of her moseyed towards the intersection at the speed of a sedated tortoise. Cassie blared her horn, then drove on to the shoulder, her front right tire slipping into a ditch and spraying mud over a group of bikers.

She tried Harris's cell again. Nothing.

Four achingly long minutes later, Cassie pulled on to Otter Creek Drive. This all had to be a mistake. A joke. A misunderstanding. She would throw open the door to their cramped two-bed, two-bath home and find Harris waiting for her, and they would kiss, and he would place his hand on her stomach and the baby would kick, and in that moment, it would all be forgotten.

Then Cassie saw their house and that dream evaporated. She opened her mouth to scream, but the only thing that came out was an anguished wail.

Their home was engulfed in flames. Orange and red fingers poked through holes in the roof, as though trying to reach the heavens. Smoke rose in the night sky. It was as if hell itself had descended over their home.

ACMs hovered above the blaze, dousing the disintegrating roof. At least twenty firefighters were combating the fire from the street. Cassie could see dozens of people pushing up against the police barricades with their cell phones out and visors on, live-broadcasting the inferno direct from Earth+.

Cassie sprinted towards her house. She could smell the acrid smoke. She felt like she was running straight into a furnace, the heat singeing her skin, scorching her bones.

'*Harris! Harris!*' she screamed. One of her heels got caught in a crack in the road, and suddenly Cassie was falling forward, her body slamming against the asphalt. The world spun. She was dizzy but managed to get to her feet. Her hands immediately went to her stomach as she stumbled forward.

'*Harris!*' she screamed. Her shoe came off, rocks biting into her heel. A young cop with red hair and freckles wrapped his arms around her and pulled her back. She tried to wriggle out of the cop's grasp, but he was stronger than he looked.

'Ma'am, you can't go in there! You have to stay back; it's too dangerous!'

'Let go of me! That's–that's my home!' Cassie said. Her mouth had gone dry, her tongue heavy, the words slipping out, barely audible. 'My husband is inside!'

The cop's eyes widened. He turned back and shouted, 'Lieutenant, I have a woman here saying this is her house. What should I do?'

An ashen-faced cop with a thick brown mustache shouted, 'Keep her there! Don't let her near the fire!'

Another cop ran up, her face pale. 'Lieutenant,' she said, 'I just got off with my brother in the St. Louis PD. He's saying they have reports of half a dozen house fires. They ran out of ACMs.'

The lieutenant replied, 'I have reports of dozens of fires all across the state.'

'Why was the EPP here before we were?' the young cop said. 'Don't they only handle Earth+ crimes? Why would they be at the scene of a house fire?'

'I have no idea,' the lieutenant said. 'Something is going on. I've never seen the EPP respond to a call before us. How the hell is this fire connected to Earth+?'

'Let me go,' Cassie pleaded, trying to pry the young cop's arms from around her. 'My husband needs help!'

They ignored Cassie. The lieutenant looked up at the ACMs. 'Forensic imaging detected residue from an accelerant, which means the house was primed to go up fast. We can't get a good thermal reading due to the fire, so we can't tell if there are any more civilians inside. Keep the bystanders back. And keep your mouths *shut*. Half the neighborhood is live-broadcasting this fire, and conspiracy nuts in Earth+ will have a field day with the EPP on scene.'

Cassie tried to free herself, but the young cop held her tight. Too tight.

'Let me *go*!' she shouted. 'Please, somebody get my husband out!'

'Miss, *please* hold still,' the cop said.

'Don't let her go near the house,' the lieutenant said, jabbing a finger at Cassie. 'We don't need her contaminating an open arson investigation. The foundation is disintegrating. We can't have the widow running into a possible collapse.'

Cassie looked into the lieutenant's eyes. Her strength left her. The word echoed in her head.

Widow. Widow. Widow.

The lieutenant saw her eyes and realized what he'd said. He put his hand on Cassie's shoulder and said, 'Oh, ma'am, I'm so sorry. I thought somebody already told you.'

Cassie cut the lieutenant off with a bloodcurdling scream. The young cop covered his ears and Cassie managed to slip from his grasp. She ran towards the house, screaming, '*Harris!*'

Then Cassie felt hands grip her shoulders and she was yanked backwards. She tried to wrench herself free, but someone slammed her face first on to the asphalt. The air left her lungs, and she felt an awful pain in her stomach. She tried to scream, but her mouth was full of dirt and blood. Cassie lay bleeding on the ground, fading in and out of consciousness, the ashes of her life drifting down around her.

TWO

March 30th, 2047

PAST CRIMES ANNOUNCES SIMULATION
BASED ON 'THE BLIGHT'
The Largest Mass Murder-Suicide in Half a Century to
Become Newest Earth+ Sensation
by Reggie Davenport, Earth+ Features Editor

At the end of the eighteenth annual CrimeCon, Past Crimes founder Crispin Lake sent millions of fans into hysterics when he closed out the hugely popular convention by announcing that the next Earth+ simulation would be none other than the Blight, the global cult murder-suicide that claimed the lives of 1,764 people on July 19th, 2037, one of the most cataclysmic days in modern history.

In a thirty-second teaser, set to Frédéric Chopin's 'Funeral March', Lake showcased a chilling sizzle reel from their upcoming simulation, including scenes from inside the mysterious Church of the Beacons, and the home at 44 Otter Creek Drive where Harris West, the 'Vertex Ignis', or 'Head Flame', radicalized hundreds around the world only to lead them to their deaths.

The brainchild of enigmatic billionaire Crispin Lake, Past Crimes is the multi-billion-dollar criminal entertainment juggernaut that has produced dozens of interactive experiences based on the most famous – and infamous – crimes in history. For the first time, your Wrap could sit next to Abraham Lincoln at Ford's Theatre as John Wilkes Booth stepped through the door, pistol in hand, listen to Jim Jones sermonizing in person at the Peoples Temple, buy a chocolate ice cream cone from John Wayne Gacy's ice-cream truck, or watch Gerald Boone dig seventeen graves for seventeen women he'd embalmed at his Idaho ranch.

At the grand finale of their week-long CrimeCon convention broadcast live in Earth+, flanked by Augmented Personas of the most infamous real-life killers, kidnappers, charlatans, and deviants in history, Crispin Lake unveiled the Augmented Persona of none other than the Vertex Ignis himself, Harris West. According to Lake, the Blight simulation will launch at midnight on July 19th, 2047, to mark the tenth anniversary. Past Crimes will also host an extravagant in-person Earth– celebration at the company's Murderland theme park in West Valley City, Utah.

'The Blight was a day that changed the world,' Lake said, standing at a podium bearing the ubiquitous Past Crimes logo of a black silhouetted outline of a crime scene victim against a red background, receding into dozens of smaller and smaller silhouettes, giving the impression of a crime echoing into the past.

Lake was bookended by Stephen Woolman, the company's Chief Technology Officer, and Maurice Wyatt, their Head of Security. 'So much about the Blight has remained a mystery, as do the motives of the self-proclaimed "Beacons" who followed Harris West and lit the fatal fires. We will bring you into the lives and homes of those "Beacons" and give you unprecedented access to the "Vertex Ignis" himself.'

'You will be able to step inside the virtual Church of the Beacons where Harris West preached his twisted gospel. And by launching on the tenth anniversary of the Blight, we hope to reinvigorate interest in this monumental event, while paying our respects to the thousands whose lives were irrevocably changed that day, and the millions, if not billions of us – myself included – who were shaken to their core.'

'As our fans know, we pride ourselves on creating the most life-like, realistic, and accurate Augmented Personas in the world. Our simulated Harris West is no exception. Our Blight simulation will be the definitive word on one of the most infamous, perplexing, tragic, and fascinating days in human history. We have pushed our already revolutionary technologies to their limits. Now, I'm proud to announce that on July nineteenth, 2047, we will go beyond those limits.'

As with all CrimeCons, visitors were treated to panels featuring Augmented Personas of some of the most diabolical minds in history, as well as dozens of new announcements, including new Earth+ merchandise (the Ed Gein Wrap skin is expected to be a top-seller), as well as patches to previously released Past Crimes simulations based on newly discovered information and biometric data. Lake also formally announced their long-rumored 'Theia' Earth+ visor, which Past Crimes claims to boast the most realistic haptics ever created. According to a press release, the Theia is the first headset to allow users to experience all five senses inside Earth+. In a stroke of marketing genius, Lake announced that all Theia pre-orders will be drone-dropped at the stroke of midnight on July 19th.

'The Theia will allow our hundreds of millions of fans around the world to feel the heat, smell the smoke, and experience the Blight the way it was intended,' said Lake.

Founded in 2027, Past Crimes has become one of the most popular and lucrative entertainment brands in the world. Past Crimes revenue topped ten billion dollars in the fiscal year ending 2046, with 97 percent of their earnings coming from the company's Earth–services. Yet despite their success, or perhaps because of it, Past Crimes has occasionally been a lightning rod for criticism.

Lake famously lobbied for Statute 486-16, which allowed for posthumous convictions and drew condemnation from many politi-cians, including Senator Randi Hayes, who called Statute 486-16: 'A heinous revocation of people's rights. Conviction without true due process, and I include these sham Earth+ InstaTrials, serves no purpose other than to line Crispin Lake's pockets. His so-called charitable endeavors are nothing more than performative philanthropy, like a thief giving a dollar back to the store whose safe he robbed. Crispin Lake's "Disneyland of Death" has made him billions, and these conventions are nothing more than ComicCons of blood, celebrating killers while victims and their families are left with shattered lives.'

Within minutes of Crispin Lake's announcement, analysts predicted that between the Blight Experience and the release of the Theia visor, Past Crimes would add $3.2 billion in revenue for the upcoming calendar year alone.

Crispin Lake launched Past Crimes at an opportune time, as the long-gestating Metaverse had evolved from curio to a fully formed virtual universe that quickly integrated into society. Earth+ now serves an estimated two billion daily users, with its annual revenue having recently surpassed China and within just a few billion of the United States.

In recent years, however, as subscribers to their simulations have exploded, the Murderland complex itself has seen its attendance dwindle as fuel costs have rendered mass travel all but obsolete, and consumers shifted their spending to Earth+-based entertainment venues. Lake said he would take the opportunity for the Blight sim launch to reinvigorate interest in his park.

'Twenty-five thousand lucky subscribers from all around the world will be chosen at random and given an all-expenses-paid trip to our park to experience our festivities in person,' Lake said. 'Humanity has spent much of the past few decades fractured and isolated. With celebrations in both Earth+ and Earth–, we will show just how much crime can bring us all together as one.'

The deal for the Blight simulation was brokered by the V.I.C.E. licensing agency, which secured rights to hundreds of NTPs of victims and perpetrators of the Blight. One notable exception is that of Cassandra Ann West, Harris West's widow. Lake acknowledged that he had made overtures to Mrs. West in the hopes that she might participate in the production, but Mrs. West, referred to by some as the 'Red Widow', declined.

'Nobody knows Harris West better than the woman who shared his life and his home,' Lake said. 'I hope one day Cassie West will share with the world her knowledge of the man behind the Blight, and provide an even greater level of authenticity to this ground-breaking sim.'

In the decade since the Blight, Cassandra West has consistently proclaimed her husband's innocence. Prior to July 19th, 2037, the widow West had worked as a licensing agent at V.I.C.E., although her employment was terminated through mutual arrangement following her husband's posthumous conviction. Mrs. West declined to comment for this article.

THREE

June 2nd, 2047

There were ninety-eight Wraps at Aly Miller's virtual graduation. Which was strange, because there were ninety-nine students in their class. It didn't take long for Aly to realize that the lone missing Wrap belonged to David Goodwin, her best friend and the only person in the Sophomore class she actually liked, despite the fact that they had actually never met in Earth−. In fact, Aly had never met any of her classmates in real life. Despite that, she had become fast friends with David − or at least with his Wrap − and his absence made her feel both nervous and alone.

Once a week, Aly and David met at a virtual movie theater inside Earth+ that had been designed to replicate the old Majestic Theatre in San Antonio, whose ornate arches and blue tile roof made it feel as though they were watching from inside a glamorous Mediterranean mansion. There they watched century-old black-and-white films, taking advantage of the theater's free Wrap customization. Aly would go as Lauren Bacall, Humphrey Bogart, and Bette Davis. David's favorites were James Dean, Marlene Dietrich, and Clark Gable. There was something dreamy about old films, the way they played with light and shadows, how every gesture and touch seemed swollen with intimacy, and one look could break your heart. She told David how, one day, she wanted to make movies like they used to, back when life was lived rather than viewed.

After the movies ended, Aly and David would hang out in her Earth+ bedroom, talking about unrequited crushes, bands they loved and bands that were totally overrated, and how much they couldn't wait to turn eighteen and gain legal control of their Wraps. Her walls were covered with digital replica posters of her favorite movies – *Psycho*, *Casablanca*, *The Maltese Falcon*. They had both been born as the world migrated to Earth+, when physical touches and gestures were being replaced by digital ones, intimacy conveyed through haptics rather than skin. Those old movies were touchstones of a world that was gone before they arrived. Still, she longed for that kind of connection. She'd even saved up some money babysitting, which meant accompanying some kid's Wrap around a virtual park or fair to make sure they didn't interact with any sketchy Wraps, and hoped to use it to visit David in person.

She'd met David four years ago, after he'd transferred over from Crichton Elementary. Aly was an introvert, David was very, very much not, and somehow those conflicting personalities fit together perfectly. David *willed* her into a friendship, brought her out of her shell, made her feel like what she had to say was important to him even if it didn't feel that way to her. She'd been his rock during his parents' divorce, and he held her hand when she vented about her unrequited crush on Regina Moore.

The school had turned on Emotional Mirroring for the day, so students could cry or blush as they said goodbye for the summer, preparing for whatever virtual summer camp or Earth+ job they had lined up. During the semester, Emotional Mirroring was banned from Earth+ schools. Which meant that whatever emotions the students were experiencing in Earth– would not be replicated on their Wrap during school hours.

Educational officials thought banning Emotional Mirroring would discourage bullying. The belief was that if cruelty didn't elicit a response, it would cease. Instead, to Aly, it felt like attending school with digital mannequins. Kids walked through the virtual halls with wide smiles plastered to their faces, even if they failed a math quiz or were called horrible names by Harrison Dawkins. It was always unnerving on the last day of school to suddenly see all these faces with red-rimmed eyes, as though the mannequins had suddenly come alive.

Yet when a digital yellow ribbon appeared on the lapel of Aly's blue-and-white lapel – signifying the completion of her Sophomore year, she didn't care. All she could think about was David. Why wouldn't he be there for the last day of school? Even if he was sick in Earth−, he could have programmed his Wrap to at least sit in the auditorium with the rest of his classmates. The fact that David was missing entirely meant something was wrong.

Once the ceremony ended, Aly sent David a private message asking him if he was OK. A few minutes later, she received an invitation to a Lockbox. That was strange. In all the time she'd known David, he'd never once invited her to a Lockbox. This was worse than she thought.

Aly immediately opened the Lockbox link. She found herself in an empty room with two chairs. David's Wrap sat in one. He was wearing a T-shirt and jeans, rather than his school uniform. And he was crying.

'Why weren't you at school today?' Aly said. 'David, you're scaring me. What happened?'

David got up, went over to Aly, threw his arms around her and sobbed into her shoulder. David was tall and lanky, and she could feel the haptic representation of his collarbones digging into her. When David withdrew, Aly's shoulder dried instantly where he'd wept.

'Yesterday was my last day at Westbury,' he said. 'That's why I wasn't there. My parents thought it would be easier for me to make the transition if I didn't attend. Tearing off a Band-Aid or some platitude crap.'

'Transition? What are you talking about?' Aly said.

'My parents are transferring me.'

'That's not funny,' Aly said.

'Do I look like I'm laughing?' David said. 'Last week, Rachel Ingersoll's dad told all the other parents at an Earth+ PTA meeting that Mrs. Whitshaw was teaching us about the Boston Riots of 2031. The whole thing turned into a giant shitshow with screaming and threats, and Demi Madison's parents even called the EPP. The next day, something like fifty parents signed a petition calling for Mrs. Whitshaw to be fired.'

'Including your parents,' Aly said.

David snorted. 'My parents spend every Sunday morning at the Heavensent Virtual Church listening to Arwin Dodgson's sermons.'

'Arwin Dodgson is the priest who said allowing people to choose Wrap settings other than Male and Female was like worshipping the devil, only worse, right?'

'Yup. So you can guess how my folks felt about Mrs. Whitshaw teaching us about the Boston Riots. They still believe the footage was doctored. So last night my folks said they would no longer allow me to attend a school that was actively trying to warp my fragile little mind. They said they want me to think for myself at a school that will show me the right way to think. So next semester they're transferring me and my sister to Rush Limbaugh Virtual High.'

'That's complete crap,' Aly said. 'Those riots were real. They happened. We all saw people broadcasting it live in Earth+.'

'*I* know that and *you* know that. But I'm still a minor and that means I can't legally do anything to stop the transfer. I told them I wouldn't go, and they said if I didn't, I'd be out on the streets.'

Aly felt a white-hot rage growing inside of her. The Higher Learning Act of 2036 had granted parents complete authority over their child's virtual schooling until the age of eighteen. Which meant they had complete authority over where their kids went to school and what they were taught at those schools. So if a parent didn't approve of what was on their kid's syllabus, they could simply set up firewalls around texts they found offensive. And if a parent didn't like the curriculum itself, they could simply transfer their child's Wrap to another virtual school at a moment's notice.

Thankfully, Aly's parents had allowed her to stay at Westbury. They never seemed to have issues with the curriculum. Aly wasn't sure if her freedom was because her parents approved of her education, or because they just didn't care. And now the one person who made her feel less alone was being taken away from her.

'When we're in the real world, we're invisible,' David said, tears sliding down his cheeks and disappearing when they hit the floor. 'In Earth+, we're just puppets.'

'I don't know which one is worse.'

'I guess I'll find out next semester.'

'So what happens now?' Aly said. 'We can still hang out outside of school, right? There are a hundred movies we haven't seen yet.'

David looked at his shoes. 'I don't know. I don't think so. My mom said they were probably going to block my Wrap from interacting with any other Westbury students. She said she doesn't want anything you guys learn to rub off on me.'

'Rub off on you? Like educational osmosis?'

'Something like that. Either way, I'm pretty screwed.'

'Can't you fight them? Get a lawyer?' Aly said. David shook his head.

'Unless you have a million bucks for a lawyer, I'm screwed until I'm eighteen. My parents have legal authority over everyone my Wrap interacts with and which Terminals I have access to. Basically, I have to live my life the way they want me to.'

'If they block you from the Majestic Theatre Terminal, I'm going to find a way to get to your house and force them to change their minds.'

'They haven't changed any of my Wrap's settings outside of education. They spend every minute outside of work in a Past Crimes sim. They're addicted to it. I think my mom is more excited about the Blight sim than she was when she got pregnant with my sister.'

'Tell me about it. My dad is convinced that if he was alive in 1865, he would have prevented Lincoln's assassination.'

David laughed. 'I'm actually OK with it. The more distracted they are, the better it is for me. Otherwise, they might ban my Wrap from every Terminal outside of school.'

Every school, business, park, and venue within Earth+ had a corresponding Terminal. Terminals were access points for your Wrap to 'jump' to. If you wanted to see a movie, purchasing a ticket would grant your Wrap access to the Terminal inside the virtual theater. Sporting event, same thing. No ticket, no Terminal. Larger virtual venues, like amusement parks, had multiple Terminals to save your Wrap from having to walk an hour and a half just to get to the log flume.

Aly gripped David's shoulders and said, 'We'll find a way to beat this. I promise.'

'How?'

'I . . . I don't know yet. I mean you just sprung this on me ten seconds ago. But have I ever given up on anything?'

David smiled. 'No. You're like one of those snapping turtles they have at the virtual San Diego Zoo. You know, they don't look like much but their jaws can crush metal and don't let go unless you pry them apart with a crowbar.'

'I take that as a compliment.'

'You know this would all be a lot easier if you were a bad friend,' David said. 'I could just walk away and say, "You know, Aly really wasn't all that nice. Not very funny. Smelled kind of weird too, and they don't even have a sense of smell in Earth+."'

'Guess that sucks for both of us that I'm pretty awesome,' Aly said ruefully. 'So who am I going to bitch to about the fact that Regina Moore doesn't know I exist?'

'If Regina Moore is too stupid to ask you out, that is decidedly her loss,' David said. He paused. Got wistful. 'I'm going to miss you like crazy, Miller. Just don't go getting a rebound best friend before we figure all this out.'

'I won't,' Aly said. And she meant it. 'I love you. We will figure this out.'

'I l—' Suddenly, David's eyes grew wide. 'Shit. They're here.'

'Who?'

'My parents. I'm not supposed to—'

And then, without warning, David's Wrap disappeared, leaving Aly alone in the Lockbox.

'David?' she shouted. '*David?*' But he was gone. Ripped from the virtual world without warning. Ripped from her life before she had a chance to say goodbye.

When Aly logged out of Earth+, her cheeks were stained with tears. She balled her hands into fists and punched her mattress over and over, opening her mouth and screaming without making a sound. It was so unfair that David's parents could rip him away from school two years before graduation, tearing him from his friends, from his *life*, without even considering for a second what it would do to him. Or the people who cared about him. She put her visor back on and opened the link to David's Lockbox, but she only got a message saying, **LOCKBOX SESSION ENDED**.

He was gone. Just like that, her best friend taken from her life on a whim. Everyone – scratch that, just adults – said Earth+ gave people freedom. It allowed you to do so many things you never could in the physical world. But for kids like Aly, this limitless virtual arena was nothing more than a digital prison.

Eighteen was three years away, but it felt like forever. Three years when her life was out of her control. And as she saw today, it could change at any moment. She could be forced on to a path without her consent. Three years. Hell, it may as well be a lifetime. After seeing what David was going through, maybe it was a good thing her parents ignored her.

She still hadn't gotten used to the whiplash of going from packed classrooms and loud hallways in Earth+ to being alone in her bedroom in the span of seconds. Or how quickly the loneliness hit when she did.

Because she was born after the infamous Hell Week, Aly Miller couldn't say for certain whether virtual schools had accurately recreated the in-person school experience as the government claimed. She knew it was odd that David Goodwin was her best friend despite the fact that they'd never met IRL. In fact, it had been three months since Aly had even seen someone her own age in person. She looked down at her rumpled shirt. Her pants that were too short for her long, skinny legs. In Earth+, she was put-together. Her Wrap wore perfectly pressed uniforms. Her hair was always combed and clean and her skin blemish-free. But in the real world, Aly felt like she was falling apart.

Both of Aly's parents worked from home, which, despite their presence, only exacerbated Aly's feeling of loneliness. Her father, Alan, remained sequestered in his office from the moment he woke up to the moment he went to bed. He'd always seemed distracted, detached from their family. It had gotten worse over the past few months. Aly barely saw him, and she knew he slept at his desk most nights.

Aly's mother, Nadine, taught virtual fitness classes in an Earth+ Lockbox and was successful enough to be a brand ambassador for FlexLetic, which paid her to dress her Wrap in the hottest new athletic gear. And when her classes were over, her mother spent the rest of the day inside Past Crimes simulations. Every Sunday, she met her friends at an Earth+ salon to do their virtual nails and argue about which husbands had definitely killed their wives, which mistresses were definitely in on it and where all the bodies were buried.

Her parents rarely spoke anymore. It was like living with two strangers. When she was eighteen, she would leave this house and her old life behind. Start fresh. See David in person. Meet a girl. Share a kiss. A *real* kiss. She wanted to know what it felt like to hold the hand of someone you loved. Share her dreams. Share her life – her *real* life.

Then Aly heard a sound she hadn't heard in a long, long time. A knock at her door.

'Um . . . who is it?' she said. She immediately wiped the tears from her eyes. There were indents in her bed where she'd pounded her fists. She smoothed out the comforter and composed herself.

'It's Dad,' came the almost unfamiliar voice on the other side. 'Are you busy?'

She couldn't remember the last time her father had knocked on her door. She quickly looked around. Her clothes were put away, her bed was made, there was no mess. Nothing to be embarrassed by. Everything that meant something to Aly was stored within her Wrap's account in Earth+. Aly's room looked much like it had when they moved in. A blank slate, waiting to be given a personal touch that never came. Everything she owned, everything that defined who she was, existed solely inside Earth+.

'Nope, come in,' Aly said. Her father opened the door slowly and poked his head into the doorjamb, as though expecting to find something that would make him uncomfortable.

'Heeeeeere's Daddy,' he said. Aly sat there, silent. 'Sorry. It's from an old movie.'

'*The Shining*. I know. It's just . . . weird to have your dad imper-sonate a serial killer. You and Mom spend too much time in Past Crimes sims.'

He laughed, but there was something strange about it, as though he found something funny that was unrelated to Aly's comment. Then he said, 'Can we talk?'

Aly nodded and her dad stepped inside.

He was wearing a sweater with three holes Aly could see and an old pair of slippers whose seams were split, cotton leaking from the sides. She wondered why he didn't just drone himself a new pair, or a shirt that didn't look like it had been a moth's dinner. His eyes were marbles inside darkened flesh, his hair was unkempt and thinning, and he smelled like the inside of a shoe. She wondered when was the last time he slept. Or showered. He looked as if he'd completely stopped taking care of himself. That worried Aly – and scared her a little.

Her father pointed at the bed. 'Mind if I sit?' he said. Aly nodded, trying to pretend this wasn't strange. He took a seat, careful not to sit on her pillows. He groaned as he sat, then rubbed his knee.

'Everything OK?' Aly said.

'Just getting older. Joints squeak a little more than they used to.'

'You need to move around more. All you do is sit in that chair for eighteen hours a day,' Aly said. 'Have you been taking your vitamin D pill?'

'Sometimes. Hard to remember.'

'Sometimes isn't enough, Dad. The doctor said you needed them. We all do. I take mine twice a day.'

When Aly was a year and a half old, she was diagnosed with rickets. In fact, rickets was commonplace these days. People rarely left the house anymore, which meant they got about as much vitamin D as a hibernating bear. Despite the supplements, her vitamin D levels were still pitiful. She even kept a UV lamp switched on eight hours a day. Virtual learning was supposed to protect kids from all sorts of ailments, but she needed medication and machinery to offset the adverse effects of virtual learning itself.

She wasn't sure how to act around her father. They hadn't had much of a relationship the past few years. He was inside Earth+ at least sixteen hours a day. He was an accountant. No accountants were *that* busy. She wondered what he was doing, but also didn't want to know. He had stopped taking care of himself. He rarely wore clean clothes, she didn't think he showered more than a couple of times a week, and if he ate, it was toast or a slice of drone-dropped pizza Aly was pretty sure had been sitting in the fridge for weeks. It was as though her father had completely stopped caring about himself. And it scared her.

'So what's up, Dad? Did you need something?'

'You haven't done much with your room,' he said, ignoring her question. 'When I was a kid, my walls were covered. Posters of bands and movies. Photos of friends. I even had some trophies. Can you believe that?'

'Trophies for what? Biggest fashion victim?'

Her father laughed again and it made Aly smile. She couldn't remember the last time she'd heard the sound of laughter in their house.

'Believe it or not, back in the day I actually had some style,' her father said wistfully. 'So how's school? Who do you spend most of your time with?'

His questions felt odd. Perfunctory. The kind of questions you asked a stranger, not your flesh and blood who lived with you under the same roof. On the one hand, she liked that he was finally showing an interest. On the other, this wasn't like him. Something had to be up.

'It *was* my friend David, but his parents are transferring him,' she said. 'They think Westbury is indoctrinating him or something. It's such crap. We get punished for nothing. Kids should be able to have control over their Wraps.'

'That's great,' her father said, nodding absently.

'Did you hear what I just said?'

'No. Sorry. What? Your friend is going to be a doctor.'

'Is everything OK, Dad?' Aly said, eyes narrowing. Her dad stared out the window but didn't respond. 'Earth– to Dad. Hello? Are. You. OK?'

He had a confused look on his face, as though for a moment he'd forgotten that he was in her room. Then a dreamy smile spread across his lips and for a moment it put Aly's mind at ease. Just for a moment, though. Until he spoke.

'I'm fine,' he said. 'More than fine, actually. I've made some new friends.'

The reverent way he spoke reminded Aly of how David Goodwin's eyes sparkled whenever his Wrap was placed next to Tyrus Jones's Wrap in AP Chem. As if his mere presence opened up a world of possibilities.

Aly raised her eyebrows. 'New . . . friends? Where? You don't leave the house.'

'We have an . . . I guess you'd call it a collective. In Earth+,' he said. 'We're just a collective of like-minded people.'

'A collective of like-minded people? That sounds like a cult.'

'It's *not* a cult,' her father said, with a little too much anger. 'We're just people who are concerned with how the world has changed. And maybe not for the best. This group . . . they've opened my eyes to a lot of things, Aly.'

'Does Mom know about these . . . friends?'

His smile disappeared for a moment, and when he spoke, it was harsh and abrupt. 'No. Your mother does not know. And I trust that this can stay between us until the time is right.'

'Until the time is right? How will I know when that is?'

Her father smiled and said, 'Trust me. You'll know. And no matter what happens, I will always love you, Aly.'

'No matter what happens? You're starting to freak me out, Dad. What's going on? Who are these people?'

Her father took her hand in his, lightly, and clasped it.

'Three-six-five-two is coming. He gave me a mission. When I leave to complete my part in it, you won't see me again.'

'A mission? Three-six what? Who is *he*? What do you mean I won't see you again? Where are you going?'

'I have a calling, Aly. It's the second calling I've had in my life.

The first was to be a father. The second is this. When my mission is over, the fires will light up the sky. But you need to know that what I've done, I've done for the good of humanity.'

Aly looked at her father, then burst out laughing. 'I get it. You're kidding. For the good of humanity. You almost had me. Better late than never to develop a sense of humor.'

Yet her father's forehead was shiny with sweat and there was a sad look in his eyes like he was preparing to never see her again, and Aly knew that he was completely serious.

'Please stop it,' Aly said. 'You're not well, Dad. You need to talk to Mom. You need to get help.'

'I don't need help,' he said. 'I am a Beacon. That is my calling.'

'A Beacon? Dad, Beacons were those insane people who killed themselves in the Blight,' Aly said. 'You're spending too much time in Earth+. The Blight was ten years ago, Dad. It's over. You're thinking about the Past Crimes simulation.'

'It isn't over. It never ended. Past Crimes doesn't know what they have. What's *really* inside their simulation.'

'What's inside it?' Aly asked.

'The truth about the Blight,' Alan said. 'And they don't even know it. When the clock strikes midnight, the world will see that the biggest fires are yet to come.'

'Yet to come? Dad, you're scaring me. Are you saying there's going to be another Blight? Who are these friends? I have to tell Mom—'

'You absolutely *will not*,' her father shouted. Without warning, he grabbed her wrist and yanked her towards him. His eyes were crazy, his breathing fast and uneven. Aly screamed and wrenched herself away. She fell on to the floor and yelped, more out of surprise than pain. Her father looked at his hand, horrified, as though he couldn't believe what he'd just done.

Aly scooted to the far side of the room, trying to get as far away from her father as possible. She eyed the door. Then the window. At that moment, Aly did not recognize the man sitting on her bed. Whatever was wrong with him hadn't happened overnight. Something had been metastasizing inside of him, taking control of his mind. Like he'd been . . . brainwashed.

'I'm sorry, Aly, I didn't mean to hurt you. I just need you to know—'

'What the hell is going on in here?' Aly's mother, Nadine, was standing at the door, wearing a sweat-stained tank top and yoga pants. Aly could still see the slight indents by her temples. The CyberBod sweatproof athletic headset always left Aly's mom looking as if she spent the day with a metal clamp fastened to her head.

'Nadine,' Aly's dad said. 'Aly and I were just doing some father–daughter bonding.'

'He told me he was going to leave and then he grabbed me,' Aly said, rubbing her wrist. Small blue bruises had embedded themselves in her skin. 'He says he's met people. That he's going on a mission to become a Beacon. I . . . I think he means there's going to be another Blight.'

'A Beacon?' Nadine said, glaring at Alan. 'Are you goddamn insane?'

'No, I'm not insane,' he replied. 'My eyes are finally open. I've been waiting for this day for almost ten years.'

'Dad, are you saying there's going to be another Blight? But Harris West is dead.'

Her father said, 'Harris West may be dead. But the Vertex Ignis is not one man.'

Nadine saw Aly rubbing her wrist. She took Aly's hand, gently, and turned it over. Her face went pale when she saw a fingerprint-shaped bruise.

'What the hell did you do, Alan?' her mother said. There was rage in her eyes. Aly shrank further back against the wall. 'Did you put your hands on our daughter?'

'Mom, calm down,' Aly pleaded. 'I'm fine.'

'You miserable bastard,' Nadine said, jabbing her finger at her husband. 'Every day I wake up trying to think of reasons not to leave you. I just ran out of reasons. Aly, get your things.'

Aly felt her breath leave her body as her mother disappeared into the hallway.

Why couldn't she have just played along with her dad's delusion? He couldn't be serious about being a Beacon. He'd become obsessed with Past Crimes. Confused the real world with the virtual one. Either way, he'd clearly lost his mind. If only she'd just shut up, they could have gotten him help. This was all her fault.

'Nadine!' her father yelled, launching himself off the bed and into the hall after her. 'Nadine, get back here!'

Aly followed him, her breath coming out in bursts as she began to cry. She was so stupid. Why did she have to say anything? She'd already lost David. She couldn't lose her family too.

'Please, Mom, Dad,' she said. 'Please stop. I'm sorry. This is my fault. I overreacted. Dad didn't do anything. Let's just start over.'

She could hear them screaming at each other in the living room. They were cursing at each other, calling each other horrible names, each one a knife piercing Aly's heart. She knew they hadn't gotten along in a long time. Maybe they didn't love each other anymore. But as long as they were under the same roof, they could be a family. They could fix this.

Aly found her parents in their bedroom. Nadine had already pulled out a suitcase and had begun haphazardly throwing clothes into it.

'Mom,' Aly said. 'Please stop.'

'What did I say?' her mother said to her, without looking at her. 'Get your bag. I want to be in a ReVolt cab in fifteen minutes.'

'I . . . I don't have a bag,' Aly said. 'I haven't gone anywhere in . . . ever.'

Nadine sighed and rolled her eyes and continued packing. 'Just throw some stuff in here then.'

'I don't want to go anywhere.'

'Nadine,' Alan said, his voice flat, emotionless. 'Let's talk about this.'

'There's nothing to discuss. The next time you see us will be in an Earth+ courtroom. My lawyer is going to cut you to pieces.'

'Mom, stop,' Aly pleaded. 'Put your clothes away. Let's have a family talk. We used to do those, remember?'

Nadine stopped shoving clothes into the suitcase for a moment, as if a memory had floated past her subconscious, but then she continued packing. Moments later, her suitcase was zipped. She hadn't left any room for Aly. Nadine lugged the suitcase into the hall, Aly trailing her.

'Nadine,' her father said. 'Let's talk. In just over a month, I'll be gone. Don't do this to Aly.'

'I should have left you a long time ago,' Nadine said, the loose wheel of the barely used suitcase squeaking with a loud *ee-oo ee-oo*. 'Expect to hear from my attorney. And the police.'

'Do *not* get the police involved,' Alan said, his voice firmer.

'There's too much at stake. The Vertex Ignis is relying on me. You cannot fathom how important this is.'

'Dad, the Vertex Ignis is dead,' Aly said. 'Harris West is dead.'

'Oh, Aly,' her father replied. 'There's so much you don't know.'

Nadine looked at Alan with a mixture of scorn and pity. 'You really are a sad, small man,' she said. Nadine dragged the suitcase towards the front door.

'Mom, please,' Aly begged. 'Just sit down. All of us. Let's have a family talk.'

'We're not a family anymore,' Nadine said. 'We haven't been in a long time. It's just you and me, Aly. Now, let's go.'

She snapped her fingers as if to beckon Aly to leave with her. Aly didn't move. Her mother rolled her eyes.

'I'll come back for you, then,' she said.

Aly opened her mouth to speak, but then she saw her father and the words disappeared in her throat.

'I can't let you leave,' he said. He was holding a gun. And pointing it at Aly's mother.

At first, her mother seemed shocked. Then the look turned to one of bemusement.

'When did you get *that*?' she said.

'You need to stay,' he said. 'Both of you.'

Aly could feel her heart beating fast in her chest like a humming-bird's wings.

'Dad,' she said, as calmly as she could. 'Put it down.'

'This is bigger than me,' he said. 'Bigger than us. Nadine, you have to come back. Don't make me do this.'

'I'm not *making* you do anything,' she said. 'I'm done with you blaming me for your own failures. Goodbye, Alan.'

She reached for the door and Alan pulled the trigger.

Aly's ears rang and she instinctively closed her eyes and covered them. When she opened her eyes, she saw her mother sinking to the floor, a look of astonishment on her face, red soaking her green yoga top.

As the ringing in her ears subsided, Aly realized that she was screaming. Her father turned to her. He still held the gun. Only now it was pointed at Aly.

'It wasn't supposed to happen like this,' he said. 'I did it all wrong. I did it too soon.'

'Dad . . .' Aly whispered. 'Dad, what did you do?'

'Nobody can know,' he said. 'Ten years is a long time to wait for the fires to light up the night sky again. I'm sorry I won't get to see it.'

Then he pulled the trigger one more time.

FOUR

July 16th, 2047

When Cassie West was in her twenties, she was in a book club that referred to themselves as 'The Beleaguered Wives', ironic given that, at the time, eight of the nine members were unattached. Lubricated with wine and stuffed with various cheeses, they devoured books where unsuspecting women discovered that their husbands or boyfriends were – pick one – a spy, a catfisher, a philanderer, a murderer, or sometimes all of the above. At the end of that week's discussion, the real debate would begin: what might they do if, after marriage, they found out the men in their own lives were not who they thought they were? Would they leave them? Divorce them? Perhaps even murder them? How would they cover those murders up? Those hypotheticals were as much fun – and sometimes more so – as discussing the books themselves.

Yet in their dozens of meetings, the club never discussed what might happen if their men were accused of being someone that they were not. In retrospect, Cassie wished they had. It might have helped her get through the last ten years of her life. After the Blight. After her husband had been accused of being the most diabolical monster in the Earth+ era, the man who had used the power of unlimited global connectivity for pure evil.

Now, ten years later, Cassie was still figuring out how to live.

The velvet curtain parted and Cassie stepped on to the Lockbox stage – or at least her perfectly manicured Wrap did. There were three hundred paid attendees in the theater tonight, the faces of their Wraps emotionless and unmoving. Three hundred people. The most she'd ever had. She checked her EPD, or Earth+ display,

and saw another two hundred Wraps on the waiting list. Two
hundred people meant another twenty grand she was losing out
on. She should have known. She kicked herself for not renting a
bigger Lockbox.

Ever since Past Crimes announced their Blight simulation, interest
in the Blight had, for lack of a better term, caught fire. Cassie had
been inundated with requests for comment on Crispin Lake's plans,
all of which she'd ignored. Amidst this, word of mouth about her
Lockbox performances had clearly spread. When the Blight sim
launched, she'd have little trouble filling a thousand-Wrap Lockbox.
Her stomach lurched at the thought of performing in front of that
many Wraps, but she quelled the nausea by thinking how much
money she could make. That kind of dough would solve a lot of
problems. Clear a lot of debt. And most importantly, give her more
money for the most important thing of all:

Convince the world that Harris was not the monster they thought
he was.

Means to an end, Cassie said, as she surveyed the sea of Wraps
waiting for her to start the show. *Means to an end.*

The stage curtain was red velvet. A crystal chandelier hung from
the low ceiling, giving the Lockbox a sense of glamour and intimacy.
A stool sat in the middle of the stage, illuminated by a single spotlight. Cassie had once seen an old photo of Bettie Page, sitting on
a stool wearing nothing but garters. The photo was sultry and inviting,
but Bettie had a look on her face that said *I have very few fucks to
give*. That was the vibe Cassie was going for.

Cassie altered her Wrap slightly for these performances. She'd
colored in the grays streaking her dark brown hair, smoothed over
the light crow's feet around her eyes, increased her skin pigmenta-
tion by 3.5 percent and purchased a 'Dance' Wrap modification to
ensure her Wrap was more coordinated in Earth+ than Cassie was
in Earth−. Not to mention that shaving her legs was a whole lot
easier when she could just update her Wrap's skin.

The curtain parted and Cassie stepped out on to the stage. Her
Wrap wore a shimmering blue robe, cinched at the waist. Her hair
was done up in bouncy concentric ringlets which cascaded down
her back. Her green eyes were practically luminescent. Her fingernails were long and red. The robe ended just above her thigh,
revealing long, toned, tanned legs that glistened like she'd spent a
month in the Caribbean sun. White tufts of virtual fur around her

collar created a V down her neck that revealed the lacy top of a black bra.

Most of the Wraps were men, along with a handful of women and several gender-neutral Wraps. They all stared at the stage without blinking, as if they were in a painting. One of the requirements to access Cassie's performances was that your Wrap's Emotional Mirror settings had to be off. No smiles, frowns, cheers, or jeers. You were there to watch. That was all.

She'd made that mistake the night of her very first show. There were only nine Wraps in attendance, but one in the front row licked his lips in a way that almost made Cassie's lunch come back up. When her performance ended and Cassie left Earth+, she cried in her bed for an hour, thinking, *This is not worth any amount of money.*

But she was desperate and broke and this was money on her terms. Her second show, she made a thousand dollars in an hour. So she kept going but smartened up. The Wraps had to be emotionless. To her surprise, more and more Wraps began paying for access. Nine became twenty, became fifty, became a hundred. She always envisioned herself climbing the corporate ladder at V.I.C.E., not climbing atop a stool in a Lockbox in Earth+ to make ends meet.

The day after Harris's death, when he'd officially been declared the Vertex Ignis, aka progenitor of the Blight, Cassie received a terse email from their homeowner's insurance company letting her know that they would not be paying a dime due to Harris's posthumous conviction of arson (among his other crimes). The day after that, Cassie's boss at V.I.C.E. let her know in polite terms that they would rather employ Satan himself than the widow of Harris West. Because Cassie hadn't been charged with a crime, V.I.C.E. couldn't fire her for cause, so they offered Cassie 'go away' money to terminate her contract, which she accepted. Between legal fees and Cassie's crappy rental apartment, the money had evaporated faster than smoke.

She'd clear fifteen grand tonight, easy. The Lockbox itself was cheap. The landlord was obsessed with the Blight, had seen every documentary, subscribed to nineteen different true crime networks, and he was constantly asking Cassie if she would sign his copy of *Vertex Ignis: The Real Story of Harris West*, a schlocky tell-all 'biography' of Cassie's husband that invented more facts than a

Donald Trump, Jr. presidential rally. He'd practically *begged* Cassie to rent the space, even gave it to her at fifty percent below market rate – provided his Wrap received free attendance to her shows.

Lockboxes were primarily used for business meetings, private affairs (business and otherwise), reception halls for virtual weddings and celebrations, and as safe, encrypted spaces where people who struggled with issues related to race, identity, gender, sexuality and culture could congregate with safety and privacy. But like any technological advancement, it was soon exploited.

People realized Lockboxes could be used to conduct just about any manner of illegal activity, safe from the watchful eye of the woefully undermanned EPP. Drug deals could be conducted in Lockboxes, sex trafficking rings could be organized hidden from the government's watchful eye, and even Earth– murders could be planned inside, making premeditation impossible to prove and even harder to prosecute. Law enforcement did their best to crack down, but virtual space was infinite. Manpower was not. For the most part, law enforcement considered Lockboxes like speakeasies during Prohibition. The cops knew they were around, but as long as nobody got hurt – or you paid the right people – they were allowed to keep doing their thing.

'Welcome,' Cassie said. The Wraps did not respond. 'Shall we begin?'

Her Wrap's robe was programmed to stay closed, no matter how fast Cassie moved or how much her performance defied the rules of gravity, which she had set to 'Low'. Cassie could have done a backflip followed by a cartwheel and triple-double axle moonsault and the robe would have stayed cinched. Hell, she could have taken a chainsaw to it and it would have chipped the blade.

For the next forty-five minutes, she danced. At least, her Wrap did. Cassie had figured out how to disassociate herself from the proceedings, separate her mind from what her Wrap was doing. At the end of the routine, she said, 'Time for the bonus round.'

Half the Wraps stayed. They'd paid an additional hundred on top of their entrance fee to see the robe finally come undone. But when Cassie began to loosen the tassel, one of the Wraps in the back began to flash red. This meant the offending Wrap was attempting to record the performance.

Immediately, Cassie froze the Lockbox and called up her EPD.

She singled out the flashing Wrap and opened its payment details. The Wrap had bought a ticket under the name Kim Wilson, but Cassie could see that the payment had been processed via multiple blockchains and several different aliases, clearly in an attempt to mask the attendee's identity. When she found the name of the payment's originator, Cassie groaned. The Wrap's real purchaser was Reggie Davenport. Goddamn him.

Reggie Davenport was a reporter at the *New Boston Tribune* and one of the banes of Cassie's existence. He'd been trying unsuccessfully to land an interview for going on ten years and was willing to do just about anything to get one. He'd been stalking Cassie in both the real and virtual world. Cassie had filed an Earth– restraining order, which had been enforced, as well as one in Earth+, which had been refused.

Davenport had dragged her in columns for months after the Blight, always quoting 'unnamed sources' from within Cassie's former company.

Cassie was always so secretive at work. Most V.I.C.E. employees realize true crimes are our business, but Cassie always seemed a little too obsessed. Like she wanted to be a part of one. I have a hard time believing she didn't know what her husband was doing or that she wasn't involved. People always say, 'Happy wife, happy life.' Well, if your husband commits mass murder, what does that say? I heard Cassie had secret Lockboxes all over Earth+ . . . who knows what went on in there?

Given how relentless and unethical he was, she wasn't surprised Davenport would commit Wrap Fraud to gain access to her private Lockbox. He could stalk her with impunity within the virtual world. There were few rules and not enough people to enforce them, and if there was one thing Cassie had learned in her time at V.I.C.E., women who feared for their safety and security were never taken seriously until they showed up in the morgue.

If Cassie hadn't paid for extra Lockbox security measures, Davenport could have sold the performance footage to any number of unscrupulous news outlets, a private collector, any one of a number of Blight media or entertainment outlets, or even used it as leverage to blackmail Cassie for that interview.

It took all of eight seconds for Cassie to expel Davenport's Wrap from the Lockbox and send an alert to the EPP. Cassie doubted the EPP would do anything other than toss the alert into her (large) digital file. Law enforcement weren't big fans of hers. After all, Cassandra Ann West was still the madman's widow.

Once Davenport's Wrap was gone, Cassie unfroze the performance.

'Sorry for the delay,' she said to the unmoving audience. 'Shall we begin?'

When her show ended, Cassie exited Earth+, removed her visor and placed it back in its charging station. Her head throbbed. The headaches had been getting worse and worse. Too much time in Earth+ was messing with her brain's chemistry. She had to be careful. Neural Flares were no joke. She swallowed two sodium tablets, then opened the VirtuCash app on her phone and let the camera scan her retinas.

A few performances ago, she'd enabled Shop+. Several Wraps had purchased the robe and shoes she'd worn during tonight's performance. Cassie received a small commission on each sale. All things told, she'd cleared 288,743 in EPC, or Earth+ Coin, a decentralized global currency that could only be used within the virtual economy. It came out to about $22,000. That would cover the rent for her 500-square-foot one-bedroom, one-bathroom apartment, and even allow her to chip away at her Replenish debt. Somehow Cassie owed the government more money now than she did a decade ago. Funny how debts worked. It was almost as if they didn't *want* you to be able to pay them off.

Shortly after the Blight, Reggie Davenport had gained access to the Harrises' financial records and used their dire financial straits to insinuate that their (mutual!) desire to start a family had pushed her husband to commit mass murder. His not-at-all incendiary headline read:

Baby Mama Monster
Was Harris West pushed to the brink by his wife's insatiable desire to procreate?

It was at that moment Cassie realized that there were very, very few things people couldn't find a way to blame on a woman. In addition to the Replenish debts, Cassie had other debts that were far more important to pay off than the government. She had no next of kin, so if Cassie died, the government would never recoup their money. A decent silver lining to take to the grave.

Shortly after Harris's death, Cassie had used every dime she had to hire six private investigators: three to cover Earth−, three to cover Earth+. All with the goal of helping her prove Harris's innocence. Their job was to scour both the real and virtual world for anything, be it crimes, confessions, clues or mysteries, that could reveal the true mastermind behind the Blight, or how her husband had become mixed up in it. Given how much the world had contracted over the last twenty years, covering the physical world was fairly easy. But she could have hired an army of Augmented Sherlock Holmeses and they'd only be able to cover a fraction of Earth+. There were infinite corners and crevasses, Lockboxes and Terminals, and hundreds more sprouted up every day. But six PIs were all she could afford, and in ten years they'd found nothing but dead ends, false confessions and leads that evaporated when investigated.

So Cassie fought against the wind, convinced of her husband's innocence with no actual proof. She couldn't tell people how they'd spent years trying to start a family. How Harris had beamed when he talked about wanting to be a father. How he cried when Cassie told him she was pregnant. How she knew deep down he would never *ever* have done those things because he had too much to live for.

Remember me like it was yesterday.

How can you prove someone *isn't* capable of something? Maybe Cassie couldn't produce any proof – yet – but her faith in Harris remained. She would find out how and why he was involved. Even if it took the rest of her life.

She transferred the equivalent of fifteen thousand dollars into her bank account and paid her rent. Another three thousand paid down her Replenish loan. The rest paid off debts to several of her PIs. Within minutes, she received texts from two of them thanking her for (finally) paying, but informing her that they would not do any more work until she could consistently pay on time.

Cassie stood up. Stretched and tightened her robe. It was faded yellow, the ugly stepchild of her flamboyant Lockbox robe, and covered in unidentifiable stains. Her hair did not cascade down her back in ringlets but was held together in a messy top knot. Her legs did not glisten, and she had an ugly purple bruise on her shin from walking into her coffee table.

But the Wraps who paid to see her show didn't want the *real* Cassie West. They wanted the Cassie West of their imaginations.

The Red Widow. The Cassie West they'd read about and whose wedding video they had seen in so many documentaries. And because Cassie had refused to participate in any Blight media, this was the only place they could see her.

Only God knew how many documentaries had been made about the Blight. There were currently ninety-six – no, wait, Farming+ just announced one that day, so ninety-seven – streaming services. At least half of them had run Blight programming. Some were straightforward true crimes. Some were laughable reenactments with wooden actors who wouldn't get cast in community theater productions. The Blight had been covered from every conceivable angle – hell, Zillow TV had a four-part docuseries about how the Blight affected home prices (and how *you* could profit from it!).

Cassie turned them all down immediately. The only one that made her hesitate was when Crispin Lake came calling. Two years ago, Past Crimes had contacted Cassie through her lawyer, asking if she would be willing to participate in the creation of the Blight sim. Past Crimes was already well into production and they were planning to create Augmented Personas of both Harris and Cassie. They didn't need permission for Harris. He'd already been posthumously convicted and they could use his likeness and biometrics freely. But Cassie's participation would add a layer of authenticity. And they were willing to pay handsomely.

She took a weekend (and several bottles of drone-dropped wine in plastic bottles) to think about it. Her apartment was a dirty shoe box. Her furniture was disintegrating. The cost of all materials had exploded after the California tsunami of 2032 when several dozen freighters lolling in the waters of San Pedro Bay overturned following a 7.8 earthquake in the ocean floor. The seventy-foot wave killed ninety-eight people and sent nearly a billion dollars of cargo to the bottom of the Pacific Ocean. Shipping and manufacturing costs inside Earth+ people didn't need furniture or baubles – at least none that couldn't be manufactured with ones and zeroes. But it also meant that Cassie would never again live in a home with a staircase or a second bedroom.

Despite her destitute situation, Cassie emailed Crispin Lake and declined his offer. He didn't want the truth. He wanted her to come to the Past Crimes complex in West Valley, Utah, and tell the world she'd been fooled by Harris. The Cassie that Past Crimes was creating for their sim was a naïve woman kept in the dark by a calculating, monstrous husband, a woman whose life had been ruined. Only the last part was true.

So she refused. She could live with performing in rented Lockboxes and living in a dirty apartment and having cheap take-out parachute down the building's delivery slot six times a week. She could live with being a fake Cassie inside a Lockbox, because that was on her terms.

Eventually, she would find a thread to pull on. A thread that would lead to the truth. A thread that would show the world that Harris West was not a demon but a scapegoat. And until then, she would shake her (virtual) thing. A means to an end.

Cassie's phone vibrated. She took it out and saw a message from Reggie Davenport.

'You've got to be kidding me,' she mumbled. 'Read message.'

Her phone read the message in Davenport's high-pitched, whiny drawl.

You're a fool not going on the record. Think about how many people have told your story because you've refused to tell it yourself. Think about how much money people are making off of you. You could own your story. Show everyone who hates you the *real* you. I think people would sympathize with what Cassandra Ann West has had to do to survive. Give me the exclusive. It'll be the biggest interview of the year. The *decade*. All you have to do is say yes and I can change the minds of millions. And maybe even change your life. Do you even still have a life, Ms. West?

When the message ended, Cassie thought for a moment and crafted an eloquent reply.

Fuck. Off.

She hit send and smiled when she saw he'd read it without responding.

Cassie went to the window and looked outside. The streets were strewn with detritus: cans and cigarette butts and empty food containers and the metal skeletons of drones that had crashed into poles and walls and each other while delivering their wares. Piles of garbage bags lined the sidewalks, high enough to be used as barricades, the cost of fuel so high that trash removal occurred once a month, at best. Many of the bags had torn open, spilling their spoiled contents on to the street where they were devoured by animals or the tens of thousands who had lost their homes. Nobody opened their windows anymore; the smell of the rotting outside world was constant.

When Cassie was a girl, her parents would take their family out to eat all the time. When she and Harris were dating, they would pop out to the neighborhood bistro for hot mussels and chilled white wine every Saturday night. Now, you could walk for hours without seeing a single restaurant. Buildings could no longer keep up with the amount of trash their tenants collected (a symptom of the populace eating 98.4 percent of their meals at home) so rather than toss their trash down garbage chutes, where they would remain uncollected for weeks, people just tossed it out the window. And so most neighborhoods smelled like a combination of rotting fish and wet leaves. People rarely left home. There was nothing out there for them. No wonder everyone, Cassie included, was vitamin D deficient.

Then she looked down and saw a dozen people standing on the street in a small crowd. Their phones were out and aimed at her apartment window. One of them shouted, 'Cassandra West! The Red Widow!'

One woman turned around and took a selfie, making sure to tilt the camera to get Cassie's window in the background. Cassie immediately shut the window, locked it and closed the drapes. They always found her. Ever since the Blight, she'd become a human tourist attraction. Everywhere she went in public, people took pictures. Asked for autographs. And that's if they were fans. She couldn't remember the last time she'd left her apartment.

Then, at some point, her Wrap's source code got leaked. It meant people could track her movements within Earth+. She could be sitting on a virtual park bench, her Wrap altered to look like an eighty-year-old man, and people would *still* berate her in public.

She'd reported the violation to the EPP and even filed to have her Wrap's source code changed. She was met with a combination of indifference and scorn. Her filing was rejected within twenty-four hours. And so Cassie had no safety or privacy in the real or digital worlds. She was no longer a person but a commodity. The brutal irony was that in order to survive, she had been forced to commoditize herself. But at least the Lockbox performances were on her terms.

Cassie opened the SkyMeals app on her phone and ordered a

tuna salad with a side of curly fries. Five minutes later she heard the ding from her apartment's delivery chute. She opened it and removed a plastic bag with a small parachute tied to the top.

The lettuce was soggy. The fish was gray and smelled like an old sofa cushion. She bit into the tuna, grimaced and swallowed. She needed the protein.

Then her phone pinged again. She rolled her eyes and picked it up, expecting to see some snarky reply from Reggie Davenport. Instead, her eyes widened. It was from Wanda McCrae, one of the investigators she'd hired and whose debt she'd just paid off. The subject line was brief.

Saved these for you. Consider them a parting gift.

A link appeared on her screen. Cassie tapped it and found a folder filled with dozens of news articles dating back three months. Cassie put on her visor and spread the files out on her EPD screen. There were tons of articles about the Past Crimes Blight sim announcement, a few interviews with Crispin Lake and profiles of Beacons who had died in the fires – and the loved ones who hadn't seen it coming.

Cassie was about to call it a day when she noticed something strange. McCrae had included a police report and a news article about a murder-suicide dated June 2nd – but she'd included two copies of the same police report. McCrae didn't make mistakes – if she sent two copies of the same report, there was a reason. Cassie read the digital note attached to the file.

C – Read the article. Then the reports. Both of them. – WMcC
Cassie opened the article and read.

June 3rd, 2047
Two dead in marital quarrel turned deadly. Teenage daughter the only survivor.

The town of Westbury was stunned when Alan Miller, 52, and Nadine Miller, 51, of Westbury were killed during a marital dispute that turned deadly. According to their surviving daughter, Allyson, 13, Mr. Miller fatally shot his wife before turning the gun on himself.

According to Westbury police, the dispute began shortly after four p.m. and escalated quickly. A suitcase in the foyer containing Mrs. Miller's clothing led police to believe Mrs.

Miller was in the process of leaving her husband. It is not known whether Allyson was planning to accompany her mother.

Friends and family of Mr. Miller said he had become withdrawn over the past few years, spending more and more time inside Earth+, and that the Millers' marriage had long been strained. Still, it is unknown what led Mr. Miller to commit such an act of violence. When asked about a possible motive, Detective Wabash of the WPD stated, 'Mr. Miller was a disturbed individual who committed a heinous act. We have not ruled out mental illness. Any other speculation is hearsay.'

Allyson Miller was remanded to the custody of the state. Funeral services for Mr. and Mrs. Miller will take place this Saturday at Westbury Digital Burials. Use the link below to donate virtual flowers.

Cassie read and reread the article. It sounded awful. Her heart broke for Allyson Miller. Cassie wondered why McCrae had sent her this story. It sounded as though there may have been red flags with Alan Miller, but nobody had done anything about it. Strangely, Cassie couldn't find any more coverage of the Miller deaths. Or any follow-up about what had happened to the daughter, Aly. It was as though two people had died, their daughter had been taken away and the story had been forgotten about.

Cassie tapped her lip. She couldn't figure out why McCrae had sent over two copies of the same police report, or why McCrae thought Cassie would take an interest. Then Cassie noticed something strange. The log dates on the cover pages were different. The first report had been filed at 10:19 p.m. on June 2nd. The second report had been filed at 1:52 a.m. on June 3rd. The details of the crime itself appeared to be the same, but the reports had been filed several hours apart.

Cassie read the first report. It contained forensic details of the Miller deaths, an interview with Allyson Miller and statements from witnesses who'd heard the gunshots. It was clear from the report that the deaths had been a murder-suicide, just as the article stated. But in the transcript of the police interview with Allyson Miller, somebody, likely McCrae, had underlined one section:

Detective Wabash: 'What did your father say, exactly, when he was in your room prior to the altercation with your mother?'

Allyson Miller: 'He said he was leaving us to become a Beacon. I was only three when the Blight happened but I know what Beacons are and what they did. He talked about the Vertex Ignis in current terms. Like he was still alive. But Harris West is dead. He said the biggest fires are yet to come. I didn't get it at first, but July 19th, 2047, is exactly ten years after July 19th, 2037. Three six five two. I think there might be another Blight coming. And I think my dad was going to be a part of it.'

(END OF TRANSCRIPT)

Cassie's heart began to race. Why would the police end the interview there? Wouldn't they have follow-up questions? And what the hell did the numbers three six five two mean?

Maybe that's not where the interview ended, Cassie realized, *but simply where they stopped transcribing it.*

Cassie opened the duplicate report and read through it. But this time, when she got to the transcript of the Allyson Miller interview, the section McCrae had underlined was gone. Not crossed out . . . just missing. It was as though someone had edited the transcript and removed Allyson Miller's comments about her father and the Blight. But why the hell would the police do that?

He said he was leaving us to become a Beacon.

Cassie's mind began to race. Where was Allyson Miller now? Did she know her remarks had been cut by the police? If this wasn't the full interview, Allyson had to know things that hadn't been included in the police report.

Cassie went into her EPD and found several social media accounts belonging to people named Allyson Miller. She compared the avatar photos in the accounts to the image of the girl in the police report and determined that the accounts with the screen name @AlyMillz belonged to the girl she was looking for.

But when she scrolled through Allyson Miller's social media feeds, she was surprised to find that they were all empty. That didn't make sense. Unless . . .

Cassie ran a search for the @AlyMillz screen name and found that people had been interacting with Allyson Miller's accounts for years. Allyson Miller had clearly been active on social media, but for some reason, after the death of her parents, her accounts had all been wiped clean. Had Aly deleted them – or had they been scrubbed?

The most frequent account that interacted with @AlyMillz belonged to a user named @BeGood2All. He'd Tweeted at @AlyMillz the morning of June 3rd, the day after the killings. He'd done the same on June 4th and 5th.

@BeGood2All: Hey @AlyMillz are you OK?

@BeGood2All: @AlyMillz Please message me.

@BeGood2All: @AlyMillz I love u. Please let me know you're OK.

Cassie checked the profile settings and found that the @BeGood2All account was registered to a thirteen-year-old named David Goodwin.

She ran a search for photos of Allyson Miller and used facial recognition filtering to ensure she only saw photos of the right girl. Most were class photos taken inside the digital half of Westbury High. She found one photo captioned *Me and @AlyMillz. Friends for life*. The photo was of two kids, their arms around each other, smiling like happy lunatics. Two people were tagged in the pic: Aly Miller and David Goodwin. The same David Goodwin whose @BeGood2All account regularly interacted with the @AlyMillz account.

Goodwin had posted the photo to his public EarthSnap account three days after the deaths of Aly's parents. It was clear the post was made in solidarity with Aly.

Cassie couldn't find any other stories about the Miller killings, no updates on Aly or her whereabouts, or anything else about the investigation. Even for a local crime, Cassie knew from experience that this one had flown suspiciously under the radar. Add to that the duplicate police reports and Aly's feeds being scrubbed, and it looked as though the circumstances surrounding the deaths of Alan and Nadine Miller were being swept under the rug. But why?

Cassie put her visor back on. She brought up her EPD's search engine and found the Terminal for the Westbury police precinct. Soon after Earth+ had become an intrinsic part of daily life, every police department in the country established virtual precincts. At Earth+ police Terminals, your Wrap could file a complaint, dispute a ticket, speak with a detective in Earth+, or even visit someone's

Wrap in the holding cells. Wrap alterations were suspended inside the virtual stations, and your identity was immediately recorded into a digital log.

After the Blight, she'd spent half her waking hours inside interrogation rooms, in both Earth+ and Earth−. *No, I didn't know what Harris was going to do until the day he died. No, I wasn't involved in the Blight. No, I don't think it's possible he was the Vertex Ignis.*

Cassie took a breath and tapped the icon for the Westbury police Terminal. Instantly, she found herself outside a two-story brick building. Even with the latest digital tools at their disposal, cops still made their precincts look as welcoming as a medieval dungeon.

Cassie entered the precinct. In Earth− police stations, there was constant commotion. In Earth+ precincts, everything was eerily quiet. Wraps of police officers sat at desks, frozen in place, like video-game NPCs waiting to be triggered when you approached the right spot.

Behind a large wooden desk sat a female police Wrap, frozen in place with a too-wide smile. As Cassie approached, the Wrap sparked to life and said, jovially, 'Cassandra Ann West. How may the Westbury Police Department serve you today?'

Cassie took the Miller police report from her EPD and handed it to the desk cop. 'I need to speak with Detectives Wabash and Merriman.'

'And what is this regarding?'

'The deaths of Alan and Nadine Miller on June second.'

'Are you friend or family?'

'Call me an interested party.'

'One moment, Ms. West. I'm going to put your Wrap on hold while I see if either of the detectives are available.' The Wrap's eyes flickered for a minute. Then she said, 'It appears Detective Merriman is out on paternity leave. Detective Wabash is available and will see you. Please be aware that all of your interactions inside this precinct are being recorded.'

'I'm aware,' Cassie said.

A Wrap materialized in the lobby. The badge on his lapel read *Det. Wabash.* Detective Wabash was a fit, middle-aged man, dark hair graying at the temples, with a severe brow. His skin was smooth and unlined, teeth a brilliant white. Even if visitors to police precincts had to turn off their Wrap alterations, it was clear the cops themselves were given that luxury.

'What can I do for you, Ms. West?' he said. Wabash did not offer Cassie his hand. Even virtual cops were rude.

'I wanted to talk to you about the deaths of Alan and Nadine Miller.'

The eyes on Wabash's Wrap narrowed into slits. 'Do you know the victims?'

'I don't,' Cassie said. 'But I read the report you and Detective Merriman filed the night they died. Both of them.'

'Both of them?' Wabash said.

'There were two reports. One filed on the night of the killings. Another filed early the next morning. In the second report, your interview with Allyson Miller was edited. Specifically, pertaining to Alan Miller's comments about being a Beacon, and Allyson raising the possibility of another Blight.'

'One moment, Ms. West.'

The eyes on Wabash's Wrap began to flicker, just as the desk cop's had. It meant the detective had frozen his Wrap inside Earth+ while he did something in the real world that Cassie could not see. A few minutes later, Wabash's Wrap returned. And it did not seem happy.

'You're Harris West's wife. The Red Widow,' Wabash said. 'What in the hell are you doing at the Westbury Terminal? You don't live anywhere near here.'

'I want to know why you edited Allyson Miller's interview.'

'Aly Miller's interview was not *edited*,' Wabash said curtly. 'We always condense reports when they're filed to isolate pertinent information while removing any that has no bearing on the investigation.'

'How in the world could Alan Miller claiming he was a Beacon have no bearing on your investigation?'

'Because Alan Miller was insane,' Wabash said angrily. 'Do you know how many cranks have claimed to be Beacons over the last ten years? Hundreds. Maybe thousands. People come to police Terminals looking for attention. One guy tried to set himself on fire with a cigarette lighter before he remembered the lighter wasn't real. Alan Miller was a kook. Just like all the rest of them.'

'That kook killed himself and his wife and left his daughter an orphan. I've read dozens of police reports on other people who've claimed to be Beacons. Most had a history of mental illness. None of them had a family. Alan Miller was a father and a husband. Something happened to him. Something – or someone – changed him.'

'The final report is the official report, *Ms. West*,' Wabash said. 'We're done here. Go back to doing whatever it is that you do and just be glad you still have your freedom. Because I have a very hard time believing you didn't know exactly what your husband was doing. And if it was up to me, I'd force a confession out of you.'

'Is that a threat, Detective?' Wabash didn't reply. 'Fine. I'll go to the press.'

Wabash let loose a hearty laugh. 'Go right ahead. The woman who buried her head in the sand while her husband planned the worst mass killing in a generation. Yeah. I'm sure everyone will line up to hear what you have to say about the tragic deaths of two people that have absolutely nothing to do with you.'

Even inside Earth+, Cassie could feel her blood beginning to boil. She clenched her fist. She wondered if she could get arrested for assaulting a virtual cop.

'Look, Detective. If Aly Miller's statements about her father are true, then it's possible another Blight is being planned at this very moment. Which means lives are at stake. I don't know why you're not taking this more seriously.'

'I've been a cop for twenty-eight years,' Wabash said. 'Eleven dealing with crimes involving Earth+. And I've never seen anything as horrible as the Blight. It was like the world was collapsing around us. No one in law enforcement will ever forget that day. Some people might believe you – that you didn't know what your husband was doing. I'm not one of them. So let me give you some advice, Ms. West. Go away. Do something with your life, which you're lucky enough to still have. Because a lot of people aren't so lucky. I don't want to ever see you again.'

'Go to hell, Robocop,' Cassie said.

Wabash's eyes flickered again. When they finished, he said, 'Your Wrap is officially barred from this Terminal. Leave Aly Miller alone. That girl has been through enough. I'm also going to put out a Terminal Alert Marker on your Wrap. This means your Wrap will automatically be flagged any time you visit another police Terminal. Harass any more cops, stick your nose in any other cases that don't concern you, and your Wrap could be banned from every police Terminal in Earth+. Goodbye, Ms. West. Have a nice life.'

With that, Cassie disappeared from the precinct and found herself back at her EPD's home screen. She ripped off her visor. She felt blood rising in her cheeks and anger burning in her chest. If Aly Miller was telling the truth, there could be a second Blight on the horizon. Hundreds, *thousands* of lives could be at stake. But she needed to know the truth. She needed to find out what happened to Allyson Miller.

FIVE

Cassie went into her EPD and ran a search for Aly Miller. She couldn't imagine the horror the poor girl had witnessed, what kind of emotional state she was in, and she had no idea where she was. The news report said Aly had been remanded to the state, but Cassie wouldn't be able to get that information unless she was family. She needed another way to find her.

Cassie found the Westbury High virtual yearbook. Aly was fifteen, which would likely place her in sophomore year. There were ninety-nine students in the sophomore class at Westbury, and each student had their own Earth+ page, complete with interactive photos, quotes and more. Cassie noticed that all the students' Wraps had clear, unblemished skin, perfect hair and straight, white teeth. Cassie had gone to school in Earth−, back when school was still held in-person. She'd had braces. Acne. A short, bob-style haircut she thought was quite stylish until she got to college and her freshman-year room-mate handed her a red Solo cup filled to the brim with cranberry vodka and said, 'You can't go out looking like a toilet bowl plunger.'

Kids like Aly Miller had grown up after Hell Week. But not Cassie. Like the rest of the country, she would never forget Hell Week. The week education and the lives of every future generation of children changed forever.

On April 3rd, 2031, teachers, students, and other school faculty around the country marched in peaceful protests against what they felt were escalating threats from politicians and parents, angry about what was taught in curriculums and the lack of practical safety measures to protect teachers and students alike. Teachers who paid for school supplies out of their own pockets despite barely making ends meet were being systematically targeted and harassed by politicians and pundits making millions. Parents came to school board meetings looking to pick a fight. Some of them came armed. Some came drunk. On special nights, they were both. The worst weren't even parents, just 'concerned citizens' willing to do whatever it took – *whatever* it took – to make sure educators stayed the hell out of education.

The peaceful April 3rd protests were met by counterprotests from those parents and other assorted demagogues and militia groups fighting what they claimed was the radicalization of the nation's youth by forcing them to read books about history – *real* history. Politicians and pundits harnessed the power of Earth+ to mobilize thousands of counter-protestors, distributing incendiary and unregulated propaganda inside Lockboxes.

The teachers came bearing signs and bullhorns. The counter-protestors came strapped with semiautomatic rifles. By week's end, twenty-four schoolteachers, eight faculty members and six students had been killed. Two counter-protestors later committed suicide.

And so, on April 16th, 2031, the President signed an Executive Order declaring that, beginning that fall, every school around the country would go virtual. Classes inside Earth+ were safer, they said. Better for kids to grow up socially maladjusted than to have their lives cut short in the middle of geometry. As though those were the only two options.

Kids like Aly had grown up inside virtual classrooms. Many had never even met their closest friends. When her parents died, Aly may have lost the only flesh-and-blood people she'd ever really known.

Cassie needed to know what exactly happened the day Aly's parents died, what her father had said and why the news had gone quiet. She couldn't simply go to Westbury High to find Aly Miller's Wrap. Schools were only legally permitted one Earth+ Terminal, and that Terminal was only accessible to Wraps of students, faculty or authorized family members. When schools first shifted towards virtual learning, anyone could access their Terminals. This quickly became a problem. Predatory Wraps began showing up inside the huddle of girls' soccer teams. Hence, firewalled school Terminals.

There was no legal way for Cassie to access the Westbury Terminal to find Aly Miller. And if anyone found out that Cassie West – aka Mrs. Vertex Ignis – had tried to bypass a school Terminal, she'd have an EPP drone crashing through her window before she could blink.

Maybe the police wouldn't help Cassie get in touch with Aly Miller. But a friend might. She opened a direct message box to @BeGood2All and began typing.

> *My name is Cassandra West. I'm the widow of Harris West. I know this is out of the blue, but I'm contacting you because of what happened to your friend Aly Miller. I think she knows things that are being ignored. I think she might be in trouble. And if she's right, I think a lot of people might be in danger.*

To Cassie's surprise, David Goodwin responded less than fifteen minutes after she sent her message. His message contained a link to an encrypted chat room. If Cassie accepted, every message they wrote would be deleted as soon as it was read by the other party. Not only did David Goodwin want to make sure nobody else could see their chat, but he wanted to make sure there was no record of it. Whatever had happened to Aly Miller had made David Goodwin wary – and maybe even scared.

Cassie joined the chat room and wrote: **Thanks for responding so fast.**

David replied: **How can I be 100% sure this is the real Cassandra West?**

Cassie grabbed a piece of paper, scribbled *It's me*, then snapped a photo of herself holding it and messaged it to David.

Good enough?

Good enough. But you really should comb your hair once in a while.

I don't think you agreed to chat in order to give me fashion tips. You're worried about Aly too.

You said Aly might be in trouble.

Because I think she is.

Why do you think that?

Because in the police report about her parents' deaths, her comments about her father were edited out. She also raised the possibility of her father being involved in another Blight. That was also edited out.

I didn't know that.

All of Aly's social media accounts have been scrubbed, and

she has undoubtedly been denied access to them wherever she is. You probably do know that.

You think it was the cops who did that?

The cops or the EPP. The only story the cops and the press have put out there is that Aly's father was insane. But if there's more to it, they might be ignoring a catastrophe.

Why do you care? Don't you kind of have enough of your own shit to deal with?

People were told lies about the Blight. If they're still being told lies, thousands of people could die. I don't want to see anybody else get hurt. And I want to know the truth.

Well, I care about Aly.

I think our goals are aligned.

Only if it ends with Aly safe. If your goals protect her, then, yeah, we're aligned.

Did you talk to Aly after it happened?

For like two seconds inside a Lockbox, but turns out my parents set up a Lockbox alert. They found out and permanently banned my Wrap from interacting with Aly. I can't message her, see her, or contact her. I wouldn't even know if my Wrap was standing in the same room as her.

Banned? Because of this?

Yes and no. Long story short, my wonderful, godly parents decided that everyone at Westbury was a bad influence. So they're transferring me to a new school and cutting me off from all my friends. Including Aly.

That's awful. I'm sorry. I'm starting to think that maybe the government giving parents total control of their kids' Wraps was a bad idea.

The joys of growing up in Earth+. Your parents can detonate your life at any moment for any reason and you can't do a thing about it. So you really didn't know what he was doing?

Who?

Your husband. Mr. Vertex Ignis.

No. I didn't.

If you're telling the truth, then that sucks royally. Must have been hell.

It still is.

When Past Crimes announced the Blight sim, my mom nearly fainted. They're both Premiere subscribers and have been to

Murderland, like, a dozen times. They said the Earth– park
isn't as cool as it used to be, but they would live in those sims
if it was possible. She's already pre-ordered the Theia visor, and
they're going to an Earth+ launch party at the Terminal near
Leimert Park in LA where they found the Black Dahlia. She
even pre-ordered the Harris West skin for her Wrap to wear
there.

I always made fun of Harris's style. Or lack thereof. Never
in a million years did I think people would pay to dress as him.

Have you watched the teaser for the Blight sim?

No. And I never will.

Guess that's understandable. I've seen it like twenty times.
Going inside the Church of the Beacons? Badass.

So do you know where Aly is now?

I have no idea. She said she'd been contacted by a social
services rep who was going to put her in touch with some government foundation that looked after orphaned kids. That's when
my parents cut me off.

Does Aly have any other family?

She has an aunt who lives somewhere in Maine, but I don't
think Aly has ever even met her outside Earth+ family reunions.
You think there's a connection between what Aly's father did
and what your husband did?

I don't know. But if this is a warning and somebody doesn't
do something, it scares me what might happen.

All right.

A virtual contact card appeared in the chat with the initials *AB*.

Here you go. Just . . . be sensitive. She's been through hell.

Cassie added Aly's info to her virtual contact list and replied.

I will be. I promise.

You know, I always thought you were a little crazy. I was
planning on doing the Blight sim the day it opens too. I usually
go for the ones where there's a kidnapping or a weird disappearance. I like trying to solve a mystery. Find someone before it's
too late.

If they're part of a Past Crimes sim, it's already too late.

My parents think you're a liar.

What do you think?

They haven't been right about much. But I'll reserve
judgment until you find Aly.

I'll find her. You're a good friend, David.

Crap. I gotta run. My stupid parents get an alert every time I use an encrypted chat room and they want to make sure I'm not doing anything terrible like thinking for myself.

Get out of here. And thank you.

Hey, Cassie?

Yes?

Find Aly. Make sure she's OK.

I will. I promise.

Cassie didn't have the heart to tell David that even if she found Aly, she couldn't change what had already happened. Cassie knew better than anyone that alive and healthy did not necessarily mean you were OK.

Cassie opened Aly Miller's virtual contact card and composed an email.

> *Dear Aly – I got your email from David Goodwin. He's a great friend. My name is Cassandra West. My husband was Harris West. I probably don't need to say more. I learned about what happened to you, and there are no words to express my sympathy. I can't imagine what you're going through right now. But I need to talk to you. What you might not know is that your interview with the police has been cut from the official record. Including what you said about your father, who he claimed to be and what he might have been a part of. I think what he said is hugely important. I think lives could be in danger. I wouldn't ask if it wasn't a matter of life or death. Tell me if there's any way we can speak. I'll do anything. Thank you, Aly. I believe you.*
>
> *Cassie West*

Cassie took a deep breath. Then she went to the kitchen, opened the fridge and took out a bottle of white wine. She had no idea how long it had been in there. She uncorked it and took a swig. It tasted like acid laced with sugar. She spat the mouthful into the sink and dumped the rest down the drain. She opened the cabinet in search of something – anything – to drink and heard a *ping* from the other side of the room.

Cassie ran, nearly tripping over her slippers, and found an email waiting for her. The sender was Allyson Miller. There was no subject. The message was just one word.

OK.

Cassie thought for a moment. She didn't have a follow-up planned. Finally, she wrote:

I'll rent a Lockbox and send you the link.

No Lockboxes. Nothing good has ever happened in Earth+.

OK. How, then?

You come here. We meet in person. Or we don't meet at all.

Cassie didn't hesitate. **Tell me where to go.**

SIX

July 17th, 2047
10:16 a.m.

When the plane landed in Dallas, Cassie absently checked her phone, expecting a text from Harris saying *Welcome home!* Instead, her screen was black. It had been over ten years since her last flight, a trip to Boise to meet with the Bruns family, the last people on the planet who didn't use Earth+. Their son, Gavin, had vanished the day after his wedding with his twenty-year-old mistress and the $4.4 million he'd embezzled from his law firm. Cassie signed the Brunses, then sold their story as an interactive drama to InterStream for $2.1 million, less than half of what their son stole.

Back then, she'd had a husband. She'd had a job. She'd had hope. A wave of sorrow washed over her, the ache she still felt every single day, just as powerful as ever. It was a wound that would never heal, never close, as long as she still drew breath.

The driverless car picked Cassie up at Dallas/Fort Worth airport and headed south on 35W to her destination: the TAP – Thoughts and Prayers – Foundation, a taxpayer-subsidized twenty-first-century orphanage that took in orphaned, abandoned and homeless children. Yet Aly referred to the TAP Foundation in one of her emails as 'a detention center, but with crappier food' so maybe the name wasn't quite so spot on.

The TAP headquarters was located in Hillsboro, about halfway between Dallas and Waco. The flight had cost Cassie $4,000, leaving enough money in her bank account to buy a salad (no protein) and a bottle of water (not purified). She'd only packed a carry-on bag with a single change of clothes, basic toiletries, a portable Earth+ visor, a charger and . . . well, that was pretty much it. If the trip lasted longer than twenty-four hours, she'd have to buy more clothes. Or at least a stronger deodorant.

When the car arrived, Cassie saw that, if anything, Aly had been overly generous in her description of the TAP Foundation as a detention center. To Cassie, it resembled nothing less than a prison.

The TAP Foundation was a large, three-story concrete slab that took up the majority of a sandblasted block in central-east Texas. The windows had thick iron bars. Half a dozen security guards wearing body armor and carrying rifles the size of Cassie's leg patrolled the roof. Two more armed guards stood outside the entrance. Cassie wondered if she should have worn body armor, just to fit in.

A little further down the road, Cassie could see the Hillsboro prison, its brick walls topped by barbed wire, patrolled by legions of armed guards. If not for the TAP Foundation sign out front – 'Thoughts and Prayers Save Lives' – Cassie wouldn't have been able to tell the difference between the two buildings.

She approached the TAP Foundation slowly, holding her hands palms up in front of her.

'I'm unarmed,' she said. The guards did not respond.

She ascended the concrete steps to the front door. The guards had still not acknowledged her presence. She looked for an intercom or doorbell but saw nothing. She went to knock, but one of the guards said, 'Don't do that.'

Cassie turned to him. 'I have an appointment.'

'Your name and the name of the Boarder you're here to see,' he said.

'Boarder? You mean the child I'm visiting?'

'Here, they're called Boarders.'

'All right,' Cassie said. 'I'm here to see *Boarder* Allyson Miller.'

'Louder,' the guard replied.

'I'M HERE TO SEE *BOARDER* ALLYSON MILLER.'

The guard put his finger to his ear and nodded twice. 'Voice checks out. You're Cassandra West.'

'I am.'

'My sister died in the Blight,' the other guard said. Even though his face was hidden behind a black visor, Cassie knew he was staring daggers at her.

'I'm sorry,' Cassie said.

'You should have burned along with your husband,' the guard replied.

Before she could respond, the front door swung open. A diminutive woman barely five feet tall stood in the doorway. Her metal-gray hair was buzzed to half an inch, and she wore large, round glasses that made her pupils look like olives in a martini glass. But it wasn't the woman's appearance that made the biggest impression. It was the fact that she was carrying a rifle nearly as tall as she was. And she was aiming the barrel at Cassie's face.

Cassie opened her mouth, but no sound came out. She was pretty sure her heart had stopped. Thankfully, the woman lowered the gun. Then she held out a tiny hand and offered a broad smile.

'Emmeline Procter,' the woman said. 'Director of Boarder Services at the TAP Foundation.'

She jabbed her hand at Cassie again. Once the shock from having the portable cannon aimed at her face wore off, Cassie took Procter's hand and shook it. The woman's grip was gentle. A teacher, not an infantryman.

'Sorry for the rude greeting,' Procter said. 'We take security very seriously at TAP. As you know, children are valuable assets.'

'Assets?' Cassie said. 'You mean kids.'

Procter smiled. 'Right. Kids.'

'Why the . . .' Cassie pointed at the rifle nestled in Emmeline's arms.

'Operation Child Barrier,' Procter said. 'The government passed it after Hell Week. It mandates that any physical entity functioning as a shelter for children under the age of eighteen requires all faculty to be trained in advanced weaponry and trauma care, and to carry a loaded, legally obtained and fully functional firearm at all times. For the safety of both ourselves and our Boarders.'

'You mean your kids.'

'Right.'

'So you're mandated to carry a bazooka with you at all times?'

Procter laughed. 'Walk softly and carry a rifle that can shoot sixty rounds per minute.'

'So *all* faculty are required to be armed?' Cassie said.

'Every single person who gets a paycheck from TAP. Even our cooks are packing twenty-four/seven,' Emmeline said. 'We're subject to random government inspections. I'd say twenty or so per year. We're fined fifty grand for every infraction. Hence, Franklin here.'

'Franklin?'

'That's what I call my AR-99. Franklin. I named it after my ex-husband. Figured it was a good name for something that causes nothing but pain. Don't worry, Ms. West. I can shoot an ant off a frog's head. If you do anything to jeopardize our assets, let's just say Franklin gets offended easily. If I shoot you, it's because you deserved it.'

'That's reassuring,' Cassie said, not reassured at all. 'Thank you for agreeing to let me see Aly.'

'I'll be honest,' Procter said, 'I was kind of curious to meet you.'

'Why?'

'Most people think they know everything there is to know about Harris West. Not much out there about you.'

'People don't know everything about Harris West,' Cassie said.

'Hard to stay hidden these days. People who hide are usually hiding something.'

'If I'm hidden, then why am I here?'

'My boyfriend thinks you're an ice queen and that you knew what was coming,' Procter said. 'Maybe even had a say in it. Me? I tend to look for the good in people. I think you got blindsided. Maybe you're even a half-decent person. Guess we'll know more once that Past Crimes sim goes live.'

'I'm not here to talk about my family,' Cassie said. 'I'm just here to see Allyson Miller.'

Emmeline's smile disappeared. 'She's a livewire, that one.'

'What do you mean?'

'Allyson Miller. Fifteen. Orphaned. Most orphans are rather subdued when they come to us. But not Aly Miller. She was quite disruptive when she arrived. Loud. Impatient. Demanding.'

'Demanding in what way?'

'Oh, just to know more about what happened to her family, what would happen to her next – just jabbering non-stop.'

'Her parents died right in front of her. I'd hope you and your staff would cut her some slack.'

'Cut some of these kids enough slack,' Procter said, 'and they'll string you up with it. Don't worry, though. We got through to her. She listens, now.'

'Got through to her? How?'

'We have our methods,' Procter said. 'If Boarders are willful, you need to find a way to break their will. They need to be told what they can and can't do, what they can and can't learn, what they can and can't be.'

'We're still talking about children, right?'

'You'd be surprised at how willful some *children* can be,' Procter said. 'Come. Ms. Miller is this way.'

The doors closed behind Cassie with a loud *clang*. She guessed the entryway was reinforced with steel. A tank would have a hard time breaking into this place. She wondered whether all this security was meant to keep people out or to keep the kids in.

They passed through several security gates. At each one, Cassie underwent a full-body scan plus a retinal and fingerprint scan, all while being watched by guards wielding progressively larger weaponry as if they were leveling up in a video game. There were walkways above the corridors, all patrolled by guards, their heavy boots clanging on the metal.

'Doesn't this seem kind of like overkill?' Cassie said, as Procter led her down a concrete hallway with a dozen cameras embedded in the ceiling. 'Don't you guys just, you know, take care of lost kids?'

'Like I said, government mandate. We house hundreds of Boarders here, Ms. West. Some of them, like Ms. Miller, tragically lost their parents. Many of our Boarders were orphaned following government-mandated forced births. Keeping all of these Boarders housed, fed and healthy costs tens of millions of dollars a year. Some of that comes from corporate donations. The rest has to be worked off by the Boarders themselves. Each Boarder has a debt when they arrive, which varies depending on their age and needs. If they don't work it off before they leave, it will be docked from any future earnings when they do. If they flee, we lose that income and face hefty fines. Hence, the security measures.'

'Some security measures, sure. But there's enough firepower in this place to take on North Korea.'

'Some people think this level of security is necessary.'

'And I'm sure those "people" receive no money from the purchase of these weapons.'

'TAP is a public institution,' Procter said. 'Without government funding or sponsorship revenue, we close our doors.'

'So the government funds you, you purchase the weapons, the weapon sellers donate money to the politicians who run the government. A perfect loop.'

'We give our Boarders clothes and food,' Procter said. 'And no *children* have died on my watch.'

'High bar you've set,' Cassie said. 'Where's the exit? I only saw the entrance.'

'That is the exit,' Procter said.

'There's only one way in and out?' Cassie said. Procter nodded. 'What if there's a fire?'

'Then you'd better hope you're a faster runner than the person behind you.'

A door at the far end opened and a pair of orderlies appeared pushing a stretcher. On top was a young man, maybe sixteen or seventeen, strapped to the gurney. He was convulsing, his eyes rolled back in their sockets, his arms and legs thrashing beneath his bonds. An IV pumped something blue into his arm. Procter and Cassie stepped to the side to allow them to hustle past. They then disappeared through the door Cassie had just come through.

'That kid was having a Neural Flare,' Cassie said.

'Most likely,' Procter replied. 'It's not uncommon, but thankfully we have a terrific medical staff at TAP.'

'How much time do the Boarders spend in Earth+?'

'Our Boarders spend six to eight hours a day in virtual school. Then we have mandatory focus testing for some of our corporate sponsors. Products, entertainment, Wrap attire. We also livestream some of the younger Boarders playing with new toys and products. It helps defray the cost of food and lodging. And yes, before you ask, they do receive a percentage of the sponsorship and advertising revenue.'

'A percentage. How magnanimous.'

'We don't have to give them *anything*, Ms. West. We shelter and feed eight hundred and twenty-nine children a day here. The cost of that is astronomical. If you'd like to question my methods or my credentials, you are free to leave.'

'Not until I see Aly Miller.'

'You know, Ms. Miller has been here almost a month and a half, and you're the first person who's even tried to come to see her.'

'Really,' Cassie said, surprised. 'Not one visitor?'

'Afraid so. The truth is, visitors are not common here. The ones whose parents . . . left them . . . have no family. Some boarders lost their parents to violence or drugs. Some are simply troubled young souls who pushed away everyone who cared about them.'

'Then they're the ones you need to work the hardest on.'

Procter said nothing. They continued walking.

A metal door slid open, revealing a long corridor with light-green tiling. Slivers of sunlight filtered down through a skylight in the high ceiling. The corridor was lined with rooms, each one housing a child – or more accurately, containing them. Each room was fronted with some sort of reinforced glass that stretched wall to wall and floor to ceiling. Some rooms housed teenagers. Some housed children who looked as young as three or four. Every child was wearing white pants, white slippers and a baggy white shirt with a number stitched on the front. The children all had hollow, vacant looks in their eyes, the product of medication, malnutrition or hopelessness. They looked at Cassie and, for a moment, a few eyes glimmered. Then, as she passed their rooms, the lights dimmed once again.

Each room was about twelve feet by twelve and contained a single bed with a thin mattress, a metal desk, a bookshelf, ancient Earth+ visors, charging stations and a sink. In the far corner of each room was an enclosed space of frosted glass, about three by three, housing a combination toilet and shower.

'We call these Homerooms,' Procter replied. 'Combination home and classroom.'

One boy, eight or nine, lay on his back on the concrete floor, unmoving except for the rise and fall of his chest. A girl of no more than four sat at a desk, alone, her face shielded by an Earth+ visor. Another boy, fifteen or so, beat against the glass as they passed. Cassie couldn't hear him – the glass was soundproof – but she could read (some) of the angry words on his lips. Eventually, he gave up and slid to the floor, defeated.

'These don't look like any homerooms I've ever seen,' Cassie said. 'They look like cages.'

'Not in the least. Each room is a hundred and forty-four square feet, which is the size of the average child's bedroom. Every Homeroom has a state-of-the-art air filtration system that prevents nincty-nine-point-nine percent of germs from entering or exiting.

Each Boarder has monitored access to Earth+, including a complimentary suite of pre-recorded educational programs and selected
entertainment programs picked by our sponsors. Boarders get to
spend two hours a day outside, weather permitting, plus three square
meals and high-protein snacks. They have two hour-long Earth+
sessions every week with our Augmented Persona child psychiatrist
algorithm. And that safety glass could stop a rail gun.'

'Let me guess. Mandated by Operation Child Barrier.'

Procter nodded. 'The state spares no expense when it comes to
protecting the life of a child from threats, visible and otherwise.'

'Those uniforms certainly don't look cheap,' Cassie asked.

'Those *uniforms* are military-grade, specially designed microbial
repellent fibers. They may not be fashionable, but they are germ-
resistant. And at the end of every day, we go over each child from
head to toe with a UV light to identify any foreign contaminants.
Same for any Boarder returning from a Road Trip.'

'Road trip? You let them outside the compound?'

'We offer short-term Road Trips to our Boarders, if, say, a distant
relative wants to take them for a weekend. Often these relatives
don't want to care for a child full-time but are amenable to a short-
term rental. We do charge a fee for these trips, to offset the earnings
lost while the child is out of our hands.'

'What if the kids don't come back?'

'If the Boarders don't return, or return in suboptimal condition
that curtails their earning potential, the renter loses their deposit
and must cover the Boarder's projected earnings.'

'So basically, you break it, you buy it.'

'In a matter of speaking.'

'How old are the children in your care?'

'The Boarders range from age two to seventeen.'

'Two? That young?'

'Bad things don't only happen to those who are prepared for
them.'

'What happens when the kids turn eighteen?'

'Once they turn eighteen, they're of legal age. They are no longer
protected by the state, and we can't mandate sponsorships on them.
So they go wherever they want, I suppose.'

'What if they have nowhere to go? Does anyone check on these
kids once they're out of your hands?'

'We have a post-Boarder security monitoring service, available to all our graduates for four thousand nine hundred and ninety-nine dollars a year. If they refuse the service, there's nothing more we can do.'

'How can these kids afford five thousand a year for security monitoring?'

'We do offer affordable loans,' Procter said. 'Well, here we are.'

At the far end of the corridor, Cassie saw a metal stool placed in front of one of the Homerooms. There were large television screens attached to the walls in between each Homeroom, each on a different channel. The children who were plugged into Earth+ or in a semi-catatonic state watched them with sunken, red-rimmed eyes.

Procter gestured to the seat in front of Aly Miller's cell. Cassie took a seat and looked inside at its occupant.

A young woman sat on the bed. She was thin and haggard, her body all angles. She was fifteen but looked several years younger. Her white clothing hung off her bones, and Cassie could see her thin wrists beneath her sleeves. Her hair was long on top and in the back and looked as if it had once been buzzed on the sides but had started to grow in unevenly. She held her head low, with an angry, almost feral look in her eyes, a fierceness that told Cassie that even if she was malnourished, she was very smart and very capable.

Procter took a device from her hip and pressed a button. 'Allows sound to pass through,' she said to Cassie. Turning to Aly, she said, 'How are we today, Ms. Miller?' Aly said nothing. 'When she got here, all she talked about was conspiracy theories. We managed to put a stop to that. Now, she doesn't say much.'

'Maybe it's because nobody listens,' Cassie said.

'Squeaky wheels get the grease,' Procter said. 'Silent ones just stay broken. Enjoy your chat, Ms. West. Ms. Miller, behave yourself.'

With that, Procter turned and headed back down the corridor. The metal door slid open, then shut noiselessly behind her, leaving Cassie alone with Aly.

'She's a piece of work,' Cassie said. 'How are you?'

Aly simply stared at Cassie. Then she offered a slight smile and said, 'Hello, Clarice.'

'I'm sorry?'

'Just something from an old movie.'

'Oh, right.' Cassie eyed the glass wall separating them. 'Took me a second. So you like the classics?'

Aly nodded. 'Used to. Now the only movies I get to watch are overblown Earth+ productions in our focus groups. Hannibal Lecter had it better. At least he got to have artwork on the walls of his cell. Maybe I should have eaten people instead of, you know, watching my parents die.'

'I'm so sorry for what you've been through,' Cassie said. 'For what happened to your parents. For this.'

Aly nodded and said, softly, 'Thanks. You'd be kind of surprised how few people have said that.'

'I mean it. Thanks for agreeing to meet with me.'

'No sweat. You're the first person I've spoken to who doesn't work here since I've been here.'

'What do you mean?'

'They don't let us talk to the other kids,' Aly said. 'Boarders, I mean.'

'How can they do that?'

'Apparently, a few kids – Boarders – escaped a few years ago. They planned it together during group exercise. So now for exercise they just plop a portable treadmill into our cells – sorry, *Homerooms*. I think they figure if they keep us apart, less chance of us planning a coup.'

'Don't you get, you know, outside time?'

'Yup. In ten-by-ten pens. Like a pig,' Aly said. 'So is your husband really innocent?'

'Right to the point,' Cassie said. 'I believe he is, yes.'

Aly nodded, as though that answer was some sort of confirmation. 'Well, if you're telling the truth, then your husband got the shit end of the stick and you've been getting fucked with it ever since.'

'Are you doing OK in here?'

Aly didn't say anything for a moment. Then she stood up, tilted her head up at the ceiling and spun around like a wobbly top and sat back down.

'I'm just peachy. I love this place. Like a five-star hotel but instead of thousand thread count sheets and room service, you get blankets that feel like horse hooves and food that tastes like the inside of someone's lower intestine.'

'What did your lawyer say? Did you have any other options besides TAP?'

'Sure. My other option was a mansion in the Hamptons with a

pool and RoboButler. I chose this place. I might have made a mistake.'

'David Goodwin said you had an aunt.'

'I do. We met for the first time ever at her lawyer's office in Earth+. How did she put it? She and her husband had life plans and those didn't include kids. She wished me luck. The whole meeting lasted less time than a shower.'

'Don't you have a lawyer? Someone on your side?'

'The state appointed me a guardian ad litem. The social services guy told me that with all the crimes in both Earth+ *and* Earth−, the government ran out of money for public defenders. I got the guardian ad litem dude for five hours. I think my time expired before he finished reading the police report. Otherwise, it's not all that different from my life in Earth−. During school hours we do a bunch of pre-recorded Earth+ educational programs. Then we do product testing for various Earth+ sponsors. Sometimes they put haptic suits and sensors on us, then make us listen to music or watch movies. They record our reactions and pass them along to . . . whoever. For every twenty hours of testing I complete, I get one hour of free time. I took two this week to watch the interactive version of *Dr. Strangelove*. There's something to be said for riding an enormous bomb into oblivion. Once I stash away another few hours, I'm watching *Double Indemnity*. I would totally let Barbara Stanwyck use me for whatever she wanted.'

'I know this is a tough subject to bring up, and I don't have a better segue. But I don't think we have much time. Can we talk about what happened the day your parents died?'

'Sure. Let's move on to happier topics.'

'In the police report I read, you told Detective Wabash that your father said he was a Beacon.'

'That's right.'

Cassie felt a chill. 'Did he say exactly what he was going to do?'

'Not exactly. But once the cops found the kerosene, it was pretty clear. He was going to burn our house down. Probably with both my mom and him inside. I figure he told me because he didn't want me to be there when he did it.'

'Kerosene?' Cassie said. 'That wasn't in the police report.'

'Yeah, well, obviously, they left a lot out. They think my dad was just some crazy person. And I guess he was, at the end. Crazy. But he was saying things. Scary things. I studied the Blight. I know what happened. I know who the Beacons were and what they did. And what my dad was saying . . . he mentioned new friends. If he was a Beacon, then he wasn't alone.'

'Who scrubbed your feeds?' Cassie asked.

'They did, I assume?'

'Who is "they"?'

'The government? The EPD? As soon as my aunt declined to take over my guardianship, my attorney said all legal rights to my feeds and my Wrap would be turned over to the state until I turned eighteen. The state's attorney said my dad was a whacko who acted alone. He also said that spreading any disinformation in Earth+ or Earth− could create an unnecessary panic and potentially be a prosecutable offense. They deleted everything. Even the pictures I took with my own EPD. It's like my life and my memories don't belong to me anymore.'

'It doesn't sound like anyone had your best interests at heart.'

'I can't remember the last time I ever felt like someone had my best interests at heart.'

Cassie felt something pull at her own heart, like a violin string being plucked.

'Did your dad say when this was going to happen?'

'He said the numbers three six five two,' Aly said. 'At first, I thought it was nonsense. Then I thought about it. And it hit me. July nineteenth, 2047, is exactly three thousand, six hundred and fifty-two days after the first Blight.'

'If he was telling the truth, we don't have much time. Did he mention who any of these friends were he met? Names?'

'My dad didn't have friends. Not in real life. Whoever he met, it was inside Earth+. People always tell you that Earth+ was this amazing thing that opened up new worlds. We could do anything we wanted, whenever we wanted. Everything would be amazing. Your dreams would come to life.'

'They told me Earth+ would change the way we lived and worked and played,' Cassie said. 'What they don't tell you is that this new world has dark corners. But they don't want to talk about all the things you can't see. They don't want you to know what people do in the shadows.'

'Everyone has said my dad was crazy,' Aly said. 'The police. Procter. Even the stupid therapist algorithms they have me talking to. I don't know. Maybe he *was* crazy.'

'He might have been crazy,' Cassie said. 'But that doesn't mean he was lying.'

'A few years ago, my dad cheated on my mom,' Aly said. 'He rode his bike twenty miles to meet up with an old girlfriend he'd run into at a convention in Earth+. At first, he denied it. But I knew he was lying. His upper lip always curled upwards when he was lying. But when he told me he was a Beacon, his lip didn't move. He wasn't lying to me the day he died. He said everything is going to change at midnight on that day.'

Cassie shivered. 'All of this points to something I really don't want to think is possible.'

'You think there's going to be a second Blight. Just like I do.'

Cassie nodded. 'I do. I think those "friends" your father met were other Beacons. And I think the second Blight is going to start at midnight on July nineteenth. The tenth anniversary of the first Blight.'

'Somebody brainwashed my dad. In there,' she said, pointing to the Earth+ visor in its charging dock. 'I want to know who.'

'They said there was a church inside Earth+ where all the Beacons were radicalized by my husband,' Cassie said.

'But your husband died ten years ago,' Aly said.

'That's right.'

'My dad said that Harris West might be dead, but the Vertex Ignis is alive. So if my dad was radicalized, it couldn't have been by your husband.'

'No. No, it couldn't.'

Aly sat there for a moment, thinking, then said, 'You know, I was kind of hoping that when I met you, you'd be crazy. Like a full-on lunatic who ate metal cans or something, with a weird mad-scientist perm and walking around muttering random numbers under your breath or smearing poop on the walls.'

'I'm about sixty percent of the way there,' Cassie said.

'I wish my dad really was crazy too. Like they're saying. At least then nobody else could get hurt. But if it's like we both think . . .' She trailed off.

'Then a lot more people might get hurt,' Cassie replied. 'More than ten years ago. Maybe much more. Ten years ago, a lot of people were still feeling out Earth+. Now, there's a much, much larger pool of potential Beacons to draw from all over the world. This could be catastrophic.'

'If there is another Blight,' Aly said, 'it means someone convinced a lot of people to die for them while they came out unscathed.'

'People in power always leave it to everyone else to do their suffering,' Cassie replied.

'So, what do we do?' Aly asked. 'My dad was the only lead we had and he's dead.'

'"We" don't do anything,' Cassie replied curtly. 'If there is a second Blight planned for July nineteenth, it's on me to figure out what to do.'

Aly stood up, fast, and approached the glass. 'No, my parents are *dead*. I want answers just like you. I want to know who did this to my dad.'

'I understand,' Cassie said. 'If I were you, I'd want those answers too. But you're staying here.'

'The hell I am!' Aly shouted. As soon as she did, a red light flashed above her Homeroom partition. Another one lit up inside the chamber.

'What is that?' Cassie said.

'We get a warning when we raise our voices above the maximum permitted decibel level,' Aly said. 'Three of those in a week and we lose outdoor privileges. Cassie. You *have* to get me out of here.'

'I'm sorry. I am. But that's not my problem.'

'When I was with the guardian ad litem, and his time was up,' Aly said, 'I told him I still didn't know where I was going. Know what he said? "Sorry, that's not my problem."'

'I . . .' Cassie began. But then she stopped. She had nothing to say.

'So where do you go now? The cops? The media? They all pretty much hate you.'

'I don't know.'

Aly was right. Nobody was going to listen to her. Then, from the corner of her eye, she saw one of the television screens turn red, the famous crime-scene logo of Past Crimes emerging in its center. Below it, a tagline read: **Prepare to Enter the Blight.**

Cassie groaned. So far, she'd been able to avoid the teaser for the Past Crimes sim, despite it being more ubiquitous than Starbucks. But this time, she couldn't look away. It showed scenes from the upcoming sim. A bizarre church. The bloodstained floor of somebody's home. And then . . . Harris's home office. Cassie got up and went closer. It was just how she remembered it. Just how Harris had left it. Except . . .

'What is it?' Aly said.

'The Blight sim,' she replied, her head spinning. 'Harris's office. It's missing something.'

'Missing something?'

Cassie nodded. 'I think I know what I need to do now.'

'What?'

'Past is prologue,' Cassie said.

'What does that mean?'

'It means I have to go back to the Blight.'

Aly's eyes widened. 'You're talking about Past Crimes. Their Blight sim.'

Cassie nodded. 'I know this company and I know Crispin Lake. They've likely spared no expense completely recreating the entire Blight. The Beacons, the church where Harris allegedly preached, everything. They use everything that's available, and even some things that aren't.'

'You think Past Crimes knows more about the Blight than the police do?'

'Without question,' Cassie said. 'The cops can't pay for information. Crispin Lake can. But somebody removed that device from the crime scene. If Lake recreated the Blight, he may have inadvertently recreated clues. If the Skin Reader is missing, what else might be missing? The Blight sim could prove that somebody didn't want the truth getting out.'

'But if the second Blight is planned for midnight on July nineteenth, the moment the Blight sim goes public, you'll be too late to do anything.'

'I don't plan to enter the sim with the rest of the public,' Cassie said. 'I'm going to go in before they do.'

'How in the hell will you be able to do that?'

'Because I can offer Crispin Lake the one thing he's never been able to have.'

'What's that?'

'Me.'

'You?' Aly said, a disgusted look on her face. 'You're going to sleep with him?'

'First of all, ew. Second of all, ew again.'

'I mean, that's what it sounded like.'

'No. I mean the virtual me, not the physical me.'

'Phew. Not that I'm judging. But I still don't get how you can convince them to let you in before everybody else.'

'A few years ago, Crispin invited me to a private Lockbox. Just the two of us. I agreed. He told me Past Crimes was developing a sim based on the Blight. This was before they announced it publicly. And he wanted me to be a part of it.'

'I take it you said no.'

'He offered me money. A lot of money. He wanted to create a full Cassandra West Augmented Persona inside their Blight sim. But Harris would still be the Vertex Ignis, and I would just be a naïve, clueless wife, oblivious to the evil her husband was planning. Lake told me it was my chance to be absolved and forgiven. That people would see for themselves that I had no part in the Blight. But even though he thought he was freeing me, he was still condemning my husband. So I said no. And I never heard from him again.'

'So why do you think he'd believe you changed your mind now?'

'Because Crispin Lake is a perfectionist. When he finds out there's an error in his sim, he'll realize somebody didn't want the truth out there. He'll want to know who. And nobody knows the world of Harris and Cassie West better than, well, Cassie West.'

'There's no way in hell Crispin Lake would be willing to let a civilian into his sim early,' Aly said.

'Those are the two things people like Crispin Lake hate,' Cassie said. 'Not being able to get everything you want and finding out that you were wrong.'

'So what are you going to do?'

'The Blight sim launches in less than three days. I have to get in touch with Crispin Lake, convince him to let me into the sim, and hopefully prevent a global massacre.'

'I have to go with you,' Aly said. 'I have the same right to be a part of this as you do. My life was ruined, just like yours. Why do you get to try and I don't?'

'Because I'm out here and you're in there,' Cassie said.

'Go to hell,' Aly said.

'I'm sorry. I really am. I appreciate everything you told me. And I believe you. Even if nobody else does.'

As Cassie turned to walk away, the door at the far end of the hallway opened. Emmeline Procter approached, flanked by a pair of orderlies armed with rifles.

'Focus group time for Ms. Miller,' Procter said. A third orderly appeared holding a straitjacket. Cassie could see a syringe sticking out of Procter's jacket pocket.

'What are you doing to her?' Cassie said.

'Ms. Miller isn't always the most agreeable Boarder. Sometimes we have to *encourage* her to work with us. So, in the event she doesn't come with us of her own volition, we have to ensure she comes anyway.'

'No!' Aly cried. 'Please. Ms. West. Get me out of here.'

'I . . . I can't,' Cassie said.

Aly pounded on the glass. Her wrists were so skinny. Even beneath the baggy clothes, Cassie could see bone. Cassie's heart broke just looking at her. Aly was clearly a fighter, but she looked as if life threw one more obstacle at her, it would knock her down for good.

'*Get. Me. Out of here!*'

'You know I can't do that.'

'Yes, you *can*,' Aly said. 'There's no one else. My parents are *dead*. I have the same right as you to find answers.'

Aly was right. But Cassie couldn't.

'I'm sorry,' she said. 'I promise that if I can, I'll come back.'

Cassie started to walk away. Procter and the orderlies passed her in the hall.

'*Please*,' Aly cried. Cassie heard her banging on the glass, the sound ringing through the hallway, the nearly emaciated girl still possessing ferocity within her. 'I need to know! This isn't just about you! This is my *life*!'

Cassie ignored the pleas, even as each cry cut her like a blade.

'Ms. West! Cassie! Come back!'

Aly stopped talking. Cassie heard the glass partition of Aly Miller's Homeroom slide open.

'Get the hell away from me,' Aly spat.

'We've been down this road before, Ms. Miller,' Procter said. 'You can come with us or we can carry you with us. Your choice.'

Cassie could hear Aly's agonizing, angry sobs. She closed her eyes, wished she could drown out the sound. She turned around. Two burly orderlies held Aly in the air by each arm, like a twig between two oaks. A third was pulling some sort of liquid into a syringe.

'Keep her head still,' the orderly said, bringing the syringe to Aly's neck.

Procter stood there, watching, a look of disappointment on her face.

'Get that away from me!' Aly said. Cassie could see the girl's neck tendons straining, could even see her carotid artery pulsing as her heartbeat sped up.

Then one more wail came from Aly's lips.

'*Please.*'

At that moment, for reasons she couldn't quite understand, Cassie thought about the family of Joy Ruiz. The last family she'd signed before Harris died and her world imploded. She thought about Hector. How he'd called her a Blood Banker. How the insult cut her deeper than the boy knew.

Somewhere in the back of her mind, when she sat across from that grieving family, she knew Hector was right, that she was, essentially, putting a price tag on a young girl's life. But she told herself it was just her job, that she had bills to pay too and that she didn't owe these people anything more than the money they would receive to turn their story over to her. Their pain would be Cassie's profit and that was the way the world worked. Cassie didn't create that system. She just worked within it.

But after seeing Aly, what was happening to this young, helpless girl, once again she felt that fingernail dragging across her heart, telling her that another girl's life was being converted into currency right before her eyes. She'd ignored that feeling before. Too many times. She'd buried it deep and covered it with denial and excuses.

She couldn't do it again. She thought about David Goodwin's last words to her.

Find Aly. Make sure she's OK.

I will. I promise.

'Procter!' Cassie shouted. The Director held up her hand just as the needle was about to sink into Aly's flesh.

'Yes, Ms. West?'

'So how much do those Road Trips cost?'

SEVEN

July 17th, 2047
12:47 p.m.
Thirty-five hours and thirteen minutes to launch

Cassie stood outside the TAP Foundation, two armed guards at her back, a teenage girl at her side, wondering just how in the hell this had all happened. In order to allow Aly a one-week Road Trip, Cassie had agreed to fork out what essentially amounted to every dime she had left to her name. Between what she would owe the TAP Foundation *and* the Replenish program, Cassie would be in debt until the year 2956, give or take. There was a modicum of satisfaction in knowing that when she died, given that she had no family and no children, those companies would be stuck footing the bill.

It would be the shortest road trip in history, though, if she couldn't get through to Crispin Lake. She had one shot at this. And she hoped to God she was right.

Thankfully, she still had the email address Lake had used when they were negotiating the Gerald Boone agreement while she worked at V.I.C.E. She'd dealt mostly with the Past Crimes' in-house counsel, Salman Jalal. Although Jalal was always responsive and respectful, for something as big as this she couldn't risk going to anyone else but Lake himself. She had no idea if Crispin Lake still used it, or if it went to some assistant who might assume it was a prank and delete it. It was probably her only chance. It had to work.

Aly held up Cassie's phone and gave her a 'three, two, one, thumbs up' countdown. She was recording. Cassie took a breath and spoke.

'Hello, Mr. Lake. My name is Cassandra West, but you knew that before I said a word. You know I wouldn't reach out to you unless it was important. Well, I can't think of anything more important. I believe there is a second Blight coming. And I believe somebody falsified the crime scene at my home after Harris's death, and that crime scene then made it into your sim. In short, your Blight simulation is not the full truth. If you want to know why, I request that we meet. In person. At your Murderland complex in West Valley. If I'm right, tens of thousands of lives are at stake – maybe more. And I believe the key to stopping it may be within your simulation. You might know the Blight better than anyone, but I know my home and my husband better than anyone. And the home you recreated is not fully accurate. I know this is highly unusual, to say the least, and I know how closely guarded your sims are. But if I'm right, we could save hundreds, maybe thousands, of lives and possibly rewrite history the way it actually happened. Now, I'm sure part of you is skeptical. So I'll make it worth your time. If I'm wrong, I'll agree to the terms you posed to me when we met a few years ago. I will agree to let you use my likeness, voice, biometrics, and everything else you want for your Blight sim. You will be able to reconfigure whatever Augmented Persona you've created of me to have it reflect the *real* me. You will have full, complete access to Cassandra Ann West. You have nothing to lose, Mr. Lake, and everything to gain. You could be a hero. You could stop a horrible act of terrorism. The choice is yours. I hope to hear from you soon.'

'Got it,' Aly said.

'OK. Let me rewatch it before I send—'

'Too late. Already sent.'

'You didn't.'

'I did.'

'Well, I guess now we wait.'

Two minutes later, Cassie's phone vibrated. Her breath caught in her chest when she saw she had a new message. The sender: Crispin Lake. And it came with a video attachment.

Cassie opened the video. Aly perched herself over Cassie's shoulder.

'Is that him?' Aly said.

Cassie nodded. 'That's him.'

Crispin Lake sat at a large, clear, sparkling glass desk. Framed photos of some of the most notorious criminals in history hung on the wall behind him. His hands were steepled on the table.

'Cassie,' Lake said. 'I always had a feeling our paths would cross again. Needless to say, if there's anything we can do to prevent a crime from occurring, we will. That said, you can understand if I do question your motives, so I accept your proposition. I'll send a first-class airline ticket to your EPD; just let me know where you're flying out of. You will be my guest at Murderland. Once we debrief, I'll evaluate whether to let you into our simulation. Regardless, I'm excited to meet you, Cassie. In person. Finally.'

Cassie hadn't expected a response so fast. Part of her hadn't expected a response at all.

'He's in,' Cassie said.

'Holy crap. He's going to let you into the sim?'

'If he believes me.'

'You mean if he believes us.'

'One more video,' Cassie said. Aly nodded and recorded it.

'I'll be flying out of Dallas,' Cassie said. 'There's one thing: I won't be coming alone. I need two tickets. For myself and a girl named Allyson Miller. I will explain more there, but her father may have been involved in this crime.'

A minute later, Lake replied. 'Done. My head of security, Maurice Wyatt, will be in touch with you to nail down the details.'

Within five minutes, Cassie had several emails from Maurice Wyatt. Their trip was booked. They were going to Past Crimes.

'This is not really how I expected my life to go,' Aly said.

'I've been saying that for ten years.'

Aly walked through the airport shaking her head in awe. 'I've never been on an airplane,' Aly said. 'I've never even seen a plane take off outside of Earth+.'

'When I was a kid,' Cassie said, 'my family took vacations in the Bahamas, Barbados, Costa Rica. We visited my grandparents in Florida every Christmas. We flew all the time.'

'That sounds horrifying.'

Cassie laughed. 'You get used to it. I'd sleep right through most flights.'

'I'm afraid I'm going to barf,' Aly said.

'They have bags for that.'

'For what? Barf?'

Cassie nodded.

'Bags,' Aly said, nonplussed. 'We literally created an entire virtual world to live in, but people are still barfing into bags.'

Security scanned Cassie and Aly's retinas. Cassie found it ironic how impressed Aly was with air travel but not with someone shooting a laser into her eyeball. She figured most kids Aly's age had taken more retinal scans than flights.

As soon as the scan was complete, Cassie felt her phone vibrate. She had an automated notification from the TAP Foundation's Road Trip Program.

> **Dear Ms. West – We have been notified by the Global Flight Alliance that Allyson Miller has completed a retinal scan at Dallas/Fort Worth International Airport. As a Boarder under your care for the next 165 hours and 23 minutes, we would like to remind you that if Ms. Miller is not returned at the end of your Road Trip, or suffers any injuries or impediments that curtail her earning potential, you will be solely responsible for the cost of any and all medical attention, psychiatric evaluations, and/or funeral preparations. Additionally, you will be required to reimburse TAP for said monetary losses. Thank you.**
> **– Emmeline Procter, Director, TAP Foundation**

'I've seen military contracts with less severe penalties,' Cassie said.

'I'm not going back to that Tupperware container,' Aly said. 'I don't care what we find.'

'Yes, you are,' Cassie said.

'You'll have to kill me to get me back there.'

'We'll cross that bridge when we come to it.'

The airport was sparsely populated. Electric planes could only hold a hundred passengers, but most topped out at fifty. Everyone waiting at the gates was encased inside IMPUs, and most wore Earth+ visors. A group of men cheered and exchanged air high-fives; no doubt they were attending an Earth+ sporting event. A woman gripped her armrest, her knuckles white, every now and then jerking to one side or another as though expecting something to jump out at her. Cassie guessed she was in a virtual theater, maybe inside an interactive horror movie being chased by someone with a chainsaw. Another man was kissing the air, his hand gently stroking the space where a face might be.

As they neared the gate, a phalanx of security guards and medical personnel, all encased in portable IMPUs, hurriedly rounded the corner pushing a gurney. A man lay on top, covered in a thin blanket. His eyelids fluttered. The skin around his eye sockets was ghostly pale. IV bags were attached to his veins.

'Have the MediCopter meet us right outside Terminal B,' one

of the guards shouted into an earpiece. 'Brainwave patterns are erratic. I spoke to his wife; she said his flight was three days ago. He never boarded. He must have been inside Earth+ that entire time.'

Aly stood there, frozen, watching the scene. 'He's having a Neural Flare,' she said. 'Isn't he?'

Cassie nodded. 'This one looks bad.'

The man's body began to shake. The guards tried to strap him to the gurney while keeping him moving. As they passed by, a pale arm shot out from underneath the blanket. Aly shrieked. Cassie pulled her away with such force that she fell to the floor. A cop cinched the strap around the man tighter as a doctor shouted, 'He's going into convulsions!'

Then the crew rounded the corner and disappeared.

'Sorry about that,' Cassie said. She helped Aly to her feet. 'You OK?'

'Yeah. You're stronger than you look.'

'Pilates,' Cassie said.

'What's that?'

'Never mind.'

'I've heard of Neural Flares but I've never seen anyone have one,' Aly said. 'What causes them?'

'Too much time inside Earth+ can alter your brain's cognitive ability. When you're inside, it's easy to lose track of time. Before you know it, you've been inside for days without having a sip of water or anything to eat. Your blood pressure and oxygenation drop. Your brain can overload. Your body can simply shut down. I've seen it happen.'

'Where?'

'My old company, a few times. People working eighteen-hour days in Earth+. Usually, it's workaholics or people who live alone. Nobody checks on them. Sometimes they're not found until it's too late. After a bunch of people got Neural Flares, my company set up biometric monitoring for employees. Most companies don't bother.'

'Why wouldn't every company have biometric monitoring to prevent Neural Flares?'

'Because if the employee doesn't know anything is wrong, they'll just keep working. They'll work until they literally drop. Most companies are OK with that.'

'That's messed up,' Aly said, clearly still shaken. 'Aren't there ways to monitor how long you've been inside?'

'There are ways to monitor your blood pressure, glucose levels, sodium and oxygen levels, everything. You can even have your EPD send a distress signal to the nearest hospital if your skin's water saturation dips below safe levels. But personal Wrap monitoring systems aren't cheap. Most people don't have them because they can't afford them.'

'Sometimes my dad would come out of his office,' Aly said, 'and he'd be all dizzy. Like grabbing-on-to-the-wall-for-support dizzy. The skin around his eyes looked like he'd fallen asleep in the sun wearing goggles. He always said he was fine. Just working too hard. We should have gotten him help.' She looked at Cassie. 'How do you get over that – knowing you could have helped someone you love but didn't?'

'When I figure that out,' Cassie said, 'I'll let you know.'

They walked towards their gate. Aly's stomach growled loud enough for the whole airport to hear.

'When was the last time you ate?' Cassie asked.

'Yesterday? Maybe?'

'All right. Let's get you fed. I'll just add it to your tab. Anything in mind?'

'Is airport pizza edible?'

'You don't want airport pizza, kid, trust me. They haven't used real cheese in airports since I was your age. Let's see what else they have.'

Cassie downloaded the AirServ app. Aly ordered chicken fingers, fries and water. Cassie got a chicken club and an iced tea. An AirServ drone brought it to their seats within two minutes. Aly inhaled her chicken in about thirty seconds, then hoovered up the fries as if she might never eat again.

'I'm still hungry,' she said.

'When you get out of the TAP Foundation and start working, you'd better pay me back for all of this,' Cassie said.

'Just add it to my tab.'

Aly devoured two bags of chips and a dark-chocolate candy bar, and Cassie swore she could still hear the girl's stomach growling. As they sat at the gate, Cassie noticed a man across the row from them. He was eyeing Cassie like he was trying to place her. He took out his phone, held it up and tapped the screen. She knew he was using a photo recognition app, which would compare a million data points from her live image to a database of billions of public photos. Cassie turned her head, trying to avoid the photo. It didn't work.

The man stood up and approached Cassie. He held out his phone and showed her a picture on the screen.

'That's you, isn't it?' he said. Cassie recognized the photo. It had been taken the day of the Blight by a reporter. In the shot, Cassie was lying on her side on the street in front of her burning house, holding her stomach, agony etched on her face. She remembered that moment. The physical trauma from her placental abruption. The emotional trauma from knowing Harris was inside the burning house. It was the worst moment of her life, captured for the world to see. And now this man was showing it to her for his own amusement.

'Get away from me,' Cassie said.

'You're Cassandra West. Holy shit. I thought it was you.' The man held his phone up again and snapped a picture of Cassie. 'Would you mind signing this pic? If I can sell it as an NFT, I'll split the money with you.'

Cassie eyed the man like she could rip out his thorax with her fingernails. 'Just leave me alone.'

'Come on. I'm obsessed with the Blight. I'm actually flying out to Utah today to do some sightseeing, then I'll be at the Murderland complex for the big Past Crimes celebration. Please tell me you're going to be there too. Oh, man, Crispin Lake said it was going to be a special day, but Cassie West appearing *live* at the Blight sim launch? Wow.'

Then Aly stood up, fire in her eyes. 'Didn't you hear her? *Back. The hell. Away.* Or so help me God, I will rip off your stupid little micropenis and throw it into the propeller blades.'

Micropenis looked at Aly as if he'd accidentally stepped into a den of snakes. He took a step back. Then another.

'Bitch,' he said, either to Aly or Cassie, or both of them. Then he returned to his seat.

Aly sat back down.

'You didn't need to do that,' Cassie said.

'You bought me chocolate.'

'Fair enough. Thank you.'

Twenty minutes later, they boarded their flight to Utah. The plane was a fifty-seater and the largest aircraft Cassie had been on since she was a teenager. Once they were seated, IMPUs slid up from the armrests and over their seating area, isolating Cassie and Aly from the rest of the plane – and each other.

'I feel like I'm a leftover meatloaf,' Aly said, pushing against the plastic. 'So, what do you do on these things?'

'There's an Earth+ visor in the pocket in front of you. Flights usually offer a bunch of free Earth+ entertainment.'

'Where's the barf bag? Just in case.' Cassie pointed to the flimsy folded paper bag in her seat pocket. Aly took it out. 'This looks like it would disintegrate if you breathed on it.'

'Then keep the contents of your stomach where they belong,' Cassie said. 'Maybe we can find a concert or a party or something. Keep your mind off the flight.'

'That sounds exhausting. Can I just do something simple? Maybe read a book somewhere relaxing?'

'Pretty sure we can do that.'

Cassie helped Aly get situated with her visor, then bought her a copy of a classic V.E. Schwab novel she'd read and loved years ago, about a girl who makes a deal with the devil for immortality, the tradeoff being that nobody will remember her.

Cassie put on her visor and linked her Wrap with Aly's. She selected a 'Springtime Meadow' Earth+ sim. Seconds later, both of their Wraps appeared in the middle of a field of rolling green grass, topped by a luminous yellow sun and clouds that floated by like cotton candy on a slow-moving stream. Aly's Wrap found a large oak tree, the ground speckled with sunlight. She sat back against the wide trunk, propped her book up against her knees and read.

Cassie stood over Aly and watched as the young girl lost herself in the virtual pages. The light breeze felt real, gently rattling the leaves, fluttering the pages of the book in Aly's hand. A sense of serenity came over Cassie. After all these years and all the innovations that had irrevocably changed the world, it was good to know that words themselves still possessed a sort of magic. Books, Cassie supposed, were the original Earth+.

'You OK here for a while?' Cassie said. Aly nodded. She was already lost in the story.

Cassie left the meadow and returned to her EPD. In-air 12G was pretty robust, but if you wanted to watch a live concert or attend a football game with 100,000 other people, the buffering time could be brutal. The sense of serenity had evaporated. Soon they would land in Utah, and Cassie would have to convince Crispin Lake to let her into the simulation. When she worked at V.I.C.E., Cassie used the Past Crimes sims almost weekly. Now, it had been ten years since she'd done one. She and Harris had been infatuated with the sims when Past Crimes first launched. Cassie pretended it was a purely professional obsession, but like the rest of the world, she found something intoxicating about being part of the most infamous crimes in history. Nothing compared to being immersed in the mystery and violence, the inimitable sensation of feeling her heart thump as a killer rounded the corner or she came upon an unmarked grave. There was a reason Past Crimes was a global obsession.

There had never been a better time to reacquaint herself.

Cassie selected 'Past Crimes' on her EPD's entertainment menu, and suddenly her Wrap appeared at the edge of a barren desert. Enormous red-hued mountains rose from the ground, illuminated by bolts of lightning. Thunder shattered the skies, as though Cassie had ventured on to the road to hell itself. There was a rumbling beneath her feet and three buildings rose from the rock of the mountains. A bright red billboard lowered from the sky, large enough to make the Hollywood sign look like a fire hydrant.

In the middle of the gargantuan sign was the legendary Past Crimes logo: the silhouetted outline of a murder victim, etched in black against a vivid red background, echoing into infinity, a crime reverberating into the past. Crispin Lake had designed the Past Crimes Murderland complex itself in the shape of that outline. If you were flying to Utah, you could look out your window and see what appeared to be an enormous crime scene victim from thousands of feet in the air. It felt appropriate that the park was referred to as 'The Disneyland of Death'.

The buildings were a combination of steel and brick, their tops ringed with rusty barbed wire. They looked like a movie theater and an old Apple store had a child and that child's au pair was John Wayne Gacy.

A placard on each building denoted which sims were available in each building: the building on Cassie's left read: *Murder*. The middle: *Mayhem*. On her right: *Crimes of Passion*. The Mayhem and Crimes of Passion buildings read: *Available to Subscribers Only*.

Cassie selected the Murder building. Immediately, her Wrap hurtled towards the entrance and through the giant, vaulted doors.

On a wall in front of her, the images of half a dozen people materialized. She recognized all of them. These were the sims available
to her as part of her complimentary Earth+ in-flight entertainment:

Jeffrey Dahmer
Abraham Lincoln
The Black Dahlia
Essie Harwood
The Mills and Hall Murders
Gerald Boone

She tapped the image of the 16th President and the other images
disappeared. A disclaimer appeared in white lettering. It read: **The**
events of April 14th, 1865, are a matter of historical record. You
will have the ability to watch history unfold as it happened – as
a Spectator – or to alter it as you see fit – as a Participant.
Enjoy your Past Crime. – Crispin Lake

'Spectator' meant she would enter the sim and experience
Lincoln's assassination as it happened. A full, immersive recreation
of one of the most infamous crimes in history. Past Crimes sims
were known to be so accurate and meticulous that thousands of
schools used them for educational purposes.

'Participant' meant she could enter the sim and alter the course
of the crime. Lincoln and the other Augmented Personas would
react to her accordingly, based on their own unique and historically
accurate behavior profiles. This was what was so addictive about
Past Crimes. You could experience the crime as it actually happened
– or you could change the course of history.

Cassie selected Participant.

The images of three other people appeared alongside Lincoln.
Cassie had the choice to enter the sim as any of the following Wraps:

Abraham Lincoln
Mary Todd Lincoln
Major Henry Rathbone
John Wilkes Boothe

Cassie chose Mary Todd Lincoln. When she did, her surroundings
faded to black. She could see nothing. Hear nothing. She could feel
her heart thumping in her chest even though she saw nothing but
darkness.

Then Cassie felt a slight chill. Instinctively, she knew it wasn't
real, just a trick of the haptics to make her body believe the temperature had dropped. Suddenly, she emerged from the darkness, like a

car nearing the end of a long tunnel, and she found herself walking down a stone street past brick buildings in a city she did not recognize in a time long before she had been born. Cassie was no longer on an airplane heading to Utah to meet Crispin Lake. She was walking towards Ford's Theatre on April 14th, 1865, heading towards the assassination of President Abraham Lincoln.

Cassie felt her hand being gently squeezed. She looked up and found herself staring into the thin, hollow face of Abraham Lincoln.

'How's your head, my dear?' the President asked. 'I know you haven't been well. Thank you for agreeing to come tonight. I've been told this play is unforgettable.'

EIGHT

I t wasn't the sight of the tall, gaunt man at her side holding her hand that most shocked Cassie. It was the feel of his fingers. They were long and bony, like twigs beneath paper-thin skin. He looked weary and walked slowly, his face thinner than it appeared in old photographs. Cassie got the sense he walked slowly so as not to limp, preferring to keep his weakness and weariness hidden. Abraham Lincoln looked like a man who'd lived a dozen lifetimes.

Yet there was still a confidence and grace about the man, and his smile was both warm and resolute. He wore a long, black woolen overcoat. Speckles of rain had begun to dot the new-looking wool. Cassie was wearing a dark cloak and could feel something in her hair, some sort of bonnet. Lincoln did not appear to notice the rain or the chill.

Cassie had been an avid Past Crimes user years ago, but after Harris's death and her 'exit' from V.I.C.E., she hadn't set foot in one of their sims. The improved technology, the realism, it astounded Cassie. She didn't feel like she was inside a simulation recreating 1865. She felt like she was walking down the street *in* 1865.

Horses pulled carriages down the street. People stopped to stare at Lincoln as he walked by. Some bowed and curtsied. Lincoln nodded at each one, offering a tip of his hat and a polite smile. Cassie kept stride with Lincoln and waved at some of the pedestrians.

'Mary, how are you feeling? Does your head still ache?'

'No, I . . . I'm fine.' She smiled warmly at Lincoln and he smiled back, giving her hand another gentle squeeze.

They walked hand in hand. Cassie matched Lincoln's deliberate gait. She could see several men standing outside a three-story brick building, dressed in soldiers' garb and wielding bayonets. They didn't take their eyes off the President as he approached. Cassie felt her body grow warm – but it wasn't her body, was it? She reached out and ran a finger along Lincoln's coat. She could feel the fabric on her finger, each thread on her skin. Every touch felt like life. It was uncanny.

Cassie remembered when Earth+ first became a reality. The earliest iterations of the virtual world were like the earliest versions of the Internet itself: slow, clunky and near impossible to find anything worthwhile. The visors were heavy and overheated easily, the medical profession referring to the burn marks they caused frequent users as 'Scalp Sear'. The EPDs froze every few minutes. Wraps were pixelated, looking more like early video-game avatars than their users, and the haptic gloves made everything feel as life-like as a wax corpse. Still, nobody could fathom just how far and how fast the technology would progress. Earth+ was a punchline – until suddenly it wasn't.

The real-world economy was collapsing like a sandcastle in a storm, and almost overnight the people who sneered at the possibility of a full-blown virtual-world economy were either searching for employment inside of it or looking for ways to make money from it. This new world gave Cassie the chance to walk down a stone street in 1865 with the President of the United States, just moments before his death changed the course of a nation.

Crispin Lake spared no expense. Made sure no detail was over-looked. She had no doubt that this simulation appeared just the way this very street would have two hundred years ago. She was disoriented but also amazed. Everything around her, from the streets to the people to the textures and sounds, seemed lifelike. *More* than lifelike. Like she wasn't merely inside this world, but that this world was being pumped directly into her brain.

The President noticed Cassie touching his jacket and smiled.

'Those lads at Brooks Brothers made a fine coat,' Lincoln said. 'And the lining is truly magnificent. If there's a chill in the air, I can hardly feel it.'

Lincoln opened the coat to reveal a fine silk lining. An eagle was embroidered on the material, holding a banner which read: *One Country, One Destiny.*

'I can only hope the bird is right,' he said, closing the garment.

'It's stunning,' Cassie said. Lincoln smiled.

'Thank you, Mary. I hope the headaches let you be so we can enjoy the play unencumbered. The good Lord knows we could all use a night of revels. In all honesty, I would have preferred to stay home tonight. I'm not feeling quite myself, but the newspapers have already reported that I'll be attending, and so I must, at least for appearances' sake.'

'I'm glad you came,' she said.

Lincoln leaned down and kissed Cassie gently on the cheek.

If I'd known I was going to be kissed by a dead President, Cassie thought, *I would have done the JFK sim.*

'Glad to see the missus back to her old self,' came a voice from behind them. Cassie turned to see a younger, severe-looking man with a hooked nose, muttonchops and a thick mustache walking arm in arm with a woman wearing a thick cloak and a bonnet on her curly black hair.

'Who are they?' Cassie whispered to Lincoln. He looked at her as if she had asked if they could fly to the moon.

'Major Rathbone and his fiancée, Miss Harris,' Lincoln said, concern in his voice. 'They accompanied us in the carriage here, my dear.'

'Right. Of course.' Cassie waved politely at Major Rathbone and Miss Harris. Rathbone tipped his cap to her.

'Are you certain you're feeling all right, Mary?' Lincoln asked.

'I am. I was just being foolish. Silly me.'

Lincoln looked at her and narrowed his eyes. 'I may ask the physician to come by after the play. I'm beginning to worry about your condition.'

A red bubble appeared in the air in front of Cassie. It read: *Learn More – Mary Todd Lincoln.* She selected it.

A voice began to speak. Cassie recognized the man. It was Crispin Lake himself.

'On July second, 1863,' the voice stated, 'Mary Todd Lincoln was in a carriage traveling from the presidential retreat at Soldiers' Home back to the White House, whereupon the driver's seat detached from the carriage, frightening the horses, forcing Mary to leap from her seat to save herself. She hit her head on a rock, which became infected and led to the beginning of the deterioration of Mary Todd Lincoln's physical and mental state. Following the accident, Mrs. Lincoln was plagued by migraines and bouts of depression, which grew more severe over time. Abraham Lincoln's concerns about his wife's physical and mental condition on the night of his assassination were not unwarranted. Following the deaths of her husband and three of her four children, Mary Todd Lincoln attempted suicide and was eventually committed to Bellevue. Following a subsequent spinal cord injury, and increasing public criticism of her personal life, Mary Todd Lincoln died at the home of her sister on July fifteenth, 1882.'

No wonder Lincoln was concerned, Cassie thought. The woman whose body she inhabited at the moment had a lifetime of pain ahead of her.

As they neared the theater, Cassie could see torches lighting the front entrance in a ghostly pallor. Six soldiers rested bayonets on their shoulders and saluted the President as he approached. Lincoln returned the gesture but seemed pained to do so. Cassie could not fathom how it was possible, but she felt sympathy for this man. She knew her mind was being tricked into thinking Abraham Lincoln was standing beside her, rather than a collection of millions of data points constructed perfectly to create an illusion in her mind. Yet with every step, she could hear Lincoln's shoes clicking on the stone, the breath being drawn into his lungs, his labored breathing as he pressed on. Cassie couldn't help but marvel at the wonder of Crispin Lake's creation.

When they stepped into the theater's foyer, a young boy approached and shyly handed a program to Lincoln.

'I'm sorry, Mr. President,' the boy said nervously. 'The play has already begun.'

'Oh, I have a feeling they'll stop for us,' Lincoln replied, patting the boy on the shoulder.

'May I see?' Cassie asked, pointing to the program.

'Of course,' Lincoln said, handing her the booklet.

The play's title was *Our American Cousin*. The name *Laura Keene* was printed in large, bold letters atop the cover. She was the lead, and clearly the biggest draw. Underneath Laura Keene were the names *John Dyatt* and *Harry Hawk*. Cassie flipped through the program as an usher led them upstairs.

As they took their seats in the presidential box, the show came to an abrupt halt. The actors stood in their places as the orchestra began to play 'Hail to the Chief'. Most of the attendees stood up and turned to face Lincoln, applauding and cheering enthusiastically. Some stayed in their seats, either refusing to acknowledge the President or staring daggers at him. Cassie wondered just how many people in attendance tonight would do just what John Wilkes Booth was about to, if given the opportunity.

When the music died down and the play commenced, Lincoln pulled out a seat for Cassie and turned it to face the stage. He sat in a rocking chair next to her. She took his hand and squeezed it, running her thumb over his calloused knuckles, again marveling at how real everything felt.

'Careful, dear, not quite so hard. Some days even my bones feel brittle.'

It wasn't just how realistic everything *felt*, but that Lincoln was *reacting* to her. His responses weren't pre-programmed. The Augmented Personas inside the sim were designed to react to Cassie.

Major Rathbone and Clara Harris sat across from them, craning their necks to view the performance. American flags were draped around the outside of the presidential box. Ornate yellow drapes hung from the ceiling, pulled back to reveal the stage.

They were alone in the presidential box. There were no ushers. No guards. Cassie knew what was going to happen and yet was still shocked at how little security had been present on that day. Within moments, Lincoln, Rathbone and Harris were enraptured by the play, oblivious to the lack of security.

Cassie could feel herself begin to sweat. She ran her finger along her neck, and to her surprise, it came away damp. She had no idea if she was sweating in real life, or if Mary Todd Lincoln's Wrap was inside the sim. At the moment, they were one and the same. Her heart was a drumbeat. The moment of fate was approaching. Should she say anything? Do anything? Simply watch the crime unfold?

Cassie turned back to the play. Tried to focus on the performance. One of the actors said, 'Well, I guess I know enough to turn you inside out, old gal, you sockdologizing old man-trap!'

Cassie had no idea what in the bloody hell 'sockdologizing' meant, but the line had the entire theater, including Lincoln, in absolute hysterics.

Then she heard it. A slight squeak behind them. It was the door to the presidential box being opened. She held her breath. She knew exactly who it was and why he was there. Neither Lincoln, Rathbone nor Harris moved. It was happening. Just the way the history books said it would. The act would be quick. In mere seconds, this performance and the fate of the nation would be changed by a single bullet.

She remembered the message from Crispin Lake that preceded her entry into the sim:

You will have the ability to watch history unfold as it happened – as a Spectator – or to alter it to your command – as a Participant.

Cassie had been a spectator as her own life went up in flames. She knew what she had to do. After all, wasn't the whole point of her going to Past Crimes to try to change the future?

'Get down!' Cassie shouted, and she shoved Lincoln as hard as she could. He was a large man, but frail and not expecting the sudden jolt. He toppled off his chair and hit the floor with a grunt. Cassie heard a deafening *boom* from just over her left shoulder. A chunk of wood on the railing exploded. Cassie felt splinters pelt her cheek.

Cassie looked back and saw a man partially obscured by a cloud of smoke. He had dark, curly hair and a thick mustache. His mouth was open in a shocked expression. He held a small pistol, aimed right where Lincoln's head had been a moment ago.

John Wilkes Booth. Perhaps the most infamous assassin in American history. He had not expected to miss.

Booth quickly dug into his pocket, looking for another bullet.

Major Rathbone did not hesitate. He leaped from his seat and charged Booth, throwing his shoulder into the would-be killer's sternum. Both men went down in a heap. Clara Harris screamed. The play halted and the entire audience stood up to see the commotion in the presidential box.

Cassie saw a glint of metal as Booth drew a dagger from a sheath. He raised it above Rathbone, preparing to slice open the major's throat, when a large boot kicked Booth in the side. The assassin fell on to his back, gasping for air yet still clutching the knife. Then the boot came down on Booth's forearm. *Hard.*

Cassie heard a crack as the bone broke. Booth cried out in pain and the blade fell from his grasp. Lincoln stood tall, his foot on his own assassin's arm. Lincoln reached down, picked up the knife and tossed it aside.

Half a dozen armed men burst through the door. They yanked Booth to his feet and began dragging him outside as he howled in pain and anger.

'The President!' an actor shouted from the stage. 'The President stopped a killer!'

The crowd erupted as Lincoln stood there, unsure of what to do. He looked at Cassie, breathing heavily, eyes full of confusion and adrenaline.

'Mary,' he said. 'You just saved my life. How did you—'

'Women's intuition,' Cassie replied.

'Women's intuition,' Lincoln said with a wry smile. The President took her hand, then leaned in and kissed her gently on the lips. The crowd erupted in applause. Cassie closed her eyes. When she opened them, she saw Aly Miller staring at her, cringing. Cassie's lips were still puckered. She composed herself, her cheeks reddening in record time.

'I had no idea porn was available on this flight,' Aly said.

'I wasn't watching . . . never mind,' Cassie said. 'How long was I in there?'

'I don't know. A while? They said we're landing soon.'

It's a ninety-minute flight, Cassie thought. *Ninety minutes that went by like a heartbeat.*

'So what were you doing in there, then?'

'A Past Crimes sim.'

'I don't remember any Past Crimes sims involving make-out sessions. Please tell me you weren't rounding first base with Jeffrey Dahmer. His breath must smell awful.'

'I was doing the Lincoln assassination sim, and the President kissed me after I saved his life. And let's be clear. He. Kissed Me.'

'Um, why?'

'As a thank you, I guess? I went in as a Participant. I stopped Booth from killing him. The Augmented Personas inside react to what you do. I was his wife – well, his fake wife. He was just reacting to me. And to be honest, it wasn't that bad of a kiss.'

'Now I'm *definitely* glad I know where the barf bags are.' Then Aly's eyes widened. She leaned across Cassie's seat towards the window and pointed at the ground coming up beneath them. 'That's it, right? Murderland.'

Cassie looked out the window and saw what Aly did. An enormous outline seemingly etched into the Utah landscape in the shape of a crime scene victim. All the years working at V.I.C.E., all the times she'd pitched other people's lives to Past Crimes, yet she'd never been to Murderland in person. The sight was incredible yet ominous, exactly the vibe Crispin Lake was going for. At night, the outline glowed bright red and could be seen from four different states.

'It looks like a god died in the middle of the desert,' Aly said reverently, 'and the cops are trying to figure out who did it.'

The plane banked and the outline dipped out of view. Cassie felt nails digging into her skin. Aly was gripping her forearm.

'Sorry,' she said. 'I've never done this before.'

'It's OK,' Cassie said. 'Just ease up a little with the talons. I'd prefer not to be actively bleeding when we see Crispin Lake.'

Aly removed her hand, leaving white nail marks on Cassie's skin.

'I'm nervous,' Aly said.

'I am too.'

'You really think Lake will let you in?'

'I hope so,' Cassie said. 'There's a mistake in his Blight sim. I saw it in the teaser they released. And there's no way Lake would release anything unless he was sure it was authentic. Which means someone else lied to him. Someone prevented him from knowing the truth. And to people like Crispin Lake, being lied to is an unforgivable sin. I think he'll want to know the truth as much as we do.'

'What if we don't find anything?' Aly said. 'What if it's all just a mistake? What if there is no second Blight and the first happened just the way everyone says?'

'I hope it doesn't happen,' Cassie said. 'Thousands of people could die.'

'It could also mean that your husband really is guilty.'

'It might,' Cassie said.

'Can you live with that?'

'I don't know what living is anymore,' Cassie said. 'So I don't know how to answer that.'

'Like I told you – no matter what happens – I'm not going back to that place. Don't try to stop me.'

'I won't,' Cassie said. 'I'm not your mother.'

'What about the money?'

'They can try to squeeze as much blood from a rock as they want,' Cassie said. 'So where would you go?'

'I don't know,' Aly said. 'I really don't belong anywhere anymore.'

Neither do I, Cassie thought as they descended, the outline of the Past Crimes complex growing closer, the fate of thousands of lives possibly resting on what they found within.

NINE

4:28 p.m.
Thirty-one hours and thirty-two minutes to launch

A man the size of a ReVolt SUV was waiting for them at pickup outside of Salt Lake City International Airport. He was six three or six four with a gleaming shaved head and an upper body that looked as though he'd spent his entire life pushing large boulders up steep hills. He held a tablet that read *West*. When he saw Cassie, he folded the tablet and slid it into his jacket pocket.

'Ms. West, Ms. Miller,' the man said, stepping forward. 'My name is Wyatt. Chief of Security at Past Crimes. Mr. Lake sent me to greet you.'

Although he looked as if he could break a tanker truck over his knee, Wyatt's voice was soft and kind. Wyatt held out his hand. Cassie shook it. His fingers enveloped hers like an adult's on an infant, but his grip was relaxed. She felt no pressure.

'Pleasure to meet you, Ms. West.'

'Thanks for arranging our flight,' Cassie said.

'Sorry we couldn't fly you on Mr. Lake's private jet. Short notice and all that.'

Aly eyed Wyatt suspiciously. 'So you're Crispin Lake's . . . driver?'

Wyatt smiled. 'I'm what you might call a jack of all trades for Past Crimes. Mr. Lake doesn't really trust driverless cars and didn't want you getting wrapped around a barrier on UT-154 because your ReVolt lost its satellite uplink. Mr. Lake wanted to make sure you got to the complex safe and sound. We're going to meet with him at the Bundy Building.'

'How long have you worked with Lake?' Cassie asked.

'Twenty years?' Wyatt said. 'I was Crispin Lake's first employee. It's either me or Steve Woolman. Woolman might have me beat by a week or two.'

'What's he like?' Aly asked.

'Mr. Lake? He's a visionary.'

'I heard he doesn't talk to anyone or meet with anyone outside of Earth+.'

'I'd say that's ninety-five percent true,' Wyatt said. 'Mr. Lake has a small group of confidants he meets with in Earth−. Mr. Lake lives and breathes Past Crimes. In twenty years, I haven't seen him leave the complex. But I think even he'd tell you that everything he cares about is within the walls of Murderland. Now, Ms. West, take out your phone.'

Cassie did.

Wyatt tapped a button on his phone. Cassie's phone vibrated with a notification. Wyatt had sent her a digital Contact Card containing his phone number, email, Earth+ EPD link, CV, dozens of photos and even a signed letter from Crispin Lake stating that Wyatt was officially employed by Past Crimes. She also noted that Wyatt was a widower.

'In case you need anything during your stay, that's how you can get in touch.'

'There's no address listed,' Cassie said.

'I live at the complex.'

'So you just live among the psychopaths,' Aly said.

'The only psychopaths at Past Crimes are, thankfully, either dead or Augmented Personas.'

'I'd rather live in my Tupperware container,' Aly said.

'Mr. Lake has wanted to meet you outside of Earth+ for a long time, Ms. West. Of course, we're aware this isn't a courtesy visit, and if we can help prevent any sort of crime, we will.'

'Glad to hear it,' Cassie said.

'And Mr. Lake is very, very sorry for your loss, Ms. Miller.'

'Thank you,' Aly said. 'Well, thank him, I guess.'

'You'll have a chance to,' Wyatt said. 'Do you have any bags?'

Cassie held up her carry-on. Aly turned around to show her backpack.

'You travel light,' Wyatt said. 'Hey, less work for me.'

He led them to the parking lot and ushered them into a ReVolt SUV the size of a Panzer tank. Cassie noticed that the lenses of

Wyatt's sunglasses wrapped all the way around the side of his head, so that even when he was standing perpendicular to them, Cassie could see their reflection in his shades.

As Wyatt drove away from the airport, Aly pressed her face against the window like she was seeing the world in color for the first time.

'I've never been this far from home,' Aly said. She pointed excitedly to the rising mountain range on their left, their peaks hidden by the clouds. 'Holy crap,' she said breathlessly. 'Are those real?'

'They most certainly are. Those are the Uinta Mountains,' Wyatt said. 'Stunning, right? I appreciate technology as much as the next guy, but it can't *quite* replicate the beauty of God's earth.'

'I've never seen mountains before,' Aly said. 'Not for real. We did a virtual hike up part of Mount Everest in Geography. It's not the same. I like the Earth– mountains better.'

'First time on a plane. First time seeing mountains. Not a bad day,' Cassie said.

They rode the rest of the way in silence. Even though the world on the ground had all but crumbled, the horizons themselves were still a wonder to behold. Aly was right. There weren't enough ones and zeroes in existence to replicate what was right in front of them.

'Here we are,' Wyatt said. Aly pressed her face to the window, mouth agape, her breath coating the glass.

'It's gigantic,' she said. And it was.

The Murderland park was about seven thousand acres, or a shade under eleven square miles, and shaped just like the famous Past Crimes logo. Each section of the 'Victim' housed a different area of the park, devoted to its villains and villainesses.

At one outstretched hand was Murderer's Row, which contained rides and exhibits showcasing the most famous killers in history. Dahmer. Gacy. Bundy. Gein. Wuornos. Lopez. Sithole. You could sit in a replica of the ice-cream van that British serial killer Fred West drove, and then explore West's home in Gloucester, dubbed the 'House of Horrors', inside Earth+.

The other hand was called Grifter's Gulch and housed amusements dedicated to the most famous swindlers, con men and white-collar criminals in history. Madoff. Abagnale. Lustig. Ponzi. Delvey. Van Meegeren. Holmes.

The left foot exhibited the Disappeared, featuring history's most notorious kidnappings and disappearances. Hearst. Ramsey. Ross.

Lindbergh. Getty. Hagerman. Sinatra, Jr. The right foot harbored Zealotville, where you could explore Jonestown, the Branch Davidian compound, the Remnant Fellowship, NXIVM, Heaven's Gate, Rajneeshpuram and the Manson Family.

At the north end of the park lay Mastermind Mountain, home to attractions celebrating evil geniuses: Adam Worth, aka 'The Napoleon of Crime'. H.H. Holmes, a former academic who allegedly constructed a building to use as a 'murder hotel' during the World's Fair in Chicago. The Zodiac Killer, who claimed thirty-seven victims, mailed taunting ciphers and cryptograms to newspapers and was never apprehended. You could even sit coach on the airplane hijacked by D.B. Cooper.

Every inch of the Past Crimes complex was a monument to the vicious and vile, evil and venomous, remorseless and unforgettable. There were statues dedicated to the most notorious criminals, stocked gift shops where visitors could purchase tchotchkes and memorabilia, and restaurants and stands devoted to filling the belly while simultaneously making it lurch (Dahmer's Delight, a meat-filled hoagie that came in a souvenir mini refrigerator, was the park's best-selling food item).

Each limb also housed numerous stations where visitors could access Earth+ and interact with Augmented Personas of the criminals themselves, and get visitors-only specials on clothing and accessories to adorn their Wraps.

Crispin Lake had harnessed the waning power of the real world and the seemingly limitless horizons of the virtual one to create a multi-billion-dollar franchise at the nexus of both.

Wyatt pulled up to the employee gate. It was unmanned. Wyatt lowered the window and a small camera extended towards the driver's side. It scanned Wyatt's retinas and then retracted. The gate opened, revealing a long underground tunnel illuminated in dark-red lighting. Images of some of the most infamous criminals in history flashed on the walls, a macabre welcoming committee.

When the car came to a stop, Cassie felt a slight rocking sensation underneath, likely a charger port locking into place. Wyatt got out and took their bags from the trunk. He led them to an elevator and pressed his palm against a console. The console chimed, a panel slid open and another camera scanned his retinas. Then the elevator doors opened.

'Welcome to the Bundy Building,' Wyatt said. He pointed to a hand-shaped panel embedded in the inside of the elevator door. He pointed at Aly. 'You first.'

'My first what?'

'Put your hand there.'

Aly tentatively placed her palm against the panel. A robotic voice said, 'Biometric analysis, commencing.' The panel hummed.

'It's warm,' Aly said. 'It's not cooking me, is it?'

The humming ceased and a panel slid open in the ceiling. A beam of green light scanned Aly up and down, turning her skin the color of a kiwi.

'What the hell is that?' Aly said, scooting back up against the wall.

'Nothing to worry about,' Wyatt said. 'Before letting anyone into the Bundy Building, we scan body temperature, oxygen levels, blood pressure and biometrics. Once it's complete, you'll get a quick UV once-over to eliminate any bacteria you may have picked up from the flight. Think of it as the world's most advanced dry shower. Mr. Lake is a bit of a germophobe, but I suppose we all should be.'

After the green light finished scanning Aly, the voice said, 'Visitor one: normal.'

Wyatt nodded approvingly. 'There. Not so bad, was it?'

'If that thing gives me a tumor, I don't care how big you are, I'm going to kick your ass,' Aly said.

Wyatt laughed. 'I just bet you would. Your turn, Ms. West.'

Cassie pressed her hand against the panel and let the elevator scan her.

'Minor symptoms of Hyponatremia in passenger two,' the voice said.

'Hyponatremia,' Wyatt said, a measure of concern in his voice. 'The sodium levels in your bloodstream are low. That means you're overly susceptible to Neural Flares. Somebody has been spending a little too much time inside Earth+. Have you had any symptoms?'

'It's nothing,' Cassie said. 'Just a few headaches. I'll be careful.'

'Mr. Lake may want to take precautions in the event your condition worsens while on our premises,' Wyatt said.

'I understand.'

'Biometric evaluation complete,' the scanner said. 'Commencing irradiation.'

The elevator was enveloped by a purple hue that lasted for about fifteen seconds. When it finished, the voice said, 'Irradiation:

complete. No viruses detected. Germ count reduced by ninety-nine-point-nine-nine-nine percent.'

'We're good to go,' Wyatt said. He pressed the button marked 8 and the elevator doors closed. When they did, the metal walls turned transparent, allowing Cassie and Aly to see the entirety of the Murderland park as they rose into the air. Cassie could see several hundred people roaming the streets of Murderland. People carried Past Crimes shopping bags, children held red balloons with the black crime scene victim in the Mylar. Visitors sat at Earth+ stations wearing visors, others were dressed in costumes of the most infamous madmen and women in history, like Halloween in broad daylight. Still, the scant number of people made the park feel almost vacant, like a shopping mall from the 2020s.

'This is the calm before the storm,' Wyatt said. 'This place will be jam-packed when the Blight sim drops.'

'I can't fathom how much it must have cost Lake to pay for twenty-five thousand attendees to come for the launch,' Cassie said. 'The airfare alone must have cost millions.'

Wyatt laughed. 'As long as it doesn't affect my paycheck, I'm happy to keep my head in the sand.'

'What's that building over there?' Aly said, pointing to a smaller, yet still sizable building directly north of them. It appeared to be a solid steel cube, about thirty feet high, and the only part of the park that wasn't decorated in some form of death or destruction.

'That's the R and D department,' Wyatt said. 'Where the real magic happens.'

'Can we go there?' Aly asked.

'Absolutely not.'

'Please?'

'This is not a tour,' Wyatt said, his voice firm, pleasantries gone. 'Mr. Lake instructed me to bring you to the Bundy Building and nowhere else. For your safety and our security.'

'We aren't here to sightsee,' Cassie said, glaring at Aly as the elevator came to a stop. 'Time is a luxury we don't have. I need to speak with Crispin – Mr. Lake – as soon as possible. Lives might depend on it.'

'I think we can arrange that.'

Cassie recognized the voice. The elevator doors had slid open noiselessly. Standing at the end of a red-carpeted hall, waiting to greet them, was Crispin Lake.

TEN

Lake strode towards them – that's the way it appeared to Cassie. He didn't just walk but *strode* – like a dignitary walking down a red carpet. His movements were fluid, his gait so smooth his feet didn't even seem to touch the ground.

Lake was tall, about six one or two, trim but not skinny, like a long-distance runner. He wore a red sport jacket over a black buttoned-down shirt – the Past Crimes colors, Cassie noted – with dark blue jeans and heavy, military-style black boots.

Lake's hair was close-cropped at the sides, black with speckles of gray, longer on top and dyed so blonde it was nearly white. A stray strand dangled from his forehead and curled around one brown eye. His beard was short and neatly trimmed, and he wore a pair of clear, wire-rimmed glasses. Cassie found it both odd and oddly refreshing that Crispin Lake, who had invented one of the premiere media companies of the last half century and had pioneered technologies that had made him a billionaire several times over, had eschewed all manner of corrective corneal implants and surgeries to stick with old-fashioned lenses.

'Mr. Lake,' Cassie said. 'Thanks for seeing us.'

'Ms. West,' Lake said. His voice was smooth and deep, baritone, as if it belonged to a larger man. 'I'd always hoped we'd have a chance to meet in person. I have to be honest: until today, I didn't think it would ever happen.'

'I'd always hoped to meet in person too. Just under very different circumstances.'

Cassie held out her hand. Lake did not take it.

'I don't shake hands. Please don't take offense. We have a state-of-the-art bacterial and viral detection system, as you're aware, but I remain more cautious than most. Separation and isolation are, and will always be, the best defense. And, well, I plan to live forever.'

Cassie couldn't tell if he was joking. As if reading her mind,

Wyatt said, 'He's not kidding. I've worked for Crispin for twenty years and I've still never shaken his hand.'

'When you retire, Maurice, I'll consider it,' Lake said. Then he turned to Aly. 'You must be Ms. Miller.'

'Aly,' she said.

'Aly,' he said. 'It's a pleasure to meet you. I'm very sorry for your loss.'

'Thank you,' Aly said softly. Then Aly scrunched up her nose. 'What's that smell?'

Cassie smelled it too – a sweet yet metallic scent, like copper and citrus.

'So glad you noticed it,' Lake said. 'That is Blüt, our very first Past Crimes scent. It can be worn by men or women.'

'It smells like . . .'

'Blood?' Lake said. 'Yes. With just a hint of orange. Blood and citrus combine to make a satisfying aroma. Now, I know this isn't a social visit. From what Ms. West has said, there's quite a lot at stake. So please. Come with me.'

Lake led them down a long corridor, lined with murals depicting notorious crimes and criminals, all of which had been adapted into Past Crimes simulations: Pritchard Houghton, who had kidnapped his eight-year-old niece Lily, brainwashed her into believing she was his daughter and managed to elude authorities for nine years. Lucius Ward, aka the Snake of Saskatoon, Raffaelo Filipacci, Ezekiel Munson and more. At the very end of the corridor was a mural that made Cassie stop in her tracks. She knew it was coming. She knew it would be here. But it still stole her breath.

Staring back at her was a life-size image of Harris West. The picture had been taken at a friend's wedding ten years before the Blight, back when they were merely dating. Cassie remembered the night vividly. She'd had one too many glasses of Chardonnay and decided that a friend's wedding was the right time and place to tell Harris that she wanted more of a commitment. Little did she know he'd already started to look at rings and that within the month they would be engaged.

He looked so young and handsome in his tuxedo, back when in-person weddings were still a thing, with an ear-to-ear smile that made her heart speed up the first time she saw him at the charming bookstore on Barrow Street, when something inside of her told her she had to talk to this man because even if it led nowhere, which it likely would, at least she would never wonder what if.

As it happened, he'd approached her first, asking if she could recommend a book for a six-year-old girl. Her heart sank, figuring he was buying a book for his daughter, but he must have read her mind because he laughed and clarified that it was for his niece. Cassie tried not to let her relief show, and so she led him to the children's section where she handed him the first three books in the Sadie Scout adventure series that she'd loved growing up. She accompanied Harris to the cash register, an unspoken agreement between them that she should, and after he paid, he thanked her on behalf of his niece and asked if he could buy her a cup of coffee as thanks. She'd never said yes to anything faster in her life – at least until the day Harris dropped to one knee and presented her with a 0.2-carat diamond ring, which was still the most beautiful thing Cassie had ever laid eyes on.

And now that picture of Harris was being used to push a lie, to convince millions that the man she loved was a monster. She turned to Lake, forcing her breath to come out even, not letting her emotions get the best of her.

'You're wrong about him,' Cassie said. 'Everyone is wrong about him.'

Lake sighed and checked his watch. 'Is that why you're here, Ms. West?' he said. 'If you came all this way to admonish me, I'm going to ask that you reimburse Past Crimes for your plane tickets.'

'That's not why I'm here. I'm here because I – we – think thousands of lives are at stake. I believe there's going to be a second Blight. And the new Beacons are being led by a Vertex Ignis, possibly the same one who led everyone to their deaths ten years ago. If we're right, it means my husband was falsely accused and there's a demon still out there. I think we can use your sim to find that Vertex Ignis and possibly stop the Blight. *That*, Mr. Lake, is why I'm here.'

'And all this is predicated on . . . what exactly? A hunch?'

'Before my father killed my mother and himself,' Aly said, 'he told me he was a Beacon. He talked about the Vertex Ignis like it was the same person. And he told me a date that would line up exactly with when your sim would launch.'

Lake's eyes narrowed. 'I read the police report. It doesn't mention any of that.'

'The reports were doctored,' Cassie said. 'I have the original in my EPD. Also – your simulation is wrong.'

'I've been called a lot of names in my lifetime,' Lake said. 'A liar is not one that I'll shrug off.'

'I'm not saying you're lying,' Cassie said. 'I'm saying someone lied *to* you.'

'Go on,' Lake said.

'In the teaser you released for your sim, you showed a scene from my old home at Forty-four Otter Creek Drive. You showed Harris's office. It looked exactly the way it did before our house burned down.'

'We spared no expense,' Lake said.

'But there was something missing. The Skin Reader. He kept it on his desk. Employer-mandated. It's not in the teaser for your Blight sim. And I can't think of any reason why you'd leave it out, unless it wasn't in the files you used to recreate his office.'

'Maurice, do you have your phone on you?' Lake asked. Wyatt nodded. 'Play the teaser.' Wyatt did. Lake watched from over his shoulder. 'Stop. Now.'

Cassie could see that he'd paused it as the teaser zoomed in on Harris's desk. Just as she'd said, there was no Skin Reader.

'I think someone removed it from our house before the police reports were filed. Before forensics came. Somebody didn't want the world to know what Harris was working on – or who he was working for.'

Lake tapped his lip. 'All right. You have my attention. Let's go somewhere private where we can talk.'

Lake led them to a large circular room with a high ceiling adorned with a massive chandelier dripping with red and black crystals. They sat at a large black marble table, Lake across from Cassie and Aly, Wyatt near the door, watching.

Behind Lake a timeline wrapped around the wall, with dates stretching all the way into history and leading to the present day.

399 BC – The Poisoning of Socrates
March 15th, 44 BC – The Assassination of Julius Caesar
April 3rd, 33 AD – The Crucifixion of Jesus Christ

Lake saw her looking at the timeline and said, 'We don't know the exact date when Socrates drank hemlock. That was his sentence after being convicted on charges of impiety and corrupting the young. So 399 BC is our best guess. And according to the New Testament, Christ was crucified somewhere between April seventh, 30 AD and April third, 33 AD. Unfortunately, my company wasn't around back then; otherwise, we'd not only have the day, but the hour, minute, second, weather, position of the sun, the exact color of Jesus' eyes, and know what that hemlock beverage tasted like. Within the next decade, I want people to experience the crucifixion first-hand.'

'You're going to create a Jesus sim?' Cassie said.

'Jesus. Caesar. Rasputin. All the great historical crimes, dating back centuries. Millennia. Technology is just now catching up to our ambitions. Sims based on recent events have fewer obstacles because we can get everything we need from the people who lived it. It's much trickier if we want to replicate crimes from several thousand years ago. Not as many photos, videos, reports or archived social media feeds. But if I'm going to recreate ancient Judea, I want people to be able to feel what it's like to have the nails driven into their palms.'

'That doesn't strike you as, I don't know, brutal? Maybe a little blasphemous?'

'*The Passion of the Christ* made over six hundred million dollars, and that was almost fifty years ago. It's one of the most brutal movies ever made. But people paid to see it again. And again. And again. Brutality is a balm. Watching someone else suffer reminds us that it's not us.'

'Maybe that's why you've been so successful,' Cassie said.

'You might not believe me, but I am anything but casual about the specter of death,' Lake said. 'Now. Tell me why you're really here.'

'Before he died,' Aly said, 'my father told me that three six five two was coming. July nineteenth, 2047, is exactly three thousand, six hundred and fifty-two days after the first Blight.'

'We think Aly's father was going to be a Beacon in a second Blight,' Cassie said. 'And we believe this Blight is scheduled for midnight on July nineteenth, 2047. Less than two days from now.'

'That would be the same moment our simulation launches,' Lake said, shifting in his seat, clearly uncomfortable at the prospect of his billion-dollar baby launching alongside a massacre.

'What if Ms. West has been right all this time,' Aly said, 'and her husband *wasn't* the guy behind it all? What if they were still out there?'

'Ms. West, Ms. Miller,' Lake said, 'if this is about Harris—'

'I know everyone thinks I'm either delusional or evil,' Cassie said. 'The Red Widow. But if we're right, tens of thousands, maybe hundreds of thousands of people have been radicalized in Earth+. Maybe more. And it's *not* my dead husband who's doing it. You could be launching your expensive new simulation on the same day of a global mass murder-suicide that will make Jonestown pale in comparison.'

She watched Crispin Lake, waiting for him to say something. Anything.

'And if you're wrong?' Lake asked, finally.

'Then the world goes on. Nobody gets hurt. That's what we all want, right? Hell, I *want* to be wrong. But if there's a one percent chance that I'm not, we need to make sure – *you* need to make sure – this doesn't happen.'

'And the reason you didn't go to the police or the media first with all this conjecture?'

'Law enforcement likes me as much as they like STDs. The media has already made me the Red Widow. Either I'm a femme fatale who was in on the crime or I'm a shrew who saw all the warning signs but ignored them. I need proof. And I think I can find it inside your sim. I watched an interview with you around the time I started working at V.I.C.E. I wanted to license a crime to your company more than anything. You said something that stuck with me. You said, "My sims aren't lifelike. They *are* life." Do you remember saying that?'

Lake's smile let her know that he did. 'That stuck with you,' he said, proudly.

'And if you were telling the truth, which I think you were, then the Blight sim you're about to launch isn't just lifelike. It is *life*. Am I right?'

Lake seemed to get where she was going with this. 'You are.'

'Then you've painstakingly recreated what happened that day ten years ago. You've tried to recreate the Blight down to the very last detail. Haven't you?'

'This simulation is the most arduous undertaking of my life,' Lake said. 'Everything inside this sim is exactly how it happened the day of the Blight. With one fairly large caveat.'

'Which is?'

'You. It kills me what we had to do in our sim given that we didn't have rights to your likeness or biometrics. The Cassandra Ann West in my simulation is a shadow of the real woman. I'm hoping we can flesh her out. So to speak.'

'None of that will matter if people don't believe your sim is the real deal,' Cassie said. 'You missed the Skin Reader.'

'We didn't *miss* anything,' Lake said.

'But you were prevented from seeing something,' Cassie said. 'Doesn't it make you wonder what else was hidden from you? What else might be missing from your simulation? Or what could be in there that isn't supposed to be, because someone planted it?'

'It's like that old movie. *Inception*,' Aly said. 'Someone could have planted evidence at any of the crime scenes, knowing you would replicate it inside your sim.'

The look on Lake's face told Cassie that he had not considered this possibility. Until now.

'And what if this is just the last, desperate attempt of an unbalanced woman who refuses to accept that her husband is the monster the world believes he is?' Lake said. 'Just because you haven't been able to live with the truth does not mean it's a lie.'

'Then you have nothing to lose by letting me enter your sim,' Cassie said. 'If we're right, we can potentially save thousands of lives. The world will love you – even more than they already do – because you were a part of it. You launch your sim and gain millions of subscribers and everyone buys a boatload of merch and you can afford a yacht the size of Peru.'

'And if you're wrong?'

'You get to fix that one caveat.'

'You will agree to provide your likeness and biometrics for the sim,' Lake said.

'If there is no second Blight, and I can't prove that Harris wasn't the Vertex Ignis, then yes. You can have my likeness. My biometrics. I'll even send you my old toothbrushes. There are details about my life with Harris that even you don't know. You'll get it all. Everything.'

'The launch is in less than five days,' Lake said. 'You'll have to agree to have a body and biometrics scan. We can re-skin your Augmented Persona inside the sim and upload a day-one patch to at least get your appearance right. The biometrics and behavior patches we can do via a rolling update. You'll have to agree to stay at the complex for as long as we need you.'

'Agreed,' Cassie said.

'What about me?' Aly said.

'You're not a part of the Blight sim,' Lake said. 'We don't need you.'

'So what does that mean for me?' Aly said to Cassie.

'Don't worry,' Cassie replied. 'You're never going back to your Tupperware container at the TAP Foundation. That's a promise.'

'OK,' Aly said, unsure as to whether Cassie was being sincere or merely placating her. Cassie wasn't fully sure herself.

'So, Crispin,' Cassie said, 'do we have a deal?'

Lake tapped a slender finger against his upper lip. Then he smiled. 'V.I.C.E. was shortsighted to terminate your employment,' Lake said. 'You're a hell of a salesman. They could have used your unique . . . position . . . to their benefit.'

'I don't think I want my vocation to be profiting from other people's traumas anymore,' Cassie said.

Lake thought for a moment, then said, 'I'll agree to your terms, Ms. West. But you have to agree to mine. Before entering this sim, both you and Ms. Miller will sign a non-disclosure agreement preventing you from discussing our sim in any way prior to its official launch. Everything you see and do here will remain strictly confidential in perpetuity. We'll have plenty of other conditions that my counsel, Mr. Jalal, will write up.'

'Done.'

'You will also sign a contract stating that if this second Blight does not take place, you will provide the services you've offered here today. Meaning full body and biometric scanning, and consultation on an indefinite number of updates.'

'Done.'

'This won't be in writing, but if you *are* right, and we *are* able to prevent a catastrophe, you will agree to give due credit to myself and Past Crimes in any and all future media appearances.'

'I will stand on a mountaintop in Earth+ and tell the world to pray to a golden idol of Crispin Lake.'

'The Jews turned their backs on Moses when he ascended Mount Horeb,' Lake said. 'I have more brand loyalty than Moses ever did.'

'What about me?' Aly said.

'You can enter the simulation too, but you'll be beholden to the same terms as Ms. West. Strict NDA, likeness, etcetera.'

'You have no need for her likeness or biometrics,' Cassie said.

'Not for this sim,' Lake replied, 'but you never know what might happen in the future.'

'Done,' Aly said.

'Aly, hold on. Think about—'

'I want in,' she said. 'I don't care what it takes.'

'Aly, I—'

'You're not my mother.'

Cassie nodded. 'No, I'm not.' She looked at Lake. 'So, are we good to go?'

'We are,' Lake said. 'Now we are still working out last-minute bugs, and some of the Augmented Personas are still being fine-tuned. Just a final coat of paint. Unlike our third-rate competitors, when we say we use biometrics to create our APs from the ground up, we mean it. Our APs aren't just sprites piled on top of each other. We literally create layers of bone, muscle and skin so our APs don't just *look* authentic but *move* authentic. If you were to remove the digital "skin" from our Augmented Personas, you would find the same thing you'd find if you removed the skin from a human – recreated faithfully in Earth+. Just be aware that what you see when you go in may be a slightly less refined version of the simulation that the public will see on July nineteenth.'

'Then let's do this,' Cassie said. 'We don't have much time.'

'One thing before we start,' Lake said.

'What's that?'

'You've asked a favor of me that I've never granted to anyone before. I believe I'm entitled to ask one question of you.'

'All right,' Cassie said. 'Shoot.'

'For the last ten years, you've proclaimed your husband's innocence,' Lake said. 'Nobody believes that Harris was innocent. Myself included. My question is simply this: why?'

Cassie looked down. The conference table went up to the middle of her torso, hiding her from the ribcage down. Only Aly saw Cassie place her hand against her lower abdomen.

'I miscarried two days after the Blight. Two days after my husband and the father of my children killed himself. We'd been trying to get pregnant for so long. We sacrificed everything. Mortgaged everything. Took on debt that could never be repaid. But we were going to have a family. I might have been the one going through all the treatments, taking all the hormones and having pint after pint of my blood drawn, but Harris was in just as much pain as I was. He held my hand through it all. He cried every time my beta never rose above zero. And he cried the day we saw our child's heartbeat for the first time. Those tears could never be replicated in a simulation. I saw the way my husband looked at me after our twelve-week appointment when my doctor told us our baby girl was healthy. And I know beyond a shadow of a doubt that there is no chance in hell Harris would have removed himself from this earth before meeting his daughter, unless he had no choice. I owe it to the family that was taken from me – both of them – to find the truth. No matter how long it takes.'

'One thing this business has taught me is that the truth does not change based on what people want it to be,' Lake said. 'I hope you're prepared if that's the case here.'

'I'll have to be.'

'All right, then,' Lake said. 'Let's get you back into the Blight.'

ELEVEN

Twenty-seven hours and forty-two minutes to launch

A young man in his early forties with dark skin, a neatly trimmed graying beard, and ear-length hair entered the room holding a tablet. He handed it to Cassie. The device was as thin as a sheet of paper and as sturdy as a sheet of metal.

'Salman Jalal,' Cassie said. 'It's been a long time.'

'I think the last time I saw you was when you were still at V.I.C.E. and we were finalizing the contract for the Gerald Boone simulation,' Jalal said.

'A lifetime ago,' Cassie said.

'Certainly was. I never thought we'd cross paths again.'

'Neither did I. How are you?'

'Busy, as always,' Jalal said. 'It's always an adventure working for a company where the dead require more legal counsel than the living.'

Cassie tapped the screen. A contract appeared. Jalal watched, patiently, as she read it. Wyatt brought water bottles and a large bowl of fruit. Aly took an apple and did a Tasmanian devil on it, leaving nothing but the core and stem in about eight seconds flat. She took a massive swig of water, then let out an earth-shattering belch. Her face turned bright red.

'Any chance you have a burger or a pizza back there?' she said.

'I like this one,' Lake said. 'Maurice, see what they're serving in the cafeteria today.'

'I could go for a turkey sandwich,' Aly said.

Wyatt laughed at the girl's moxie and went to explore the food options.

As promised, the NDA was brutal. If Cassie breached the contract or, in some cases, even *thought* about breach of contract (she would be subjected to a weekly Skin Reader test in perpetuity), Crispin Lake would basically own her, own everything she owned, and even everything she *might* own. It amused Cassie more than it bothered her. She didn't own anything of value, and given that her whole life the last ten years had been singularly devoted to trying to clear her husband's name, if, in the end, she came up short, she didn't feel she'd have much reason to live anyway. Lake could have her money (what little she had) and her life (wasn't much of a life anyway). If it turned out that Harris had, after everything, been the Vertex Ignis, and had led all those people to their deaths, then Cassie would probably be happier below ground anyway.

'I don't fully understand,' Cassie said. 'Why does the NDA exist in perpetuity? I get why you want it until the sim launches. But after that, won't everything be public anyway?'

'Not everything,' Lake said. 'Just being here, you're going to see things that nobody else has ever seen. And there are people out there who would go to great lengths to hurt Past Crimes.'

'Don't get me started on the Found,' Wyatt said.

'The who?' said Aly.

'Some cult that thinks the world owes them something because something bad happened to them,' Wyatt said.

Lake added, 'The Found is a group of sad-sack wannabe revolutionaries who see themselves as victims. But in reality, they have more in common with terrorists. They all lost someone under truly terrible circumstances, to killers, maniacs, and deviants, and for that I sympathize. But they now feel the world owes them something.

They formed what might charitably be called a cult to "get back" at people they feel have wronged them or exploited them. Somehow, we ended up in their sights. They're well funded, and not always peaceful. They're constantly trying to hack into our servers, and one even posed as a visitor and tried to break into our R and D building.'

'It's run by this couple,' Wyatt said. 'Psychopaths, both of them. I'll feel safer when they're both in prison, or underneath it.'

'Some people experience tragedy and channel their remorse and anger to better the world,' Lake said. 'Others . . . go down a different path. I believe it all stems from jealousy. Any time a successful company comes along, there will be people who try to either steal from them or bring them down. But that kind of excitement for our product, that kind of passion, can never be duplicated.'

Lake was bragging, but Cassie knew he was right. Any time Past Crimes announced a new sim, the anticipation was second only to the coronation of a new Pope at the virtual Saint Peter's Basilica inside the Vatican+. People ate, slept and *breathed* Past Crimes. It wasn't hyperbole to say that some people lived in Lake's sims. In fact, Cassie knew from her previous work at V.I.C.E. that Neural Flares were quite common for Past Crimes devotees. People would enter a sim and simply stay there, their catatonic body found days later by the EPP.

Decades earlier, when MMO, or Massively Multiplayer Online, games became popular, there was a rash of hospitalizations and even deaths as people became so addicted that they literally forgot to eat and sleep. South Korea in particular had seen a number of MMO-related deaths: a twenty-eight-year-old man who died from organ failure after playing games for fifty straight hours without so much as a sip of water. The young couple who raised a cherubic virtual infant, while their real infant starved. Things got so bad that the South Korean government instituted the Youth Protection Act, which made it unlawful for gamers under sixteen to play between the hours of midnight and six a.m. in order to protect its young populace. The law led to a spate of identity theft and was soon abolished.

Things had only become worse once Earth+ became the dominant economy, and the vast majority of both professional and social interactions began to take place inside. Neural Flare 'cures', usually just pure sodium tablets, were a billion-dollar economy in themselves. The EPP tried to get Lake to add a disclaimer to his sims, as well as an hourly timer that reminded users to hydrate. Lake refused their request. Adults could make their own decisions, Lake said. Cassie knew this added to the mystique of Past Crimes. The more people who had an obsession – especially an unhealthy one – with his products, the more people wanted to lose themselves inside it. Controversy created cash.

Cassie finished reading the contract, then signed with her finger. Jalal linked a retinal scanner to the device and scanned Cassie's eyes.

'Done,' he said.

'Terrific,' Cassie said. 'If I breach this contract, you have the legal right to about eighteen cents, my collection of cheap jewelry and an ugly yellow sofa. Now, let's get inside.'

'First things first,' Lake said. 'I want you to meet my head programmer, Stephen Woolman. Past Crimes wouldn't be Past Crimes without him.'

'Giving credit to someone else?' Cassie said. 'That's very unlike you.'

'There are two people I trust with my life,' Lake said. 'Maurice Wyatt is one of them. Steve Woolman is the other. And if you end up . . . staying . . . you'll be working with Steve a great deal. Come with me.'

Lake and Wyatt led Cassie and Aly down a glass-lined corridor that overlooked the Past Crimes park. Digital magazine covers, clips from Lake's many interviews and features about the company flashed on the glass like digital hallucinations. At the end of the hall, above the door, there was a counter that read *Past Crimes Subscribers*. The number read *One hundred and twenty-one million* – and it kept climbing. Cassie did some quick math.

A yearly subscription to Past Crimes cost a thousand dollars. That meant Past Crimes was raking in over twelve *billion* dollars a year – and that was on Earth+ subscriptions alone. They were surely raking in hundreds of millions, if not billions, more on Murderland admittance, merchandise, Wrap gear and more. If you wanted to, say, enter the Ed Gein sim wearing an exclusive Ed Gein Wrap (no pun intended), it would run you five hundred bucks. The Blight sim could blow it open even wider. Cassie wouldn't be shocked if they passed a hundred and fifty million subscribers in the next two years. That kind of cash influx could give them the resources to fully revamp the comparatively obsolete theme park.

'Do you know why I named this the Bundy Building?' Lake asked as they walked.

'Why?' Aly said.

'Because right here, in this very spot, is where Ted Bundy was arrested in 1975. Back then, West Valley City was called Granger. Right where we stand, a state Trooper named Robert Hayward was sitting in his car when he noticed a suspicious tan Volkswagen drive by. Responding to an unrelated call for assistance, Hayward passed by a house where he knew the family, and also knew that their teenage daughters were home alone. And idling there, in front of that house, was that very same tan Volkswagen. Hayward suspected the driver was casing the house. So Hayward tailed the VW, pulled it over at a gas station and held the driver at gunpoint while he waited for backup. The driver of that car was Ted Bundy. He was going to kill those girls – and probably many more if Robert Hayward hadn't followed his instincts. This site is legendary in the annals of true crime. So when this lot came up for sale, I knew it was the perfect place to build my park. And the spot where Hayward pulled Ted Bundy over was the perfect place to build my command center. Hence: the Bundy Building.'

'So why not name it the Hayward Building instead of the Bundy Building?' Aly asked. 'I mean, Hayward was the hero.'

Lake smiled. 'Bundy has more name recognition.'

He knocked on a door whose nameplate read *Stephen Woolman*.

'Enter,' came a voice from inside.

Lake opened the door, revealing a large office-slash-workroom. A middle-aged Black man sat behind a Lucite desk, his eyes focused on four floating monitors arranged in a row in front of him. If he noticed his visitors, he either didn't show it or didn't care. The office walls were some sort of glass and covered with digital schematics and diagrams. Electronic equipment, tools and parts lay scattered on tables. It looked as though someone could build a space station inside Stephen Woolman's office.

'Hey, Steve,' Lake said.

'Crispin,' Woolman said absentmindedly. 'I'm almost done with the dental biosensors for the Theia.' He spoke without removing his eyes from the screens.

'That's wonderful news,' Lake said. 'I'm sorry to intrude, but we have a matter that's quite pressing. Stephen, I'd like you to meet Cassandra Lake.'

Woolman paused. He took his face away from the monitors and stood up. He had short, graying hair, a neat goatee, and green eyes that conveyed a fierce intelligence. He approached Cassie with his hand outstretched.

'Ms. West,' the man said, with a reverent smile. 'It is an *honor*.'

She took his hand. 'Why is it an honor?'

'Why?' Woolman said in disbelief. 'Because you had front-row seats to one of the most important historical moments any of us have ever lived through. I know Crispin had tried to get you to be a part of our sim, and when you declined, I assumed that was the end of it.'

'I wasn't involved in it,' Cassie said. 'I might have survived, but part of me died. It's not quite as romantic as you're making it seem.'

'Of course. I meant no disrespect.'

'Steve,' Lake said. 'Ms. West isn't here as a tourist. She has pointed out a flaw in our sim.'

'A flaw?' Woolman said with a laugh. 'I don't think so.'

'Not a flaw,' Cassie said. 'But I think someone manipulated the crime scene after my husband died. Your simulation only replicates the room as it was presented to you. Incomplete.'

Woolman's eyes narrowed. 'So you want us to . . . fix it?'

'Ms. Miller suffered a terrible tragedy,' Lake said. 'But we have reason to believe her father may have been involved in the planning of another Blight. Possibly timed to coincide with the tenth anniversary of the first and the launch of our simulation.'

'Jesus Christ,' Woolman said, his smile disappearing. 'What . . . what can we do?'

'Based on what Ms. Miller's father said, and Ms. West's intimate knowledge of the crime scene at Forty-four Otter Creek Drive, they believe there may be other errors or clues within that could prove whether or not there will, in fact, be another Blight.'

'And give us the information to stop it,' Cassie said.

'They want to enter our simulation now?' Woolman said, confused. 'But it's not public yet. It's not ready.'

'I'm aware of that, Stephen. I run this place.'

'We've never let a civilian into a sim before launch before.'

'Rules are made to be broken. How close is it to being release ready?'

'Ninety-eight percent? I would never release it to the public until I nailed down that final two percent – critics would savage us for its lack of polish – but for a casual user, yes. It's good to go. We're ironing out some bugs, tweaking the biometric trackers and haptic sensors and making sure they connect with the Theia visors, but those are all mostly bells and whistles. The recreations themselves are in place. Now, you said Ms. Miller's father may have been involved? Was he planning it?'

Aly replied, 'No. He said he was a Beacon. He was following someone else.'

'Someone else,' Woolman said. 'But your husband, Ms. West – he was the Vertex Ignis. And he's dead.'

'I think the Vertex Ignis is still alive,' Cassie said. 'I think the same person who planned the first Blight pinned it on my husband and has been working in the shadows ever since.'

'I hope to God you're wrong,' Woolman said. 'The alternative is . . . horrifying.'

'We all hope she's wrong,' Lake said. 'But if she's not, it's our duty to help prevent it.' He turned to Cassie. 'Steve has led the team recreating the Blight. He was my first hire at Past Crimes.'

'I think I have Mr. Wyatt beat by about two weeks,' Woolman said.

'Steve Woolman is the Wozniak to my Jobs,' Lake said.

'Every band needs a charismatic frontman,' Woolman said. 'I'm happy to be the drummer in the background.'

'Steve is modest. He helped pioneer the new frontier of augmented reality,' Lake said. 'He recognized what Earth+ could be before just about anyone. Before Steve, Earth+ was a curiosity. Stodgy elitists and obtuse technocrats laughed at it the way people laughed at the Internet in the eighties. But people like Steve – and myself, of course – had the vision and helped it grow into what it is today.'

'You two, plus a number of global catastrophes, tragedies and economic meltdowns,' Cassie said.

'Necessity is the mother of invention. The world needed a new way to live. The economy was in the Stone Age, shipping millions of pounds of cargo across the globe on freighters, forcing children to go to schools just so they could be mowed down by a psychopath with an itchy trigger finger. We've helped make the world cleaner, better and safer.'

Woolman nodded. 'If we can do anything to help prevent another tragedy, we will.'

'Thank you,' Cassie said to Woolman. 'So what did you do before Past Crimes?'

'I was a video-game developer,' he said.

Lake laughed. 'Steve was a video-game developer like Thomas Edison didn't want to shave in the dark. Steve was creating new virtual worlds before anyone understood the possibilities of Earth+. Did you ever play the "Beyond the Beyond" games?'

'Didn't they make those into movies?' Aly said.

Woolman said, 'Three movies. Made almost four billion at the box office.'

'Steve created the most detailed dystopian worlds in the history of augmented reality,' Lake said. 'He was able to layer his creations on to our everyday world, so that each and every building looked like it was crumbling in front of your very eyes, so that mile-long fissures appeared in the highway in front of you. Stephen extrapolated what our planet would look like not just post-apocalypse, but post-post-*post*-apocalypse. Thousands of years after civilization had crumbled and had been rebuilt literally from the ground up. For everyone who always said they'd be able to survive in the dystopia, Stephen Woolman gave them a chance to prove it.'

'When we released the first Beyond the Beyond,' Woolman said, 'it changed the game for augmented reality. I chose augmented reality over virtual reality because I wanted people to be able to see *their* world through *my* lens. The month we launched, twenty people were hospitalized. They were literally fainting from fright when the Rippers – that was our name for the feral creatures that humans had devolved into – tore them limb from limb. Some people felt it was too realistic. That only proved to me that we needed to go *further*. To achieve the next level of reality, we needed to combine the real world with the virtual world.'

'I've never actually had my femur chomped on by a Ripper,' Lake said with a laugh, 'but with the revolutionary haptics and sensors Steve created, I'm pretty sure he captured exactly what it would feel like to have your bones gnawed on by a post-apocalyptic humanoid. That's exactly what I was trying to do with Past Crimes. Make people *feel* these stories, not just view them through the glass of a television screen or minuscule speakers in their ears. I wanted to remove all boundaries. People were tired of two-dimensional participation. Tired of only using three of their five senses. The Theia will enable people to use all five.'

Woolman went to the back of the room and pressed his palm against a metal cabinet. A mechanism unlocked and Woolman took out a device. He unfolded the thin metal frame to unveil what looked like a cross between sunglasses and swim goggles. It fit in the palm of his hand. The eyepieces were convex and covered in some sort of blue glass. Two small earbuds were attached to the frame.

'This is the most advanced Earth+ visor ever created,' Woolman said with pride. 'I named it the Theia, after the goddess of vision.'

Lake added, 'Past Crimes is not just an edutainment company. We're a *technology* company. We've created the most advanced simulations in the world, and to experience that we needed the most advanced visors in the world. Stephen has created them with the Theia.'

Cassie turned it over in her hand. It weighed less than a bottle of water. 'It's so light,' she said.

'Six-point-four ounces,' Woolman said.

'What's the Theia made out of?' Aly asked.

'It's a complex, flexible polycarbonate,' Woolman said. 'Stronger than steel but more flexible than mesh. It's not dissimilar to what the military uses in bulletproof vests, only far lighter, and with incredibly high-thermal conductivity. Our simulations require a truly staggering amount of data to process at lightning speed. Each sim chews up enough energy to power a small city.'

'What does that do to the environment?' Aly asked. Woolman laughed.

'You're a sweet kid. I haven't heard anyone pretend to care about the environment in a long time. We do have to be careful, though. If you send that kind of energy through an ordinary headset, the plastic would melt into your skin in less than six seconds.'

'I'm afraid to ask how you know that,' Aly said.

'Every day that ends in "Y" is a day that someone tries to rip us off,' Woolman said. 'But we have good lawyers, plus our competitors use budget materials and are run by people with budget brains. One company I won't name killed two people during its R and D phase when their headsets literally burst into flame during testing. We didn't even need to sue them. The EPP shut them down, and their founder killed himself in prison eighteen months later. We're the only people in the world who can create something as advanced as the Theia – and do it safely. The only injuries at Past Crimes are virtual.'

'Can I try?' Cassie asked. Woolman held it out to her, and Cassie took it. She turned the Theia over in her hands, then slipped the device on and placed the earbuds in her ear canals. To her surprise, she felt the buds enlarge until they molded to the shape of her ear.

'What just happened?' Cassie said.

'You like?' Woolman replied. 'Theia's proprietary inner ear materials automatically expand and contract to give the user a perfect fit. The sound quality is like real life, only better, and our OLED screens are the best in the world. The first smartphones had displays containing maybe a million pixels. Now even the lower-end models can display a billion pixels or more. The Theia displays nearly one trillion pixels per inch.'

'It's like real life,' Lake said, 'only—'

'Better,' Cassie interrupted. 'I get it.' She took the visor off.

'When you put Theia on for the first time, our optic sensors map your eye,' Woolman said. 'Pupil, lens, cornea. If you have astigmatism, the visor will adapt and correct any sight imperfections. What you see in Earth+ with the Theia will be clearer than if you had twenty/ten vision in Earth–. But what I'm most proud of is that with Theia you will be able to utilize all five senses. Each house in our Blight simulation has its own textures, and even its own scent. You'll know the difference between a Beacon who lived in New Jersey and a Beacon who lived in Marrakesh just by smell. Coffee will taste different when you buy it fresh-brewed in Nicaragua versus having a plastic tub drone-dropped. We have perfected the art of thermal taste simulation.'

'So you'll be able to *taste* Earth+?' Aly said. 'That sounds . . . unsanitary.'

'The tongue is actually connected directly to the brain stem,' Woolman said. 'What you taste goes directly to those receptors. But it also goes the other way. There are three cranial nerves that supply stimulation to the tongue: the vagus, the glossopharyngeal and the facial nerve. By stimulating these nerves, we can create actual sensations inside your mouth that correspond to taste. We use specially calibrated sensors to provide heating and cooling sensations to the taste channel, or TRPM5, on your tongue. Think of it like playing a piano, only for your senses. The right keys create a literal symphony of taste.'

'This is all absolutely fascinating,' Cassie said, 'but thousands of lives are at stake. I'd like to get into the sim.'

Woolman looked at Lake and said, 'I need to run a full diagnostic before I let anyone inside.'

'How long will that take?' Cassie asked.

'This simulation and the Theia weren't supposed to be used by the public for a few more days. That may not sound like a lot of time, but to our team it means a few thousand more working hours to fix any bugs and make sure the hardware will be able to handle the software. Give me one night. I want to make sure that when you go in, the Theia won't cook your brain.'

'Ooh, I saw a movie where Hannibal Lecter did that,' Aly said.

'Not funny at this current moment,' Cassie said.

'I know time is of the essence,' Lake said, 'but so is your safety. As I said, we want to make sure that all injuries at Past Crimes occur only in Earth+.'

'So what do we do for the night?' Aly said. 'Check into a Past Crimes hotel? Order some fava beans and a nice Chianti?'

'I'm afraid, for confidentiality reasons, I can't let you leave the complex until the sim launches,' Lake said. 'Lucky for you, my employees work pretty much around the clock. They all live in housing on or near the park. I built a pretty nice lounge for the slackers who can't hack an eighteen-hour work day. We call it the Crash Pad.'

'You want us to sleep . . . in your break room?' Cassie said.

'I promise, the Crash Pad is far more than a break room. Our beds are ergonomically and biometrically designed to both give you a good night's sleep and align your spine correctly. There are private showers and plenty of snacks. I hope you at least brought your own clothes, because all we have are Past Crimes T-shirts and sweatpants. And you know what they say about wearing the T-shirt of the band you're seeing.'

'I'm guilty of that,' Cassie said. 'Rolling Stones back in 2033 at the virtual Hollywood Bowl.'

'Keith Richards is a big fan of ours,' Lake said. 'In fact, he came to Murderland last year to celebrate his hundred-and-third birthday.'

'Well, I'm not here to celebrate. First thing tomorrow morning, I'm in,' Cassie said. 'Otherwise, I'll break your NDA with just a little too much enthusiasm for your liking.'

'I'll get you in tomorrow morning,' Woolman said.

'Wyatt, send out a company-wide EPD memo. The Crash Pad is closed for the night to give Ms. West and Ms. Miller some privacy.'

'I'll get working. I wasn't planning on sleeping much the next week, anyway,' Woolman said. He looked at Cassie and Aly. 'I hope you're wrong.'

Wyatt led them out of Woolman's office. Aly yawned. Her eyes were red and bleary. Cassie had no idea when she last had a full night's rest. Cassie checked her watch. It was nearing eleven. Sleep was beginning to pull at her eyelids too, a fog settling over her brain. Aly yawned again, then looked back at Cassie with an embarrassed smile.

'I think I hit a wall,' Aly said.

'I think we both did.'

Wyatt stopped in front of a metal door and pressed his palm against a sensor. A red light scanned his hand up and down. When it finished, another green biometric sensor emanated from the ceiling and scanned all three of them. Aly shuffled nervously as the machine read her biometrics.

Wyatt smiled at Aly. 'I know, I know, if you get a tumor—'

'I'll beat you to death with your own arms,' Aly said.

'My arms are thicker than your waist,' Wyatt said with a smile.

'I guess I'll have to work extra hard to pull them off then.'

Wyatt laughed. The scan finished and the door slid open, revealing a large common room with two overstuffed sofas, eight full-size beds, an industrial-size fridge, several coffee machines and even a bookshelf. The recessed lighting was dim, cozy. Cassie had expected some sort of space-age lounge, with drones zipping through the air, maybe a robot that gave you free back massages, or a cyborg chef that made omelets on demand. Instead, the Crash Pad looked more like a swanky hotel combined with a teacher's lounge.

'Where are the visors?' Aly asked. 'No Earth+ hookups?'

'I don't think you understand how tired an employee must be to sleep in the Crash Pad instead of going home,' Wyatt said. 'In my tenure at Past Crimes, not a single employee has ever requested we add visors. If you're here, you're here because you can't keep your eyes open or your body is on the verge of shutting down. We prefer that not to happen.'

'I don't know the last time I saw an actual bookshelf,' Cassie said. She walked to the chest-high wooden shelf and ran her thumb along the spines. It had been at least a decade since Cassie had seen an actual printed book. They'd become too costly to produce, and once all the manufacturing jobs dried up and workers found new jobs in Earth+, printed books had largely become relics of the past. When she was a little girl, Cassie had shelves teeming with books. Seeing this shelf was a reminder of a different time. Aly was eyeing one of the beds like a desert wanderer who'd come upon a sparkling blue lake.

'Women's bathrooms are down the hall to the left,' Wyatt said. 'I've already keyed in your biometrics, so all you have to do is place your palm on the door to open it. There are showers, towels, and fresh toiletries, including women's products. If there's anything you need, just press the red button above your bed.'

'You really don't want people to go home, do you?' Cassie said.

'It's not that we don't want people to go home,' Wyatt replied. 'But Crispin likes to hire people who are as passionate about what we do as he is. He encourages them to work long hours, and if they need a place to sleep after eighteen-hour days, he wants to make sure it's comfortable.'

Aly was already getting under the covers. 'Holy God, this bed is amazing,' she said, emitting a groan of pleasure. 'What thread count are these sheets? A million? Whatever you did to make them so comfy, *that's* the technology you should be selling.'

Wyatt laughed. 'I'll let Crispin know. I'll leave you two alone. If you need anything—'

'Red button,' Cassie said.

Wyatt left the lounge. Cassie sat down on the bed adjacent to Aly's and took her shoes off, flexing her stiff ankles and joints. Aly's eyes were fluttering open and closed as she burrowed into the mattress. Cassie felt a tightness in her chest, like a long-forgotten scar that had opened fresh. It had been ten years since she'd shared a room with anyone. Even longer since she shared a room with someone who was not her family.

Within seconds, Aly was asleep. She made a light snorting sound, and for some reason it made Cassie smile. Cassie went to the bathroom, washed, then got into bed. Aly was right. It felt like she was resting on air. As she got comfortable, she noticed Aly's eyes had opened.

'Everything OK?'

'Not really.'

'What's wrong?'

'Just thinking about tomorrow. About what we might find. Or not find.'

'I am too. If we do find something, I'm scared about what it means. And if we don't find something, then . . . it's like my parents just died and that's all there is.'

'I'm scared too,' Cassie said. 'I'm scared that there will be another Blight. But I'm also scared that we don't find anything. And if we don't, then it means Harris really was . . .' She trailed off.

Aly nodded. 'Can I tell you something?'

'Of course.'

'Please don't be mad.'

'I won't.'

'Promise?'

'I promise,' Cassie said. 'I don't have any anger left.'

Aly sucked in a breath.

'I hope we don't find anything,' she said. 'I hope there's no second Blight. I hope my dad was just a crazy person and he killed my mom, and even though that means my life is basically ruined, at least nobody else's will be. It means nobody else will get hurt.

Aly sat up and looked Cassie in the eye. She continued.

'I hope your husband really was behind the Blight. I hope he was guilty. Because that means the only Vertex Ignis is dead and can't hurt anyone else.'

Cassie said nothing.

'Are you mad?' Aly said.

'No,' Cassie said. She wasn't mad. She felt something, but it wasn't anger. 'Can I tell you something too?'

Aly nodded.

'I still visit him sometimes.'

'Who? Harris?'

'Yeah. After he died, I held a funeral in Earth– for him. There was nothing in his coffin because his body burned up in the fire. There was nothing left to bury. The day after his coffin went into the ground, his gravesite was dug up. His headstone was smashed. Photos of the victims of the Blight were placed in his empty coffin. So I had his coffin reburied in an unmarked grave in the middle of nowhere. I don't visit his grave because people will follow me and do it all over again. I bought him an encrypted grave in an Earth+ Lockbox. Only I have access to it. I still go there sometimes. I bring virtual flowers. I bring the ultrasound photos of our daughter who was never born. And I'll just stay there for a while. Sometimes I think about staying there until I just shrivel away. Or my Neural Flares become so severe I won't remember anything anymore. I don't believe that Harris was the Vertex Ignis. But sometimes it feels like I'm holding on to that because I have nothing else to hold on to.'

Aly nodded. 'I miss them. It hurts every day. I hate my dad for what he did, but I can't stop thinking about who he used to be. He would take me to parks in Earth+ and push me on the swing for hours. We had a virtual dog. He wanted me to learn responsibility, and he promised that if I could take care of it, he'd get me a real one. I'm trying to remember *that* father. Not the one at the end.'

'Maybe someone will invent a visor that will let us pick and choose our memories,' Cassie said. 'Keep the good ones and get rid of the bad ones.'

'I'd buy it,' Aly said. 'I bet when you woke up ten years ago, you didn't imagine this.'

'I imagined a lot of things. Traveling thousands of miles with a strange girl to try to stop a global catastrophe while hoping to clear the name of my dead husband who's accused of being a cult leader-slash-genocidal maniac was not one of them.'

'So what did you imagine?' Aly said. 'Before all this.'

Cassie took in a long, slow breath and said, 'I imagined being happy. I imagined having a family. Having one of those marriages that make other people both angry and jealous. Maybe some travel. *Real* travel, not just in Earth+. Knowing I was loved and loved back. And I had that. I wish I'd known how fast it could all go away. I would have appreciated it more.'

'I would have appreciated my friends,' Aly said. 'I don't know if I'll ever see them again.'

'What about you?' Cassie asked. 'What did you see for yourself?'

'I wanted to make movies. *Real* movies. The way they used to make them a long time ago. Movies that were dark and mysterious. Where the effects are just the actors and the light and shadow and the writing, instead of capes and monsters and things that explode. I mean, there's room for all of that, sure. But I like the movies where what they don't say is just as important as what they do say. Where people have two shadows: one on the wall and the one they keep to themselves.'

'You can still do that,' Cassie said, but her voice lacked conviction. She knew Aly could tell.

'I guess it didn't work out the way we'd hoped for either of us, did it?'

'There's still time for you,' Cassie said.

'Maybe,' Aly said. 'Maybe there's still time for you, too.'

'Maybe there is.'

'Goodnight, Ms. West.'

'Cassie.'

'Goodnight, Cassie.'

Aly closed her eyes again. Within seconds, she was snoring. Cassie watched Aly for a few minutes, wondering if there really could be a life for her. As she drifted off to sleep, she wondered just what that life might be.

TWELVE

They sat at their small, round dining-room table in the kitchen. The cabinets and appliances were dated. They never had the money to replace them. Two steaming bowls of Coq au Vin sat on the table. Cassie wore a sleeveless yellow blouse. The small diamond on her ring finger glowed brilliantly, brighter than she even remembered, like there was a sun embedded within the tiny gem.

Harris sat across from her. His beard was neatly trimmed, full and brown, and his eyes – God, those brilliant eyes that she'd fallen in love with the day she saw him in that bookstore, which she'd fallen in love with before she'd fallen in love with the man himself – they gazed at her with such love and devotion that it nearly made Cassie cry.

Harris cut off a piece of chicken, dipped it in sauce and brought it to his mouth. When the morsel touched his tongue, his eyes practically rolled back in his head.

'Cass,' he said. 'Taste this. You're going to want to marry me all over again.'

She took a bite and, of course, he was right. The chicken tasted more tender, like it was real poultry rather than the chicken breasts and thighs grown in labs they often ate to save money.

When she was young, Cassie's mother always complained about her birthdays. Their celebrations were muted. But Cassie savored hers. Every year on March 30th, she would return home from work to a delicious homecooked meal, a bottle of wine alternative, the perfect jazz playlist, and a night that ended naked in each other's arms. And as much as she enjoyed the meal – and she did – the ending was always her favorite part. She loved feeling the bristles of his beard against her neck, against her thighs, against her breasts. There were times she'd gotten home from a trip and wanted to skip right to dessert, but she knew how hard he'd worked preparing the meal, and Cassie wanted to make sure Harris knew she appreciated it. Patience was its own reward. And she was glad that despite all the technological advances of the last few decades, they still made love the old-fashioned way.

Cassie looked at this man across the table and felt her heart swell as he ate a forkful of food, sauce dribbling down his chin.

'Can't seem to get it all in my mouth,' Harris said, playfully.

'I don't mind you dirty,' Cassie replied. She looked down at her belly, just starting to swell. The first trimester had been rough, but she wouldn't trade all the morning sickness, all the strange cravings or all the sleepless nights for the world. 'Do you know that I lost the baby?'

Harris nodded, sadly. He put the fork down and met Cassie's eyes, his own filled with remorse and pain.

'I'm so sorry I couldn't be there for you,' he said. 'You had to go through all of that alone. You had nobody. No family. No friends. Everybody turned their back on you because of who they thought I was.'

'You wanted this so badly,' Cassie choked out, her voice cracking. 'You wanted it just as much as I did, didn't you?'

'Just as much.'

'Then *why*?' Cassie demanded. 'Why did you leave me? Why did you leave *us*? When we were about to have everything we ever wanted?'

Harris did not respond. He picked up another forkful of food, but this time the meat turned to ash and blew away before he could get it in his mouth.

'Did you do it?' Cassie said. 'Are you the monster everyone says you are? Have I spent the last ten years of my life defending evil?'

'You know I can't answer that,' Harris said.

Behind Harris, an orange flame began to lick at the drapes.

'I miss you,' Cassie said. The food on the table and the wine in their glasses had all turned to ash. '*Should* I miss you? Even if you're not who they say you are, you *knew* about it. Who made you do it?'

Harris said nothing. The flames continued to spread, climbing up the walls and crawling towards the ceiling.

'Some days I hate . . . I goddamn *hate* that I miss you. It would be easier if I didn't. At least then I could have moved on. Started a new life. I don't even know if that would have been possible, but at least I could have *tried*.'

'Maybe you should have tried either way,' Harris said. 'Ten years is a long time to be chained to a ghost.'

Cassie nodded. 'I need to know if this is all worth it. I need to know that you're the man I believe you are. I need to know you're the same man I fell in love with, the man I was going to start a family with, the man I wanted to grow old and die with.'

Harris reached his hand across the table. Cassie leaned forward and his palm closed around hers.

'I love you,' he said. 'Forever.'

'I love you too,' Cassie said. 'Even though I wonder if I should.'

Harris took her hand and brought it to his lips and kissed her skin, and she wept. The flames encircled the whole room, a bright, orange cage around them, and then Harris's body turned to ash and blew away. She watched this, her life once again turning to ash, but then somewhere beyond the flames, Cassie heard a scream.

She woke up looking at an unfamiliar ceiling. It was not on fire. There was no table. No food. No ash. It took a moment for Cassie to remember where she was. This was the first time she'd slept in a bed not her own in years. She knew it had been a dream, even when she'd been inside it, and that was why, she supposed, she had not been afraid.

Then she heard the scream again. Cassie turned to her side and saw Aly in the bed next to hers. The girl's face was pale and coated in sweat, her hair stringy and plastered to her face. She was rolling back and forth, her eyes shut but somehow pained at the same time.

Then she screamed again.

Cassie sat up, looking at this young girl, her mind clearly overrun by the horrors she'd witnessed. And Cassie sat there, unsure of what to do.

This was not her daughter. This was not her flesh or blood. She was, until this week, a total stranger. This girl was not her responsibility. She had allowed Aly to come with her because she had given in to her emotions and because she understood the girl's need for answers, because they had a shared goal. That was all. Answers were all she could give to this girl. All she owed to this girl. Nothing more.

But Aly's howls of pain shook Cassie somewhere deep inside, each sob making her heart feel like it was being squeezed. Cassie closed her eyes and tried to ignore it, tried to tell herself that this was not her pain to fix, but before she knew what she was doing, Cassie was out of her bed and kneeling by Aly's side and holding the girl's sweat-coated hands. She brought Aly's head to her shoulder and gently brushed the hair from her eyes.

Aly cried for a few more minutes, but soon the cries softened, an echo receding. Eventually, they stopped altogether and Aly grew quiet, the only sound in the room her breathing, steady and strong. Cassie knelt there for what seemed like hours, not caring that her legs ached, not caring that she would be exhausted come morning.

So this is what it's like, Cassie thought. *This is what was taken from me.*

At some point, when her knees began to hurt, Cassie tried to remove her hand and return to bed. But Aly held firm. So Cassie moved Aly over, gently, then slid beside her and pulled the soft blanket over them both. Aly's head rested in the small nook between Cassie's shoulder and chest. Cassie closed her eyes, hoping that sleep would come but the dreams would stay away.

THIRTEEN

July 18th, 2047
5:47 a.m.
Eighteen hours and thirteen minutes to launch

When Cassie woke up, she was alone. Her shoulder was sore and her leg was dangling off the bed. There was an indent in the mattress where Aly had slept. She wiped the crust from her eyes and sat up. There were no windows. She had no idea if it was morning or night. She had no idea what kind of schedule people at Past Crimes kept, but that question was answered when a booming voice came through an intercom somewhere in the lounge.

'Glad to see you're both awake. We've been waiting for you.' It was Crispin Lake. She wondered if the man ever slept.

'What time is it?'

'Five forty-eight.'

'How did you know we were up?'

'The Crash Pad takes biometric readings of its inhabitants every fifteen seconds,' Lake said. 'Breathing patterns change between sleep and waking. That way, if an employee's heart rate spikes abnormally from stress, exhaustion, anything, we can get them immediate medical attention. Both of your heart rates were elevated most of the night. Bad dreams?'

'I already see a therapist algorithm, but thanks for asking,' Cassie said.

'Well, get dressed. The Blight is ready when you are.'

'All right,' she said.

'Your pulse just went up several beats,' Lake said. 'Take a deep breath. Let us know when you're ready.'

Cassie put her fingers to her neck. Lake was right. Her pulse was racing.

Aly came back from the women's room wearing gray sweatpants and a loose-fitting red T-shirt with the Past Crimes logo on it. She toweled off her damp hair and nodded at Cassie.

'Morning,' Cassie said.

'Morning. Sorry if I hogged the bed.'

'Sorry you had to smell my armpit most of the night.'

'I'll live,' Aly said. Cassie pointed at Aly's Past Crimes shirt. Aly's face reddened. 'There were like a million of these in the bathroom. I didn't think I'd put Crispin Lake out of business by taking one. I used to make fun of people who wore the T-shirt of the band they were seeing. This is like next level.'

Aly took a seat on the bed across from Cassie. She put the towel down.

'I had a dream last night. About the day my parents . . .' she said, trailing off.

'I figured that's what it was.'

'I have that dream a lot. Almost every night.'

'That must be awful.'

'I don't know how to get them to stop. I try to think happy thoughts and all that bullshit when I go to bed. Going to old movies at the recreated Majestic in Earth+ with David. The feeling in my stomach when I sit next to Regina Moore in Social Studies. I try not to think about that day, but it always just pops into my head. Does that make sense?'

'More than you could possibly know,' Cassie said.

Aly took a deep breath, as though expelling the thoughts, then went to the fridge and took out an organic yogurt. Cassie showered and changed. Ten minutes later, the entrance to the Crash Pad slid open and Crispin Lake entered the room, Wyatt following behind him.

Lake saw Aly spooning yogurt into her mouth and said, 'I see you found the snacks.'

'I wuz hungwee,' Aly said, her mouth full of strawberry goop.

'Ms. West? Can I get you anything before we begin?'

'Maybe just a coffee,' she said.

'I would recommend having something to eat before you go in. Your biometric scan when you arrived showed minor Hyponatremia. We'll be measuring your oxygen levels, brain patterns, heart rate, sodium levels, and blood sugar while you're inside. If any of your readings spike, we'll pull you out. We take Neural Flares very seriously. Now, are you ready?'

Cassie took a deep breath. She'd come all this way to enter the Blight sim, but there was something gnawing at her.

'I'm going to see him. Aren't I?' Cassie said. 'Harris.'

Lake nodded slowly, sympathetically. 'Yes. We have created a highly detailed Augmented Persona of your husband, right down to every pore.'

'Statute 486-16,' Cassie said. 'Right? Because he was posthumously convicted of his role in the Blight, you were able to use his NTP without needing to obtain any approval.'

'That's correct,' Lake said. 'I pushed hard for that statute. I firmly believe it's in the public interest to know as much about its criminals as possible, and for enterprises like ours to have the unencumbered rights to be able to use the NTPs of people whose despicable actions necessitate the forfeiture of their rights to privacy. If you don't learn from the past, you are doomed to repeat it.'

'Just so we're clear, I do not believe that the Harris West you created in your sim is the Harris West I knew.'

Lake clucked his tongue and sighed.

'If you deliver me proof, I'm all ears. But at some point, you either have to find the holy grail or accept that it doesn't exist.'

'I'll find it,' Cassie said. 'I guess I'll see myself inside the sim, too.'

'You will,' Lake replied. 'The law permits a certain amount of . . . leeway . . . when it comes to creating APs of people who have not given permission and have not been convicted of any crimes. Similar to how television shows used to "recreate" crime scenes with actors. So you are in there; you're just – how do I put it? – altered.'

'Altered in what way?'

'Likeness. Demeanor. I would call your AP "Cassandra West-adjacent". You'll see for yourself. Obviously, if you agree to let us use your likeness and biometrics, we would perform a full overhaul of the current Cassandra West AP and patch in the real deal.'

'If I'm wrong, I'll stick to my word that I'll participate. But if I'm right, you'll have to "overhaul" your entire simulation.'

'We never refer to anything as an "overhaul",' Lake said. 'We simply update our simulations to provide the most accurate historical representations in order to provide our valued customers with the most satisfying experience possible.'

'You sound like you're selling condos,' said Cassie. Lake did not reply.

Wyatt entered carrying a tray containing bagels, scrambled eggs, fruit, baked goods, assorted jam and spreads, and a large pot of French press coffee. Cassie downed two cups and nibbled at a bagel while Aly ransacked the pastry tray.

'I haven't eaten real food in weeks,' Aly said.

'Thank you,' Cassie said to Lake. 'You didn't have to do this.'

'I'm in the hospitality industry too, in a sense,' Lake said. 'Happy customers keep coming back.'

'I'm not a customer,' Cassie said.

'You were,' Lake replied. 'I checked our records. You had a Past Crimes subscription for nearly eight years through V.I.C.E. It was terminated right after the Blight.'

'To be fair, my finances were a little bit strained after the Blight.'

'Well, when this is over, I'm restarting your membership. Gratis, indefinitely.'

'You sure you can afford that?' Cassie said. Lake offered a thin-lipped smile.

At that moment, Stephen Woolman appeared at the door. His eyes were bloodshot and he was unshaven, and Cassie was pretty sure he was wearing the same clothes as yesterday.

He looked at Cassie, then at Aly. 'It's time.'

FOURTEEN

6:32 a.m.
Seventeen hours and twenty-eight minutes to launch

They rode an elevator to the eighteenth floor, then followed Woolman through a series of narrow gray corridors, barely wide enough for one person to walk. Cassie's heart drummed in her chest. She could hear Aly breathing behind her. She turned back.

'You OK?' Cassie said. Aly nodded, but her eyes were wide, cautious.

'Yeah. Just nervous.'

'Me too.'

When they arrived at the end of the corridor, Woolman approached a metal door, turned to the side and slid his sleeve up to his shoulder.

'What's he doing?' Aly whispered to Cassie.

'I don't know,' Cassie said.

A small metal compartment slid open and a retractable arm extended out towards Woolman. At the end of the arm was a thin needle attached to a small vial. A red light emanated from the arm, pinpointing a spot near Woolman's shoulder. Then, quicker than a breath, the needle plunged into Woolman's arm, then retracted, its vial containing a sample of Woolman's blood. Five seconds later, the metal door opened with a hiss.

'Follow me,' Woolman said, passing through the doorway.

'What was that?' Cassie asked.

'Blood analysis and recognition,' Lake replied. 'We take the security of our pre-launch simulations very seriously.'

'It can analyze his blood that quick?' Cassie said.

'In five seconds, that machine can determine blood type, hemo-globin count, cancerous cells, even cholesterol,' Lake said. 'Thanks to this machine, I knew I needed to add more folic acid to my diet.'

They entered a narrow hallway with backlit white walls that seemed to almost be glowing. Two men stood at the end of the hall. They wore red uniforms with the black Past Crimes crime scene victim logo in the center. And they both held large rifles at their sides.

The guards nodded as the group entered.

'Ryerson. Trautman,' Lake said.

'Mr. Lake,' the guards replied in unison.

The guards stepped aside, giving Woolman access to the door. Woolman raised his shirt sleeve again and another needle drew blood. A door slid open and they all went inside.

'Welcome to the Maternity Ward,' Woolman said. 'You are the first non-Past Crimes employees to ever set foot here.'

'Whoa,' Aly said.

The large room was pristine white, with a tissue-thin 360-degree screen in the center mounted to the ceiling. Six spotless white leather chairs surrounded a circular console, each one facing a bank of monitors. Each chair had an Earth+ visor in front of it, docked in a charging station.

'Have a seat,' Lake said. 'Anywhere you like.'

Cassie sat down in one of the chairs. Aly took the seat next to her. The padding seemed to contour to her body, perfectly aligning her spine. Lake and Woolman took two seats. Wyatt lingered at the back of the room. One of the guards – Ryerson? – stood next to Wyatt, his rifle reflecting off the sparkling white walls.

'Why do you call this place a maternity ward?' Aly asked.

'This is where my children are born,' Lake said, matter-of-factly. 'I love every one of my simulations like a parent loves a child. I probably spend more time raising my creations than most parents do with their children. Not to mention that I spend far, far more money on my children.'

Must be nice to be rich enough that people are willing to over-look it when you say things that are totally insane, Cassie thought.

'The Maternity Ward is where we test out our simulations before they are released to the public,' Woolman said. 'It's the final chance to catch any bugs, make any last-second improvements and ensure all the APs are functioning properly.'

'So what do I do?' Cassie said.

'Put your visor on like you normally would,' Woolman instructed. He pointed at the large screen hovering above the work stations. 'This screen transmits data directly from your visor. It allows us to see exactly what you're seeing inside Earth+ and records what happens within the simulation.'

Woolman took out a tablet. His fingers danced around the keypad. Cassie took the visor from its charging station and fit it over her head. The buds nestled into her ears. She felt a slight tingling in her jaw and her soft palate.

'What is that?' Cassie said.

'Those are our patented cranial sensors,' Woolman said. 'First of their kind to be used inside Earth+. They allow us to transmit data directly to your tongue and olfactory canal. They're baked into every Theia device.'

'We're going to start you somewhere familiar inside the sim,' Lake said. 'Your home. After that, you'll be free to experience the sim and find what you're looking for.'

'I think you'll find that your house has been painstakingly and, dare I say, lovingly recreated,' Woolman said.

Aly removed a visor from the docking station and slid it over her face. 'Oh, that's weird,' she said. 'Feels like my tongue is being electrocuted.'

Woolman said, 'Once you enter the sim, that feeling will pass. Now, just to be clear, you'll both have the ability to be either Participants or Spectators. Cassie, if you choose to be a Participant in your home, the AP Harris will react to you unless the AP Cassie is there. Make sense?'

'Harris will defer to the virtual me.'

'That's right.'

'One last thing,' Lake said. Salman Jalal entered the ward carrying a paper-thin tablet.

'What's this?' Cassie asked.

'Since you're already experiencing effects of Hyponatremia,' Jalal said, 'I need you to sign a waiver that any adverse physical or psychological effects you experience inside or as a result of the simulation are not the responsibility of Past Crimes.'

'Fair enough,' Cassie said. She skimmed the document and signed it. Jalal looked it over, nodded and stood next to Woolman.

'Good luck, Ms. West,' Jalal said. His gaze lingered on her for an extra moment. It unsettled Cassie, but before she could question it, Jalal left the room.

'Ready?' Lake said.

'Yes,' Cassie said.

'I think so,' Aly added.

'I sincerely hope you *don't* find what you came here for. But if you do, we will use our considerable resources to do whatever it takes to keep people safe.'

'Thank you,' Cassie said. She took a deep breath.

'Here we go,' Woolman said. 'Ms. West, Ms. Miller. Prepare to enter the Blight.'

Cassie saw nothing but black. Then her Wrap appeared in the middle of the desert. Aly's Wrap was beside her. Red-hued mountains came into view in the distance, the massive buildings of the virtual Past Crimes complex rising out of the earth, monoliths in the void. Their Wraps hurtled through the doors of the middle building, passing the images of the most notorious crimes and criminals in history.

They sped down a long, dark corridor. Cassie felt wind in her hair, a chill lancing down her spine. The walls burst into flames, the faces of the demons of the past smiling from within the fire. She could see Aly's mouth open, as though trying to scream, but her voice was drowned out. Then, at the very end of the tunnel, she saw the silhouette of a man. As they got closer, Cassie recognized him.

He stood there, smiling, hand outstretched as though welcoming her. She knew his smile. She knew his eyes. She knew his face.

'Join me,' Harris West said, 'and experience the Blight.'

FIFTEEN

9:04 a.m.
Fourteen hours and fifty-six minutes to launch

t's just Harris's Augmented Persona, Cassie told herself. *He's not real. He's not real. He's not—*

Then the world around Cassie went white. And when the white

faded, and Cassie's eyes adjusted to the virtual world around her, she recognized where she was in an instant.

She was standing in the foyer of her old home at 44 Otter Creek Drive. She smelled bacon. She looked around. Everything was exactly how she remembered it, how she'd left it the morning of July 19th, 2037.

'Is this . . .' Aly said.

Cassie nodded. 'My home.'

She walked into the kitchen. The scent of bacon grew stronger. Her mouth began to water. She smelled something else as well. Something heavenly. Coffee. She smelled fresh-brewed coffee.

'Are you OK?' Aly said. Cassie hadn't even realized Aly's Wrap was beside her. She shook her head.

'I don't know why I thought this would be easy,' Cassie said. The house. The aromas. It was as if the past ten years had evaporated, and she was back in those precious moments where her life still felt full of love and hope and possibility. It looked like a normal, happy home, but the trick was this was a recreation of a nightmare.

She took a deep breath and went into the kitchen. When she saw the man standing by the stove, a single word escaped her lips.

'Harris,' she said.

He wore a pair of khaki shorts and a gray T-shirt with a hole in the armpit. His hair was disheveled and he had several days' worth of grayish-brown scruff. She could smell the faint tang of body odor. They'd had sex the previous night and she knew he hadn't showered yet. She remembered his face as they made love, how he seemed strangely emotional, resting his cheek against her breast at the end and saying, 'You know I love you, right? Both of you. Forever.'

At the time, it had seemed sweet. Loving. Now, Cassie knew Harris was aware it was the last time they'd ever be intimate. He was saying goodbye.

This Harris turned around. He had a soft, loving smile on his face. He held a pair of tongs, several strips of crispy bacon clamped in their jaws.

'Hey, hon,' Harris said. 'Bet you're hungry after last night.'

He walked towards Cassie. She took a step back. She knew this wasn't real. *He* wasn't real. This was the Harris that Crispin Lake had created. But God, he looked and he smelled just like the man she'd married, the man she'd loved, the man whose child she'd been carrying when her world erupted in flames.

He moved quicker than she could react and, suddenly, Harris's lips were on hers, and her eyes closed involuntarily and she felt his strong hands around her waist and she melted into him and kissed him back deeply, tasting the combination of minty toothpaste and coffee on his breath. She felt dizzy and everything fell away. How could a dream and a nightmare coexist so seamlessly?

When he let go, Harris looked into her eyes, then went back to the stove. He knew he'd be dead in twelve hours.

'You have the meeting with the Ruiz family today, right?' Harris said, turning back to the stove. He asked the question in a manner that was confirming details he already knew. He was making sure Cassie would be out of the house during the day. Cassie hadn't picked up on all the loaded questions and looks and statements ten years ago because, well, why would she? She had hoped to lock down the Ruiz deal and be home for dinner. But Harris knew this was the last time they would see each other. He knew *something*. Even if he wasn't responsible for the Blight, he woke up that morning knowing he would not live to see the day's end.

Harris scooped a small mountain of bacon on to two plates then added eggs to both. The toaster rang, and he slid two pieces on to one plate, and four on to another.

'For you,' he said to Cassie, placing the lighter of the two plates on the table. He began to wolf down his food, barely stopping to take a breath.

Like he's eating his last breakfast, Cassie thought.

'You look cute,' Cassie said, without thinking. Harris looked up, grease dotting his chin.

'Are you trying to seduce me over breakfast?' he said, with an egg-flecked smile.

'That's exactly what I'm doing,' Cassie replied.

'Last night was nice,' he said.

'It was.' That night ten years ago was the last time Harris had touched her. The last time anyone had touched her. She felt an ache deep within her, an old pain flaring up. The conversation had been recreated faithfully, taken from police reports and Cassie's dozens of interviews with law enforcement.

'"Last night was nice"?' Aly said. 'Were you two always like this?'

'Yes. We were,' Cassie said. 'And it was wonderful.'

It shocked her how easy this was. To fall back into their old pattern.

Harris laughed and came over, pressing his lips against her cheek. Cassie felt dizzy. This didn't just *feel* real – it *was* real. The food. The conversation. She remembered it as if it had just happened. A nightmare wrapped in a dream.

This whole morning – the food, the conversation, everything – was exactly what Cassie had told the police when they interviewed her after the Blight. She'd spent weeks in precincts, real and in Earth+, answering every conceivable question a dozen times over. She'd walked them through the last few weeks of Harris's life in excruciating detail. Lake had recreated that horrible day to absolute perfection and with terrifying detail and realism.

This was the day Cassie's life – and maybe even the world – had changed forever.

'He looks thinner than in his photos,' Aly said.

'He does,' Cassie said.

Harris had lost weight in the few months before his death. Not enough to raise her concern. Enough to let her think he was eating healthier. Working out more. But looking at him now, it was clear he was thinner than she'd remembered. She didn't know if he'd really been this thin the day he died, or if Lake has constructed him this way inside the sim.

'I need to nail this meeting,' came a voice from behind Cassie. 'I think the Ruiz family is on board, but their son Hector is an X factor. He hates me. But we need this commission.'

'Oh my God,' Aly said. Cassie turned around, a sinking feeling in her stomach telling her she already knew who it would be.

There she was. Cassandra Ann West. Her own Augmented Persona. Harris was talking to the Past Crimes version of Cassie herself. Only this wasn't Cassie. This was Cassie+.

The AP of Cassandra Ann West was several inches taller than Cassie was in real life, elongated yet fuller, bustier. Her rich chestnut hair cascaded down her back, her statuesque figure stretching the limits of her tight outfit. Everything about this Cassie was augmented in every way. Crispin Lake had given Cassie the perfect digital makeover.

'You look like Jessica Rabbit,' Aly said. 'That's from *Who Framed*—'

'I know what it's from,' Cassie said. 'This is what he did because he couldn't use my actual likeness in the sim.'

'It kind of makes me want to hate you. But I bet guys will love it. I guess that's probably why he made you look like . . . that,' Aly said, making an hourglass shape with her hands.

'I'm going to be home early for dinner tonight,' AP Cassie said. 'I swear.'

Harris stood at the counter. He didn't look at her. 'No rush,' he said.

He knew she never came home early. And on this day, he was counting on it.

Cassie watched their conversation, mouthing the words as each AP spoke them. She'd replayed their final conversations so many times, wondering if there were signs she'd missed.

The other Cassie went to the stairs, but Harris came over and put his arms around her waist and kissed the other Cassie on the lips, slow and deep. She remembered leaning into it, not wanting it to stop, and if she'd known it was the last time they would ever kiss, she wouldn't have let it.

'I have to get into Earth+,' Harris said. 'You're going to crush it today. I love you. Forever. Goodbye, Cass.'

'Love you too,' the other Cassie said, in a way that did not carry the finality that Harris's words had. Then she went upstairs. Cassie knew exactly how the rest of her day would go. She would review the Ruiz contract while she got dressed. Then she would head out to the V.I.C.E. office. Later that day, she would sign the Ruiz family and feel hope for her future.

They watched AP Cassie flit about the house with a grace Cassie had never possessed in real life. She seemed less like a woman than a performer, created for entertainment purposes within the sim. Finally, she left, stopping to give Harris a peck on the cheek, wiping away ruby-red lipstick from his jawline with a napkin. The virtual Harris was still seated at the kitchen table, picking at the last of his breakfast.

When he was done, he went into his office, sat in his desk chair and took a deep breath. Ran his hand through his hair. On his desk was a computer hooked up to two razor-thin monitors bookended by two framed photos: a selfie from their third date at Lloyd's ice cream shop, a dollop of peanut butter cup ice cream dripping from her nose, a pinch of sprinkles and chocolate sauce embedded in

Harris's beard. Their first dance as a married couple, in front
of Harris's mother, their only living relative. They'd been married
by a priest who appeared via hologram, the service having been
conducted in the living room of their 600-square-foot apartment.

'Today,' Harris said, 'the fires will rise.'

He did not appear disturbed or hesitant in the slightest. Then he
put his visor on and disappeared into Earth+.

'I cannot in a million years picture Harris ever saying that,' Cassie
said.

'You don't need to,' Aly said. 'Everybody else can.'

Cassie approached the seated Harris. His hands were so lifelike.
She could see the scar on the webbing between Harris's thumb and
pointer fingers. He'd gotten it as a kid after a fishing accident where
he'd cast his hook haphazardly and accidentally impaled himself.
The flesh was slightly raised, just as it had been in real life.
Everything was just how it had been in real life.

With one exception.

There was no Skin Reader on Harris's desk. Just like in the teaser
video. In real life, Harris had to press his index finger into a slot
at the beginning and end of each day, then answer a dozen or so
questions about his work and employment. If his biometrics were
outside normal readings, he could be fired and possibly prosecuted.
Given the level of detail in the sim, Cassie was certain Lake hadn't
overlooked the Skin Reader. It had been taken from the crime scene.

And if that was wrong, what else was?

Cassie went upstairs to their bedroom. Memories came back to
her. The day they'd moved in. The first time they'd made love. The
day her Beta rose above 50. Ghosts of hope and promise, lingering,
taunting her. The room was just as she remembered. Dark gray
duvet. Mismatched nightstands. Off-white rug that shed constantly.
Most of their furniture and furnishings were cheap. Every spare
dime went towards paying back their Replenish loan, and the material shortage meant decent furniture cost tens of thousands of dollars
and would take months, if not years, to arrive. Cassie never minded
the shabby decor. This was home.

'Are you OK?' Aly said. Cassie nodded.

'It's just a lot to process. I've thought about this house so many
times. I never thought I'd be back.'

She remembered the day she and Harris had gone on an Earth+
tour of 44 Otter Creek Drive. It was common for brokers to 'spruce

up' their virtual listings, then force the buyers to close before having seen it – or smelled it – in real life. They'd made an offer without ever seeing it in person, eventually paying thirty percent above the asking price after a ferocious bidding war. They knew they couldn't afford it. They had hope and faith, and though neither could pay the mortgage, it gave them a reason to believe.

They'd gone into the bedroom and held hands. Harris had leaned down and kissed her. 'This is our forever home,' he'd said.

And it was supposed to be. Now, in Earth–, that home was nothing but an empty lot. After the charred remains of 44 Otter Creek Drive had been cleared, the space had remained untouched. Nobody wanted to live where the Blight originated. Cassie and Harris's forever home now existed only on Crispin Lake's servers.

Cassie walked around the room. When she got to her nightstand, she stopped. She reached down and touched the drawer handle. She felt her hand shaking. Even in Earth+, she was afraid. Then, slowly, she slid the door open. There it was. Just as she'd left it. She reached in and took it out. Aly came up beside her and looked at what Cassie held in her hand.

'Is that a watch?'

'It's called an OvuBand,' Cassie said. 'I wore it when Harris and I were trying to get pregnant. It tracks your hCG, FSH, estrogen, ovulation days, everything related to your fertility. I froze its face when I found out I was pregnant.'

She showed it to Aly. There was a number in the upper right corner – 57. Below it was the digitized face of a smiling baby.

Cassie put the watch back in the drawer.

'I'm sorry,' Aly said. Cassie nodded. Then she saw something else. Something strange. Something she *didn't* recognize. A folded piece of paper below the watch, amidst other random junk. She picked it up.

'What is it?' Aly said.

She unfolded the paper to find a map of Murderland.

'This isn't mine,' Cassie said.

'But it's in your drawer,' Aly said.

'Yeah. But I didn't put it there.'

'Maybe it's just promotional material?' Aly said. 'Like an easter egg for visitors in the sim to find. Lake coding it in so if people find it inside the sim, they'll want to come to the park too?'

'I don't know. That doesn't seem like something Lake would do.'

'Look here,' Aly said, pointing at the map. 'All of the entrances and exits are marked with red Xs. Maybe your husband did it?'

'Harris never went near my nightstand,' Cassie said. 'He once told me there was so much junk in there I could be hiding a severed head and nobody would ever know.' Aly grimaced. 'It was funny at the time.'

The presence of the map bothered her. Sure, Lake could have left it there as promotional material. He was a hell of a marketer. But why were the entrances and exits marked?

They went back to Harris's office. His face was hidden behind a visor.

Aly went to the closet and slid the door open. Sitting on the floor was a suitcase. A suitcase Cassie didn't recognize. A brand-new suitcase.

What the hell . . .

Cassie unzipped it. A dozen canisters of acetone fell out. In the pile lay a gun.

'Holy crap,' Aly said. 'This is exactly like what my dad had. Kerosene and a gun. He was going to set our house on fire before killing himself.'

She looked at Cassie with concern, then added, 'Tell me this is a mistake. That you know for a fact your husband didn't own any of this.'

Cassie wanted to say that. To tell Aly that Harris had never bought accelerant. Never owned a gun. But the truth was she rarely set foot in his office, and she had certainly never opened the closet door. She never needed to. She'd never been suspicious or jealous, and Harris kept everything clean. He could have kept it all in his closet for weeks. *Months.* And Cassie never would have known.

'I can't say that,' Cassie said.

'If all this might be his,' Aly said, 'how can you be so sure he wasn't the Vertex Ignis?'

After a moment, Cassie said, 'I can't be.'

Then she noticed a paper-thin tablet on the table. She tapped the screen. A notepad app came up. It read: **Edward D'Agosta. Penny is a loose end. Make sure he handles her before today's sermon.**

'Who's Edward D'Agosta?' Aly said. 'And what does that mean – "make sure he handles Penny"?'

'D'Agosta was another Beacon. If I remember correctly, Penny was his wife. They both died in the Blight.'

'So why did your husband write his name down? And what does he mean by "loose end"?'

'I don't know,' Cassie said. 'But we have to find out.'

Cassie brought up her EPD. The menu read: **BLIGHT SIMULATION: CURRENT BEACON – HARRIS WEST.**

Below that was another button. **VISIT NEW BEACON.**

Cassie tapped it. A menu appeared on her EPD, listing hundreds of names. She recognized most of them. They were all people who had died in the Blight. Lake had outdone himself. In addition to the West home, he had recreated the homes of hundreds of other Beacons. Visiting all of them would take days. Weeks. *Months.* And people would do it. They would want to witness every single death. Meet every single Beacon. People would spend *thousands* of hours inside this sim, soaking up every last detail. They would never leave. They would keep renewing their subscriptions. This simulation was a living, breathing attraction.

And it was going to make Crispin Lake *billions*.

'Here he is,' Cassie said. 'Edward D'Agosta. Send your Wrap there too.'

'On it.'

Cassie tapped the name and chose 'Spectator'. Immediately, the foyer of 44 Otter Creek Drive faded out, and Cassie found herself in what appeared to be the master bedroom of a home she did not recognize. Aly's Wrap appeared a moment later.

The bedroom was large, with peeling, wood-colored linoleum floors. An old ceiling fan whirred noisily over a queen-size bed with a threadbare comforter. The room smelled musty. The furniture had likely all been purchased used, the wood secondhand.

Two desks sat at opposite ends of the bedroom. At one desk sat a man in his mid- to late forties. He had dark brown hair peppered with gray and wore an Earth+ visor. He was sitting so still that Cassie only knew he was alive by the sounds of his breathing. Edward D'Agosta.

At the other desk sat a woman. Same age as Edward. She was working on a paper-thin tablet, its projectile sensors reading and responding to the movements of her fingers without her ever touching the glass. She appeared to be designing clothing patterns. A red bubble appeared over the woman's head, its lettering in the recognizable Past Crimes font. Inside the bubble were two words: **Learn More.** Cassie selected the bubble.

'This is Penny Adelaide D'Agosta.'

'That's Crispin Lake's voice, right?' Aly said.

'He narrates all of his sims,' Cassie said. 'It must have taken him years to record everything for the Blight.'

Lake's narration continued. 'Born Penny Adelaide Morris in 1992 in Athens, Georgia, Penny D'Agosta ran a clothing shop in Earth+ where she sold bespoke outfits for Wraps that she designed herself at the very desk you're looking at right now. Penny married Edward D'Agosta on March twenty-sixth, 2031, in St. Louis, Missouri. They had no children. They lived in their two-bedroom, two-bathroom house in St. Louis until both were killed in the Blight, following Edward's radicalization at the hands of Harris West.'

Another bubble appeared. It read: **Testimonials.** Cassie selected it. Three options appeared: **Mother. Father. Brother.** Cassie selected **Mother**.

The D'Agosta house faded away and Cassie found herself sitting in front of an elderly woman on a dark-gray couch. A ribbon appeared below her that read: **Angela Morris – Mother of Penny D'Agosta.** The woman's withered, veiny hands trembled as she spoke. Her eyes were red and full of sorrow and regret.

'I never liked Eddie,' Angela said. 'He was always late. Late to everything. Their first year together, all of their dates were in the virtual whatsit. What kind of man does that? But Penny was in love, and as her mother, I had to bite my tongue. If Penny was happy, I was happy.' Angela looked into the camera, a tear streaking down her face. 'But I don't think she was truly happy. I think she wanted to love Edward more than she actually loved him. But I never could have imagined . . . maybe I shouldn't have bitten my tongue.'

When Angela Morris was finished talking about her daughter, a bubble appeared over her head that read: **Learn More About Edward D'Agosta.** She selected the bubble and found herself sitting in a theater below an enormous wraparound screen that reminded her of the planetariums she visited as a child. The screen featured photos and videos from the forty-plus years of D'Agosta's life, swarming and swooping around like he was the center of the cosmos.

'Edward Linus D'Agosta was born in 1989 in New Orleans, Louisiana. He moved to Los Angeles in 2015 to work as a film scout, until his job became obsolete when film production began migrating to virtual stages. He held menial jobs within Earth+, but after the death of his father, Willis D'Agosta, Edward inherited enough to buy his own home and launch a subscription-based Lockbox inside Earth+ called "Menbership".'

There was one 'Friend' testimonial. Cassie selected it and found herself sitting in a coffee shop across from a man named Simon Echeverria. Simon Echeverria was thick with a bald head and small, twitchy eyes.

'We met inside Menbership,' Simon said. 'It was guys only, so Eddie felt like he could open up a little more without Penny around. All I can say is there's no way he would have killed Penny if she didn't always push his buttons.'

Simon paused to take a sip of milk-colored coffee.

'I mean, I liked the chick, but she just nagged the hell out of him every day. Some people didn't like the idea behind Menbership, a guys-only club and all that, but he needed to get away. We all did. Simon . . . I loved the guy, but he felt beaten down. And I guess Harris West gave him something to believe in. A cause that was bigger than himself. I wasn't all that surprised Eddie fell in with the Beacons. He got a little angry sometimes. Felt like the world left him behind. Then someone comes along and tells him that he's important. I'm not saying I condone what Eddie did . . . but I understand.'

Cassie closed Simon's testimonial and returned to the D'Agosta master bedroom. When she did, Penny swiveled around in her chair to face Edward. 'I think we should take a trip. A *real* trip. I think we need it. I feel like there's been a distance between us.'

Edward did not respond. Penny walked over and tapped Edward on the shoulder.

'Earth to Eddie?'

Nothing.

She tapped him harder. Again, nothing.

She shoved him with her palm. Not hard, but enough to show her irritation. Still nothing.

'You're kind of proving my point,' Penny said. 'Bad enough we haven't had sex in a year. I think you need to talk to someone. I sent you the Terminal location for a therapist algorithm my friend Reena's husband used. She said it really helped him. I insist you set up a session, Ed. Because if this is the way it's going to be from now on, this isn't going to work.'

Edward did not respond.

'Don't tell me you're going back to that church you keep talking about,' Penny said. 'I'm starting to think all these people are toxic. I mean, I grew up in a pretty religious family, but I've never heard of anyone spending this much time at church. What do you even know about these people . . . what do you call them again?'

'Beacons,' Edward said, his back still turned to his wife.

'I'm going to ask the police if they've ever heard of these *Beacons*,' she said. 'Sounds more like a cult than a religion to me.'

Penny waited another moment, then sighed with contempt and sat back down.

Aly tapped Cassie on the arm and said, 'How does the sim know what they said to each other if they both . . . you know . . .'

'They owned a Horizon home assistant,' Cassie said, pointing to a blue, quarter-sized speaker on the ceiling. 'After the Forced Birth Act, home assistants were mandated to record all conversations within speaker range. Certain words, when spoken, automatically notified law enforcement. Everything the D'Agosta family said was recorded. That's how they were able to replicate my conversations with Harris, too.'

'How the hell would Crispin Lake get access to those recordings?'

'If you're a convicted felon,' Cassie said, 'all of your recordings, no matter who's in them, become a matter of public record.'

'Everything we say or do makes everyone else money,' Aly said. 'You got that right.'

One minute later, Edward got up from his chair. He went downstairs. Cassie knew what was about to happen.

'You might want to leave,' Cassie said to Aly.

'Not a chance.'

The girl followed Edward, Cassie trailing behind her. 'Aly . . .'

'I need to see it,' Aly said. 'I need to see what they did to people other than my father.'

Edward went into the kitchen and picked up a thick wooden cutting board. He ran his hand over the grain, then weighed it in his hands. Then he went back upstairs, Aly and Cassie following.

He approached Penny at her desk. Her back was still to him. She was scrolling through designs, mixing and matching different pieces to create unique looks, then dragging the ensembles over a digital replica of various Wraps, stretching and tightening them over all different body shapes. Edward stood behind her, clutching the cutting board. Finally, Penny turned around.

'What the hell are you doing?' Penny said.

'The fires will burn forever,' Edward said, 'but thankfully you won't have to feel them.'

Then Edward raised the cutting board and brought it down on Penny's head.

The impact made a sickening crunch. Penny toppled off her chair. She must have been either dead or unconscious before she hit the ground, because she made no effort to break her fall. Blood began to soak the carpeting. Aly shrieked and covered her mouth. Edward brought the cutting board down again. And again. And again. The thuds grew wetter. Cassie turned away. She heard a clattering sound and the cutting board came to rest by her feet, cracked in half and coated in blood.

Then Edward D'Agosta went to his closet and opened it. He carried out six containers of kerosene and arranged them around Penny's prone body. Then Edward sat back down in his chair and put his visor back on, leaving gruesome red streaks on the plastic.

'We didn't commit suicide,' he said softly, the body of his wife limp on the floor next to him. 'We committed an act of revolutionary suicide protesting the conditions of an inhumane world.'

Then Edward began to sing.

'Never mind what they say,' he said. 'Never mind what they do.'

'What's he singing?' Aly asked.

'The song is "I'm Sorry" by the Delfonics,' Cassie said. 'From their album *La La Means I Love You*, released in 1968.'

'Why is Edward D'Agosta singing it?'

'On the night of November eighteenth, 1978,' Cassie said, 'James Jones urged his followers to commit what he called "revolutionary suicide". D'Agosta is repeating Jones's exact words from the death tape that was recovered from Jonestown after nine hundred and nine people died. At the end of the tape, after Jones's followers drank the poison and the children have stopped crying and everything has gone silent, you can hear the Delfonics singing "I'm Sorry". On the recording, the music was altered. Slowed down. It sounds almost . . . demonic.'

Aly looked up at Cassie. 'How do you know all this?'

'For a long time, it was my job.'

Then D'Agosta spoke again. 'At my church, I will find salvation.'

'The church,' Aly said. 'That's what Penny was talking about. It's the Church of the Beacons, right?'

'Pretty sure,' Cassie said. 'Maybe we can find something there. Something that ties all this together.'

'We're going to go there?' Aly asked, fear in her eyes. 'That's where all the Beacons met.'

'It is.' She studied Aly. 'You should go back to Earth–.'

Aly took a breath, steeled herself. 'No chance in hell I'm staying behind. I owe it to my parents to find the truth.'

'All right, then.'

Cassie pulled up her EPD menu and scrolled until she found a tab that read: **THE CHURCH OF THE BEACONS.**

The Church of the Beacons. The Earth+ Lockbox where Harris had allegedly radicalized hundreds of Beacons, poisoning their minds into committing one of the greatest atrocities in modern history.

In her EPD, Cassie tapped **Church of the Beacons** and then selected **Participant**. The D'Agostas' bedroom faded away and Cassie found herself sitting in a wooden pew inside a large, square room. The walls were gray marble and the floors were covered with red carpeting. At the front was a wooden pulpit atop a raised dais. A massive chandelier hung from a vaulted ceiling at least twenty feet high, the red carpeting reflected in hundreds of crystals. Hundreds of Wraps were packed into at least fifty pews, shoulder to shoulder. Men and women of all ages, all shapes, sizes, backgrounds, races, and ethnicities. They were all silent. All were facing the front of the church, as though waiting for something. Or someone.

Aly appeared in the pew next to Cassie. She was breathing fast, terrified.

Then, without warning, the space was plunged into darkness. The church was silent. Cassie's heart began to speed up. A song began to play: 'I'm Sorry' by the Delfonics. There were no speakers Cassie could see.

'What's going on?' Aly asked, eyes shifting around nervously.

'I have no idea,' Cassie said. 'Nobody has ever seen the inside of the Church of the Beacons. Not even Crispin Lake. Everything you see here had to have been assembled from testimonies and assumptions. I have no idea how much of this is based on reality. Or virtual reality based on myth.'

After thirty seconds of darkness and silence, twin flames appeared on either side of the pulpit, each at least six feet high. They seemed to be coming from the ground itself, burning on their own. Cassie knew this was virtual, but she could *feel* the heat. She could *smell* the smoke.

Then she heard a female voice next to her whisper, 'He's coming.'

She turned to see a Wrap staring at her, a dreamy smile. She was strikingly beautiful, an Asian woman in her early thirties, with straight black hair and ruby-red lipstick. The flames danced in her irises.

'Who's coming?' Aly asked.

'The Vertex Ignis,' the woman said. 'We've all been waiting for this day for so long.'

Cassie felt someone take hold of her left hand. She turned to see an older man, rail-thin, with kind eyes and sunken cheeks sitting next to her. He patted the back of her palm like he was comforting a child.

'I stayed awake all night wondering if I would have the courage to go through with it,' he said. 'But now that I'm here, I know that my purpose is to be a Beacon. I will leave both this world and the real world spreading the Vertex Ignis's flame. I've lived a good life. It is a blessing that I get to end it today with all of you.'

The music stopped. Then a voice rang out from the dais that chilled Cassie to her core.

'Welcome, Beacons,' a man said. 'Today is the day we light up the world.'

Cassie knew that voice.

Harris West appeared between the twin flames. He stepped to the pulpit. He wore a long red robe with a bright yellow belt that glowed like a sun. The light from the flames cast his shadow against the back wall, making him look like something otherworldly. He raised his hands as if embracing the hundreds in attendance. And then he smiled.

The devil, Cassie said. *He looks like the devil.*

Several pews away, she saw Edward D'Agosta's Wrap. In real life, he would have been sitting at his desk, plugged into Earth+, the battered body of his wife at his feet.

'I know you have waited for this day for a long time,' Harris said. 'I know many of you are scared. Scared about what you have to do. Scared about what comes next once we leave this Earth – the Earth that God created, the Earth that man destroyed. The only thing I can promise you is that when today is over, you will be remembered. By me. By those left behind. You are my family. Your memory will last far beyond this lifetime. The fires we light today will illuminate the world, and the smoke will rise to the heavens. And it is in heaven that we will all find each other, once again. We are Beacons. We are the ones who light the way. Say it with me. We are the ones who light the way.'

The entire gathering spoke in unison: '*We are the ones who light the way.*'

Harris continued: 'Our fires will illuminate the path to everlasting life.'

'*Our fires will illuminate the path to everlasting life.*'

'In 168 BC, the armies of Antiochus IV invaded Jerusalem,' Harris continued. 'After years of brutal warfare, the small, underequipped Jewish armies managed to drive out the Greek invaders and reclaim their temple. It was there that they found one small jug of oil remaining. They expected the oil to burn for just one night. Yet the oil miraculously burned for eight days and nights. My friends, each of you is just one person. But your fires will burn far longer than eight days. They will burn forever. Say it with me. My fire will burn forever.'

'*My fire will burn forever.*'

'I am a Beacon in the night.'

'*I am a Beacon in the night.*'

'Yes. Yes, you are. You are my friends. You are Beacons.'

The audience was enraptured by the man – Cassie's *husband* – preaching from between the columns of fire. Cassie looked at the woman to her right. She selected the **Learn More** button hovering above her head. Crispin Lake's voice said, 'This is Rinako Ngata. Born April second, 2004, in Osaka, Japan. Died in the Blight, after murdering her boyfriend, Haruto Kimura, at Rinako's home in Osaka.'

Cassie did the same to the man on her left.

'Jakub Zielinski, born in 1968 in Wroclaw, Poland. Died in the Blight, along with his daughter, Maja.'

'They all understand Harris,' Aly said. 'The Wraps here must speak fifty different languages. But they all understand him.'

'Every Past Crimes sim has iBabel technology,' Cassie said. 'Instantaneously translates your Wrap's primary language and alters the speaker's facial features to match the pronunciations. So a Wrap could be speaking in Polish or Japanese or Hebrew, but if your

Wrap is set to English, iBabel makes it seem like English is their native language.'

'My first few years at school,' Aly said, 'all the teachers and parents ever talked about was how Earth+ would bring the world together. How it allowed people to come together without supervision or intrusion. I wonder if any of them thought it could lead to something like this.'

'If there's enough money in any technology,' Cassie said, 'people will always overlook the dark side. Or they'll be forced to.'

'Did anyone here survive?' Aly said. 'If they did, maybe they'll know what's going on right now. Maybe they'll know if there was another Blight planned.'

Cassie tapped on the **Learn More** button on other Beacons in the church.

Walter Needham, 74, died in Chicago, IL.
Svetozar Meszaros, 60, died in Visegrad, Hungary.
Tyrese Washington, 44, died in Huntsville, AL.
Kathryn Garrick, 28, died in London, England.
Emily Murtagh, 51, died in Boise, ID.
Adebola Okoro, 36, died in Lagos, Nigeria.

She went on and on. Beacons after Beacons. There were no survivors.

'I need to see them,' Cassie said. 'Before they came here. I'll meet you back here.'

Cassie pulled up her EPB and selected Svetozar Meszaros. She found herself in a small house with old furnishings. Seated on a couch were an older man, Svetozar, and a woman around his age. Cassie selected **Learn More**.

'Svetozar Meszaros and his wife Lilla died together in the Blight. They were found in the burned wreckage of their cottage in Visegrad, their bodies still holding hands. Based on their autopsies, authorities determined that Svetozar doused their home in gasoline before he and Lilla each took a handgun and shot each other at the same time, the fire raging around them.'

Cassie watched as Svetozar and Lilla caressed each other's hands. They leaned in for a small kiss. Then they each brought a gun up to the other's temple. Cassie left their house before she could see what happened next.

She then visited the homes of Adebola Okoro. Emily Murtagh. Tyrese Washington. And more. At each stop, she felt an ache in her heart. In some homes, the Beacons killed only themselves. In others, they killed loved ones or friends before taking their own lives. In one home, she saw an entire family, children included, singing hymns as the fire engulfed them.

Finally, she went back to the church. Aly was seated there already, her eyes wide, face pale, as though she'd seen things she would never forget.

'Are you OK?' Cassie said.

'I . . . I don't think so.'

'How many did you visit?'

Aly looked at her. 'Too many.'

'Me too.'

Cassie did not feel like she was surrounded by Wraps. This simulation did not feel like a virtual representation of a crime. There was no digital buffer between what Cassie saw and what was fed into her brain. Everything felt real. She could smell skin and breath. She could feel the wood of the pew creaking underneath the seated Wraps, the intense heat coming off the flames surrounding the Vertex Ignis. This church did not feel like a simulation. It felt like a séance. Cassie was not surrounded by virtual Wraps. She was surrounded by the echoes of ghosts.

Meanwhile, Harris continued his sermon.

'The world has forgotten we existed,' he said. 'We have become nothing more than ones and zeroes, nothing more than Wraps and bank accounts to fatten the wallets of the people who banished us from the real world. But we Beacons resist. We are blood and bone and brain. Today is the day we remind the world of that. Today is the day we deny what they have tried to make us. Today is the day we reclaim our freedom, our independence, our free will.'

There was a great, rousing response from the crowd. Many stood up and clapped. Others nodded in agreement. Some were crying.

'After today, they will never forget us,' Harris said, his voice loving yet firm. 'After today, we will be bonded together, forever. The world has been consumed by darkness. But you – all of you – you will be the beacons in the night. Say it with me brothers and sisters. What will you be?'

The Wraps chanted in unison, '*Beacons in the night.*'

They chanted again: '*Beacons in the night.*'

And again: '*Beacons in the night.*'

All these people preparing to follow this man – who could *not* be her husband – into the depths of hell.

'Today we ignite the flame,' Harris said. 'And that flame will continue to burn. Three six five two will be our continuance.'

'*They will be our continuance.*'

'Three six five two,' Aly said, tugging on Cassie's arm. 'That's exactly what my dad said the day he died. That's ten years to the date of the original Blight. This was planned. This was planned all along. It's going to happen.'

'That means this dialogue was already programmed into the simulation,' Cassie said. 'Lake has to know about it. We have to tell the police. We have to tell—'

Before she could finish her sentence, Cassie felt a searing pain rip through the right side of her head, as if someone had taken a knife to her temple. Suddenly, the Church of the Beacons disappeared, and all Cassie saw was a white, searing light, and then she felt nothing at all.

SIXTEEN

10:29 a.m.
Thirteen hours and thirty-one minutes to launch

'She's having a Neural Flare!'

Cassie recognized the voice. Stephen Woolman. She opened her eyes. Or tried to. Her eyelids fluttered, a strobe light somewhere inside her brain. She was out of Earth+ and back in the Maternity Ward. But she hadn't exited the sim on her own. She'd been pulled out.

Then Cassie felt her stomach roil and she doubled over. Strings of saliva dripped from her mouth. Her head felt as though she'd just spent a month in a salad spinner. Wyatt appeared at her side with a thermos. Cassie took it, her hands shaking. She drank greedily from the bottle. Wyatt handed her a towel and she wiped her lips. The drink tasted salty and slimy, like ocean water. Slowly, the room stopped spinning and Cassie managed to open her eyes.

'What . . . what happened?' Cassie said.

'You had a Neural Flare,' Woolman said. He was standing over her. 'We had to pull you out of the sim. Your biometrics were going haywire. Sorry if it was . . . abrupt.'

Aly knelt next to her, eyes wide with concern and fear. 'Ms. West, are you OK?'

'I don't know. I think so.'

Woolman took a silver packet from his pocket and handed it to her.

'Eat this,' he said. Cassie tore open the foil and squeezed out some sort of brownish paste. It looked as appetizing as the gunk she cleaned out of the bottom of her dishwasher.

'What is this?' she said.

'Our own proprietary nutrition paste,' Lake said. 'It helps combat the effects of Neural Flares. It's calibrated with the right amount of carbs, fats and protein, with extra sodium and potassium.'

'That looks like the stuff my dad used to clean off our tires after a rainstorm,' Aly said.

'The taste does leave something to be desired,' Lake replied. 'But right now, getting Cassie's biometrics in line is more important than satisfying her sweet tooth.'

Cassie squeezed the pungent gunk into her mouth, grimaced and forced it down. It tasted like the underside of a shoe. Then she washed it down and held the bottle back to Woolman.

'More.'

Woolman shook his head. 'Too much hydration can dilute the effects of the nutrients. Thankfully, Ms. Miller's biometrics are fine. We had to pull Ms. West out before Submergence kicked in.'

'Submergence?' Aly said.

'The brain is the central hub for all of your senses,' Woolman replied. 'It acts as something of a buffer between Earth+ and Earth−. When you're inside, even if everything *seems* real, your brain knows it isn't. Neural Flares eat away at that buffer. If Flares become strong enough, it can destroy the buffer, leaving half of you tethered to reality, and half of you tethered to the digital world. That's Submergence.'

'We have preventative measures to keep all our employees safe,' Lake said. 'When our sims are in Beta, every visor is coded to our employees' biometrics. If an employee is showing signs of Hyponatremia, they have to take a mandatory twenty-four-hour break. If, while inside the sim, their blood sugar levels or mucus membranes become depleted, we have neural haptics that can, essentially, snap them out of it. Like we did to you.'

'What about her?' Aly said, pointing to Cassie. 'How close is she to Submergence?'

'If she was an employee,' Woolman said, 'we would restrict her from any Earth+ activities until her levels evened out.'

'Cassie,' Aly said, 'maybe you should—'

'Should nothing,' Cassie said. 'Inside the Church of the Beacons. My husband said three six five two. Three thousand six hundred fifty-two. Aly's father said the same thing the day he died. That's the exact number of days between the Blight and the tenth anniversary. And the launch of your sim. Why was it in there?'

Woolman looked concerned. 'These are the most advanced Augmented Personas we've ever developed. Every AP has a nearly infinite amount of reactions and dialogue. I've never heard our AP Harris say that. And if I did, I can't say I would have thought anything of it. He was insane. Marshall Applewhite told the followers of Heaven's Fate that they could transform themselves into extraterrestrial beings and ascend to heaven.'

'Alan Miller used the same phrase that your AP Harris did. He called himself a Beacon. We need to alert the authorities.'

'A sequence of numbers seems like a very thin branch to hang your entire theory on,' Lake said. 'And I'm going to need more before I jeopardize years of work and hundreds of millions of dollars.'

'What are you saying? You won't report this?'

'Ms. West,' Lake said, 'with all due respect, if I report this to the authorities, they will tear my sim code apart line by line. Our launch will be scuttled. Our celebration will be canceled. It could put thousands of people out of work. If we have absolute, concrete proof there will be another Blight and that we can save lives, I will move heaven and earth to do that. But I will not jeopardize this company – and this company's employees – for such a lightweight hypothesis.'

'That hypothesis could save lives,' Cassie said. 'Don't you want to know what those numbers mean? Your judgment is clouded.'

'*My* judgment is clouded?' Lake said with a laugh. 'Ms. West, I refuse to make rash decisions based on conjecture from people who may have ulterior motives.'

'Ulterior motives? What the hell are you talking about?'

'If we bring the authorities in, they may reopen your husband's case. And that's what all this is really about, isn't it?'

'I want to save people. If doing that means people realize Harris wasn't the Vertex Ignis, so be it. I think you're afraid.'

Lake barked out a laugh. 'Afraid? Of what?'

'Afraid that if I'm right, it doesn't just cost you millions. It costs you your company.'

'I'm not sure how you're arriving at that conclusion. So do tell.'

'If my "theory" holds up, and the same Vertex Ignis planned both the first and the second Blight, it means your entire simulation is a lie. I've been inside. I've seen your recreation of the Church of the Beacons. Your entire sim is predicated on Harris being the Vertex Ignis. But if he isn't, people will realize this sim is based on a falsehood. And if people question the authenticity of this sim, what's to stop them from questioning every other sim?'

'People will know we created a simulation based on the absolute best information available to us at the time,' Lake said, but the uncertainly in his voice told Cassie this was a can of worms he did not want opened.

'Everything you've done for the past twenty years could evaporate. You're telling me I have ulterior motives. Well, I'm telling you you're more interested in saving your own ass.'

'You do realize that even if there is another Blight, it does not absolve your husband. Marshall Applewhite had Bonnie Nettles. Keith Raniere had Nancy Salzman. It's possible your husband had a second in command.'

'What if I found them?' Cassie said.

'That would mean your husband was guilty. Is that something you're willing to accept?'

Cassie paused, then said, 'I might have to.'

Lake nodded. 'If you find proof, and it is absolutely conclusive and convincing, then I will call the head of the EPP myself.'

'Then I'm going back in,' Cassie said. 'If there's an accomplice, I'm going to find them.'

'Whoa, hold on a second,' Woolman said. 'You just had a Neural Flare, Ms. West. You need to rest. Your brain is an engine. If it overheats, you don't just fire it back up.'

'Since it's my engine, I'll decide what I do with it,' Cassie said.

Woolman looked at Lake, as though waiting for his agreement.

Lake considered it for a moment, then said, 'If she wants to go in, she can go in.'

'Sir, I—'

'She signed a contract stating that she had Hyponatremia when she got here. Because of that, Past Crimes is not responsible for any adverse effects from her time in the sim. If Ms. West wants to go in, she is responsible for what happens. And on the chance she is right, time is ticking away. We might need her to go in.'

'Thank you,' Cassie said. 'And if I find what we need, you'll contact the authorities.'

'You have my word,' Lake said.

'Mine too,' Woolman added.

'I'm going back in with her,' Aly said.

'Stop,' Cassie said. 'There are things in there you can't unsee. You're just—'

'You're not my—' Aly said.

'I know. I know.'

'I'm going back in.'

'OK.'

Woolman asked, 'How are you feeling, Ms. West?'

'A little better,' Cassie said. Her stomach had settled a bit, and her heart rate had slowed down. The sludge she'd eaten had tasted like pet food, but the headache had subsided.

'That was a minor Flare, but it was still a Flare,' Woolman said. 'I don't love the idea of sending you right back in. And if we see another biometric spike, I'm pulling you back out.'

'Neural Flares have been known to cause violent outbursts,' Lake said.

'Remember the guy at the airport?' Aly said.

'I know all of this,' Cassie said. 'I'll be careful. Crispin, let me ask you something. There were no survivors of the Blight, at least not among the Beacons. So that means there's nobody alive who actually heard what my husband allegedly said inside the church.'

Lake waited a moment. 'I'm sorry. Was that a question?'

'How do you know what Harris said inside the church if there were no witnesses?'

'We interviewed thousands of family members and friends of those who died in the Blight. We combed through more pages of police reports, interviews, Earth+ activity logs and biometric data than any of our other sims, combined. What is inside that church is the absolute closest to the truth there ever has been, and there ever will be.'

'But how true is it?' Cassie said. 'Can you honestly say that what's happening inside your sim is what happened in real life? I mean, the woman you have playing me doesn't look anything like me.'

'That's your choice,' Lake said. 'Listen. Do we know the exact thickness of the blade Jack the Ripper used? Or the brand of pen the Zodiac Killer used to write his ciphers? As with any crime, we use whatever knowledge we have that is fact, and combine it with the absolute best research team and programmers in the world. Every sim is a combination of fact and impeccable research.'

'But you have no firsthand knowledge. You're guessing on at least some of it.'

'It's not a guess if you have ninety-nine percent of the information.'

'I'll argue semantics with you once this is over,' Cassie said. 'Now get me back in there. If Harris did have an accomplice, I need to know who it was and where they were. I still think there's more inside for me to find. Give me another shot of that crud.'

Woolman handed her another packet of brown goop. Cassie sucked it down, took a sip of the salty slime drink, then put her visor back on. Aly did the same. When they were both sitting, the door opened and another guard came into the room.

'I want more security here in case you have another Flare,' Lake said. 'A more severe one.'

'Whatever you need to do to feel safe,' Cassie said. 'Now I want to do what I can to keep other people safe.'

She selected **HARRIS WEST – HOME** from her EPD and their Wraps were back at Otter Creek Drive.

'Let's split up,' Aly said. 'You're too close to all of this. I might find things you'll overlook.'

'I don't love the idea of you snooping around my house.'

'It's not "your" house. This house doesn't exist.'

'Fine. But if you find anything, come get me.'

Cassie started in the den. There wasn't much. Their possessions were few, and nearly all of their files had been contained within Earth+. She went into their bedroom. They each had their own nightstand, made out of shoddy particleboard. Cassie opened up Harris's nightstand drawers. Nothing out of the ordinary. She went to the closet and rifled through his jackets and pants pockets. Nothing. She noticed that on one side of his closet were size-38 jeans. In the middle were 36s. On the right, 32s. Had he really lost that much weight? Or was this another guesstimate from Crispin Lake?

'Hey, Cassie?' It was Aly. Her voice sounded . . . disturbed. 'Can you come here a sec?'

Cassie found Aly in the bedroom. The contents of Cassie's night-stand had been emptied.

'What is it?'

Aly held out a small notepad. 'Look.'

Cassie took it from her. Written on every single page were the words 'Three Six Five Two'. Over and over and over again. Dozens and dozens of pages of the same number.

'This is insane,' Aly said, her voice accusatory.

'I didn't write that.'

'It was in your room.'

'But I didn't write that.' She didn't. At least she didn't remember writing it. But the words. She recognized her own handwriting.

'It's like you were obsessed with this number,' Aly said. 'The same number my father said before he killed my mom. The same number your husband said in that church. Why were *you* writing it?'

'I wasn't,' Cassie said. She could tell from the look on Aly's face that the girl's confidence in her had been shaken.

'I'm going to keep looking,' Aly said. 'Don't follow me.'

Aly left the room. Cassie kept flipping through the notebook. Then she tossed it to the ground. She turned towards her closet. It had been ten years since she'd opened it. She slid the door open.

'What the hell . . .'

Her closet was empty. A few metal hangers, but otherwise it had been packed up. Not a single dress or jacket or blouse. It was like someone had stolen all of her clothing – or packed it up before—

'Where are all your clothes?' Aly said. Cassie hadn't seen her return.

'I . . . I don't know.'

'Did you pack them up the day of the Blight?'

'Of course not. I went to work that day and everything was normal. My clothes were still here when I left.'

Aly's face told her she didn't fully believe it. 'Come here,' the girl said. She left the room and Cassie trailed her. This wasn't right. This wasn't the house she'd left that morning.

Aly led her into Harris's office. She pointed to a piece of paper on his desk.

'I found that in his drawer,' she said. 'Look.'

Cassie picked it up. On the paper was drawn a picture of a room. Two large scribbles were at either end.

'They look like flames,' Aly said. 'Like the flames we saw in the church.'

Between the flames were the outlines of two people standing behind some sort of desk. Both were in shadow. No facial features were visible.

'It's the pulpit,' she said. 'Harris was sketching out his vision for the Church of the Beacons. And there are two people giving sermons.'

'That doesn't make sense,' Cassie said. 'If Lake knew there were two people, he would have said something. He might have known there was another Vertex Ignis out there.'

Then another thought occurred to her.

'Lake left things out of the sim that were there in real life,' Cassie said. 'What if he added things that weren't?'

'Isn't his whole deal making his sims authentic?' Aly said.

'Yes, but . . .' She didn't know what else to say. Something here felt very wrong.

'I'm going back to the church,' Aly said. 'Harris used the same numbers my father did. The same numbers I found in your notebook. And Harris also clearly meant for there to be two people giving sermons inside the church. I want to see if that person is there.'

Then Aly's Wrap disappeared.

Cassie looked around. She felt dizzy. There were so many things wrong. So many things that she didn't remember or were out of place. She looked at the picture again. It was crude, but there were clearly two people. One was meant to be Harris. The Vertex Ignis. The other . . .

Cassie brought up her EPD. She selected **CHURCH OF THE BEACONS**. Within moments, Cassie was back in a pew inside the Church of the Beacons.

Harris was still standing between the twin flames. The hundreds of Wraps in attendance were still watching him, rapt. Aly was in a pew a few aisles over. Cassie slid past the Wraps in her pew and managed to squeeze in next to Aly.

'Somebody put all that back in my house,' Cassie whispered. 'I don't know if it happened right after Harris died, if someone put everything else and took my clothes, or if Lake added it to the sim himself.'

'And why would he do that?' Aly said. 'You're suggesting Crispin Lake deleted your clothes from the Blight sim for fun?'

'I don't know. But I intend to ask him as soon as we're done here.'

Then the flames beside Harris went out, leaving him alone on the dais.

'My friends,' Harris said, 'our physical lives end today. But our cause will live on. Our journey is not complete. We will ensure that our flames never die. We will reignite them. Three Six Five Two.'

The Wraps chanted in unison, '*Three Six Five Two*.'

Aly looked at Cassie. There was suspicion in her eyes. There was no way Lake couldn't have known about this. She had to get back to the Maternity Ward. She had to confront Lake about all of this. He knew about Three Six Five Two. He had to know about the drawing, the notebook. He had to—

Harris continued.

'I will be joining you today. Just like you, my body will turn to ash and that ash will reach the heavens. But our work will continue. I have entrusted Three Six Five Two to the hands of another. Someone who will guide the next Beacons, who will help them ignite a new flame. I am not the Vertex Ignis, because the Vertex Ignis cannot die. The name will live on. Just like all of you.'

A glowing yellow light illuminated the dais where Harris stood. The twin flames reignited. A shadow appeared behind Harris.

'The drawing,' Aly said. 'That's the same image from the drawing I found in your house.'

Someone stood behind Harris. Cassie craned her head to see.

'Meet my successor. A savior. A fellow Beacon. The Vertex Ignis.'

Harris stepped to the side. The second figure was still in shadow. After a moment, the figure stepped forward into the light. The shadow disappeared, revealing the next Vertex Ignis.

Aly gasped. Cassie's jaw dropped.

Standing between the twin flames was Cassandra Ann West.

SEVENTEEN

'Cassie?' Aly said, turning to Cassie. 'Why are you up there?'

'I . . . I have no idea. We need to get out of here. I need to talk to Crispin Lake.'

Cassie tried to call up her EPD – but nothing happened. There was no menu. No selections available. No list of Beacons to visit, Cassie's home or even the church.

What the hell . . .

'Why can't I access my EPD?' Aly said. She grabbed Cassie's shirt. 'Did you lock us in here?'

'No, I swear. I can't get out either. Lake must have disabled the EPD. We need to be let out manually.'

'He can do that?'

'Legally, no. Technically . . . he can do anything.'

'What the hell is going on?' Aly shouted. 'Did you do this?'

'No, I swear to God.'

Aly did not appear convinced.

The AP Cassie West stepped forward until she was between the twin flames, just like her husband had been moments before. She smiled at the Wraps in attendance. This was not the Cassie they'd seen earlier at Otter Creek Drive. This was Cassie from ten years ago. The *same* Cassie from ten years ago. Young. Vibrant. Cassie felt like she was looking into some sort of funhouse mirror, seeing herself as she used to be.

'I thought you never gave Lake permission to use your likeness,' Aly said.

'I didn't.'

'Then why are you up there? How is he able to use you?'

'He can't. He shouldn't be able to. I don't know why.'

'Well, what *do* you know?' Aly said. 'Because my father talked about Three Six Five Two before he died. Harris West talked about it here. And I found a notepad in *your* house with that number written a hundred times like some crazy person, and a drawing of two people standing at a podium *just like this one* and here you are. And you can't explain any of it?'

'Lake did this,' Cassie said. 'He had to.'

'Why?' Aly said. 'Why would he do all of that? What, just to frame you?'

A sick feeling rose in Cassie's stomach. *Just to frame you.*

Then Cassandra Ann West raised her hands, as though about to bestow a blessing over the congregants.

'My fellow Beacons,' she said. Cassie shivered. It was her voice. 'Today, my husband lights the flame. In ten years, we will make sure it continues to burn. And it will burn, brighter than it will today. Three Six Five Two.'

'*Three Six Five Two*,' the Beacons repeated.

'Get me out of here,' Aly said.

'I can't.'

'*Let. Me. Out.*'

'I *can't*. I'm not the one doing this!'

'You're Harris's accomplice,' Aly said. 'It was you all along. *You're* the next Vertex Ignis. It all makes sense now. You're going to ki—'

And then Aly's Wrap disappeared.

Cassie was alone in the pew. One moment Aly's Wrap had been there; the next it was gone.

'Aly?' she said.

There was no response. Cassie's AP continued to preach at the pulpit.

Cassie knew one thing for sure: Aly hadn't left the sim. She'd been removed from it.

Cassie stood up. She inched her way out of the pew and into the aisle. The other Wraps paid her no attention, riveted to the speech of her virtual doppelgänger. She wandered up and down the aisles looking for Aly, but her Wrap was gone. She ran to the back wall, looking for an exit she knew wasn't there, and found nothing but solid virtual marble. There were no exits. No way out. She was stranded.

Cassie ran up the dais. Up close, she was shocked by how much the AP Cassie looked exactly like her. They were the same height. Same hairstyle. Same eye color. Same freckles and birthmarks. They even breathed in the same cadence. She had to get out of here. She had to alert the authorities. She had to get Aly the hell away from Past Crimes and Crispin Lake.

Cassie went wall to wall to wall, pounding on the virtual marble. None of the Wraps paid her any attention. Cassie stood at the pulpit, preaching to the Beacons, a smile on her face that made Cassie sick.

'Hello?' she shouted. 'Get me out of here! Lake? Woolman? Hello?'

She stumbled around the church for what felt like an eternity. It could have been minutes. It could have been hours. She had lost all concept of time. Finally, exhausted, she sat back down in a pew. Her head pounded. Could Lake conceivably keep her inside the church forever, letting her physical body wither away in the real world? There had to be a way out. There had to be—

Then, without warning, the church disappeared and Cassie's world turned black. Suddenly, she saw white. White walls. A white floor. A chair. A monitor. And . . . red. Why did she see red?

Cassie tried to stand but couldn't. Her feet were bound at the ankles and her hands were tied behind her back. Then she heard a voice through the haze.

'Don't move a goddamn muscle, Ms. West, or I will shoot you between the eyes.'

EIGHTEEN

12:45 p.m.
Eleven hours and fifteen minutes to launch

Wyatt had a gun aimed at Cassie's forehead. He spoke into an earpiece. 'Subject is restrained.'

Cassie looked around the room. Woolman was cowering in the corner. His face was ashen and he looked like he might vomit. He pressed himself up against the wall, as though Cassie might rip through her restraints and tear his head off.

Salman Jalal ran into the room.

'Police are on the way,' Jalal said. He was out of breath, eyes wide and terrified.

'What the hell?' Cassie said, struggling against her bonds. 'What's going on? Where's Aly?'

She followed Woolman's terrified eyes, which were focused on the floor near Cassie. She looked down. And choked back a scream.

A man lay at Cassie's feet, unmoving, a pool of thick blood spreading beneath him.

He had a security guard suit on. His own blood staining his Past Crimes shirt an even darker red.

'Aly?' Cassie shouted.

The seat the girl had occupied was empty. Cassie felt a sharp pain in her leg and noticed her right pant leg was torn. Blood trickled down her calf in a steady rivulet.

'Somebody *please* tell me what's going on,' Cassie said. 'I was in the sim. The real me. Lake put me there. He thinks *I'm* Harris's accomplice. Let me go!'

Woolman crouched in the corner, babbling.

'Crazy . . .' he said, looking at Cassie like she was some sort of demon. 'You went crazy. You killed him. You killed Ryerson.'

'I didn't kill anyone,' Cassie said, desperately. 'I've been inside the sim the whole time.'

'You had a Neural Flare,' Woolman said. 'You lost it. You . . . you killed Andy Ryerson.'

The door slid open and Crispin Lake walked into the room. He looked at Cassie with a mix of disgust and remorse.

'Police are on their way?' Lake said.

'Any minute now,' Jalal said.

'Have we uploaded evidence for the InstaTrial?'

'Already done.'

'Thank you, Salman. We don't want to waste any time locking this piece of garbage away for the rest of her natural life.'

Lake walked over to Cassie, gingerly avoiding the blood on the floor. He knelt down and looked at the dead guard.

'This man's name was Andrew Ryerson,' Lake said. 'He worked for me for five years. He had a wife. A son. I've met a lot of cold people in my life, Ms. West. But you would freeze hell itself.'

'I didn't do anything,' Cassie shouted. 'You . . . you did this. You put those numbers in the sim. Three Six Five Two. You put that drawing in our home. You removed the Skin Reader. You used my likeness. You did all of that.'

Lake listened to Cassie with a look of pity. 'You're insane,' he said. 'And anyone who doesn't agree with me will change their mind within the hour when they learn what you've done.'

'This has to be a mistake,' Cassie said. Her mind was swimming. She felt nauseous. 'This is all part of the Neural Flare, right? My mind is making all of this up.'

But she could smell the scent of blood and sweat. Her leg hurt. She could hear a pitter-patter as droplets of her own blood hit the floor. It *seemed* real. But there was no way she could have . . . no way she would have . . .

'Police are five minutes out,' Jalal said.

'Wyatt, set up a press conference in Earth+. I need to let the world know that Cassandra may have orchestrated a second Blight.' Lake pointed at Cassie and sneered. 'But right now, all I want is to get this piece of shit out of my park.'

'Where is Aly Miller?' Cassie said.

'I have no idea what you're talking about,' Lake said.

'Aly Miller. *Allyson Miller*. She came here with me. She was inside your sim with me. You *met* her. She was *in this room*.'

'You came here alone,' Lake said. 'I gave you a chance because I believe in justice and truth. And this is how you repay my generosity? With murder?'

'I didn't kill anyone. What did you do with Aly?'

'What did *I* do with her?' Lake said, angrily. 'I've never heard of this girl. If she's real and she's missing, then you're the only one who knows where she is.'

'No,' Cassie said. 'I . . . I got her out of the TAP Foundation after her father killed himself and Aly's mother. I brought her here to find out who was responsible for her parents' deaths.'

'Maurice, have you met this girl?'

Wyatt hesitated, ever so briefly, then said, 'I don't know what she's talking about.'

'You're lying. You met her at the airport,' Cassie said, desperately. 'You were *kind* to her.'

'I drove *you* here, Ms. West, and you alone,' Wyatt said, his voice even. Maybe a little too even.

'You set me up,' Cassie shouted at Lake. 'You knew I'd see the Skin Reader was missing. You knew that would get me here. There's going to be a second Blight, and you're going to pin it on me.'

'You are delusional and ill,' Lake said. 'The only thing you've proven since you came here is that you're every bit as psychotic and remorseless as your husband was.'

Wyatt pressed a finger to his ear and nodded.

'Cops are here,' he said to Lake. 'Arrest vehicle is coming through the Bundy gate right now.'

'Wyatt, please escort Ms. West outside. I need to call Ryerson's wife before the press conference. Salman, is Ms. West's InstaTrial set?'

'All set,' Jalal said. 'It's a half-hour drive to the precinct. We should have a verdict before she gets to the station.'

'If she is convicted,' Lake said to Woolman, 'I want her likeness and biometrics patched into the sim *immediately*.'

'Done,' Woolman replied.

'Don't you see what's happening?' Cassie shouted at Wyatt, Woolman, Jalal. 'He's going to pin it on me! Where is Aly? Let me *go*!'

Another guard entered the room. He and Wyatt lifted Cassie out of her chair like a rolled-up rug. Lake, Woolman and Jalal watched. Woolman cowered against the wall. Lake looked angry. Jalal looked . . . calm. Like somehow none of this was a surprise.

Cassie struggled but the bond dug into her skin. Her head pounded, her leg ached, and her energy was waning. They must have drugged her. The 'nutrient' packets.

'Where is Aly?' she shouted. Past Crimes employees stared in horror as Cassie was hauled out of the complex. 'What did you do with her? There's going to be another Blight! Don't you get it? If you take me away, everyone is going to die! Everyone! Let! Me! Go!'

She had a brief moment of realization, thinking about how this must have looked to everyone watching the spectacle. A hogtied woman ranting about mass murder while being carried out on the shoulder of two burly guards. She could see Crispin Lake standing at the end of the hallway.

'Crispin,' she implored. 'Don't do this. Just let the girl go. You can do anything you want with me. I'll participate in the sim. Just let Aly go.'

'I want nothing to do with you now or ever again,' Lake said. 'Whatever happened to that girl is on you. I hope today you take your last ever breaths as a free woman.'

'Did you *see* me shoot him?' Cassie said to the guard.

'Excuse me?' the guard replied.

'Did you see me take Ryerson's gun and shoot him? Did you see me, a woman who's left her apartment maybe six times in the past ten years, with no military training whatsoever, disarm that security guard who works for the multi-billion-dollar company and murder him in cold blood?'

The guard said nothing.

'Did you see it, Wyatt?'

'If you don't shut up, you won't even make it to the precinct, Ms. West.'

'What does Lake have on you?' Cassie said. 'It must be bad if you're willing to frame me for murder and genocide. I'll bet you—'

Then, before she could say another word, Wyatt threw Cassie to the ground. She landed on her side and immediately all the air was driven from her lungs. She gasped for breath, inhaling dust. She coughed over and over, stirring up more dust. Her head spun. She rolled on to her back and gulped down air.

Cassie could see the sun descending through the clouds above her. For a moment, she thought about how beautiful it was, and she thought about Harris, how they'd spent a weekend renting a cabin on Lake George what felt like eons ago, how they swam and drank delicious red wine and made love, and how every night they would sit outside and watch the sunset and think about everything the future held for them. Cassie figured they would have years, *decades*, to drink up everything life had to offer. How had it come to this, writhing in the dirt, trying to breathe, ten years after having buried Harris's remains in an unmarked grave? After Harris died, after she'd lost her child, Cassie didn't think her life could sink any lower. As she lay there, face on the ground, arms and legs shackled, she realized she'd been wrong.

Cassie heard a siren in the distance. Moments later, a boxy car pulled up. It was blue and white with the letters WVPD on the side. The siren went quiet and the back door slid open. There was no driver.

The guards picked Cassie up and tossed her into the backseat. The door slid closed and a video monitor in the metal divider flickered on. A stern older man with a thick, gray mustache wearing a blue WVPD uniform appeared on the screen.

'Good afternoon, Ms. West,' the cop said with a slight Southern drawl. 'My name is Sergeant Revis Wells. Please sit up straight so we can secure you for your own safety. If you refuse to obey, we will do it for you, but it'll be a lot less pleasant.'

Cassie managed to get herself into an upright position. A harness extended from the door and clicked into a clasp by Cassie's hip. The strap tightened around her waist, barely giving her room to breathe.

'The doors of this law enforcement vehicle are sealed with electrical current,' Wells said. 'I strongly advise you not to try to open them. There are better ways to spend your day than getting thirty thousand volts coursing through your body.'

Cassie could hear a faint buzzing sound coming from both back-seat doors, like a generator coming online. Sergeant Wells clearly wasn't bluffing.

'Cassandra Ann West. You are under arrest for the charge of murder in the first degree, conspiracy to commit murder, kidnapping, aggravated assault, child abandonment and Wrap fraud. Please remain still as we begin the process of your arraignment and InstaTrial.'

A panel opened in the car's ceiling and an Earth+ visor lowered. It centered itself in the middle of Cassie's forehead and slid on to her face.

Cassie found herself inside a virtual courtroom seated behind a wooden desk. A heavy-jowled judge sat before her. To her right sat a man she had never seen before. His features were bland, skin perfectly smooth, hair unmoving. He had a pleasant smile that reminded Cassie of a toothpaste commercial. The man turned to Cassie and said enthusiastically, 'Hello, Cassandra Ann West! My name is Ernest J. Law, and I'm the court-appointed Augmented Persona attorney for your Earth+ InstaTrial.'

'You've got to be kidding me,' Cassie said. She looked down. Her Wrap was wearing a perfectly tailored black pantsuit and sensible shoes.

'Ms. West, based on my analysis of this case, I recommend you plead guilty,' Ernest J. Law said.

'Oh really? And what do you base this analysis on?'

'If you choose a jury InstaTrial, all evidence against you will be fed into the EPP's judicial algorithm. That algorithm randomly determines the makeup of the jury and, based on that and the evidence against you, determines the probability of your conviction. I can tell you, the odds are not in your favor.'

'This is a joke, right? Evidence? I was arrested thirty seconds ago.'

'Yes. And Past Crimes has already uploaded several videos and statements to be entered into evidence against you.'

'Videos? What videos?'

A screen appeared in the air in front of Cassie. A clip began to play. It had been taken from a security camera inside the Past Crimes Maternity Ward.

'Aly Miller isn't in this video,' Cassie said. 'She was there. Lake must have edited her out.'

'Keep watching,' the lawyer said. Suddenly, the Cassie in the video lunged at a guard. She pulled his weapon from its holster and then, without hesitating, shot him point blank in the chest. She turned the gun towards Crispin Lake but was subdued by several guards. Then the clip ended.

'If Aly Miller wasn't at Past Crimes,' Cassie said, 'as you claim, then why am I being charged with kidnapping and child endangerment?'

'Because we have surveillance footage and testimony from Emmeline Procter that you took Allyson Miller from the TAP Foundation. At some point between there and Utah, she vanished. No body has been found. However, law enforcement is currently looking for her body, and once they find her, you'll face a second count of murder.'

'I didn't kidnap anyone,' Cassie said. 'Lake doctored all of it. He edited Aly out of that footage. They all met her. If they find Aly's body, it's because Crispin Lake killed her.'

'If you choose a jury trial, the algorithm will take that . . . theory . . . into account.'

'So what are my options?'

'Well, you have the option of pleading guilty by confessing to the charges,' Law said. 'The algorithm will take your confession into account for sentencing, as well as your level of remorse based on biometrics, vocal intonation, and heart rate. If your confession is deemed legitimate, it could lessen your sentence. If the algorithm decides that your remorse level is below accepted measurements, it could negatively affect your sentencing.'

'What kind of sentence am I looking at?'

'If convicted on all counts? Thirty-seven consecutive life sentences. If you confess, I may be able to knock that down to twenty-eight.'

'Is there a judicial algorithm that determines just how bullshit this all is?'

'There is not,' Ernest J. Law said.

'Great. Bang-up job you're doing for me, Matlock.'

'Is Matlock a character witness you plan to call on your behalf?'

'Oh, this is really not good.'

At that moment, Cassie saw a Wrap materialize in the previously empty gallery. It was Reggie Davenport.

'You've got to be kidding me,' Cassie said.

Somebody – Lake, of course – must have tipped Davenport off about Cassie's arrest and given him the link to the InstaTrial. The reporter watched the proceedings with a self-satisfied smirk.

'Cassandra Ann West,' the judge said. 'You are charged with murder in the first degree, conspiracy to commit murder, kidnapping, aggravated assault, child abandonment, and Wrap fraud. How do you plead?'

'Not guilty.' She heard Ernest J. Law sigh next to her.

The words **Loading Judicial Algorithm** appeared above the judge's head. A bar beneath it slowly filled up. When it got to the end, the judge said, 'Ms. West. You have been convicted on all charges. You are hereby to be remanded to the custody of the West Valley Police Department to await sentencing.'

'Your honor,' Cassie said, feeling silly upon realizing that the judge himself was nothing more than an AP. 'Crispin Lake framed me. You have to let me go. He's the one you want.'

'Mr. Lake, would you like to respond?'

Crispin Lake appeared in the gallery next to Reggie Davenport. He wore a nice suit, his hair neatly combed, a solemn look on his face.

'Although I made a terrible error in judgment in giving her a chance, it is abundantly clear that Cassandra West has continued the work of her husband and put many lives at risk,' Lake said. 'She is a danger to others, to herself and to society at large. I recommend the maximum penalty at sentencing.'

'We will certainly take that under advisement,' the judge said. 'Thank you for taking the time to appear here today, Mr. Lake. We know how busy you are.'

'He's setting me up!' Cassie shouted.

'Mr. Lake has been a friend of law enforcement for many years,' the judge said. 'He has donated millions of dollars to worthy police causes, and his word in this court carries considerable weight. These proceedings are now complete. Have a nice day, Ms. West.'

Right before the courtroom disappeared, bringing Cassie back to

Earth– where she was bound in the back of an automated police car, she turned to see Crispin Lake sitting in the gallery, looking at her, the corner of his lip upturned ever so slightly, hand raised, as if he were waving goodbye.

NINETEEN

1:16 p.m.
Ten hours and forty-four minutes to launch

The car merged on to the highway, every swerve and turn sending Cassie reeling, lurching around the backseat of the unmanned car, unable to brace herself with her hands and ankles still bound. A GPS tracker in the divider showed that she was nine minutes from the precinct. Nine minutes before her freedom was taken from her. For a decade, Cassie had felt like she was in mental lockdown. In nine minutes, that lockdown would become real as a heart attack.

Her fingers felt tingly, the blood flow restricted by the bonds on her wrists. As they sped around one curve, Cassie's face came within six inches of the door. A buzzer went off and a robotic voice said, 'Caution. Electrical current thirty thousand volts. Touch at your own personal peril.'

Cassie definitely did not want to touch at her own personal peril.

She couldn't move. Couldn't reach anything. There was no way to get out. The divider between the back and front seats appeared to be solid steel. She looked around the car, desperate, searching for anything to free herself. She had to get out. Had to find Aly. Had to prove that this was all a setup, that there was no way in hell she could have, or would have, killed that guard. Aly had to have seen it. She could back Cassie up. Together, they would alert the world that a second Blight was coming, and Crispin Lake had set her up so that the world would think she was carrying on the horrifying work of her husband.

But the moment she got to the precinct, she'd be thrown in a cell. And she wasn't likely to leave it while she was still upright.

'Hello?' Cassie said. 'Sergeant Wells? Anyone? I would like to speak to my lawyer.'

A message appeared on the screen. It read: **Would you like to speak to your public defender in Earth+? Press Yes or No.**

'You've got to be kidding me,' Cassie said. At the moment, she didn't have any free appendages to scratch an itch, let alone tap a screen to make a decision that would impact her freedom. Then a second message appeared on the screen.

If you are currently restrained and cannot reach the touchpad, you may speak your command. You have ten seconds to respond.

Bingo.

'Ye—'

Before Cassie could finish the word, the car took what must have been a ninety-degree turn at eighty miles an hour, launching Cassie against the door. Instantly, she felt electricity surge through her body. Her body twitched involuntarily. Her lungs and heart felt as though they were on fire. Her teeth clattered against each other. She couldn't speak or breathe.

This is what it must feel like to get hit by lightning, she thought.

Finally, the shock subsided and she was able to regain her breath. She opened her eyes just in time to see a message on the screen which read: **Your time has expired. Have a good day.**

Cassie screamed with every ounce of energy she had, which, at that moment, wasn't very much. She was about to spend the rest of her life rotting away. And what the hell had they done with Aly? At first, she thought her time stranded in the Church of the Beacons was some sort of glitch. Now she knew that while she was stranded in the Church of the Beacons, Lake was setting the stage to frame Cassie for murder. At least one, if not thousands.

The GPS showed that the police car was five minutes from the precinct. Soon the entire world would think she was a madman, just like her husband. She should never have contacted Aly. Never have gone to Dallas. Never contacted Crispin Lake. Died alone in her shitty apartment. Nobody would have known. Nobody would have cared. The world might have even been better off if she'd just . . .

She saw the silver SUV pull ahead of the unmanned police car, noticed it was going well over the speed limit, but so were they – and really, who the hell cared anymore?

But then she saw the rear window of the SUV slide open. A man hung halfway out and brought up some sort of device Cassie had never seen before. It had a long metal handle that ended in a wide conical shape, like a speaker. Was it some kind of megaphone? Then the man aimed the device at the police car.

In less than a second, Cassie realized it wasn't a megaphone. It was a gun.

The man pulled the trigger, and Cassie braced herself – at least, as best she could considering she couldn't move her arms or legs. She closed her eyes, expecting the car to be blown to smithereens, and all Cassie could hope for was that she wouldn't feel the end.

But there was no explosion. In fact, there was no sound at all. There was . . . nothing.

Cassie opened her eyes. The man was still there, holding the gun. He didn't act like something had gone wrong. He was just . . . waiting.

And then Cassie felt it. The cop car. It was slowing down. But not in a controlled manner, like someone was gently pressing the brake. It was slowing down rapidly, as if the engine had suddenly disappeared, leaving the car to fend for itself on the highway.

Problem was, the car went from eighty miles an hour to twenty in about three seconds. The car began to drift towards the median. The front tire clipped the divider and Cassie felt the front of the car pitch forward and the back – which contained her bruised and bundled body – lift clear off the ground. The rear of the car rose in the air and Cassie along with it, and for a moment she felt weightless, held in her seat by the strap and nothing else, while the car flipped end over end and landed upside down on the highway in a crunch of metal and glass.

The impact jarred Cassie's already bruised brain. Her back and neck and shoulders and tailbone hurt like hell. But she was alive. Upside down in a police car that had just been disabled by some guy with a high-tech megaphone gun. But she was alive. For how long, she didn't know.

She looked out the window. It was splintered but still intact. They must have used the same indestructible glass on police cars that they used on the latest cell phones. The asphalt floated above her. There were no sounds in the car. She couldn't even hear the crackle of electricity from the security doors. It was as if somebody had just flipped the car's switch to *Off*.

Then she heard footsteps. A pair of boots appeared outside of the window. Cassie's heart sped up. She wasn't just a fish in a barrel. She was a fish in a barrel whose tail and fins had been cut off.

'Close your eyes,' came a man's voice.

'What?' she said.

'This is going to be bright. Close your eyes or it will burn out your retinas.'

She closed her eyes. A moment later, she heard a high-pitched squealing sound, like metal being ripped apart.

'Keep them closed,' the man said. 'I'm almost done.'

A minute later, she heard a clang as something hit the ground.

Cassie opened her eyes. The door was gone. It lay flat outside the car, a crude hole where it had been. The man held a small device the size and width of a pen, obviously some sort of laser that had sliced through the metal frame like a hot knife through warm butter. The man leaned into the hole where the door had been. He wore goggles with black lenses that concealed his eyes over a balaclava that covered his face.

'I didn't say to open your eyes yet,' he said, irritably. 'You haven't changed much, Ms. West. You've never been much of a listener.'

Ms. West. He knew her. 'Who are you?'

He held up the small device again. Its tip glowed red.

'What is that thing?'

'I call it the Devil's Fingernail,' the man said. 'Your eyes. Close them again.'

She did. Cassie felt an intense heat near her ankles, and then her wrists.

'OK. *Now* you can open your eyes.'

Cassie did. He'd used the Devil's Fingernail device to cut through her bonds. If he was there to kill her, he was certainly doing it very inefficiently.

'Hold on one second,' the man said. He knelt down and touched the wound on Cassie's leg, probing it gently.

'Goddamn,' he said with a satisfied smile. 'The asshole pulled it off.'

'OK, enough,' Cassie said. 'What's going on? Who pulled what off?'

The man removed his goggles and then his face mask and shoved them into his coat pocket. He looked young, late twenties or early thirties, Hispanic, with a goatee and long, dark hair tied back in a

ponytail. He held out his hand and helped Cassie crawl out from
the wreckage. He had striking blue eyes. And he looked at her in
a way that said she was not a stranger to him.

'Who are you?' she said.

The man smiled. 'It's been a long time since that Lockbox, Blood
Banker.'

Those blue eyes. She'd seen them before. They were a little older.
A little wearier. But they belonged to the same young man she'd
met a decade ago.

'Hector Ruiz,' Cassie said. 'Joy Ruiz's brother.'

Hector merely nodded and said, 'Let's get you the hell out of
here, Ms. West.'

TWENTY

1:40 p.m.
Ten hours and twenty minutes to launch

Ruiz led Cassie away from the police car and tossed a small,
circular device into the wreckage. He pointed at his SUV and
said, 'Get in.'

Figuring the only other option was to wait for the cop cavalry to
come and smear her all over the highway, Cassie obliged. Hector
got in on the passenger side. A woman sat in the driver's seat. She
was Black, around the same age as Hector, with curly hair that fell
to her shoulders. She wore a gray tank top, which revealed a long,
thick scar that ran from the base of her neck down her arm to her
elbow.

Ruiz got into the passenger seat. The woman turned back to
Cassie, looked her over, then said to Ruiz, 'Does she have it?'

'She does,' Ruiz said.

'What do I have?' Cassie said.

The woman ignored Cassie, yelled and slapped the steering wheel
in excitement. She leaned over, placed her hands on Hector's cheeks
and kissed him deeply. 'I didn't think he'd be able to do it on such
short notice.'

'Ye of little faith,' Ruiz replied.

'Excuse me, I seem to remember you freaking out all day,' the woman said.

'Freaking out is a little strong,' Ruiz replied. 'Moderately anxious.'

'I'm going to be moderately anxious if we wait here another second. Let's get the hell out of here.'

The woman sped off, leaving the cop car behind. Ruiz took out a phone, tapped the screen and began counting down from ten. When he reached zero, he tapped the screen again. Cassie heard a loud explosion behind them.

'You just blew up the cop car, didn't you?' Cassie said. 'What was in that little pumpkin bomb you tossed inside it?'

'Napalm,' Ruiz replied.

'Napalm? Are you serious?'

'Napalm is a pain in the ass to extinguish,' Ruiz said. 'Should shut down the highway and keep the cops occupied for a little while.'

'You knew I'd be in that car,' Cassie said.

'That's right,' Ruiz said.

'How did you know I was arrested? Nobody even knew I was at Past Crimes except the people *at* Past Crimes.'

Ruiz didn't respond. They swerved off the highway into a residential area. They drove past a building with a mirrored façade, and Cassie realized she couldn't see the car's reflection in the glass.

'Why can't I see our car in the windows?' Cassie said.

'Reflective paneling,' the woman said. 'Makes the car almost undetectable to the naked eye. And our LiDAR-busting tech either absorbs or redirects electromagnetic waves from radars. The military invented it for stealth bombers. Which lets us get away without being detected by the cops. I'm Vivian, by the way. Vivian Adair. Nice to meet you.'

'Cassandra West.'

'I know who you are,' Vivian said. 'We all do.'

'What did you do to stop the cop car back there?'

'Portable EMP,' Ruiz said, holding up the megaphone gun. 'Electromagnetic pulse. Completely shuts down anything running on electricity within a fifty-yard radius in half a second.'

'That's very cool. And I don't want to seem ungrateful. I appreciate you getting me out of there. But I want to know what the hell is going on *right now*. *How* did you know I'd be in that car, and why did you want to rescue me?'

'Who said we intercepted that car to rescue you?' Vivian said.

Hector turned around. The goggles had left faint imprint lines around his azure eyes. The baby fat had melted off him, revealing a handsome young man. But Cassie still saw in those eyes a glimmer of the angry young man who'd lost his sister, who felt her life and memory were being sold off like cheap jewelry at a yard sale. A young man who'd been let down by everyone. Including Cassie.

So what the hell was Hector Ruiz doing here, now, napalming a car and busting her out of police custody?

'We're almost there,' Hector said. 'A few more minutes. I'll explain everything.'

Five minutes later, Vivian pulled the car on to a side street. Vivian stopped the car in front of a rusted metal gate. Hector hopped out and pressed his hand against a panel at the side. The gate slid open noiselessly, revealing a small garage inside. Vivian pulled in, Hector following, and the wall slid closed behind them. Vivian got out of the car and motioned for Cassie to do the same.

'We good?' Vivian said. Ruiz checked his phone. The screen showed the alley they'd just entered. They must have had well-hidden cameras set up outside.

'We're good,' Ruiz said.

'We got it, babe,' Vivian said. She kissed Hector deeply. When they finished, Hector turned to Cassie and said, 'I said I'd explain everything. Come with us.'

Ruiz placed his hand on a sensor at the far end of the garage. Another door slid open. Ruiz and Vivian went inside and motioned for Cassie to follow.

They led her into a darkened room. A green light scanned Hector and Vivian, then overhead lights flickered on. Cassie was in some sort of makeshift lab. There were a number of computer terminals along one wall, and half a dozen Earth+ visors hanging from metal jacks. Assorted gadgets lined wooden shelves. Cassie recognized several of the napalm balls and a few more of the EMP guns, along with an assortment of other devices that did not look like they were meant for recreational use.

'Are you . . . terrorists?' Cassie said.

Hector looked at Cassie as if offended.

'What do you think, Viv?' he said to Vivian. 'Are we terrorists?'

Vivian snorted. 'Last I checked, most terrorists didn't save people's lives.'

'We are not terrorists,' Hector said. 'We're disruptors. We don't hurt anyone. When we see a company like Past Crimes making millions, *billions*, off the suffering of other people, we step in. Try to level the playing field. Occasionally, we see the police about to bury someone who doesn't deserve it, and so we step in. I bet you already had your InstaTrial by the time we got to you, right?'

'I did.'

'Convicted?'

'Yup.'

'How many life sentences were you going to get?' Vivian asked.

'Enough that I'd still be in prison in the year 3000,' Cassie said. 'So you're not going to kill me or hold me for ransom.'

'Nope,' Hector said. 'Actually, we need you.'

'And since you're now officially the most wanted woman in the country,' Vivian said, pulling a clean T-shirt, pants and undergarments from her bag, 'put these on.'

'Why?'

'Number one, there's video of you getting arrested. I'd advise against wearing the same clothes. Number two, even if they can't see you, you're more than a little ripe, and I don't want to take a chance that anyone downwind can smell you.'

'Well, you're polite.'

'My number-one priority is to keep you alive,' Vivian said. 'Being polite didn't make the list.'

Vivian led her to a small bathroom and handed her a towel and a bottle of hand soap, then stepped out to give her privacy. Cassie washed her face and body the best she could, then slipped on the clothes. They were a little big and a nondescript gray, but they did what they were intended to. When she was done, she met them back in the warehouse.

'So what is all this?' she said.

'Before we get into it,' Hector said, 'I think you'd want to know that we found her.'

Cassie paused. Then her eyes widened. 'Joy. You found your sister.'

'I figured you hadn't heard.'

'Was she . . .'

'Yes.'

'I'm so sorry.' Cassie shook her head in shame. 'After Harris died, I pretty much shut the world out. Anything that didn't have to do with him or the Blight just fell off my radar. But it shouldn't have.'

'I understand,' Hector said. 'I was the same way. After Joy died, I became angry. I became obsessed. Nothing else mattered. Her death ruined my life.'

'That's something I can understand,' Cassie said. 'Where did you find her?'

'We found her remains two years after my parents signed with you at V.I.C.E. The licensing agent who replaced you made a deal with InterStream Entertainment to produce an interactive documentary. They created a sim of Carafe, the bar where Joy met Waltermeyer, so people could look for clues themselves. I mean it was a total third-rate sim, like a bootleg of a bootleg of a bootleg of Past Crimes. They even offered prize money to anyone who found clues within the sim that led to an arrest. It became some sort of sick treasure hunt. But it was all bullshit. They made up clues that were never there. Fingerprints, patrons who were never at the bar. When my family complained, they called it a "dramatization" and told us to check the contract. The one you had us sign. Sure enough, anyone who licensed the rights to Joy's story could "dramatize" it however they wanted. My sister's disappearance made InterStream a lot of money. And caused my family a lot of pain.'

'Nothing I can say will change any of that,' Cassie said. 'But I want you to know I'm sorry.'

'You've paid your price.'

'I did,' Cassie said. 'So how did you find her?'

'By the time the documentary premiered in Earth+, my parents had burned through all the InterStream money on lawyers, private investigators and the pretty brutal Flashpoint drug addiction my dad developed to help him cope. But I wanted to keep looking. I asked InterStream if they would donate some of their profits from Joy's deal to help me look for her. Even if she was dead, I needed to know. I needed closure. They said they didn't have the budget to help. A few weeks later, I read that Isaac Frakes, CEO of InterStream, got a seventeen-million-dollar bonus.'

Vivian took Hector's hand. He continued.

'So I left home and started looking myself. Turns out it was random. Joy had tried to call her friend Deondra but couldn't get reception. We can create a whole goddamn virtual earth, but some areas in this country still can't get cell reception. Anyway, Joy went into an alley where a guy named Jarvis Leigh was suffering from Neural Flares after a ninety-six-hour Earth+ binge. Leigh strangled her, then buried her body. The Flares had turned his brain to mush. He died in his home, and when the cops were investigating, they found Joy's shoes in his closet. There were crushed Ponderosa pine needles embedded in the rubber treads. Cibola Forest was close by, and they have a ton of Ponderosa pines. We must have dug up half the forest looking for her. But we found her. Underneath the biggest Ponderosa pine in the forest. And we were able to give my sister a proper burial. Like she deserved.'

'I'm glad,' Cassie said. 'She deserved that. And you deserved that closure.'

'After we buried Joy,' Hector said, 'I hacked into InterStream's corporate email server. As it turned out, they actually had batted around the idea of donating money to help me find her. The talks went all the way up to Isaac Frakes. Frakes sent an email to their senior staff saying that InterStream stood to make more money if Joy stayed missing. His exact quote was, "If she's found, the mystery ends. People stop going into the documentary. Advertisers pull out. But if she stays gone, we have a revenue stream in perpetuity."'

'Jesus,' Cassie said. 'I swear, I didn't know.'

'I was very lost,' Hector said. 'I had two roads and I needed to choose one. The first was to live angry. And trust me, that path was really, *really* tempting. I would have ended up in jail or dead, but part of me would have preferred either of those. Instead, I found a second road. I found other people like me. People who'd lost loved ones. Who had been told their loved ones were just a dollar sign. Who were hurting. And it was on that second road that I found my angel. And she saved me.'

Ruiz squeezed Vivian's hand and she pressed closer to him.

'Hector and I found each other through pain,' Vivian said. 'And we helped each other find a path through it. My mother was killed by Drayden Downs.'

'The Seattle Strangler,' Cassie said.

'Past Crimes licensed the Drayden Downs story for a sim. They made millions off the Seattle Strangler, while my broken family ate pre-boiled pasta with synthetic milk six nights a week. So while our lives were falling apart, these criminal media executives are living it up on Earth+ yachts, made off ours and other families' blood.'

'I was a part of that equation for a long time,' Cassie said.

'For a long time, I wanted to find Drayden Downs and kill him myself. Then I stopped. I realized that taking pleasure from someone else's death made me no better than any of them. And when Downs was killed in prison, I didn't feel much of anything.'

'Crispin Lake is about to make millions – maybe billions – off of the Blight sim,' Hector said. 'I don't want him to enlarge his empire off of other people's blood.'

'That's part of the reason we saved you,' Vivian said. 'We've tried to get to Lake and Past Crimes for a long time. This – you – were the first real opportunity we've had.'

'What do you mean?'

'I hated you for a long time,' Hector added. 'But now, you're like us. You're lost. It's time for you to be found too, Cassie. Just like we were.'

Vivian went over to a bank of computers and took an Earth+ visor from a dock. She held it out to Cassie who took the device.

'I need your help. I need to get Allyson Miller out of there. She knows the truth. People won't believe me. But they'll believe her.'

'If she can help take down Crispin Lake,' Vivian said, 'we'll do whatever we can.'

'Before we do that, I need you to know you can trust us. For that, you need to meet us.'

'Us?'

'Are they ready?' Vivian asked Hector.

'Sent out the EPD notification before we left to get Cassie.'

'OK, then. Cassandra Ann West,' Vivian said. 'I'd like you to meet the Found.'

Vivian pressed a button and the storeroom around Cassie disappeared. She found herself in what appeared to be some sort of barn. She couldn't smell anything – the Theia visors at Past Crimes were a technological leap beyond the one she was wearing – but everything else looked real. Felt real.

The barn door opened and a line of Wraps began to enter. They all had warm, welcoming smiles on their faces. Cassie squinted. Then her eyes widened.

She recognized many of these Wraps from her time at V.I.C.E. The man approaching her was Vikram Das. His entire family had been killed by Leonard Elby in Laredo, Texas. Das's daughter, Sita, had briefly dated Elby years before his killing spree, before becoming one of his victims. She was posthumously, and controversially, convicted of being an accessory to murder, despite not having seen Elby for four years prior to his killings, which meant Sita's AP could be used freely for entertainment purposes. Conservative estimates put the money made from Sita's 'participation' in these projects at fifty million – not a dime of which was seen by her family.

Vikram came up to Cassie and took her hand in his. He smiled warmly, then gave her a gentle hug.

'Welcome,' he said.

Vikram walked away. The next Wrap to approach her was Sharon Lazenby. Lazenby had been kidnapped at eight years old, then found ten years later in an abandoned trailer, chained to a radiator. Her abductor was never caught. Sharon was living in a homeless shelter the same week a hugely popular interactive prestige drama about her abduction premiered. Sharon was thin and her hair was stringy. Neither she nor Vikram appeared to have altered their Wraps. Sharon put her hands on Cassie's shoulders and said, 'You are found, Cassie West.'

Wrap after Wrap came up to Cassie and embraced her. She recognized most of the Wraps from the sensational and horrific crimes that had been committed against them or their loved ones. Once all the members of the Found were done greeting Cassie, they held hands and formed a large circle, with Cassie in the center. Vivian and Hector entered the barn last. They did not greet Cassie, just took places in the circle among the other Wraps.

Hector said, 'My friends, this is Cassandra Ann West. Like us, she has lost and been lost. But now she is one of us. She is our family. She has been found.'

Hector left the circle and joined Cassie in the middle. He took her hands in his and said, 'Through love and strength we heal each other. When you are lost, you can come to any of us. And you will always be found.'

Hector tilted his head closer to Cassie and said, 'Through love and strength we heal each other.'

He nodded. She understood.

The circle then closed around Cassie, wrapping her in the tightest, most-needed hug of her life. She could almost feel her heart expanding, a sob escaping her lips as the group embraced her.

'Look at me,' Hector said. Cassie did. 'I'm going to say something to you I wish somebody had said to me after Joy disappeared. I was blinded by hate and consumed by grief. You can't overcome that alone. But you can with help. We are not blood, but we are a family. We remind each other that there is more to us than our traumas. By helping others find their strength, we find that strength in ourselves.'

'This is . . .' Cassie said, choking up. 'I don't even know what to say.'

Hector stepped back and rejoined the circle.

'Thank you,' Cassie said. 'All of you.'

'Now we have a lot of work to do,' Hector said, 'and not much time. But from this day on, the Found will be here for you, Cassie. As they have been for Vivian and me.'

The next time Cassie blinked, she was back in the warehouse in Earth−. She removed her visor. She felt dizzy. Her head pounded. Vivian brought her a cup of salted water which she drank in two quick gulps.

'How are you feeling?' she said.

'Like I was just adopted.'

Vivian smiled. 'We all carry the guilt of what happened to our loved ones, or, in some cases, what our loved ones did to us or to others. We've all wondered what we could have done to prevent it, or shouldered the blame when it wasn't ours to carry. I know you've had to carry that weight ever since your husband died.'

'I have. But I also know you didn't bust me out of police custody just to bring me here for a big virtual group hug.'

'No, we didn't,' Hector said. He knelt down next to Cassie, pointed at her leg, and said, 'Do you mind?'

'Go ahead. It kills. Something must have cut me, but I don't even remember it happening.'

'Something didn't cut you,' Hector said, rolling her pant leg up. 'Somebody did.'

'And you knew about it?'

'Yes. And I'll show you why.'

Cassie shrieked as Hector cleaned the wound with an alcohol swab.

'What are you doing?'

'One second,' Hector said. 'I need to find it.'

'Find what?'

Hector pressed his finger against her skin, right below her calf muscle. Then he pressed harder. The pain was hot and unbearable. Hector looked at Vivian and nodded. 'Found it.'

'Found what?'

Vivian handed Hector a pair of tweezers. Then she handed Cassie a small orange ball and said, 'Squeeze this.'

Before Cassie could ask another question, she felt Hector slide the tweezers into her leg. Cassie screamed and squeezed the ball. She held her breath as he rooted around in her leg for what felt like an eternity. She felt Hector pinch something inside of her leg.

'Got it!' Hector said triumphantly. He removed the metal from Cassie's leg and held up the bloody tweezers. They clasped what appeared to be a small microchip sheathed in a plastic casing. The casing was coated in Cassie's blood.

Vivian brought over a damp cloth that smelled like alcohol and said, 'This is going to hurt like a mother . . . you know.'

She pressed the cloth against the open wound. The pain was bright and Cassie gasped.

'I'm going to pass out.'

'Just another second,' Vivian said.

After far too many more seconds, Vivian removed the cloth. She then applied a bandage to the wound, wrapped it in gauze and taped it all together.

'This,' Hector said, wiping the blood off the plastic, 'is why we busted you out.'

'What is that, and why the hell was it in my leg?' Cassie asked, still catching her breath.

Hector brought the case over to the bank of computers. He put on a pair of thin latex gloves and gently opened the case. He dropped the chip into his palm. It was the size of a dime. Both Hector and Vivian stared at it with reverence.

'This,' Hector said, 'could change everything.'

He inserted the chip into a reader attached to the computer. A loading bar appeared. When it finished, a window opened displaying thousands of lines of code.

'Are we golden?' Vivian asked.

'I think so,' Hector replied. He turned to Cassie. 'Crispin Lake has built an empire on the blood and suffering of others. He donates tens of millions to law enforcement and politicians. Far more than he's ever given to the victims of the crimes he exploits and profits from. And in turn, they create laws that have made Past Crimes millions, if not billions.'

'Like Statute 486-16,' Vivian said.

'When Earth+ exploded, so did the number of crimes committed. The judicial system simply couldn't handle all the criminal cases in both Earth+ and Earth−. Hence, InstaTrials.'

'That statute is allowing him to use your husband,' Vivian said.

'And now it's going to allow him to use me,' Cassie replied.

'Crispin Lake makes monsters, because monsters make money. And you're his latest creation.'

'What do you mean?'

Vivian brought a paper-thin tablet over to Cassie and opened a video.

There was a photo of Cassie on the screen. It had been taken just the other day at the Dallas/Fort Worth airport. A banner below the picture read: **SECOND BLIGHT IMMINENT?**

An anchor came on the screen and Cassie's image retreated to the upper right-hand corner.

'Authorities are searching for Cassandra Ann West, the so-called "Red Widow" of infamous Blight mastermind Harris West, after she escaped from police custody this afternoon following her conviction on charges of murder in the first degree, conspiracy to commit murder, kidnapping, aggravated assault, child abandonment, and Wrap fraud. And in a shocking development, the EPP claims Ms. West may have followed in her husband's footsteps and planned to unleash a second Blight on the tenth anniversary of the first.'

The broadcast then showed footage of police and EPP vehicles all over the world searching homes, setting up barricades and leading people away in handcuffs. It was absolute chaos.

'Around the world, local law enforcement has joined with the Earth Plus Police to attempt to prevent a second Blight. However, with nearly three billion registered Earth+ users, plus millions more who are unregistered, the task at hand is impossible.'

'Jesus Christ,' Cassie said. 'The whole world is going to think . . .'

'That you're the new Vertex Ignis,' Vivian said.

The anchor continued: 'Cassandra West was arrested at the Past Crimes complex in West Valley City, Utah, where she allegedly murdered a security guard. Ms. West was allegedly traveling with a young female companion, believed to be Allyson Miller, fifteen, whose parents, Alan and Nadine Miller, were killed last month. Ms. West removed Ms. Miller from her residence at the TAP Foundation, and authorities are concerned she may have killed the young woman before reaching Utah. When asked whether Ms. West may have been involved in the deaths of Alan and Nadine Miller, in addition to the disappearance of their daughter, Sergeant Revis Wells of the West Valley Police Department said, "That is a possibility, however unfathomable, that we are looking into." We have just received new footage of Cassandra Ann West and her alleged victim, Allyson Miller. I warn you: this footage is shocking.'

The screen then cut to what appeared to be security footage taken from the airport. It showed Cassie yanking Aly to the ground, which had happened, but it had clearly been doctored to edit out the man suffering from a Neural Flare who'd reached out for Aly. The edited video made it look like Cassie was assaulting Aly.

'That's not what happened,' Cassie said.

'That's what the public is seeing,' Vivian said. 'And when it comes to crime, the first impression is the only one people remember.'

They then showed another video taken from the airport, of Aly threatening the man who tried to take Cassie's photo. Aly looked crazy, waving her hands at the man.

'It is believed Cassandra West may have radicalized Allyson Miller's parents,' the anchor said, 'and may have been in the process of radicalizing Allyson Miller herself. Reporter Reginald Davenport was present at Ms. West's InstaTrial conviction earlier today.'

The screen cut to a video of Reggie Davenport sitting in a chair in front of a grand fireplace surrounded by many leatherbound books. It was clearly filmed inside Earth+. Cassie doubted Davenport owned a single book.

'Cassie West didn't show a shred of remorse at her sentencing,' Davenport said. 'There is no doubt in my mind that Cassandra West is capable of unspeakable evil. There is little doubt in my mind that Ms. West murdered that poor girl. I just pray for all the people she may have radicalized to further her family's insane teachings.'

The anchor continued: 'In a statement, Past Crimes founder Crispin Lake said, "We are all mourning the loss of a member of the Past Crimes family today. I welcomed Cassandra West into our complex to meet with her about her possible participation in our Blight simulation. I am a trusting man and I wanted to give Ms.

West the benefit of the doubt, that she may have been unaware of her husband's machinations. I always feel sympathy for the destroyed families that psychopaths leave in their wake. I felt sympathy for Cassandra West. I was wrong. If there is a second Blight planned, I pray the police can stop this atrocity before it takes place, and that Allyson Miller is found safe and sound. God help the families of these new Beacons."

'When asked whether these developments might delay the imminent launch of the Blight simulation, Lake replied, "Absolutely not. People need to know the truth about the West family now more than ever. They need to experience what the world experienced, and what Cassandra West has been trying to shield us from since that terrible day ten years ago. With her conviction, we now have the right to use Cassandra West's full likeness and biometrics inside our sim. We will be updating our Blight sim accordingly to ensure that Cassandra Ann West – the *real* Cassandra Ann West, the second coming of the Vertex Ignis Cassandra Ann West – is ready for our launch."'

The anchor appeared back on screen and said, 'The EPP is asking for your help in preventing a second Blight. If you suspect a friend or family member may have been radicalized, please visit your local Earth+ police Terminal.

'Past Crimes shares rose thirty-two percent in end-of-day trading.'

'Lake has the EPP wrapped around in his finger,' Cassie said. 'They'll spread his lie because he's funded them for years. We need to get Aly Miller out of there. She knows the truth.'

'We may have a way to do that,' Hector said.

'How?'

'We have a mole inside Past Crimes,' Vivian replied. 'Somebody who's been working with us for about two years now. He's how we knew about your arrest. He knew Lake was planning something when you visited the park. He didn't know why, and he didn't know anybody would die. All we knew is that we had a very narrow window of time, and we needed to be ready.'

'Lake already had my AP programmed inside the Blight sim,' Cassie said. 'All he had to do was frame me and wait for my conviction to use it legally.'

'It's evil genius,' Vivian said. 'Right before the Blight sim goes live, Lake basically gets the media and the EPP to act as his publicist. The whole world believes you're the new Vertex Ignis, and if they subscribe to Past Crimes, they'll be able to see you inside the Blight sim.'

'Makes you wish he'd dedicated his "talents" elsewhere,' Cassie said. 'Maybe creating the world's greatest cup of coffee. Something a little less . . . evil.'

'Getting information out of that complex has been like trying to get a tank out of a mousehole,' Vivian said. 'Employees are scanned upon entry and exit to make sure they don't take anything with them. But you were, essentially, a ghost in the machine.'

'So you used me as a mule,' Cassie said, tapping the bandage on her aching leg.

'It was the only way.'

'So what did you smuggle out?'

'Code,' Hector said. 'Specifically, the master code for all Past Crimes simulations.'

Cassie looked at the screen. The code for each sim was marked by a green silo.

'Past Crimes has only released sixty-three sims,' Cassie said. 'There are sixty-four silos.'

'That's odd,' Hector said. He pressed a few keys. 'There's code in one silo that's never been made public. Looks like it can only be accessed by authorized users.'

'Maybe a sim they canceled?' Vivian said.

'I don't think so,' Cassie replied, 'It's green, which means it's active code but it's not live on their network. It's only accessible to specific users.'

'Why would they have an active sim they didn't release to the public?' Hector asked.

'I don't know,' Cassie said. 'But if there are sixty-three other silos, this means you have access to the Blight sim.'

Hector said, 'This also gives us a direct uplink to their servers. When Past Crimes launches a sim, the encrypted code is fed out across the globe, allowing everyone to access it when they log into Earth+. Now we have access to the code *before* it goes live. Which means we also have the ability to alter the code before it feeds out.'

'We can corrode billions of lines of code in minutes,' Hector said. 'So when the sim goes live, we can essentially tie a bomb to a rising aircraft. If they feed out corrupted code, it'll cost Lake billions.'

'This mole. You can get messages to him on the inside, right?'

'We can.'

'Good. Because I need you to coordinate with him.'

'Coordinate what?' Hector said.

'Aly Miller is still inside of that complex. She's the only one who can tell the world that Lake is behind all of this. He'll never let her out. So we need to get her the hell out of there.'

'And just how are you going to do that?' Hector said.

'I need you to find a way to smuggle me back inside Past Crimes.'

TWENTY-ONE

2:11 p.m.
Nine hours and forty-nine minutes to launch

Hector and Vivian laughed at the same time. They stopped once they realized Cassie wasn't joining in.

'You're serious,' Hector said.

'As a heart attack,' Cassie replied. 'Aly came with me to Past Crimes to find out who radicalized her father. I made her two promises: that I would find the truth and that I would keep her safe. I failed her. Now I need to fix that.'

'You realize going back in there, you'll end up dead or in prison,' Vivian said. 'And given the state of the prison system, I'm not sure which I'd prefer.'

'I don't care,' Cassie said. 'You help me get inside Past Crimes or I walk out that door right now, put my hands in the air and tell everyone that you've just committed industrial espionage against evil Walt Disney.'

'We would never let you walk out that door alive,' Vivian said.

'Then you have a pretty easy choice. Get me in. Or get out of my way.'

'Since I really don't want to have to kill you, I guess that doesn't leave us many options,' Hector said. 'We'll do it. But on one condition.'

'Which is?'

'I'm coming with you.'

'You are not,' Vivian and Cassie said at the same time.

'Non-negotiable,' Hector said. 'Viv, none of this matters if more people die. If we can prevent that and don't, then all of this is for nothing. Every life matters. Or no life matters.'

Vivian looked down, then said, 'All right.'

'I haven't agreed to this,' Cassie said.

'You go alone, you die.'

'I'm OK with dying.'

'Check your ego, Cassie. How are you going to infiltrate a multi-billion-dollar company alone when the whole world knows your face?'

'Well, when you put it like that. Welcome aboard.'

'Hector,' Vivian said, 'this isn't just about us. You know that.'

'I know,' he said. 'But she can't do this alone. And if getting this girl out safe means we can bring down Lake, it's everything we fought for.'

Vivian nodded reluctantly. 'All right.'

Cassie looked at the screen. 'Some of the code is red. Why?'

'Redlined code is code that was written but not used,' Hector said.

'Think of it like deleted scenes in old movies,' Vivian added. 'Lake and his team write millions of lines of code for each sim, but don't use all of it.'

'Is there any redlined code for the Blight sim?'

'I can filter the redline code by sim,' Hector said. 'Otherwise, it would probably take twenty or thirty years to do it manually.'

Cassie leaned in and saw that Hector had filtered the silos so that only the redlined code appeared on the screen. It was all gibberish, letters and numbers.

'So all of this,' she said, 'is material that Lake created for the Blight that won't be in the final sim released to the public.'

'Exactly,' Hector said.

'You said it's like deleted scenes. So can I see it?'

'You mean inside Earth+?'

'Yes.'

Hector tapped his lip. 'I should be able to isolate the redlined code and feed it directly into a visor. I don't know what this redlined code makes up. It could be hours. It could be minutes. It could be seconds.'

'But if Lake wanted it cut from the sim he releases to the public, it might have clues to the next Blight.'

'It might,' Vivian said. 'Or it could be an AP of a Beacon sitting on the toilet for twenty minutes.'

'One way to find out,' Cassie said. She put on a visor. 'Feed it through and send me in.'

'OK. Give me a second.' Hector tapped the screen a few times, and when Cassie blinked, she was back inside the Church of the Beacons. Or at least *part* of the church.

Three of the four walls were a bright light blue, and the wall behind Cassie didn't even exist, it was just an infinite gray, pixelated space. This code seemed to be a digital placeholder for the intricate designs Lake would eventually have in the final, polished sim. There were no pews. No fire. But then Cassie turned to her right and gasped.

There were still dozens of Wraps throughout the church, but whereas before the Wraps looked like real people, these Wraps looked like people who had been flayed alive. They were nothing but muscle and bone. No hair. No skin. She could see the muscles in their chests rising and falling with each breath. And while they had no skin, they all had eyes, eyes that seemed to float in lidless sockets. This wasn't a horror movie, she had to remind herself.

She remembered what Woolman had said. In order to create the most lifelike Augmented Personas, Past Crimes used actual biometrics to create layers of bone and muscle underneath the digital skin. This would ensure these APs moved and looked just like real people, not sprites or blocky video-game NPCs. These Wraps were like the church itself, unfinished digital placeholders for the Beacons that Lake would eventually design.

Lake had obviously begun to build the APs for this scene in the Blight sim but scrapped it before he got far enough to layer the Wraps with skin and features.

After a minute of silence, a Wrap appeared at the front of the church, standing on a blue riser and bracketed by two sedentary pillars of low-resolution blue fire. This was a very early build of the scene Cassie had witnessed back at Past Crimes, before all the details were baked in.

The Wrap said nothing. Just looked out among the congregation. It also had no skin, no hair, just a terrifying skull looking out over a sea of fellow skulls. The Vertex Ignis. But why would Lake have 'deleted' this scene from the finished version of the Blight?

'Beacons,' the Vertex Ignis said. 'Today we light the flames of eternity.'

But it wasn't Harris's voice that came from the Wrap's mouth. The voice was robotic yet still had inflections and intonations. As though someone had run their own voice through a synthesizer. The Wrap kept speaking. Someone had obviously used their own voice as the template for the simulated Vertex Ignis. But if Lake had the right to use Harris's voice, why wouldn't he just use that from the start?

Cassie pulled up her EPD and exited the sim. Her breathing was fast and raspy. She tried to slow it down but felt like she was hyperventilating.

'Easy,' Vivian said. 'Your Hyponatremia is getting worse.'

Hector brought her a cup of saltwater. Cassie swallowed it, then nearly coughed it all up.

'There's a voice inside that code,' Cassie said. 'I can record it on my EPD. When I get the recording, can you isolate and reverse engineer it to see who it belongs to?'

'I should be able to,' Hector said.

'OK. Hold on.'

Cassie went back inside. The Vertex Ignis continued his sermon in the same robotic voice. Cassie recorded thirty seconds on to her EPD, then left the sim again.

'I got the audio file,' Hector said. 'Hold on a minute. There are a dozen different levels here. I'll need to isolate the base. Give me a bit.'

Cassie caught her breath while Hector worked. After a few minutes, Hector said, 'OK. Think I got it. This was the original voice that was manipulated and placed back inside the redlined code.'

Hector played the audio. The Vertex Ignis said, 'Many of you have followed me for months. Some, for years. Our journey together ends today.'

'Holy shit,' Hector said. 'That's—'

'Crispin Lake. That's Crispin Lake's voice.'

'Why would Lake have used his own voice inside an early build for the Blight sim if he had the right to use your husband?' Vivian asked.

'I had the same question,' Cassie said. 'Hector, can you find out the date that redline code was created?'

'One sec,' Hector said. Cassie watched as Hector tapped more keys. 'That's strange. The creation date of this code is January fourth, 2037. Six months before the Blight took place. But that's impossible. How could it have . . .'

'The early builds of the Blight sim didn't use Harris,' Cassie said, 'because they were built *before* the Blight even took place. Lake knew the Blight was coming because *he planned it*. Lake used his own voice as a placeholder because Harris was still alive when Lake began to build the sim. *Crispin Lake* was the Vertex Ignis.'

'Oh my God,' Vivian said.

'At some point, Lake mapped Harris's voice, likeness and biometrics on to the digital placeholder. That's why this code was redlined. Once Harris was convicted, Lake could freely use his likeness and biometrics inside the sim. All he had to do was swap Harris for himself.'

'We need to get this to the police and the press,' Cassie said.

'Hold up,' Hector said. 'We obtained this code illegally. The EPP is basically on Lake's payroll. Nobody will believe we didn't steal this code and then manipulate it.'

'If we can get Aly out,' Cassie said, 'and get your mole to come out publicly, that might be enough to convince people.'

'It might,' Vivian said. 'Now we just need to find a way inside the—'

'Shhh,' Hector said, holding a finger to his lips. He held up a tablet for them to see. The screen showed the alleyway they'd pulled the car into. There were flashing lights at the street entrance. Cassie's breath caught in her chest as a police car pulled into the alley.

'They found us faster than I thought they would,' Hector said. 'None of this will matter if we're in prison or dead. We need to get the hell out of here *now*.'

TWENTY-TWO

3:01 p.m.
Eight hours and fifty-nine minutes to launch

Hector grabbed Cassie's hand and pulled her towards the back of the storeroom. As they went, he and Vivian grabbed as much as they could carry from the shelves and tossed it into a pair of backpacks. Vivian pushed metal shelving out of the way to reveal a door. She pressed her thumb on a keypad and it slid open.

'Come on,' she said, beckoning Cassie. Cassie went through the door, followed by Vivian. Hector went last, still typing on the tablet.

'Ninety seconds,' he said.

'Ninety seconds to what?' Cassie asked.

'Until this place is vaporized.'

'Is ninety seconds enough time?' Cassie asked as the door closed behind Hector.

'Depends how fast you move.'

The trio jogged downhill along a narrow corridor with a dirt floor and concrete walls.

'Where the hell are we?' Cassie said.

'This tunnel went down into the subway system,' Vivian replied. 'When public transportation became mostly obsolete, the tunnels were abandoned.'

As promised, a minute and a half later Cassie felt a rumble behind them and an intense wave of heat.

'Napalm?'

'You catch on quick.'

The corridor opened up into a large, circular space, lined with brick and held up by concrete beams. Rusted metal tracks led into the darkness. A hulking subway car lay on the tracks in front of them. The tunnel was filled with detritus, the tracks rusted and bent. Hector flicked a light on, illuminating the tunnel for fifty feet. 'Don't worry. These routes haven't been active since 2029.'

'Where do they go?' Cassie asked.

'Technically, they could take you anywhere within a fifty-mile radius of the city,' Vivian said. 'Thankfully, we're not going nearly that far.'

Piled next to the subway cars were thousands of broken and junked electronic devices. Enormous, chunky televisions from before paper-screen technology was perfected. Old Earth+ visors. Tablets and phones with cracked screens. Clunky drones with damaged rotors. Computers and desktops from back when Cassie was a young girl. They had to step carefully among the detritus.

'What is all this?' Cassie said.

'Once visors became more prevalent,' Hector said, 'and tech-nology rendered most of the old devices obsolete, the amount of electronic waste we produced outgrew what we could recycle or destroy. Subway tunnels became something of an old electronics graveyard.'

'Between new virus variants and the ease of working from home, revenue from public transportation dried up,' Vivian said. 'Subways went years without repairs. The cost of fuel for buses was ten times what the transit authorities took in fares.'

'Is that a . . . bus?' Cassie said. It was. Lodged on either side of a broken-down subway car was a pair of buses, the likes of which Cassie hadn't seen in twenty years. 'They junked entire buses down here?'

'Buses. Cars. Construction equipment. I think I've even seen a few jet engines. The cost of breaking things down is higher than the cost of just, well, leaving it. In this country alone, there are tens of thousands of abandoned subway tunnels reaching tens of thousands of miles. I'd venture to say most of them look just like this.'

'I had no idea,' Cassie said.

'Most people don't,' Vivian replied. 'Out of sight, out of mind.'

Cassie picked up a visor, careful to avoid its jagged, broken edges. It was a massive thing, nearly five pounds, looking more like a shoebox than one of the slim, sleek Theia visors she'd worn at Past Crimes.

'This was the first visor I ever owned,' Cassie said, turning it over in her hand. 'The first time I used it, it ran so hot it singed the hair on my temples off.' She tossed it back into the pile and continued on.

They walked for two hours in silence. Cassie's head throbbed. She drank more saltwater, which eased the pounding.

'Here we are,' Hector said.

At the end of the tunnel, a subway car was wedged against the brick, blocking off further progress. Hector and Vivian climbed up the steps and slid through the subway doors. They motioned for Cassie to follow. She shimmied through the empty car, its plastic seats blackened with age, poles rusted and flaking. At the far end of the subway, Hector slid a car door out of the way, revealing a low, narrow passage through the brick.

'Come on,' Vivian said. The three of them crawled through the passage. Hector stayed behind to slide the car door back into place. The passageway opened into a small room that held two metal cots, a generator, a small fridge and various supplies. Hector and Vivian dropped their backpacks and sat on one cot. They motioned for Cassie to take the other.

'Always helps to have a backup plan,' Vivian said. 'And a "Go" room.'

'How'd you get all this in here?' Cassie said.

Hector pointed to the ceiling. There was a large air duct, about five feet by five feet.

'We should be OK here for a little while,' he said.

'No,' Cassie replied. 'We need to go. The Blight sim launches at midnight.'

She stood up, but her head swam, as if her brain had been set on a spin cycle, and she fell back down on to the cot.

'You need rest,' Vivian said, pushing Cassie's head on to the cot. 'You don't do anyone any good if you suffer a debilitating Neural Flare before we even get to the complex.'

'Fine,' Cassie said. 'But just a little rest. Your mole. Can he help us get inside?'

'I hope so. I have a Lockbox on standby and I'll set up a meeting,' Hector said. 'It'll take a bit of time. Our mole rotates false Wraps to avoid clueing in Lake and his minions, like that lunkhead Wyatt. Should be enough time for you to get a little rest before we meet.'

'I don't know how I can rest right now.'

'Try,' Vivian said. 'Any more substantial Neural Flares and you risk permanent brain damage.'

'Close your eyes,' Hector said. 'I'll wake you when it's time for the meeting.'

'Fine. But I'm doing this under protest.' Cassie lay down on the cot. The mattress was thin and there was no pillow or blanket. 'This isn't all that comf . . .'

Cassie was asleep before she finished her sentence.

She felt someone pushing her. Rocking her body back and forth. Gentle, at first, then firmer.

'Go away.'

'Cassie? It's time.'

She opened her eyes. Vivian stood over her.

'I just fell asleep.'

'No, you've been out for three and a half hours.'

It hadn't felt like three and a half hours. Three and a half minutes, maybe. Still, she managed to sit up. Her head killed. Vivian brought

her more saltwater. She drank greedily. Vivian took a visor from her
backpack and handed it to Cassie.

'The meeting is set,' she said. 'Our mole is waiting for us in
Earth+. I'll patch you in.'

Cassie put the visor on and found herself in what appeared to be
an upscale hotel suite. There were four plush leather chairs set up
around a coffee table. She took a seat next to Hector and Vivian's
Wraps. A moment later, another Wrap appeared in the last chair.

The Wrap was a heavy-browed, stocky man with dark, frizzy
hair and an almost childlike face. He wore a blue work shirt over
a white T-shirt, with a tuft of curly chest hair poking out from the
collar. Cassie recognized the Wrap immediately.

'David Berkowitz,' she said. 'Son of Sam.'

'Hector,' the Son of Sam Wrap said. 'Ms. West. I was hoping
you were still alive.'

The Wrap's voice was high-pitched, slightly nasal, with a thick
Bronx accent. 'I hope the Wrap settings don't upset you,' he said.

'I think in our first meeting you came as Lee Harvey Oswald
without letting me know ahead of time,' Hector said. 'I thought I'd
interrupted some weirdo's secret JFK assassination sex fantasy.'

'Who are you really?' Cassie asked.

'Nice try,' the Berkowitz Wrap said. 'I can't stay long. The Blight
sim is scheduled to go live in less than twelve hours. The park is
absolutely packed. Security is high. I don't have much time. So let
me know how I can help.'

'Where is Aly Miller?' Cassie said.

'I don't know for certain,' Berkowitz said. 'But if she's still alive,
she's in R and D. That's the brain of the complex, where they
develop new sims, and it's where Lake keeps everything he doesn't
want the public to know about.'

'So how can we get inside?' Cassie asked.

'No idea,' Berkowitz replied. 'I don't have access.'

'Somebody must. Who would have access?'

'Off the top of my head? Maurice Wyatt. Stephen Woolman.
Maybe a few guards or technicians. But that's it.'

'So the billion-dollar question is how do we get into the park?'
Hector said. 'The main gate is out of the question. And there must
be a thousand cameras.'

'Lake likes to tell people he chose this spot in West Valley because
it's where Ted Bundy was arrested,' Berkowitz said. 'That's what

Lake says to market the complex, but it's not the real reason. The truth is that when Lake built Murderland, he needed an enormous amount of power to run it. Building both an entire electrical grid and generators to back it up was impossible given the cost of materials. Lake found an aerospace security and defense firm along the northwest edge of the Oquirrh Mountains that had shut down. They abandoned everything. Including their generators. Lake bought the land for pennies.'

'So how does this help us?' Cassie asked.

'There are underground access tunnels that run from the generators all the way inside the complex. If you can get into one of the access tunnels, it'll take you straight into the park.'

'So how do we get into those tunnels?' Hector asked.

'Each generator station has an access door. The doors themselves are locked with hand and retinal scanners, and there's security guarding each one. You'll need to circumvent the security – electrical and personnel.'

'What about the thingy you used on the cop car?' Cassie said to Hector. 'The EMP. Wouldn't that knock out the electrical security?'

'It could,' Hector said. 'But it would also knock out the generator. Wouldn't that be a problem?'

'The generators are for backup power only,' Berkowitz said. 'Ordinarily, the park is only at ten to twenty percent capacity, so we only need to keep a few running at a time. But with the park at full capacity, Lake will need them all operational. The generators are old. There are constant brownouts. One generator going offline temporarily won't raise eyebrows. The closest one is in sector four. I'll send the map to your EPD. Once you're through the access tunnel and inside the complex, I'll find you.'

'All right. So that takes care of the electrical security measures,' Hector said. 'But even if we shut down the electrical, there are still security personnel. We'll need a diversion at the generator station.'

'Let me handle that,' Vivian said.

'Why are you doing this?' Cassie said to Berkowitz. 'I'm sure Lake pays you well. Why risk your job and your neck to help us?'

Berkowitz thought for a moment, then said, 'When I started at Past Crimes, I was just . . . enraptured. I loved what Crispin Lake did, how he created new worlds and harnessed cutting-edge technology so anyone in the world could live history. I thought Lake was a disrupter. A revolutionary. But then he started donating millions of dollars to police funds and political campaigns, and then he pushed through Statute 486-16 and I realized he wasn't a revolutionary; he was using people. Lake has donated nearly fifty million dollars to the Earth Plus Police alone. And if that's what he's doing legally, it scares me to think what he might be doing illegally.'

'So why not quit?' Cassie said.

'Two reasons. The unselfish reason is that you can do more from the inside. I never would have been able to get Hector those codes if I wasn't working for Lake. The selfish reason is, as you said, Crispin Lake pays, and pays well. I have a family. The unemployment rate in Earth– is forty-eight percent, and lawyer algorithms have made me obsolete in Earth+.'

'It's the same playbook rich people have been running for years,' Vivian said. 'Use money to gain influence, use that influence to gain leverage over people who stand in your way, and crush anyone who resists. Lake just found a way to do it in the virtual world as well as the real one.'

'We have to get in there today,' Cassie said. 'There could be a second Blight in just hours. Thousands could die. There will be global chaos. We have to tell people who Crispin Lake really is. And if we don't get Aly out before the sim launches, I don't think we'll ever be able to. That doesn't give us much time to get inside the park, find her and get her out.'

'Lake is focused on the sim launch and park celebration,' Berkowitz said. 'His attention is spread thin. Security will be occupied dealing with the thousands of parkgoers. Use the chaos to get lost. Just be inside the park by five thirty. I have a meeting at six p.m., and my lack of attendance would not go unnoticed.'

'We'll be there,' Hector said.

'Good luck, Mr. Ruiz. Ms. Adair. Ms. West. I'll be waiting for you. Move fast and stay hidden.'

'Thanks,' Cassie said. 'Whoever you are.'

The mole smiled. 'Son of Sam. At your service.'

The mole departed the Lockbox. Cassie, Vivian and Hector followed suit.

The hotel room faded away and Cassie found herself back in the Go room. As Cassie stood up, her head spun and her legs buckled underneath her. Hector managed to get his arms under Cassie before she hit the ground.

'How much time do you spend inside Earth+?' Hector asked, easing Cassie on to the bed.

'I don't know. Most of it?'

'You're suffering from adrenal insufficiency and antidiuretic hormone secretion,' he said. 'The amount of sodium in your bloodstream is diluted. That causes your cells to swell which, to put it simply, wreaks havoc on your brain, causing Neural Flares.'

'You need sodium and rest,' Vivian said. 'The first we can help with. The second – well, it's going to be a long day.'

Vivian pulled a bag out from under the cot. She took out a black medical kit and a bag of IV fluid. She hooked the fluid up to a nail on the wall then opened the bag and took out a needle. She swabbed Cassie's arm with alcohol, tied a rubber tube around her bicep, found a vein, and inserted the needle.

'Got the vein on your first try,' Cassie said, impressed. 'When I had blood drawn during fertility treatments, it always took my doctor at least three or four tries. He always claimed I had tiny veins. I think he just didn't know what he was doing.'

'I was in medical school when Drayden Downs killed my mother,' Vivian said, as she connected the fluid bag to the needle in Cassie's arm. 'I wanted to be a thoracic surgeon. I would have been a good one, too. But when my mother died, I just lost it. It was like my brain wasn't connected to my body anymore. My hands shook every time I picked up a scalpel.'

'Your hands weren't shaking right now,' Cassie said.

Vivian smiled. 'It was like a switch went off,' she replied. 'Helping other people who were lost and hurting and angry, like I was. One day, I couldn't put a straw in a water bottle. The day I met Hector, when he told me about his sister, I felt like I hadn't just found my person, but my purpose. From then on, my fingers have felt as nimble as the day I started med school. I was never a big believer in fate, but sometimes the universe works in ways that make you question everything you thought you knew.'

Vivian held her palm out to Cassie. There were no shakes. No tremors. It was as if her hand had been frozen in time.

'Anyway,' Vivian continued, tapping the bag of fluid, 'this is sodium chloride. It should ease the Flares while we get ready.'

Cassie took Vivian's hand and squeezed it as hard as she could. Which, at that moment, wasn't terribly hard.

'Thank you,' she said. 'For this. For all of it.'

'Don't thank me yet. You might be heading off to die.'

'You would have been an amazing doctor,' Cassie said, 'but your bedside manner is absolute shit.'

Vivian laughed. 'I kind of like you, Cassandra Ann West. Let's see if we can't keep you alive until tomorrow.'

Cassie took a deep breath. 'Tomorrow feels like such a long time away. Aly could be dying right now. And I'm just sitting here.'

'If you tried to save anyone right now in the condition you're in,' Vivian replied sternly, 'you'd both be dead.'

'She could be dead already,' Cassie said. 'This whole thing could be for nothing. I don't even know who or what to believe anymore.'

'What do you mean?' Vivian asked.

Cassie looked at Vivian. Her gaze was unsteady. 'I've spent the last ten years telling people I'm not crazy,' she said. 'But what if I am? What if what they're saying happened is what happened, and I . . .' Cassie trailed off.

Vivian shook her head. 'Stop that. You have hope. Keep it alive.'

Cassie looked up at Vivian. 'Why?'

'Because hope is a compass. It always leads you in the right direction.'

'I haven't had hope in a long, long time,' Cassie said. 'Think it's too late for someone like me to find it?'

'It's never too late to find it,' Vivian said. 'Now rest up. That bag will be done in an hour.'

'Then let's go in an hour,' she said. 'And I leave Past Crimes with Aly Miller. Or not at all.'

TWENTY-THREE

4:10 p.m.
Seven hours and fifty minutes to launch

Once the bag of sodium chloride was empty, Vivian unhooked the tube from her arm, placed a piece of gauze over the hole and taped it down. Physically, Cassie felt better than she had in a long time. At some point, she'd stopped taking care of herself. Maybe she hadn't just forgotten how to live, but she'd refused to remember.

'How're you feeling?' Hector asked.

'Like I got flattened by a truck and then re-inflated,' Cassie said. Vivian handed her a cup of foul-smelling green liquid. 'What is this?'

'I call it Brain Fertilizer,' Hector said.

'Sounds delightful. What's in it?'

'Basically, a mixture of ingredients that are high in electrolytes, sodium and assorted nutrients. Great for Hyponatremia, Neural Flares, and raging hangovers.'

Cassie took a sip. It tasted like sugary vinegar cut with formaldehyde.

Cassie forced herself to down the entire cup, then shuddered. 'If I'm alive when this is over, I'm drinking nothing but champagne for a year.'

'Take a look at this,' Hector said.

He handed her a tablet that showed what appeared to be satellite imagery of the Past Crimes complex.

'This is a time-lapse video of the last two hours,' Hector said.

Cassie watched as thousands of small, black grains of sand – people – scurried about Murderland. Small black dots filled the outline of the crime scene victim, like ants in a colony.

'I've never seen this many people in the park before,' Vivian said. 'It's like the Fourth of July meets *Helter Skelter.*'

Hector moved the tablet's satellite view to an area a few miles west of the Past Crimes complex. He zoomed in on a large fenced-in area with a huge metal box in the center.

'This is generator four, the one Mr. Berkowitz suggested we target. We've counted eight people, a mix of guards and technicians. Thankfully, there are more of the latter than the former.'

'So we use the EMP device to shut the generator and access security down.'

'That's the plan,' Hector said. He unzipped his backpack and took out the megaphone-gun they'd used to disable the police car.

'Can I see it?' Cassie said.

Hector held it out. Cassie took it. The device was heavy. There was a small trigger. Cassie touched it, and the moment she did, Hector grabbed it away from her like she was a child picking up a butcher knife.

'You accidentally set that off, you might as well broadcast our location to the EPP.'

'Think I'll let you handle all the James Bond devices,' Cassie said.

'You have less than two and a half hours to get into the park,' Vivian said. 'After that, the mole won't be able to help you.'

Cassie looked at Vivian. 'Sure you aren't coming?'

'I need to be here to keep the guards off your asses once you get to the generator. And Hector told me someone should stay behind in case . . . well, you know.'

'In case our plan goes to shit so someone knows the truth,' Hector said to Cassie. 'But I intend to make it back. For both of them.'

'Both of them?' Cassie said. Vivian touched her abdomen gently.

'For both of them,' Hector said.

'I'll make sure he gets back to you,' Cassie said. 'To both of you.'

Vivian smiled. 'Thank you.'

'So what's the diversion you have planned? Some sort of satellite laser? Maybe a nuclear-powered hovertank?'

Vivian just smiled and said, 'Sometimes the old-fashioned diversions work the best. Now let's get you two out there.'

'We're really doing this, aren't we?' Cassie said.

'We are,' replied Hector.

Cassie took a long, deep breath. Her head still throbbed, but the pain was manageable. It was all becoming real. The last ten years of her life were coming down to the next few hours.

'I just want you to know I'm sorry,' Cassie said to Hector. 'About Joy. I could have done more for your family. For other families. I *should* have done more.'

'Remember that if we survive,' Hector said.

'I will,' she said. 'Just promise me one thing.'

'You got it.'

'If anything happens to me, promise that you'll find Aly. She knows the truth. Make sure Lake pays for what he's done.'

'I promise,' Hector said.

'Me too,' added Vivian.

'OK,' Cassie said, standing up. 'Now give me another cup of that fermented acid and let's break into evil Disneyland. Just one question. How do we actually get to the generator? You blew up our car, remember?'

'I hope you're a strong bike rider,' Hector said.

'Rode ten miles to and from work every day for nine years,' Cassie said.

'And I hope you don't mind a haircut,' Vivian added.

'A haircut?'

'That's right,' she said, holding up the Devil's Fingernail. 'Unfortunately, I don't have any scissors.'

TWENTY-FOUR

4:21 p.m.
Seven hours and thirty-nine minutes to launch

With Cassie trembling in fear, Vivian used the Devil's Fingernail to sear off about six inches of hair from her earlobe to her nape, creating a very unfortunate-looking bob.

'Is that *really* necessary?' Cassie said. 'I had short hair in college and swore I'd never go back.'

'Extenuating circumstances,' Vivian said. 'Every little bit we can do to make you look just a little less like you did yesterday helps. It could mean someone sees you and doesn't turn back for a second glance. Because that second glance could end this before it starts.'

'Short hair it is, then,' Cassie said. 'College me would be laughing her ass off.'

They then used a stepladder to climb into the air duct in the ceiling and, after fifteen minutes of shimmying, exited out to the street where there were two bicycles and two helmets chained to a fence.

Cassie went to adjust her bike, when Vivian said, 'I wouldn't do that yet. Step back.'

She did. Hector took out his phone and tapped it twice. He approached the bikes, leaned in as though listening for something, then said, 'Good to go.'

'What did you just do?'

'Decent bikes go for ten grand on the black market,' he said, climbing on to his. 'These were electrified. No sense having them if anyone with a lockpick can steal them.'

'Thanks for the heads-up. I've been electrified enough this week.'

Cassie put on her helmet, which covered her unfortunate haircut. Hector handed her a pair of oversized riding goggles.

'Better people think you just have terrible fashion sense than that you're Cassandra West,' Vivian said.

'The generator is about six miles away,' Hector said. 'If we don't get stopped, we can cover it in forty-five minutes. You ready?'

'No. But let's do it anyway.'

After ten years of desperately trying to be seen and heard, Cassie's life – and the lives of many more – depended on her avoiding both.

Hector and Vivian shared a passionate kiss. Cassie watched their embrace with an ache, remembering what that kind of intimacy felt like. Missing it.

'I'll make sure he gets back to you,' Cassie said.

'You come back too,' Vivian said. 'Now get moving. You don't have much time.'

'We'll see you tomorrow,' Hector said.

'You'd better.'

They rode off and quickly merged on to the highway with dozens of other bike riders. Where cars used to sit bumper to bumper, bikes sped down the road. And with so many riding, nobody paid Hector or Cassie any attention.

Hector rode in front, and Cassie followed. Her legs felt stiff, her head still a bit woozy. The roads were cracked, flowers and trees and weeds springing up from beneath. There was something peaceful, even beautiful, about the way nature seemed to be reclaiming the earth. It was as if the migration into the digital world meant the earth could now recover the spaces it had been driven from, without fear that it would be taken back by bulldozers and blowtorches. People didn't care much about what happened to the world they'd largely abandoned. Mother Nature could have it all back.

Enormous screens hung from buildings that overlooked the roads, forcing riders to view nonstop advertisements as they pedaled. To Cassie's horror, every single screen seemed to be promoting the Blight simulation.

The ad showed videos from all over the world, fires raging in Los Angeles, Sydney, Hong Kong, London, Berlin and more. The ad ended with a photo of Harris from their wedding, beaming with joy.

The screen turned red, and Crispin Lake appeared, thirty feet tall, wearing a red-and-black suit, holding his hand out as though beckoning the viewer to join him.

Beneath Lake, twenty-foot-high type read:

THE FIRES STILL BURN. THE BLIGHT IS COMING. THE VERTEX IGNIS AWAITS ON 7/19/47.

'The crimes may be in the past,' Lake said, 'but you can experience them today.'

Then the screen dissolved into the ubiquitous Past Crimes logo.

'Three miles out,' Hector said, raising his voice over the wind. 'Stay focused.'

Then the Past Crimes advertisement faded away. A news report began. Cassie nearly fell off her bike when she saw an enormous image of herself, hogtied and being carried out of the Past Crimes complex by Maurice Wyatt. Her face was full of rage, the veins in her neck bulging, lips curled back in an angry sneer. The headline below her photo read:

Cassandra Ann West, 'Red Widow' of Blight mastermind Harris West, still at large. Has she carried on her husband's dark agenda?

'Authorities caution that if you see Ms. West,' the anchor said gravely, 'consider her armed and very dangerous. Do not attempt to approach her. If you believe your friends or loved ones may have been radicalized by Ms. West, please visit your local Earth+ police Terminal immediately.'

Stay calm, Cassie thought. *Stay calm. I'm just breaking into a billion-dollar company with more people looking for me than Harrison Ford in that old movie where the one-armed guy killed his wife. Aly would know its name. She loved the classics. Just let me stay alive long enough to find her and maybe we'll get to watch it.*

At that moment, Cassie noticed a bike to her right was keeping pace with her. Her heart began to beat in time with the spinning wheels. There was no way he could recognize her, was there? Her hair and face were hidden. Her clothes were Vivian's. But still, the rider seemed to be motioning for her to acknowledge him.

She looked ahead at Hector. He either hadn't noticed or was pretending not to. Then the man pointed at her bike. He shouted something Cassie couldn't hear. She was about to panic. What would this guy do if he recognized her? Would they have to incapacitate him? She'd promised not to hurt anyone, but if it was this guy versus thousands who could die in another Blight . . .

He shouted at her again. She yelled back, 'I'm sorry, what?'

He yelled louder. She heard him this time, and her heart slowed. 'Your back tire needs air!'

She looked back and, sure enough, the tire was going flat. She'd been so distracted by the ads she hadn't even felt it. Cassie gave him a quick thumbs up and shouted, 'Thank you!'

The man waved, then sped off. When he was far away, Hector turned back.

'I almost had a heart attack just now,' he said. 'He didn't recognize you?'

'Just pointed out a flat tire,' she said. 'Never been so happy to have a flat.'

'We don't have time to get it pumped. Just a little further. We're almost there.'

They turned off the main road and headed towards the plains that rode along the northwest border of the Oquirrh Mountains. The tire made the ride more difficult, and she had to concentrate in order to avoid wiping out on the gravelly roads. The remnants of an aerospace company dotted the brown landscape, abandoned planes ripped apart for their metal and engines, trucks whose gas tanks had gone dry long ago. There were dozens of small generators, large warehouses and shacks, and several fenced-in areas with large generators.

'There,' Hector said, pointing out into the distance. He slowed his bike to a stop on the side of the road. Cassie pulled up next to him. He handed her a pair of high-magnification binoculars. 'That's our generator.'

She could see a large, square container inside a ten-foot-high metal fence. The fence itself looked rusted, but almost uniformly so, as though it had been cosmetically aged to fit in with the rest of the abandoned buildings. But the gray metal generator inside looked like it could have been installed yesterday. Lake had kept it in tip-top condition.

'It's about half a mile away,' Hector said. 'We go on foot from here.'

Hector opened his backpack. He had the EMP gun, Devil's Fingernail, two thermoses filled with the disgusting Brain Fertilizer concoction, sodium tablets, a cloned cell phone and other assorted items that looked decidedly unsafe.

'Some of these we'll need if we actually make it inside the complex,' Hector said. 'The others, let's pray we won't.'

'What's that?' Cassie said, pointing to a syringe capped with a plastic tip and wrapped in gauze.

'Succinylcholine,' Hector said. 'It's a pretty powerful nerve-blocking agent. Just in case. This is a concentrated dose, so only use it if you really need to knock someone out quick. I hope you don't have a fear of needles.'

'I was on fertility hormones for four years,' Cassie said. 'I've injected more drugs into my stomach than you have in your whole life.'

'Fair enough,' Hector said. He handed Cassie a small black earbud. 'Put this in.'

Cassie did. The foam expanded, nestling perfectly into her ear canal. Hector did the same.

'Viv, can you hear me?' he said.

'Gotcha,' came the reply from Vivian. 'Cassie, say something.'

'Something.'

'All right. You're good,' Vivian said. 'I might lose connection when you're in the access tunnel or if you're in a building with jammers. If you don't hear from me, assume you're on your own. Just make sure to stay away from anyone who doesn't like you. Which is everyone.'

'I've been staying away from people who don't like me for ten years,' Cassie said. 'I can handle a few hours.'

'I'd better see you both again,' Vivian said. 'I'm not raising this kid alone.'

'I'll make sure you don't,' Cassie said.

'You know, this girl is tougher than she looks,' Hector said with a smile.

'Just remember you need to be *in* the park by five thirty,' Vivian said. 'Otherwise, you're stranded.'

'We'll be there,' Hector said. 'You ready?'

'As I'll ever be,' Cassie said.

They left their bikes behind an abandoned building and headed toward the generator.

There was no turning back.

TWENTY-FIVE

4:42 p.m.
Seven hours and eighteen minutes until launch

Suddenly, Cassie was alone in the middle of Utah with a man she barely knew. She didn't have time to think about how in the hell she'd ended up here. She could either overthink the insanity of her current situation and freeze, possibly damning both Aly Miller and thousands of others to their deaths, or she could move.

She moved.

Cassie and Hector walked swiftly towards the generator station, keeping to the shadows alongside the abandoned shacks. The air was dry and windy, the sun hot and bright. When they were a few hundred yards away, Hector took out his binoculars and scanned the generator station.

'I see three people inside,' he said. 'They're unarmed. I don't think they're security.'

'That's going to change pretty quickly,' she said.

'Yes, it is.'

The fence around the station was ringed with barbed wire.

'How do we get in?' she asked.

'The fence is probably electrified, but the blast should take care of that. Just looking for the right place for us to get in . . . there.' Hector pointed to several large spools of cable inside the fence. 'We cut a hole, use those to cover it back up from the other side.'

Hector crept forward and Cassie followed. The electric hum from the generator grew louder as they got closer.

'Over there,' he said. She could see a metal door embedded in a rock outcropping, a red light blinking above a panel. 'That's the access tunnel.'

Hector took the EMP from his backpack. 'When this goes off,' he said, 'we have to move with a purpose.'

'And I was going to take the scenic route.'

He raised the EMP, pointed it in the direction of the generator and whispered, 'No turning back.'

'No turning back.'

Then Hector pressed the trigger.

At first, nothing happened. Cassie wondered if the device had failed. Her mind swam trying to think of how else they could get into Past Crimes, but she came up blank. But then she heard it. Or precisely, didn't hear it. The electric hum of the generator. It was gone.

'Time to go,' Hector said.

He grabbed her hand and they sprinted forward. They knelt down beside the fence and Hector took the Devil's Fingernail from his bag.

'One second,' Cassie said. She picked up a small twig and tossed it gently at the fence. Nothing happened. 'Just making sure.'

Twenty-two seconds later, Hector cut a three-by-three hole, just large enough for them to crawl through. Hector slid through first, pushed the spools out of the way, then helped Cassie through. Once they were both inside, they pushed the spools back into place to block the hole.

'The hell happened?' came a voice from the other side of the generator.

'Goddamn thing fritzed out again,' came another voice. 'The amount of power we're using today, I told Woolman to run diagnostics on all the generators *before* the launch. He's gonna be pissed, and I am *not* taking the blame for this.'

The other man spoke into what must have been some sort of communications device. 'Yeah, hi, Mr. Woolman, it's Billingham over at generator four. The power here just conked out. Second time this month. No, that's not my responsibility, sir. I'm not sure whose it is; I figured it was yours. Yeah, send some people over and we'll get it back up. Thank you, sir. Sorry to bother you. I know it's a big day.'

Now all they had to do was wait. Every heartbeat was as loud as a drum, and every breath as loud as thunder. Several minutes later, they heard a door open, then slam shut. Cassie peeked her head out. The red light beside the access tunnel door was off. Two men were standing near the entrance. They both had guns strapped to their chests. There was no way they could get to the door without being seen.

Come on, move, she thought. Hector put his hand on her shoulder as if reading her mind. He widened his eyes and nodded. *Stay calm.*

Then Cassie heard another sound. An electric humming. Her heart stopped. If the generator came back online too soon, they'd be locked out of the access tunnel. But then she realized the sound wasn't a humming. It was a whirring. Rotors. A drone.

She looked up and saw a drone approaching from the northeast, about twenty feet above the ground.

'What in the hell?' one of the technicians said.

'Who ordered lunch?' said another.

Cassie watched as the drone came to a stop above the generator station. It hovered in the air, then its hatch slid open and a container fell from the sky, attached to a small red parachute. The package floated to the ground and the parachute draped itself atop the box. Cassie took out her binoculars. There was a logo on the chute. It looked like a . . . pizza?

One of the technicians unwrapped the parachute and opened the delivery container. Three pizza boxes slid out. He plucked a piece of paper from one of the boxes and read a note. 'For helping us get to the big day. Chow down. CL.'

One of the men said, 'How about that? I always thought Lake was a giant asshole. Maybe I was wrong. He's only a medium asshole.'

The guards and technicians descended on the boxes like ravenous vultures.

Hector tapped Cassie on the shoulder again and mouthed, *Now.*

They crept around the generator towards the door. They were twenty feet away. Fifteen. Ten.

And then she heard it. An electric crackle, low, but unmistakable. The power to the station was coming back on.

Without thinking, Cassie dashed towards the access tunnel door. She gripped the handle, said *Please God* under her breath and turned it. The handle rotated. Hector helped her pull the heavy door open and they slid inside. The door shut behind them with a *whump*. And then they were alone in the darkness.

TWENTY-SIX

4:59 p.m.
Seven hours and one minute to launch

The darkness was so thick Cassie couldn't see her hand in front of her face.

Her breathing, which had seemed loud as they made their way towards the generator station, now sounded like cannon blasts. She had to remind herself that this was all in her head. Her breathing could not wake the dead, and her heartbeat could not be heard through the rock, steel and concrete.

Still, this was absolute madness. Before this week, Cassie could count on two hands the number of times she'd left her apartment in ten years. She was not some 'Found' revolutionary like Hector or Vivian, and she was not some trained operative who could snap a person's femur using nothing but a toothpick.

When you're inside the madness, she thought, *you might as well keep going.*

'Viv, can you hear me?' Hector said. There was no response. He looked at Cassie. 'We're on our own.'

He took out two flashlights and handed one to Cassie. Their strong beams illuminated the void, enough to make out the tunnel's dimensions. The access tunnel was about twenty feet wide and fifteen feet high, bracketed by concrete walls and an unpaved rock floor. Steel cables ran along the ceiling. There was no ventilation to speak of, and within seconds Cassie could feel a river of sweat trickling down her back.

There was a small electric car about the size of an old-school golf cart plugged into the wall outside the tunnel entrance. Cassie inspected it but didn't see a key or any sort of FOB to get it running.

'That's what the guards use to get from one end to the other,' she said. 'Would save us a lot of time if we could get it running.'

'Not worth the risk,' Hector said. 'Anyone sees this thing missing, we have a not so welcoming party waiting for us at the other end.

We go on foot. Keep the flashlight low. We don't know if someone might be coming from the other side.'

'You sound like you've done this before.'

'Nothing like this,' Hector said. 'Nothing with these kinds of stakes.'

They set off. Cassie kept the flashlight angled at the ground like Hector said. She walked carefully, the rocks crunching under her feet. Every few minutes, they would stop, listen, try to hear if anyone else was inside the tunnel. It must have been at least a hundred degrees. There was no air conditioning, no air to speak of. It felt as though they were walking deeper into an oven. Every breath felt heavy, every step like she was wading through soup. Sweat leaked from every pore.

'I don't get GPS down here,' Hector said. 'Either this tunnel has jammers or Lake had them installed.'

An hour into the walk, Cassie began to feel claustrophobic. She began to shine the flashlight further ahead, drawing Hector's ire, hoping to see a glimpse of a door, an auxiliary tunnel, anything other than the endless cave. She saw nothing.

Hector checked his watch. 'We're taking too long,' he said. 'It's already after five. We have less than half an hour or we lose the mole.'

They picked up their pace. Cassie's leg throbbed. Her head pounded. She pressed on.

There had to be an end. *Had* to. Her breathing became more ragged, wetter. The tunnel felt like it was closing in around her. She knew it was just her mind playing tricks and her body responding in kind, but still, she had to get the hell out of this place.

Then she saw it. A few hundred yards away. What looked like an outline in the black. A door-shaped outline. That had to be it. The exit. Thank *God*.

Cassie picked up her pace, feeling less like a human and more like a sweaty mess of frayed nerve endings. She could see three electric carts plugged into charging ports, two on one side of the door and one on the other. There was an empty spot where the technicians had taken the one they'd seen at the other end.

'I think I'm getting a signal,' Hector said with a smile. He tapped his ear. 'Viv? Viv, can you hear me? Hello?'

Vivian's broken voice came over the earpieces. 'Hec . . . Cas . . . hear . . . signal . . . time . . .'

Then Cassie heard the unmistakable sound of squealing metal. The access door was being opened from the outside.

She grabbed Hector and swung him against the wall as the door creaked open. She flattened herself next to him, feeling the rock wall digging into her back. She clicked her light off and held her breath. The door opened slowly, coming within an inch of their noses. She could feel Hector next to her, his arm slick with sweat. Their eyes met. For the first time, she saw fear in his.

Footsteps. Two people entered the access tunnel.

'No way Lake drone-dropped pizza to the station,' said a woman's voice. 'I bet it was that kiss-ass Woolman. Always trying to get on the boss's good side.'

'Given how much money he's going to make off the Blight sim,' a man said, 'he could have at least splurged for, I don't know, lobster?'

'I wouldn't eat anything that came out of the water,' she said. 'I used to work in maritime security. If you see what they dump into the oceans these days, you'd never eat a fish again.'

'Billingham said the generator came back online. I don't see why they need us.'

'Because in a few hours this place is going to use up more power than Dubai and Times Square put together, and we need to make sure they don't conk out again,' she said. 'Just drive slow. If we're lucky, we can stretch this out. I want to spend as little time as possible inside the park today. That place is a goddamn zoo, and I am *not* getting trampled to death by a tourist wearing a Ted Bundy mask.'

Cassie heard the sound of shoes on metal and realized they were climbing into one of the carts. The access door had already begun to swing back, revealing Cassie and Hector inch by inch, but thankfully the technicians were focused on the tunnel ahead. Cassie hadn't taken a breath in nearly a minute. She could feel the blood pounding in her temples. Her lungs ached for air.

'Hold on to your butt,' the man said sarcastically. With a faint electric whir, the cart sped off. The door closed behind them. Cassie stayed plastered to the wall until the cart's headlights disappeared around a curve. Then she allowed herself a grateful breath.

'You OK?' she said to Hector. He nodded.

'Good reflexes, West. Thanks.'

Cassie took a moment to gather herself, taking slow breaths and letting her pulse steady.

'Here we are,' she said. Hector grabbed the door handle and pulled the access door open. Then Cassie stepped into the daylight of the Past Crimes complex.

The moment the sunlight hit her eyes, Cassie felt a hand grip her shoulder from behind. Before she could scream, another hand covered her mouth.

TWENTY-SEVEN

5:36 p.m.
Six hours and twenty-four minutes to launch

Before she could react, a voice said, 'Quiet. You're late.' Cassie turned to see the face of Salman Jalal. The attorney. The guy who kept looking at her funny during her arrest. Cassie wondered why the hell Crispin Lake's lawyer was there when Cassie had supposedly killed the guard inside the Maternity Ward. Now she had her answer.

The access tunnel had led them right outside the Wuornos Wave Pool. Cassie's eyes widened. The park was absolutely packed. Hundreds of people were bobbing up and down in the water as the killer's weather-beaten face glowered at them. Every few seconds, Wuornos's mouth would open and more water would pour into the pool, people shrieking with delight as the waves rushed over them.

'It's madness here. Put these on,' Jalal said. He handed them both a Past Crimes sweatshirt and logo hat. Hector tucked Cassie's shortened hair under the brim. Then Jalal handed them each an Earth+ visor. 'They're not logged in, so the lenses will be transparent. The less people see of your face, the better. Especially you, Ms. West. I've never seen this many people in the park before. Lake outdid himself. And that's saying something.'

'Thank you,' Hector said, slipping the visor on. 'For everything you've done.'

'We still have a lot to do,' Jalal said. He sniffed the air.

'Though I'm afraid I can't do anything about your general lack of hygiene.'

'Excuse me?' Cassie whispered.

'You two smell like you've been marinating in swamp water. Now come on. And hold hands. You're a normal loving couple enjoying a trip to Murderland courtesy of Crispin Lake.'

'Honey,' Hector said, holding out his hand.

'Sweetie,' Cassie said, taking it.

They followed Jalal into the complex. Cassie couldn't remember the last time she'd seen this many people in person. There were thousands upon thousands swarming the park. Every ride had a line a mile long, everyone carried gift bags, everyone had food in their hands, gleeful and enraptured by the manufactured carnage. Jalal led them through Murderer's Row and into Grifter's Gulch. The streets were lined with fake dollar bills featuring the faces of the most infamous swindlers in history, and the cobblestones were painted green, as though the Yellow Brick Road had been built by an investment banker.

There were families pushing strollers, couples walking arm in arm. People wearing Charles Manson masks posed for photos next to the eight-foot bronze statue of Bernie Madoff himself outside the Museum of Thieves and Swindlers.

Cassie watched the tourists through the visor, waiting for the terrifying moment someone recognized her. Thankfully, everyone was quite preoccupied with the attractions.

'Tonight is going to be epic,' Jalal said. 'I hear they're going to have a firework display that looks just like Harris West. Isn't that wild?'

He widened his eyes, letting them know to play along. They walked at an unhurried pace, just a normal couple enjoying a leisurely stroll through the Disneyland of Death.

'Oh, yeah,' Cassie said. 'Nothing like an expensive firework display to celebrate the anniversary of a mass murder.'

Hector squeezed her hand lightly.

'I know what you mean,' Jalal said. 'I'm going to broadcast the whole thing so my parents in Mumbai can watch it live. They're big Harris West fans.'

'I'm definitely going to need a triple espresso to stay awake until midnight,' Hector said, loudly. 'I've been waiting for this sim for such a long time. Can't believe it's going live tonight!'

'It'll be epic,' Cassie said. 'And there's nobody I'd rather experience it with than you, honey.' Hector smiled, playing along.

Throughout the park were holographic advertisements for the brand-new Blight simulation, as countdown clocks ticked away.

MEET THE VERTEX IGNIS IN
6 HOURS 12 MINUTES 19 SECONDS

Everywhere Cassie looked, her husband's face stared back at her. People were taking pictures next to holograms of Harris. Some were taking selfies pretending to kiss him. Others held up lighters. Pretending to set fires like the Beacons had ten years ago.

Hector squeezed her hand again, as if reading her mind. *Stay focused.*

Jalal turned back and mouthed, *Keep moving*. He led them to a doorway on the side of a building in Grifter's Gulch along the Charles Ponzi Promenade. Jalal pressed his palm against a scanner, at which point a small panel slid open revealing a retinal scanner. He pressed his face to the optical lens, and after another scan, the door opened.

They entered a glass-walled hallway, portraits of history's most famous con men and women flashing on the glass like apparitions. Jalal led them to an office door with his name on it. He did another palm and retinal scan, then opened the door and ushered them inside. Jalal's office was plainly furnished, with a thin desktop computer, a few air tablets and floating photos of his wife, children and parents.

Jalal said, 'That was the longest twenty minutes of my life.'

'I think I'm going to throw up,' Cassie said.

'Please don't,' Jalal replied. 'The last thing we need is to be interrupted by the cleaning staff.'

'Thank you,' Hector said. 'I know how much of a risk you're taking.'

'We all are,' Jalal said. 'By the way, I'm sorry about your leg, Ms. West. It was the only way.'

'I never thought I'd say "I understand" about being stabbed, but . . . I understand.'

Hector and Cassie placed their bags on the floor and sat down to catch their breath.

'You don't look much like David Berkowitz,' Hector said to Jalal.

'I'll take that as a compliment. Now, are you two OK?' he asked.

'Emotionally or physically?' Cassie said. 'Because both have been better.'

'Well, I hope you can push through it. There's more going on here today than even I knew.'

'What do you mean?' Cassie said.

'This morning, Woolman's team began a system-wide update of all the Augmented Persona codes in our sims,' Jalal said. 'Thousands of them. It had to have been in the works for a long time. Maybe years.'

'What does that mean?' Cassie said. 'And why today of all days?'

'I don't know yet,' Jalal replied. 'AP codes are updated and debugged fairly frequently. Sometimes they stop responding to visitors inside the sim, or we need to add more dialogue trees, or we license biometrics or likenesses we didn't previously have rights to use. When that happens, we edit each individual AP code, then reinsert the modified code back into the sim. But this isn't just one AP. It's *all* of them. Every single sim, and thousands of APs. Including your husband.'

'Why would they alter Harris's AP code before the sim even launches?'

'Again, I don't know,' Jalal said. 'But it means that the sim they release to the public might be very different from the sim anybody has seen or tested so far.'

'You said they changed the code when they added new biometrics or likenesses,' Cassie said. 'Lake had a "placeholder" Cassie in the Blight sim. Now that I've been convicted, he can legally use my likeness and biometrics without my permission.'

Hector said, 'That would mean Lake has been planning to pin the second Blight on you for a long time.'

'But why?' Cassie said.

'Lake is a brilliant businessman,' Jalal said. 'He knows if you have a big hit on your hands, it's never too early to start work on the sequel.'

'You think he's planning a sim based on the second Blight. Which hasn't even occurred yet,' Hector said.

'He started building the first Blight sim before July nineteenth, 2037,' Cassie said. 'That's absolutely what he's doing.'

Jalal checked his watch. 'Good thing you got here when you did. We have a company-wide all-hands-on-deck Lockbox meeting that's scheduled to start in five minutes. If I was late, Lake would know something was wrong. I'd be locked out of our system in the blink of an eye.'

'What's the meeting about?' Hector asked.

'I don't know. The invite simply says: "Join Crispin Lake and learn about the future of Past Crimes." If I know Lake, he's announcing something big at this meeting.'

'Something else?' Cassie said. 'The Blight sim launches tonight. There are billions of dollars at stake.'

'Sometimes,' Jalal said, 'a billion dollars is just the starting point.'

'Lake might give us a clue to where we can find Aly,' Cassie said. 'I need to get into that meeting.'

Jalal looked at her as though she'd sprouted a second head.

'Not a chance in hell.' Jalal took a seat at his desk and removed his visor from its charging dock. 'Past Crimes Lockboxes are encrypted. Employees only. You appear inside that Lockbox, neither of us will ever see the light of day again. I can try to help you find Ms. Miller. But I can't let you in.'

'You're right,' Cassie said, unzipping her backpack. 'I can't appear inside that Lockbox. Please don't take this personally.'

Before Jalal could react, Cassie plunged the succinylcholine syringe into his thigh and depressed the plunger. Jalal's eyes widened.

'What the hell are you doing?' Hector said.

'You heard him. Employees only. I can't go into the Project Corinthian meeting as myself,' Cassie said. 'So I'm going in as Mr. Jalal.' She looked at Salman apologetically. 'If this doesn't work, you can tell the EPP that you didn't let me in.'

'You could have just . . . asked me . . . to tell you what happened,' Jalal said, as he slumped down in his chair. His breathing steadied. Cassie checked his pulse. Strong.

'Help me with him,' she said.

Hector scowled as he gripped Jalal underneath his armpits and helped Cassie prop him gently against the wall.

'Need to make sure he stays upright,' Hector said.

'Why?'

'He could choke on his own tongue,' Hector said. 'Next time you're going to drug someone, let me know first.'

'Will he be OK like that?'

'Yeah. Pulse is strong. Breathing is steady. I'll keep an eye on him and look out for anyone else.'

Cassie removed Jalal's visor from the dock and slid it into place. The EPD's screen came on, and the Past Crimes logo appeared in the center. The main menu appeared, and Cassie saw a notification in the Calendar section on the right of the screen.

THE FUTURE OF PAST CRIMES – NOW

Cassie tapped the link to enter.

TWENTY-EIGHT

6:01 p.m.
Five hours and fifty-nine minutes to launch

She waited to enter. Instead, the screen turned yellow and a blinking message appeared.

RETINAL SCAN FAILED. USER NOT RECOGNIZED.

Shit. Of course Past Crimes visors would have a retinal scan built in. She looked at Jalal, unmoving against the wall and staring daggers at her.

'I'm sorry,' she said to the lawyer. 'Trust me when I say this makes me feel way worse than it does you.'

She took the visor off and placed it over Jalal's head. She heard a tinny voice say 'Retinal scan accepted'. She took the visor off Jalal, apologized again and placed it over her head, Jalal glaring at her as she did.

Her view immediately changed from Jalal's office to the visor's EPD. She saw a loading bar at the bottom. When it finished, Cassie found herself in a massive conference room, seated at an enormous round table. There were already several dozen Wraps in the Lockbox, also seated around the table. She did not recognize any of them. They all wore perfectly coded suits of varying colors. She recognized several languages being spoken among the various attendees. German. Russian. Chinese. Spanish.

A Wrap came up to Cassie and held out his hand. He was in his fifties, with short graying hair and a dark mustache. He wore a suit with a pin on the lapel that Cassie recognized as the French flag. Light-gray text appeared above the Wrap's head. It read **François Gilot, Past Crimes Chief of Operations, France**. A severe-looking woman in her sixties standing nearby had a nametag that read **Franke Müller, Past Crimes Chief of Operations, Germany**.

Another man in his mid-forties with jet black hair and intelligent blue eyes had a title that read **Hiro Ikeda, Past Crimes Chief of Operations, Japan**.

It looked like the department heads from every global division of Past Crimes were attending this meeting. Whatever this Project Corinthian was, it would clearly have global ramifications.

'Mr. Jalal, it's a pleasure to see you again,' Gilot said. Cassie looked down. She remembered she was wearing Salman Jalal's Wrap. 'Your family? Are they well?'

'They're doing very well,' Cassie said. She just had to play along and pray Gilot didn't ask her any of their names. 'And yourself?'

'Pretty sure my wife is having an affair,' Gilot said, with a sad smile. 'Not in Paris, but in Earth+. But that's just as bad, don't you think? Losing someone's heart is maybe even worse than losing their body.'

'I . . . yes. That's terrible. I hope you two can reconcile,' Cassie said, hoping that was the response Gilot would have expected from Salman Jalal. Obviously, the two were close enough for Gilot to share such personal information.

'Maybe it's for the best,' Gilot said. 'So, what does Mr. Lake have in store? I would think the launch of the Blight is enough for one day.'

'I wish I knew. You know how much Mr. Lake prizes his secrets.'

'That he does,' Gilot said with a laugh. He patted Jalal's Wrap on the shoulder and walked off. Dozens more Wraps appeared in the conference room, each taking a seat like some sort of ad hoc United Nations session orchestrated by Crispin Lake. Cassie didn't know the exact number, but Past Crimes had virtual offices in more than thirty countries. It was important to Lake that his sims attract a global audience, hence the licensing of killers and thieves from around the world, all with the shared purpose of making Past Crimes into EPCOT Center for the damned.

Then three Wraps appeared at the front of the room: Maurice Wyatt, Stephen Woolman and finally Crispin Lake. Woolman and Wyatt quickly took seats. Crispin Lake remained standing.

'If you would please take your seats,' Lake said, and everyone did, Cassie included. 'Thank you for joining me on the eve of such a monumental launch. I know you all have many responsibilities today, so I won't take up any more of your time than I have to. I asked you all here today to talk about the past, present and future of Past Crimes.'

The lights in the Lockbox dimmed. The Past Crimes logo hovered over the center of the table. Scenes from dozens of simulations played on the walls around the room. The attendees swiveled in their chairs to watch, pointing and murmuring with glee and recognition. When the clips concluded, Lake continued.

'Over the last two decades,' Lake said, 'I have built one of the world's foremost global entertainment brands. For years, people were starving to experience the most mysterious, violent, surprising and unforgettable crimes in history. Crimes they had previously only read about or watched or listened to. They were kept as outsiders to history. Superficiality, to me, is death. I wanted to take people *inside* these crimes. I wanted everyone, all around the world, to live those extraordinary moments. I wanted them to meet their antiheroes, the masterminds and killers, charlatans and thieves, icons and legends. Thanks to you, I've been able to do just that.'

The employees applauded rapturously. Cassie joined in.

'I'm sure each of you has your favorite sims. Your favorite legends,' Lake said. The attendees all nodded. 'Tell me. What are some of yours?'

Hiro Ikeda raised his hand. 'I enjoy the Tsutomu Miyazaki and Rebecca Staub simulations.'

Lake clapped his hands together once. 'Ah, the Otaku Murderer and the Connecticut Catfisher,' he said, approvingly. 'Two very different but very memorable criminals. Miyazaki gruesomely murdered four young girls in Tokyo and Saitama. And Staub who married not one, not two, but *three* billionaires, then vanished along with forty-seven million dollars. Who else?'

Franke Müller said, 'The Vampire of Düsseldorf.'

'Ah, the infamous Peter Kürten,' Lake said. 'Allegedly tried to drink the blood of his victims. Beheaded in Cologne in 1931 after being convicted of nine counts of murder. One of my personal favorite simulations.'

A Black man wearing a yellow Aso-Oke hat stood up. His title read **Banjoko Musa, Director of Licensing, Past Crimes, Nigeria**. Musa said, 'I was very happy to help you develop the simulation for Moses Sithole.'

'The ABC killer,' Lake said solemnly. 'Terrorized South Africa in the mid-1990s. A frightening man. And your family had a personal connection to Sithole, didn't you?'

Musa nodded. 'My father lived in Johannesburg in 1995. The Sithole killings had the entire nation of South Africa terrified. So much so that Mandela himself made a public plea to help apprehend the killer. The police said Sithole claimed thirty victims. But when he confessed to the crimes, Sithole said the true number was seventy-six. *Seventy-six.* It has been a personal mission of mine to educate my people about this terrifying man. Tourism in Nigeria, in both Earth+ and Earth−, has increased exponentially since the Sithole simulation launched. You've provided many of our citizens with jobs.'

'And we have the good people of Atteridgeville, Boksburg and Johannesburg to thank for helping us perfect our experience,' Lake said. 'Thank you for your kind words. Mr. Musa.'

Musa nodded respectfully and sat back down.

'That, my friends,' Lake said, placing his palm against his heart, 'is why I do what I do. That my life's work can not only entertain and educate the masses but provide jobs for so many is pride I will take with me when it is finally my time to see the other side. Lucky for all of you, I plan to stick around for quite a while.'

The room laughed and applauded. Lake basked in the adulation.

'As you know, this company began with the Murderland complex in Earth−. We built our simulations to complement our park, so as to give people an unforgettable experience in both the physical and digital world. Yet it was always my dream to find a way to merge the physical and digital worlds. Wouldn't it be extraordinary if both could exist on the same plane? If we could somehow harness the technology of the future to bring the past into the present?'

There were murmurs around the room. Lake paused for dramatic effect. When the Wraps quieted down, Lake continued.

'I've never been a particularly religious man. But certain Bible passages have stuck with me over the years. When I created Past Crimes, I thought about Corinthians chapter fifteen, verse forty-two. "Our earthly bodies are planted in the ground when we die, but they will be raised to live forever." The Augmented Personas in our simulations will live forever, much like the legendary criminals from our past. You all know what we've done. Today I'm here to show you what we *will* do. Mr. Musa. Please turn around.'

Banjoko Musa eyed Lake curiously, then spun his chair around. When he did, a man appeared. He was thin and in his early thirties, with dark brown eyes and an intense gaze, with a smile that chilled Cassie to her core. The moment Musa saw the man, he shrieked and toppled backward in his chair.

'Moses . . . Sithole?' Musa said, in fear and awe. Moses Sithole reached down and extended his hand to Musa. Musa eyed it warily, then took it, as the mass murderer helped him to his feet.

'It is a pleasure to meet you, Mr. Musa,' Sithole said. He spoke with a South African accent, but in perfect English. 'I believe I met your father a long time ago. You're a lucky man. If I'd chosen him, you may have never been born.'

'How . . . how does he know who I am?' Musa said.

'In due time. Ms. Müller,' Lake said. 'Would you please turn around?'

The German woman did, only to find herself face to face with a slim man with a square mustache and dark, neatly parted hair, shaved below the temples, and an eerie, malevolent grin.

'*Sheisse!*' Müller shouted. She reached out to touch the man. Without hesitation, he grabbed her wrist and brought it to his lips.

'Ms. Müller,' Lake said. 'Meet Mr. Peter Kürten. The Vampire of Düsseldorf.'

Kürten smiled coldly at Müller. 'I am willing to wager,' Kürten said, 'that your blood tastes *delicious.*'

Müller screamed and wrenched her hand away.

'Friends, colleagues, everyone, please turn around.'

The contingent of Past Crimes employees turned in their seats to find dozens of the most infamous criminals in history surrounding the table. Aileen Wuornos. Drayden Downs. John Wilkes Boothe. Rebecca Staub. Scott Peterson. Jeffrey Dahmer. Billy the Kid. And many more.

There was silence, followed by a hushed whisper. Then Lake spoke.

'These,' Lake said, waving his hand like a game show host presenting the winner's prize, 'are our gods.'

There were whispers among the Wraps.

'I know what you're saying. These are murderers. Thieves. Rapists. Charlatans. Deviants. But we all come from different cultures. Different backgrounds. Not all gods are benevolent. In fact, many of them are cruel and vindictive. Yet they are worshipped all the same. Now, I'm not saying you should worship these people. Still, many do. Like Moses coming down from Mount Horeb, we are their messengers. We present the word and deeds of these gods to the world inside our simulations as Augmented Personas.

'For years, these gods have remained shackled inside our simulations,' Lake continued. 'Until now. Soon, our Augmented Personas will be free of their virtual prisons inside our sims. It is my dream to create a physical world that will allow our Augmented Personas free rein – just as they did when they were alive. Maybe one day, as technology progresses, these APs can even become sentient.'

There was tentative laughter. But Lake did not smile.

'I know, I know. Fully sentient APs may be a pipe dream. Still, our APs will be just as brilliant, diabolical, evil, mysterious and seductive outside their sims as they have been inside. Only now they won't be limited to the confines of a simulation. My dream is to build a park with the kind of technology that enables the criminals of the past to walk among us in the present. They will still be in digital form – for now – but as we all know, what's most frightening about these men and women are their minds. Imagine being a visitor and being able to have a conversation with a perfect digital replica of Ted Bundy.'

Cassie saw many of the invitees smiling. Seeing their giddiness made her feel queasy.

'Creating a physical plane where our digital criminals can exist is truly a revolutionary advance in technology. But this is just the appetizer. Now, before we get to the main course, let me introduce you to our guest of honor.'

With that, Harris West materialized next to Lake. Cassie stifled a gasp. She had to react the way Salman Jalal might. In this case, it meant not reacting at all.

'This, my friends,' Lake said, 'is Harris West. You know him better as the Vertex Ignis. The man who orchestrated the Blight. Starting at midnight, Harris West will be visited in Earth+ by millions of Past Crime devotees around the world, many of whom will be wearing our brand-new Theia visors. As you know, this week Harris's widow, Cassandra Ann West, visited our complex under false pretenses. She murdered a guard. Kidnapped a girl. We believe she was planning a second Blight to coincide with the anniversary of the first. With the launch of our simulation that we have spent years perfecting. Let me tell you this: we will not cower in the face of evil. We will stand up to it. Our simulation will launch as planned. Our customers *demand* it.'

The assembled contingent applauded. Cassie joined in.

Lake continued. 'We are praying that young Allyson Miller is found safe. With her conviction, we are legally permitted to use Cassandra West's likeness and biometrics within our simulations. And we have updated our Blight sim to do just that. Cassandra Ann West, the *real* Cassandra Ann West, the second Vertex Ignis, will be waiting for our subscribers starting at midnight tonight.'

Fortunately for Lake, they were in Earth+, because if he had been standing in front of Cassie in flesh and blood, she would have strangled him.

'With the launch of the Blight sim, we will also be releasing our Theia visors with their cutting-edge sensors and haptics. Based upon the most advanced electroencephalographic technology ever created, which we have spent a decade perfecting, our subscribers will be able to not just see, hear and touch, but taste and smell. As a great man used to say, there's just one more thing. We have harnessed the future to create a new technology that, for the first time, allows this valuable biometric information to go two ways.'

'What exactly does that mean?' Franke Müller asked.

'In the past, augmented and virtual reality visors have sent signals to the user,' Lake said. 'However, the Theia will send signals from the user back to *us*.'

An image of the Theia visor appeared above the table. It was sleek and minimalist, white trim with black lenses. It looked cool. Expensive but not ostentatious. Everyone in the world would want one.

'With our Theia visors, we have the ability to record our users' responses to any and all stimuli. We will know when people's pleasure centers are hit – and learn how to target them. We will know what excites them, disgusts them, even what turns them on. The possibilities are limitless. With this new technology, developed by my brilliant colleague Stephen Woolman, we can literally scan, record and map the human mind.'

There were murmurs among the crowd. They were all impressed, but perhaps confused. As was Cassie.

'I know. You're wondering how exactly this works. Well, allow me to demonstrate. Ms. Müller. Would you please stand up?'

Franke Müller eyed Lake suspiciously but did as she was asked.

'Ms. Müller, I asked you personally to wear our Theia visor for the past six months as a Beta tester, correct?'

'You did.'

Peter Kürten's AP walked over to Franke Müller and, with a cold, emotionless tone, said, 'Four months ago, you clipped a bicyclist near Unter den Linden in your ReVolt automobile. You did not stop. Nor did you notify the police.'

Franke Müller's face went ashen.

'What . . . that is preposterous,' she said, but the tremble in her voice told Cassie it was most certainly not.

'Our Theia visor was able to map, read and decode your mind, Ms. Müller,' Lake said. 'Don't worry. Your secret is safe with us. Your turn, Mr. Sithole.'

The Moses Sithole AP spoke to Banjoko Musa and said, 'Mr. Musa, two years ago you had an affair with a woman named Abigail Wallace, a British diplomat visiting Nigeria. After she threatened to tell your wife, Ms. Wallace disappeared.'

Banjoko Musa's jaw dropped. There was a commotion among the Wraps. Cassie looked at Lake. Never in her life had she seen a man more contented with himself. In just a few hours, tens of millions of people would be using Theia visors. The Blight launch wasn't just about a new sim. Lake would be able to scan the minds of millions – and gain access to everything they knew.

'That is a lie,' Musa said, with such force that Cassie knew Sithole was telling the truth.

'Please,' Lake said, raising his hands as though putting his attendees at ease. 'Rest assured my employees' secrets are my own. Everything we have learned with the Theia stays right here.'

'Will people be aware of the Theia's capabilities?' Musa asked. 'Why will they use our device if they know what it can do?'

'Global revenue from cigarette purchases was nearly a trillion dollars last year,' Lake said. 'And these are products people *know* can kill them.'

'But is this ethical?' Franke Müller added.

Lake laughed. 'You know the difference between what I've done and Tetris? Nothing but a few lines of code. The universe has many secrets. Unlocking them is possible to anyone with the will and ambition.'

'How did you achieve this?' Hiro Ikeda said. 'Our sims alone take years of development and testing.'

Lake said, 'And we have spent years developing and perfecting this new technology.'

'How? Where?' Musa asked.

'We have the greatest research and development department on the face of the earth,' Lake said. 'We have also had access to donors whose contributions have allowed us to unlock a great many secrets of the human mind.'

Donor minds, Cassie thought. *That has to be what Lake is planning to use Aly for.*

'Now, I know you all have a lot of work to do as we approach the launch of our Blight simulation. In just a few hours, drones will be flying all over the world delivering our new Theias. Our advancements in AP technology and the capabilities of the Theia mean the future of Past Crimes is brighter than it has ever been. Remember: the future lies in the past.'

Then the room disappeared and Cassie found herself back in Salman Jalal's office. Lake had terminated the Lockbox.

Jalal was sitting on the floor, flexing his hands and fingers. The drugs were wearing off.

'I'm trying to regain enough energy to spit in your face,' Jalal said. 'But you look like someone drained all the blood from it. What happened in there?'

'The Blight sim isn't just an ordinary simulation,' Cassie said. 'It's also a vehicle to promote the Theia. By this time tomorrow, Lake will be able to map the minds of tens of millions of people around the world.'

TWENTY-NINE

7:08 p.m.
Four hours and fifty-two minutes to launch

As Jalal began to regain his sensation and muscle movement, Cassie filled them in on the meeting. At first, she was fairly certain that once Jalal regained feeling in his extremities, he would either call security or strangle her with a visor cord. But, to her surprise, he did neither. She watched as his face went from anger to surprise to concern to fear. And when she was done, Jalal sat in silence for a long, long time.

When he finally spoke, he said, 'This was all developed in secret. Did he say where he was planning to have this . . . *merging* of the physical and virtual worlds? Murderland doesn't have the technological capabilities for something of this magnitude. And to the best of my knowledge Lake hasn't begun development anywhere else.'

'He didn't say.'

'And these "donors" Lake spoke of. Who are they?'

'I don't know,' Cassie replied. 'But that has to be what he's using Aly for. She's not dead. She's going to be his guinea pig.'

'If he's really done what he claims,' Hector said, 'Lake could access bank accounts. Social security numbers. Government secrets.'

'Not to mention what it could do for targeted advertising,' Jalal said.

'Advertising?' Hector said. 'Really?'

'Trust me, Lake has thought of every potential application.' He rubbed his leg. 'Tingles.'

'Call us even for you burying that chip in my leg and allowing me to be thrown into a cop car like a bag of meat.'

'Fair enough,' Jalal said. 'If the Theia really does what Lake says it does, and he has found a way to essentially "download" the human mind, then he would have direct access to over a hundred million subscribers.'

Jalal gingerly stood up. Cassie helped him to a seat.

'Once people find out what the Theia does,' Hector said, 'why would they buy it?'

'That's unbearably naïve,' Jalal said. 'For decades, people have been willing to give up their freedoms for entertainment and convenience. If Lake provides an unforgettable experience, which I'm sure he will, people will buy the Theia by the millions.'

'I think Lake has also begun laying the groundwork for a second Blight sim. Whatever happens tonight, he's behind it.'

'Like I said,' Jalal said, 'if you have a hit, it's never too early to start work on the sequel.'

Cassie sat there, her head throbbing, unsure of whether it was another Neural Flare or the fear of what was about to come.

'You must have contracts for each sim, right?' Cassie said. 'For everyone who licensed their likenesses and biometrics?'

'Thousands.'

'What about files for people who were posthumously convicted and fall under Statute 486-16. I want to see your files on Harris West.'

Jalal sat up straighter. 'All right. At least this time you asked me first.'

'I'm growing as a person.'

Jalal tapped his monitor. A clear keyboard rose from the desk, no more than a quarter inch thick, the letters nothing more than touchpads. Jalal pressed his index finger against the desk. The computer unlocked and Jalal's desktop appeared. His screen saver was an image of a boy and a girl, somewhere between eight to ten, both smiling.

'They're beautiful,' Cassie said.

'Thankfully, they take after my wife. I desperately want to see them again.'

'You will,' Cassie said.

Jalal typed Harris's name into a search bar, flexing his fingers as feeling returned to his extremities. The search brought up dozens upon dozens of files.

'Start there,' Cassie said, pointing to the first folder.

Jalal opened the folder. It contained a single document. Jalal pinched the air in front of the screen and a hologram of the document floated in front of them. Jalal pinched the hologram to enlarge it.

'That's our marriage certificate,' Cassie said. She remembered signing it. How special that moment was. And now it was stored on a hard drive inside a maniac's amusement park.

Other folders contained Harris's high school diploma. Old resumes. Photos from a vacation they took nearly fifteen years ago. Bank statements. Workout summaries he'd logged on various apps, including calories expended, heart rate and oxygen levels. There were even messages he'd exchanged on dating apps from before he'd met Cassie. Every text. Every photo. Interviews with dozens of friends and family members, some of whom Cassie had never even met. There were photos of Harris playing baseball as a kid. Photos of Harris drinking from a bottle of vodka in college. Employer reports. Earth+ logs. Even a photo of Harris naked that he must have sent to a paramour (Harris had a full head of dark hair and a lack of wrinkles in the photo, which gave her a modicum of relief that he hadn't sent it while they were married).

Lake. Had. *Everything.*

He knew as much about Harris West as Cassie did – maybe even more.

'Employment,' she said, pointing to one of the folders. 'What does that mean?'

Jalal opened the folder. It contained dozens of files. He opened the first one. It was an NDA form. And it was signed by Harris West. Strangely, there was no company name on the NDA. Whoever Harris had agreed to work for was only referred to as 'The Company'. Cassie read the contract.

Harris had signed it in 2034, thirteen years ago. Three years before the Blight. The terms of the contract were clear: Harris agreed to a five-year employment term where he would work on the EPD interface for a company's Earth+ division. He would be paid a hundred and fifty thousand dollars a year. Cassie remembered a conversation with Harris where he said he'd gotten a new gig. A hundred and fifty grand didn't buy what it used to, but it would help chip away at their debts. Between their two salaries, they could pay off the Replenish program within three years, and even start to put some money aside for their family.

She'd asked who the company was, but the NDA required Harris to use a Skin Reader every morning and night. Failing the Skin Reader's assessment meant termination of his contract, not to mention a lawsuit that would bankrupt them.

Then the truth hit her like a wrecking ball to the gut.

'Harris was working for Lake,' Cassie said. 'He was a goddamn *employee* of Past Crimes.'

Jalal looked at the contract. 'It seems so. These are our standard NDAs. Lake is so paranoid that he won't even put the company name on them.'

'So Crispin Lake hires Harris,' Cassie said, 'then the Blight happens, Harris takes the blame and Lake creates the biggest sim in history.' Cassie tapped her lip. It still didn't make sense.

'What are you thinking?' Hector said.

'The day of the Blight,' Cassie replied. 'Harris knew he was going to die. I don't believe he was the Vertex Ignis. But it's not a coincidence that Harris was hired by Past Crimes, then blamed for the Blight, which subsequently made his employer billions. There's a link between Harris's employment and Crispin orchestrating the Blight that we're not seeing yet.'

They kept combing through the files. There were samples of the interface work he'd done for Past Crimes. Mainly cosmetic adjustments. Logos and functionality. A little bit of work reskinning older APs like Lincoln and Gacy. Harris had apparently done a great deal of work coding the interior of the closet Patty Hearst was kept in after her kidnapping by the Symbionese Liberation Army.

'That file,' Cassie said, pointing to Jalal's screen. 'It says "Medic". Open it.'

Jalal did. Cassie's eyes widened.

'This is the report from Harris's last physical,' Cassie said. 'Blood pressure, cholesterol, glucose, testicular exam, lipids and a complete blood panel and urinalysis.'

'Why would Lake have your husband's medical files?' Hector said.

'I have no idea,' Cassie replied. '"Medic Two". What's in that file?'

Jalal opened Medic 2. It contained test results, images, CT Scans, MRIs, PET scans and bone scans. She felt a lump rise in her throat as she read.

On one X-ray, Cassie could see a very large, white mass in the center of the patient's abdomen. Half a dozen smaller white dots were sprinkled throughout the image, like Christmas lights separated from their cord. The date on the X-ray was April 29th, 2037. Two and a half months before the Blight.

In the doctor's notes accompanying the X-ray, the physician wrote: *Metastatic stomach cancer has progressed to Stage IV. Scans show cells have spread to surrounding lymph nodes, as well as the peritoneum, liver and lungs. Inoperable. Patient lifespan will likely not progress beyond three to six months.*

'Harris was dying,' Cassie said. 'And Lake knew it.'

THIRTY

8:07 p.m.
Three hours and fifty-three minutes to launch

Cassie felt a thickness in her throat, as though her esophagus had swelled, making it hard to breathe, hard to speak.

Jalal reviewed the scans.

'Let me see something,' he said. He pulled up Harris's NDA. 'There's an addendum to the contract. Verbiage I've never seen and definitely didn't approve. Look.'

Jalal pinched a section to enlarge it, then underlined it with his finger.

'Look here,' Jalal said. '"Company will have the right to review Employee's medical reports on a quarterly basis. If said reports show any underlying conditions that may prevent Employee from performing their duties – or jeopardizes the Company's faith in Employee's ability to keep their work confidential – then the Company will have recourse including, but not limited to, suspension until medical treatment is completed or, at company's sole discretion, immediate termination of their employment."'

'How is this legal?' Cassie said. 'Doesn't that violate just about every HIPAA law?'

'Twenty years ago, yes,' Jalal said. 'But once people started taking jobs within Earth+, the rules were thrown out the window. Every time a lawmaker has tried to institute guardrails to prevent this kind of violation, companies like Past Crimes spend tens of millions of dollars to lobby against it. In the end, the laws that govern Earth+ are like the Wild West. Few people follow them, and there really aren't any penalties for violating them. And these days, people are so desperate for work they'll agree to pretty much anything.'

Cassie could feel all the elements rattling around in her head, like an eggshell in a thousand pieces that would make a cohesive whole, but only if you could figure out how the various shards fit together. Harris's medical records. Harris working for Past Crimes.

The strange, draconian NDA. The Blight coming so soon after Harris's diagnosis.

'Lake knew Harris was dying,' Cassie said. 'Maybe even before Harris himself did. Harris never even told me he was sick. Why would he hide it? Why would a man not tell his wife he was terminally ill? Not to mention when he knew he was going to be a father? Harris kept it from me for a reason. He killed himself for a reason.'

'What reason?' Hector asked.

'The NDA. The medical reports. Harris was going to die and leave me with nothing to raise our child. The only way Harris would do any of this is if he knew I – *we* – would be taken care of.'

Hector said, 'You think Lake paid Harris?'

Cassie nodded. 'Harris's life insurance was worthless. Lake knew Harris was dying. So he made him an offer. Let me use your likeness and biometrics, and I'll take care of your family.'

'Do you think Harris knew what Lake was planning to use his likeness for?' Jalal asked.

'I doubt it. All Harris had to do was die the way Lake wanted him to. Say what Lake wanted him to say. The day he died, Harris sounded like someone in a hostage video. There was no conviction behind his words. Now I know why.'

'But you never received any money after he died, right?' Jalal said.

'Not a cent. But I doubt Lake had any intention of paying. Why would he? Money leaves a trail. Only two people knew about the deal, and one would be dead.'

'I didn't know about any of this,' Jalal said. 'I swear on my family.'

'How much is enough?' Hector said. 'How much money do you need to make off other people's blood?'

'For men like Crispin Lake,' Jalal said, 'no such number exists.'

'I want him to pay,' Cassie said. 'I want everyone to know what he did to Harris. I want them to know he took Aly Miller. I want them to know he was behind the Blight and orchestrated a tragedy to create an entertainment franchise.' She looked at Jalal. 'After today, you're not a mole. No more shadows. The truth needs to come out.'

'I'll talk,' Jalal said. 'You have my word.'

'So who has access to R and D?' Hector asked. 'If that's where Lake is keeping Aly, we need to get inside somehow.'

'Lake. Woolman. Wyatt. That's all I know for sure.'

'Look at this,' Hector said, pointing to the desktop on Jalal's computer. 'There are sixty-four sim folders. That matches up with the number of silos for the codes you smuggled out.'

'Inside of me,' Cassie reminded them.

'Right. The sixty-fourth was never made public. It's labeled "TW".'

'When was that sixty-fourth file created?' Hector asked.

'That's odd,' Jalal said. 'The TW simulation was created in 2030. Two years *before* Lake launched Past Crimes. It was never made available to the public.'

'So TW was actually the very first sim,' Hector said. 'Why would Lake have kept it private? You'd think he would have marketed the hell out of his very first sim.'

'Maybe it was just not technologically advanced enough for Lake's tastes?' Jalal said.

'No,' Hector said. 'Lake has overhauled and reskinned nearly every sim he's ever created. I think if TW was kept private, it's because he never wanted anyone to see it. Except exactly who he *wanted* to see it.'

'I want to go in,' Cassie said. 'Can we access the TW sim?'

'I can stream the code directly to my visor. But this time, I'm going in first.' Cassie opened her mouth to protest. 'Unless you have more paralyzing agents, you don't have a choice.'

'Fine,' she said. 'But do it fast. We're running out of time.'

Jalal put the visor on and loaded the sim. A few minutes later, he took the visor off. Jalal appeared confused.

'What is it?' Cassie said. 'What's the sim?'

'It's just a house,' Jalal replied.

'What kind of house?' Hector asked. 'Are there bodies? Captive women? Heads in the fridge? Whose house is it?'

'I don't think so. I don't recognize it from any of our other sims, or any crimes we've been pitched and turned down. The house just seems . . . I hate to say this . . . like a normal house.'

'Normal? That's impossible,' Cassie said. 'Give me the visor.'

'You know you really need to work on your manners.'

'Fine. Can I please have the visor so I can see for myself?'

Jalal removed the visor and handed it to Cassie. 'Was that so hard?'

Cassie slid the visor over her head, blinked and found herself in the living room of a cozy farmhouse. She did not recognize the home from any crimes she could recall. She was sitting on a gray couch facing a roaring fire. Two Tom Collins glasses sat on a coffee table next to a bottle of good whiskey. The house could have used a little TLC – the hardwood flooring needed some sanding, the walls needed a touch-up, and some of the screens needed to be replaced. But there was something soothing about the house. Like Jalal said, it felt too normal. It looked lived in and loved. Not the home of a criminal. The home of a family.

There were floating shelves over the fireplace lined with photographs and keepsakes. Two lit candles flickered, casting shadows on the wall. Cassie picked up one of the photos. She recognized the man in it. Then she heard a voice from somewhere upstairs.

'Babe, is that you?'

A woman came downstairs. She had auburn hair and wore a purple sweater, and her smile lit up the room brighter than the candles. She walked over to Cassie and took her hands.

'I missed you so much,' the woman said. She leaned in and kissed Cassie gently on the cheek. She stepped back and let go of Cassie's hands. 'Do you want to cook tonight or should I?'

Cassie pulled up her EPD and left the sim.

'Contact Maurice Wyatt right now,' Cassie said, handing the visor back to Jalal.

'Why?'

'He's going to get us into R and D.'

THIRTY-ONE

8:47 p.m.
Three hours and thirteen minutes to launch

Cassie sat in the front seat of a replica 1975 Volkswagen Beetle outside the Mausoleum of Madness. The car was faded yellow, with meticulously repainted rust and grime dotting the front hood. The passenger seat had been removed and lay across the backseat. Seventy-two years ago, Ted Bundy had driven a car just like this one and removed the seat in order to provide more room for his victims. Littering the car were a mask made out of pantyhose, a crowbar, garbage bags, an ice pick, gloves, a ski mask, a pair of handcuffs and more.

Hector stood at a nearby vendor selling slices of Cianciulli cake, named after Leonarda Cianciulli, the infamous Italian serial killer who murdered three women, baking the first into a cake and boiling two more into soap. Hector nibbled at his cake, frosting and dark-red filling coating his lips. She nodded at him as if to say, *I'm OK.*

Another vendor sold toy whips, replicas of those used by serial killer Albert Fish to torture young boys. At a nearby photo booth, you could have your visage custom-printed on to a rubber mask to mimic the skin worn by Ed Gein that he took from his victims.

There was a line hundreds of people long for Cannibal Canyon, an enormous rollercoaster where, after reaching the summit, you plunged hundreds of feet down into the enormous, gaping maw of Jeffrey Dahmer. Cassie was surrounded by murder, madness and mayhem, all packaged and sold to the thousands of tourists loving every second of it.

Cassie herself was wearing an Earth+ visor over an Aileen Wuornos mask. The synthetic hair was stringy and the fake flesh wrinkled and sallow. In truth, after what she'd been through the last few days, Cassie felt like the mask might be an improvement on her complexion.

People passed by the car without thinking twice. Just another Ted Bundy fanatic. The crowds inside the park were still thick; come midnight, the streets would be packed. There was an electric buzz, everyone waiting for the big Blight launch. They all knew Crispin Lake was a showman. And there would be no better show than what went on inside his park tonight.

Cassie hadn't been waiting long when she heard a deep voice say, 'Give me one reason why I shouldn't rip this door off its hinges and throw you off a bridge.'

She looked up. The imposing figure of Maurice Wyatt loomed outside of the passenger side window. She did not doubt that, if motivated, he could make good on his threats.

'Get in,' Cassie said.

Wyatt looked around, then opened the door and slid in, his frame nearly the entire length of the Beetle.

'You couldn't have picked a more comfortable place to meet?' Wyatt said, shifting uncomfortably. 'How much are you paying Salman Jalal to turn on Crispin?'

'Paying him?' Cassie said. 'Obviously, you haven't seen my most recent bank statement. Jalal knows Crispin Lake is responsible for the deaths of hundreds of people. And maybe more after tonight. I have a feeling that you know that, too.'

'Get to the point,' Wyatt said, 'or you'll never see daylight again.'

'I met your wife,' Cassie said. Wyatt took in a sharp breath. Tonya. 'Lake created a sim for you to visit her. That's why you stay loyal to him. Because he could take Tonya away from you.'

'If you say her name again,' Wyatt said, 'I will *end* you.' His hands were so big he could pop her carotid artery like a blueberry, but there was a tremble in the big man's voice. It reminded Cassie of a bridge shaking in a strong wind.

'Your home reminded me of my home,' she said. 'The way it used to look before my life burned to the ground. A home with love and promise and possibility. And that home was taken from you. Tonya was taken from you.'

'Please stop saying her name.'

'She's beautiful. And she clearly loves you with all her heart.'

'Loved,' Wyatt replied softly. 'She loved me with all her heart.'

'How did she die?'

'Bicycle accident,' Wyatt said. 'She had a seventeen-mile bike commute every day. One December morning, a driverless car lost connection with its satellite. Skidded on an icy road that hadn't been plowed or salted because there was no money for it. It hit her at eighty miles an hour. The doctors say she didn't feel it. I guess that's one thing to be thankful for.'

'I'm sorry,' Cassie said. She paused. 'But we both know I didn't kill anybody. We both know Lake set me up, and that if there is a second Blight, it's Lake who's behind it, not me. Lake built Tonya's sim before he launched Past Crimes. You and Tonya were his proof of concept. You gave him permission to use your family, and he gave you your wife back.'

'He gave me her ghost,' Wyatt said. 'But I would take a ghost over nothing.'

'How often do you visit her?' Cassie asked.

'I kiss her goodnight every evening,' Wyatt said. 'That sim is the last twenty-four hours we spent together. They weren't a particularly special twenty-four hours. I cooked dinner, then we watched some interactive rom-com. We were guests at some fancy wedding where it turns out the bride had made out with a groomsman during her virtual bachelorette and . . . it was stupid. But wonderful. Then we fell asleep. Woke up. Had coffee and breakfast. I took days like that for granted. The days that don't feel special – those are the ones you miss the most.'

Cassie nodded. 'I saw my husband for the first time in ten years the other day inside the Blight sim. And when I saw him, I thought I would give everything I owned, every penny, every drop of blood, *everything* to be able to see him whenever I wanted. Even if it was just his ghost, I would still take it.'

'How can you still love him?' Wyatt said. 'Tonya was an angel who never hurt anybody. Your husband was a monster.'

'My husband's name was Harris,' Cassie said, 'and the only person he ever hurt was me the day he took his life. Crispin Lake ruined the name of a good man. For money.'

'If you think your husband was a good man, then you're delusional,' Wyatt said. 'Crispin just made the sim. He used your husband's likeness and biometrics *legally*. Your husband made his choices, and I'm sorry you have to live with the consequences, but it's not my problem.'

'Actually, it *is* your problem,' Cassie said. 'Do you want to know the truth about what your boss, the entertainer, has done?'

She told Wyatt about the NDA, how Harris had been working for Past Crimes, how Lake had begun collecting Harris's files and medical records.

'I think your boss orchestrated the Blight,' Cassie said. 'My husband was the perfect scapegoat. Lake didn't care who he hurt or who was going to die because the Blight would be worth billions. Thousands more could die around the world tonight. Do you really want to sell your soul for this man?'

'If it means being able to see my wife, then yes.'

Cassie went silent. She was not expecting that response. She was expecting to confront Wyatt and, like in the movies, he would see the error of his ways and suddenly come to her side. *So naïve*, she thought. If life worked that way, she would still be waking up next to Harris and their child would be ten years old.

So if emotions didn't work, pragmatism just might.

'What if I told you that even with Lake out of the picture, you could still see Tonya?'

Wyatt eyed her suspiciously. 'I don't follow.'

She pointed at Hector, still chewing on a piece of cake. She told Wyatt how Jalal had smuggled out the sim codes – including sim sixty-four.

'You don't need Crispin Lake anymore,' she said. 'If you help me, that man will make sure you will have access to your wife's sim every day for the rest of your life. You won't need to carry the guilt of what Lake has done. The alternative is you turn a blind eye to everything Lake is doing. You can let all these people die. And keep your head buried in a home that doesn't exist anymore.'

'Go to hell,' Wyatt said.

'I've been there for ten years,' Cassie said. 'And if you let another Blight happen, or if you let Aly Miller die, then I hope you enjoy the heat because you'll be joining me.'

Wyatt's face was stone. His eyes revealed nothing. Finally, he said, 'What do you want?'

'Get me into the R and D building.'

Wyatt sat there long enough to make Cassie think he was about to grab her, toss her over his enormous shoulders and throw her down a deep hole. But he didn't. Instead, he looked off into the distance towards the R and D building and said, 'Keep your mask on. And follow me.'

THIRTY-TWO

9:48 p.m.
Two hours and twelve minutes to launch

Wyatt, Cassie and Hector threaded between visitors, the park packed elbow to elbow in the gloom. The lights had dimmed, the attractions cloaked in shadow and moonlight. Faces of killers and criminals leered at them from every corner. Hundreds wore lifelike masks, like an outdoor gathering of the damned.

Cassie could see the gleaming metal cube of the R&D building at the north end of the park, directly in the center of Mastermind Mountain, the section of the park devoted to 'Evil Geniuses'.

Whereas most of the park was covered with synthetic grit and grime, the R&D building looked as if it had been dropped from space – all polished walls and razor-sharp edges, a solid piece of steel. The Past Crimes logo glowed red in the building's center, the crime scene victim laying in repose against the metal.

Wyatt led them to the front of the cube and placed his hand against the wall. A small panel opened and a needle emerged. Wyatt turned to the side and the needle pricked his triceps, drawing a minuscule amount of blood before retracting. Cassie heard a faint humming, then a green light appeared and a door slid open noiselessly. Wyatt stepped inside. Cassie and Hector followed.

A long hallway stretched out in front of them, with two guards stationed at the end. Each had a rifle strapped to their chest. When they saw Wyatt, they nodded.

'Friends of Lake,' Wyatt said. The guards nodded skeptically.

The guard on the left said, 'Ma'am, please remove your mask.'

Cassie looked at Wyatt. He nodded. 'Go ahead.'

Cassie sighed and removed the Aileen Wuornos mask, dropping it to the ground in a pile of fake flesh. The moment she revealed her face, both guards raised their weapons and aimed them at Cassie's chest. She stepped back, expecting to have a hole the size of an apple blasted through her.

'Put your weapons down,' Wyatt said firmly. The guards didn't move. Their guns remained pointed at Cassie.

'What the hell are you doing with *her*?' the guard on the right asked. 'That bitch killed Ryerson.'

'No, she didn't,' Wyatt replied.

'The hell do you mean?' the other guard asked.

'Do you trust me?' Wyatt said. They both nodded. 'Then lower your weapons.'

'With all due respect, sir, trust or not, she doesn't have authorization to be here.'

'But I do. And I'm telling you to stand aside.'

'Does Mr. Lake know about this?'

'By now?' Wyatt said. 'Probably. Look. Ryerson was a good man. And this woman did not kill him. You both know me. Have I ever lied to you?'

'No, sir,' the guards replied in unison.

'Then put your weapons down and stand aside.'

The guards looked at each other. Then they holstered their guns and moved aside. Wyatt approached the security door and allowed a sensor to scan his hand and eyes. Another door slid open. The guards eyed Cassie warily as she and Hector followed Wyatt.

'I hope you know what you're doing, sir,' one of the guards said.

Wyatt did not respond before the security door closed behind them. They were now inside the central nervous system of Past Crimes.

Cassie expected there to be an army of security guards and technicians and people running around and monitors and test tubes and all sorts of mad-scientist creations and maybe sentient robots scooting around, and she figured when they recognized her, they would vaporize her in half a picosecond. But instead of that madness, there was . . . nothing. Just quiet.

Cassie looked around. Then she noticed something.

'There are no cameras,' she said to Wyatt.

'No, I guess there aren't.'

'Whatever goes on in here,' Hector said, 'he doesn't want it recorded.'

Cassie walked from one end of the hall to the other. There were five metal doors, each with a sensor in the wall. They had no markings on them, just barely noticeable indents in the otherwise flawless steel.

'What's inside those doors?' she asked Wyatt.

'I have no idea.'

'Do you remember what you said to me when we met?' Cassie asked. 'You said, "Long as it doesn't affect my paycheck, I'm happy to keep my head in the sand."'

Wyatt stayed silent.

'There's a young girl here somewhere. You stuck your head in the sand just long enough for Lake to take her and do God knows what. If staying ignorant means Allyson Miller dies, are you OK with that?'

'No,' Wyatt replied. 'I'm not.'

'So let's find Aly, get her the hell out of here and let the world know what Lake has done.'

Cassie approached the first door. There was no handle or knob or control panel. She looked back at Wyatt. 'No backing out now.'

For a moment, Wyatt looked as though he might hurl her across the room, but instead he walked up to the door and pressed his hand against the metal. There was a humming sound and the door slid open. They entered the room.

What Cassie saw took her breath away. The walls and ceilings were a pristine, gleaming, glowing white, with nothing but a single, solitary chair in the center of the room, almost like a dentist's office in a space station. The chair was attached to a thin, black rod that protruded from the floor. It had a black leather headrest and armrests. Attached to the armrests were metal restraints.

Cassie looked back at Wyatt. For the first time, she saw confusion on the man's face. As if he couldn't quite believe what he was seeing. He turned to Cassie and said, 'What . . . what goes on in here?'

'You're the one cashing those paychecks,' she replied.

She approached the chair. It was spotless. Not a smudge or fingerprint. Attached to the crown of the headrest was an adjustable restraint.

'Restraints for the patient's wrists and forehead,' Cassie said. 'So whoever is in these chairs can't move. Or escape.'

'The people in here aren't patients,' Hector said. 'They're prisoners.'

The rest of the room was bare. Not a chair or couch, not a monitor or screen. Cassie walked the perimeter, looking for something. Anything.

At the far wall, she noticed that the white paneling appeared to be a slight shade darker than the rest of the room.

'Glass,' she said, tapping the wall. 'It's a screen.'

A moment after she tapped it, the entire wall lit up black. A green light passed over Cassie, then a message appeared in black letters, the length of the entire wall.

RETINAL SCAN FAILED

'Let me try,' Wyatt said. He stepped next to Cassie and tapped the wall. There was another flash of green light.

RETINAL SCAN FAILED

Cassie didn't see a way around the safeguard. There was nothing else they could do in this room. She left, Hector and Wyatt trailing her, and opened the second door. It was the same as the first. Strange dentist's chair in the center, a far wall that doubled as some kind of screen or monitor, and a retinal scan that wouldn't give either of them access to the building's system.

Cassie did a lap around the room, making sure she didn't miss anything. When she was convinced the room was empty, she went to leave, but Wyatt was standing by the chair, staring at the floor.

'What is it?' Cassie said. Wyatt pointed at a red spot half the size of a dime. 'Is that . . . blood?'

'I think so,' Wyatt said.

'Is it Aly's?'

'I don't know,' Wyatt said. 'We need to check the other rooms right now. Come on.'

Cassie practically had to jog after the big man to keep up with his loping strides. He went up to the third door – only when he scanned his retinas, it didn't open.

'What the hell . . .' Wyatt said. He tried again. Still nothing. Wyatt looked around for an answer. Then he stomped back down the hall to the security door. It opened, revealing the two guards.

'You,' Wyatt said, pointing at the one on the right. 'Come with me.'

'Sir, I don't think I should. Mr. Lake could—'

Before the man could finish his sentence, Wyatt had backed the guard up against the wall. The other guard took a step forward, gun raised.

'You don't want to do that,' Wyatt said. 'There doesn't need to be violence here. But if there is, I've never lost a fight.'

Wyatt was five inches taller and looked like he could stop a bullet with his biceps, so the guard lowered his weapon. Wyatt led the first guard to the door and said, 'Put your face here. Or I will remove your eyes manually and do it myself.'

The guard, firmly believing Wyatt was at the very least capable if not motivated to follow through with the threat, went to the third door and leaned forward. The scanner read his retinas. The guard then placed his palm on the wall. After another humming sound, the third door slid open. When it did, Cassie's heart leaped into her throat.

In the middle of the room, strapped to a chair, eyes closed and unmoving, was Aly Miller.

THIRTY-THREE

10:52 p.m.
One hour and eight minutes to launch

Cassie ran to Aly and put two fingers to her neck. She was unconscious, but her pulse was strong. Cassie could hear her breathing, could see the comforting rise and fall of her chest. She was alive.

Aly wore a thin gray robe that hung off her loosely like a hospital gown. Wireless electrodes covered her body. One on each of her temples. One on her forehead. Two in the soft crevasses where the top of her neck met her jawbone. One on each bicep and triceps, her calves and thighs, atop each breast, on the sides of her stomach, and two just above her pelvic bone.

Behind the chair holding Aly, the wall glowed. There was a floor-to-ceiling outline of a person. Within that outline were hundreds of glowing lines and darker masses.

'What is all that?' Wyatt said.

'They've mapped Aly, from the inside out,' Cassie said. She traced the outlines, the branches, the shapes. 'I think those are her nerve endings. Those are capillaries, bones, muscles and organs.'

The organs glowed a dark yellow. The blood vessels, a light red. The bones, a neutral gray. Muscles, orange. Her system moved, flowed. A list of numbers at the bottom of the wall refreshed every few seconds.

Hector said, 'It's measuring her heart rate, oxygen levels, organ health, bone density, synaptic responses, glycogen. Everything. They're reading her biometrics in real time.'

'Aly!' Cassie said, gently shaking the young girl. Aly didn't respond. She sat there like a doll, her limbs loose and unresponsive as Cassie tried to rock her awake. Cassie looked back at Wyatt. His face was blank. 'You knew she was here, didn't you? You knew Lake was lying to the world. You let him do this.'

Wyatt seemed to shudder, the big man looking as if he could be knocked over by a leaf. 'Lake just said he was going to run some tests. I didn't know he was doing . . . *this*.'

'Just help me get her the hell out of this thing.'

Aly's arms, legs and forehead were locked into metal restraints. Cassie tried to pry them apart but, shockingly, her muscles weren't as strong as tempered steel. Wyatt joined in but couldn't get the metal to budge.

'Let me try something,' Hector said. He unzipped his backpack and pulled out the Devil's Fingernail. Then Hector knelt beside the chair where Aly's ankles were shackled. He aimed the device at the first hinge, took a breath, steadied himself and pressed the button.

A red light shot out. Smoke rose from the metal. Hector released the button and yanked the clasp away from the hinge. It came apart, freeing Aly's right leg. Hector repeated it on the other hinge and on Aly's wrists.

'I think I can slide her out,' Wyatt said. 'I don't want that device anywhere near her head. Give me a hand.'

Hector slid his arms under Aly's legs while Wyatt did the same under her neck and shoulders. He gently slid her head from its restraint. But as they began to lift her, Cassie saw what was underneath Aly's body.

'Stop!' she shouted.

'What is it?' Wyatt said, the girl unmoving in his arms.

Cassie knelt down until her head was below Aly's body. A tube ran up through a small hole in the floor, ending in a needle that was embedded in Aly's spine. Fluid flowed through the tube, up from the floor and into Aly's body.

'Some sort of anesthetic or sedative,' she said.

'Phenobarbital or thiopental,' Hector said. 'She's in an induced coma.'

'Can you get it out?' Wyatt said.

'I think so,' Cassie said. 'Just lift her a little higher . . .'

They lifted Aly's prone body. Cassie gently pried several pieces of adhesive tape from the small of Aly's back where the needle was embedded. Once those were gone, she placed her palm on Aly's skin. It felt dry and cool. Then she gently slid the needle from Aly's back and dropped it on the floor. Fluid began to slowly spurt from the dislodged tube, pooling in a clear puddle.

Cassie put her ear to Aly's mouth. She was breathing but unconscious.

'What now?' Wyatt said.

'We go back out the way we came in,' she said.

'Which is?'

'The generator access tunnel. There's no way we can make it past the exits without being recognized. Once we're clear and Aly wakes up, we need to contact the police and tell them what Lake is really doing here. What he did to Harris. That he's responsible for the first Blight. That he's not a visionary. He's a murderer.'

'Can you do all that?' Hector said.

Wyatt nodded. 'If I do all that, you'll let me see Tonya again.'

Cassie said, 'You have our word.'

Hector carried Aly out of the room, her head resting on his shoulder.

'It's gonna be OK,' he whispered. Even if Aly couldn't hear him, Cassie knew he meant it. Hector was going to be a good father. She knew at that moment that she would die to make sure he got out alive.

When they got back to the hallway, the guards' eyes widened when they saw Aly in Hector's arms.

'That's Aly Miller,' the first guard stammered. 'Lake said *you* kidnapped her. What the hell is she doing here?'

'Lake lied. He brought her here,' Wyatt said. 'We're getting her out.'

'I . . . I didn't know,' the guard stammered.

'If your boss was lying about Aly Miller,' Hector said, 'just imagine what else he's been lying about.'

Cassie looked at the other two unopened doors.

'We should check,' she said. 'Make sure nobody gets left behind.'

Wyatt scanned his retinas in front of the fourth door. The door slid open.

'Jesus,' Hector said. 'Is that who I think it is?'

A man was strapped to the chair in the center of the room. His head was shaven. His face was gaunt, sunken. Skin hung from his flesh. Electrodes were fastened to his skull and exposed skin. Cassie recognized the faded brown tattoo of a noose around the man's neck.

'Drayden Downs,' Hector said. 'The Seattle Strangler. He killed Vivian's mother. He was supposed to have died in prison eight years ago.'

'Downs is the donor Lake talked about in the Project Corinthian meeting,' Cassie said. 'Lake has donated tens of millions of dollars to law enforcement causes. But they weren't a donation. They were a transaction. He's getting live criminals shipped to him.'

Hector walked up to the body. Peered into the man's face. 'This . . . man . . . brought so much pain to so many people. He doesn't deserve to be alive.'

'Hector,' Cassie said. He looked at her. His fist was clenched, held above the man's throat.

'I could kill him right now,' Hector said. Then he released his fist. 'But Vivian wouldn't. So I won't.' He looked at Cassie. 'I won't kill him. But I don't have to save him.'

Cassie nodded. 'I understand. Come on. One more room.'

They exited and went to the fifth and final door. Wyatt scanned his retinas, but his access was declined.

'I got it,' the guard said. He scanned his eyes and the final door slid open with an audible hiss. As soon as it did, Cassie smelled something. Chemicals. Something else, too. It reminded her of the critical care unit in a hospital. Something was very, very wrong in here.

There was no chair. Instead, a long, cylindrical metal tank stood in the middle of the room. To Cassie, it looked like one of those old iron lungs from the 1950s. It was about seven feet long, with small, circular windows dotting the side, like ports on a boat. Whatever the pungent chemical scent was, it was coming from inside the tank.

'What the hell is in there?' the guard asked, covering his nose.

Cassie stepped forward. She could feel her pulse quickening in her temples. Slowly, she moved around the container. The small windows were fogged so she couldn't quite make out the details, but she could see something floating inside the tank. It looked like a—

Body.

There was a body inside. Or at least what was left of it.

The large cylinder tapered off into a smaller, enclosed metal cylinder. The larger container held a body. The smaller, windowless upper part housed the head. The upper cylinder was attached to the lower by a metal hinge.

She needed to know who could have been subjected to such an awful fate. And why.

'Give it to me,' she said to Hector.

'Cassie—'

'*Now.*'

He held out the Devil's Fingernail. Cassie took it. She held it up to the hinge holding the small cylinder to the larger body. A hiss of metal and she burned through it. Then, gently, she pulled the two halves apart, revealing the head inside the container.

When Cassie saw the man's face, the device fell to the floor, leaving a burn mark on the gleaming white. Cassie stumbled back, tripping over her own feet. Her lips opened but nothing came out.

The world around her had faded into the background. She put a hand to her mouth and felt her stomach lurch. She thought she could hear Wyatt yelling but had no idea what he was saying.

Oh my God, she thought. Over and over. *Oh my God. Oh my God. Oh my God.*

She felt strong hands on her shoulders. She shrugged them off, walking backwards until she hit the wall. Tears spilled from her eyes. A low moan escaped her lips.

Hector approached the container. When he saw whose body it held, he turned back to Cassie, mouth agape in horror.

'Cassie,' Hector said, 'is that your husband?'

THIRTY-FOUR

11:17 p.m.
Fifty-three minutes to launch

The world swam around Cassie, as if she'd been caught in a massive undertow and was being dragged to the bottom of the ocean. Her stomach heaved, but it was empty. Hector squeezed her shoulder and she felt herself surface.

'Cassie?' he said. 'Are you OK?'

'I . . .' She didn't know how to respond. She didn't know how long it took, but eventually the world stopped swimming. She still felt woozy, the sensation reminding her of when she was a girl and her father would spin her around and around, and then when he stopped, it felt like the world was moving without her, and it took every ounce of focus she had not to fall over.

She got up. Wobbled. Took Hector's hand.

'I need to see him.'

'No, you don't,' he said. 'It's not pretty.'

'Yes. I do.'

She took a step forward. Felt her balance stabilize. Took another. Then another. Until she was standing next to the tank that housed the body of her husband. Harris.

His face was gaunt, skeletal, as though he'd been slowly starved for years. His head was bald. Electrodes covered his scalp. She put her palm on his crown, felt a hint of stubble and recoiled. She put her hand on his face. Rubbed it. Felt the slight bristle beneath her skin.

He was still growing hair. *He was alive.*

But how was that possible? She'd looked inside the tank. The image of what she'd seen would be seared into her mind as long as she lived. There was no way he could still be alive based on what was here. At least not naturally. She held her hand beneath his nostrils and felt a puff of air. She looked back at Hector, tears in her eyes.

'Is he . . .' Hector said.

Cassie nodded.

She'd always thought it was strange that the EPP had arrived at her home before the Earth–police. Now it made sense. Lake had donated tens of millions to the Earth Plus Police. Pushed through Statute 486-16. The EPP wasn't there to investigate the fire at 44 Otter Creek Drive. They were retrieving the body of Harris West for Crispin Lake to use as a donor.

Cassie knelt down and looked underneath the cylinder housing Harris's head. There was a wire running up from the floor, embedded just below the base of his skull. There was no tube, no fluid pumping into him like there had been for Aly. Harris was not receiving any anesthetic. Harris was breathing, yes, but Cassie knew, based on what she'd seen inside the tank, the ruins of his body, that while he was still breathing, for all intents and purposes, Harris West was dead.

'This is what they were going to do to Aly,' Cassie said. She placed her hand on Harris's cheek. A tear fell on to his lip. Then another. And another.

'I didn't know,' she whispered. 'I'm so, so sorry. I love you. Always.'

She knelt down and gripped the wire embedded in her husband's head. Then she heard a familiar voice say, 'If you do that, the girl dies.'

Standing in the doorway was Crispin Lake.

Cassie stood up. Stepped forward, ready to drive Lake's nose right through his face. Then Lake held up a gun and aimed it at Aly, and Cassie stopped.

'Crispin,' Wyatt said. 'What in God's name have you done?'

'God had nothing to do with this,' he said. 'He wasn't ambitious enough.'

'You orchestrated the Blight,' Cassie said. 'You stole Harris. You stole my *life*.'

'Everything I did was with your husband's approval,' Lake said.

'He didn't know you would make him into a monster. He didn't know you would use him for *this*.'

'He gave me permission to do whatever I wanted to him,' Lake said. 'It doesn't matter whether he would approve of it or not. Harris feels no pain. He doesn't care what's been done to him or what people think of him. It's the perfect state of being. Just think about everything we were able to accomplish. He is just as responsible for the Theia as we are. His is the most famous stolen brain since Victor Frankenstein's little science experiment.'

'And just like Frankenstein, you created a monster.'

'I've made a lot more money from my monster than Mary Shelley ever did.'

'You stole Harris,' Cassie said, the rage spilling from her lips. 'You stole his legacy and you stole my *life*.'

'I didn't force Harris to accept my terms. Do you know how much your husband's name is worth now? How many people his name has employed and provided for?'

'And how many people died for that to happen?'

'Fair trade if you ask me.'

'What did you promise him?'

'I placed ten million dollars in an escrow account, earmarked for Harris's next of kin. All he had to do was die the way I wanted him to, rather than the way God intended,' Lake said. 'The terms of our deal made it clear that the money would be put into escrow and disbursed ten years after his death, provided that next of kin has not been convicted of any crimes. I originally told him eighteen years. He negotiated me down to ten, which I agreed to because

I'm a sympathetic man. Unfortunately for you, your conviction has you in breach of that contract.'

'You mean the conviction where you set me up?'

'You are a convicted felon,' Lake said, 'and therefore entitled to nothing.'

'So, what, are you just going to shoot us all?' Wyatt said.

'I'd prefer not to,' Lake replied. 'Even though I should. I didn't think you'd be this ungrateful, Maurice. I gave you your life back. I gave you your *wife*.'

'And you lied to me.'

'Would it really have made a difference?'

'Yes.'

'Keep telling yourself that. Now you'll never see Tonya again.'

'We're leaving,' Cassie said. 'The world is going to know what you did.'

Lake pointed the gun at the unconscious girl. He checked his watch and grinned. 'Almost launch time.'

Cassie moved between Lake and Aly.

'You'd take a bullet for this girl you barely know?' Lake said, surprised.

'In a heartbeat.'

Lake's smile faltered. 'There's no reason for anyone to get hurt. It's just minutes to midnight. If you stay here, you'll be able to see the fireworks.'

'I don't care about your stupid celebration,' Cassie said. 'We're getting out of here.'

Cassie took another step forward. To her surprise, Lake took a step back.

'Stop,' he said. 'You don't want this to go any further.'

There was a tremor in his voice. Cassie could hear it. He was bluffing. Lake was the kind of man who had someone else do his dirty work.

Cassie took another step towards Lake. And another. He kept backing up until he was nearly at the door. He still held the gun, but now Cassie was close enough to see the black muzzle just feet away from her face. Close enough to know that if Lake fired, he wouldn't miss.

Close enough to see that Lake's finger wasn't even on the trigger.

Without warning, Cassie closed the gap between them and reached out to grab his hand. She expected one of two things: she would keep him off balance long enough for Wyatt to turn him inside out. Or she would be dead before she knew if she'd even succeeded. But even if Lake got a shot off, Wyatt would be on him, and he and Hector could still get Aly out of there.

What actually happened was not anything Cassie expected.

Her aim was true. She would have slapped the gun right out of Lake's hand. Instead, her hand passed right through the space where Lake's arm should have been. Like she was trying to punch a shadow.

'What the hell?' she said.

She tried again, and again her hand passed right through his arm, *right through Lake himself*. Lake had an odd grin on his face. This time Cassie swung at Lake's face. Her fist sailed right through the air where Lake's nose would have been. A chill ran down Cassie's spine.

'He's not real,' Cassie said, turning back to Hector and Wyatt. 'Lake is a goddamn AP.'

THIRTY-FIVE

11:41 p.m.
Nineteen minutes to launch

'Who are you?' Cassie said. She ran her hand through Lake's entire body – or lack thereof. He was an Augmented Persona. A shadow. A hologram. A code. *Something*. What he was definitely not was a living, breathing person.

'My name is Crispin Lake. Founder of Past Crimes.' He took a small bow. 'At your service.'

'But you're not human,' Hector said.

'If humans can be judged on their accomplishments, then I'm just as human as you are, if not more so,' Lake said. 'In fact, I've achieved far more than almost any human in history.'

'You don't let anyone touch you,' Wyatt said, the terror of realization hitting him. 'You hold every press conference and meeting inside −+.'

'I had to keep a few things close to the vest,' Lake said. 'My apologies for the little white lie, Maurice.'

'*Little white lie?*' Wyatt shouted. 'I sold my *soul* for you!'

'If there is anything you should have learned working for Past Crimes,' Lake said, 'it's that people are as real as you want them to be. All the criminals in our sims – they are as real to our customers as anyone with blood running through their veins. I'd even say more so.'

'But if Crispin Lake doesn't exist,' Hector said, 'who created him? Who runs Past Crimes?'

'Woolman,' Wyatt said. 'It must have been Stephen Woolman from the beginning.'

Woolman had been so unassuming. He'd deferred to Lake on everything. He'd all but disappeared during the Project Corinthian meeting. He'd seemed so meek, even cowardly. It was brilliant, actually. Woolman created a lightning rod in Crispin Lake. Lake would be the 'face' of Past Crimes. The brash frontman. He would take all the heat. All the credit. All the controversy. Lake could boast and brag and let everyone from politicians to people like Hector and Vivian come after him; meanwhile, Woolman was in the shadows, playing everyone like a goddamn puppet.

Cassie included.

'This is the Augmented Persona program Lake talked about in the meeting,' Cassie said. 'He wanted to merge the physical and virtual worlds into one, cohesive whole. Crispin Lake was simply the first iteration of that promise. But Crispin Lake could only exist somewhere that Woolman fully controlled the environment.'

'Like the Bundy Building and Earth+,' Hector said. 'In the outside world, Woolman can't control the environment. For the plan to be viable, Woolman would need to create a physical environment on a huge scale where his virtual creations could exist.'

A wave of terror washed over Cassie. 'Oh my God.'

'What is it?' Hector said.

'It's going to be here.'

'What is?'

'Murderland is all but obsolete. Woolman would need to create a new environment. Somewhere he could start over fresh. Somewhere he could control the environment completely.'

Cassie remembered the map of the Past Crimes complex she'd

found on her bedside table inside the Blight sim. How all the entrances and exits were marked. She'd thought it was a glitch, a mistake, an oversight. But it was none of those. It was a breadcrumb.

'Woolman is going to burn this park to the ground,' Cassie said, as the full horror of what was about to happen occurred to her. 'That way he can rebuild a new complex with the technology to merge the real and virtual world. Where virtual criminals can roam the streets. We were wrong from the start. The second Blight isn't going to be global. It's going to be *right here.*'

'Woolman didn't pay for twenty-five thousand people to come here to celebrate,' Hector said. 'He brought them here to die.'

Cassie tore through the projection of Crispin Lake and back into the main hallway. Hector followed her, still carrying Aly. She groaned softly.

'She's stirring,' Hector said.

The guards were in the hallway, looking confused.

'What the hell is going on?' one asked.

'We need to get everyone out of the park *now*,' Cassie said.

'What the hell is she talking about?' the guard asked Wyatt.

'Woolman is going to destroy Murderland,' Wyatt said. 'And if we don't get everyone out, thousands will be dead by morning.'

Aly's eyelids began to flutter. She was coming out of her anesthetized haze, her brain clearing away the cobwebs.

'She's waking up,' Cassie said. 'We need to get the hell out of here.'

Wyatt motioned to the guards. 'You both. Come with me.'

The group exited R&D. Crowds had begun to line the streets, waiting for the celebration Crispin Lake had promised them. There were so many children . . .

'So how the hell do we get everyone out?' the guard asked. 'The celebration starts at midnight. That's in ten minutes. Nobody is going to just leave.'

'Can't you cancel it?' Cassie said.

Wyatt shook his head. 'Not on such short notice. There are at least a thousand employees involved in the celebration, from entertainment to security to fireworks and vendors. There's no universal comms system. There's no way we have enough time to get word to everyone. And even if it's canceled, people won't just leave the park. They'll get angry.'

'They're all going to die.'

Cassie turned around. Crispin Lake was standing just inside the doorway to the R&D building. He was watching them with a bemused smile.

'You would kill your fans?' Hector said.

'If everyone in this park dies tonight, that's less than one one-thousandth of our subscription base. We took a bigger revenue hit when we ran out of replicas of Gary Ridgway's glasses.'

'Fuck you, ghost,' Cassie said. Cassie picked up a rock and threw it at Lake. It sailed through him and clattered to the ground.

'I really hate that guy,' she said. She put her hand on Wyatt's shoulder. 'The access tunnels. There are six, yes?'

'That's right,' Wyatt said.

'OK, if we can herd the people towards the tunnels, maybe we can—'

Then, out in the distance, came the sound of an explosion. It rattled the air and shook the ground. A massive fireball erupted into the night sky. Cassie looked at Aly. The girl's eyes were open. She could see the flames reflected in her irises.

The crowds began to cheer. They assumed this was the start of Lake's celebration. The start of what they'd come to see. But this wasn't going to be a celebration. It was going to be a massacre.

Cassie looked at Hector and said, 'The second Blight is beginning.'

THIRTY-SIX

July 19th, 2047
12:01 a.m.
One minute post-launch

The screams began seconds after the second explosion. People were quickly realizing they were not part of the celebration.

'The Beacons are attacking the park,' Cassie said.

Wyatt pressed his earpiece and said, 'Control, what's that? Oh, Christ.' He looked at Cassie and Hector. 'Cars loaded up with explosives are driving through the gates. People are dousing the gates with gasoline and setting them on fire. It's a goddamn kamikaze attack and we're being sealed inside.'

'Are there security measures inside the park?' Hector asked.

Wyatt shook his head. 'Not for something of this magnitude.'

'Why wouldn't Lake just detonate a bomb?' Hector asked. 'Destroy the park and kill everyone all at once?'

'Lake is a businessman,' Cassie said. 'Look how many people are broadcasting this live. If Lake killed everyone all at once, there would be nobody left to do that. This will be the single most recorded crime in human history. Lake has started marketing his sim for the second Blight while it's still happening.'

Wyatt spoke into his earpiece.

'Control. We need all security personnel – hell, all personnel *period* – to start leading all guests into the generator access tunnels.'

'What . . . what's going on?' Aly said. She looked at Hector. 'Who the hell are you?' Then she saw Cassie and she began to thrash and scream. 'Get her away from me! She's the Vertex Ignis! She's going to kill us all!'

'Aly,' Cassie said, in her most calming voice. 'It was Lake. From the beginning. Or Woolman, actually. It's a long story.' She brought Wyatt over so Aly could see him. 'You remember him. He worked for Lake. He knows the truth. Lake is just an AP. Stephen Woolman created him. Woolman was behind the Blight. He's behind all of this.'

Aly looked at Wyatt, confused, scared, groggy.

'It's true,' Wyatt said. 'Cassie had nothing to do with any of it. Neither did her husband. And we're going to get you out of here and tell everybody what they did to you.'

Aly looked at Wyatt. Then Hector. Then Cassie.

'Put me down,' she said.

'You were just sedated and—'

'I said *put me down.*'

Hector sighed and put Aly down. She took two steps, wobbled, and Hector caught her before she could fall. 'I'm Hector, by the way. Nice to meet you.'

'OK. Fine. *Hector*. You can carry me. But just for a little bit.'

Hector tapped his earpiece. 'Viv. Can you hear me?'

There was a crackling on the other end, and Cassie heard Vivian's voice. 'Here.'

'Did you catch all of that?'

'Most of it. What do you need from me?'

'The second Blight isn't global. It's right here.'

'My God. Get the hell out of there! What can I do?'

'Contact the police,' Hector said. 'Not the EPP. They're working with Lake. The Earth– police. Tell them to send every firefighter and ACM they can spare to Past Crimes. Tell them we need emergency services inside and outside the access tunnels.'

Just as she finished speaking, Cassie heard two more explosions, followed by more screams.

'Is that what I think it is?' Vivian said.

'The Beacons are sealing off all the exits,' Hector replied.

'Hector, please, get out.'

'Working on it.'

Cassie turned to Wyatt. 'Each access tunnel is several miles long. If we can get people into them, they can get away from the park. But would the blasts cause them to collapse?'

'Those access tunnels are walled in by three feet of steel,' Wyatt said. 'They were built to keep the desert from collapsing in on them. A missile wouldn't breach those walls. The bigger problem is oxygen. Or lack thereof. You have thousands of people down there, with just two doors five miles apart, the air is going to get pretty thin.'

'Not to mention they'll be walking right into a fenced-in area,' Hector said. 'Vivian. The fence around the generators. We need to bring them down.'

'I'll inform the cops, and if they're too slow, we may have enough of our people to help out,' Vivian said.

'Let's move,' Wyatt said to the guards. 'I'll start funneling people towards the Grifter's Gulch access tunnel. Get security in each section to open the access tunnels and start leading people underground.'

'On it,' the guards said, running off.

'At some point,' Aly said, 'someone is going to need to do a much better job of explaining to me just what the hell is going on and why I'm wearing a hospital gown.'

'I will,' Cassie said, as another explosion rocked the complex. 'But now's really not the time. Do you trust me?'

Aly looked off in the distance, fear in her eyes, and nodded. 'I do.'

Cassie felt something inside of her chest tear. She looked at the girl, teetering, but strong. Stronger than Cassie would have thought. Maybe stronger than Cassie had ever been.

I always wished I'd gotten the chance. Maybe this is that chance.

'OK,' Cassie said. She took a bottle of Brain Fertilizer from her backpack and gave it to Aly. 'Drink this. It tastes horrible but should help a bit.' Aly downed it in two gulps, grimacing.

'I think I can walk,' she said.

'You sure?' Hector said.

'Let me try.' He put her down. She wobbled but stayed up. 'I'm OK.'

'Head towards the tunnel,' Wyatt said. 'I need to take care of some unfinished business.'

'Where are you going?'

Wyatt pointed at the Bundy Building. 'Woolman isn't walking out of here without answering for all of this.'

Cassie took his arm. Wyatt looked at it, his face softening.

'Thank you,' she said.

'I don't deserve thanks,' he said with a sad smile.

'No, you don't. Not yet. So go get that asshole. Make Tonya proud of you.'

Wyatt laughed. 'You're something, Ms. West.'

'I'll see you on the outside, Maurice.'

Wyatt smiled, then ran off.

There was another explosion, this one louder than the rest, and close enough that Cassie could feel the rumble beneath her feet.

'Let's go,' Cassie said. They ran towards the access tunnel, Cassie keeping pace with Aly. Cassie turned back once, only once. She could see flames reflected off the perfect steel walls of the R&D building, orange and red tendrils dancing in the night sky. The building itself stood unblemished. Lake built it to withstand this. To protect what he had inside.

'Come on,' Hector said. 'We're not safe.'

'Goodbye, Harris,' Cassie said, whispering the words she never thought she would get to say.

THIRTY-SEVEN

12:16 a.m.
Sixteen minutes post-launch

Aly ran slowly, but her balance seemed to get better with every stride. Fires raged throughout the park. The explosions at the gates had quickly burned through the trees and lawns, creeping up the attractions and buildings, the wood crackling around them, flaming dollar bills with the visage of Bernie Madoff and Ivan Boesky floating through the air like red and green fireflies, masks of criminals and killers melting into puddles on the asphalt.

A few petrified stragglers had joined up with Hector, Cassie, and Aly, but thousands were simply running around screaming, shouting into phones or just curling up on the ground, sobbing. Cassie saw a man, his jacket on fire, leap into the wave pool. A man stood over a woman on the ground, beating flames out of her smoking hair with a Past Crimes gift bag. Broken Earth+ visors were scattered all over the park. Guards herded hundreds towards the access tunnels. Cassie just prayed the other sections were doing the same.

ACMs began to zoom overhead, water pouring from their bladders. Every time a fire went out, more seemed to ignite in their place.

At that moment, six guards ran up to their group. One of them said, 'Jim Mullins, park security. Maurice Wyatt told us to find you. What can we do?'

'Make sure all the access tunnels are open,' she said. 'And start funneling people inside.'

'You got it,' Mullins said. He said to the other guards, 'Use your flares. Create a path.'

The guards nodded and ran off. Mullins walked with Cassie, Hector and Aly to the Grifter's Gulch access tunnel. Dozens of people were frantic outside, parents huddling with their children and praying.

'What's going on?' Mullins asked one woman.

'We can't get in,' she wailed.

Mullins placed his hand on the door, but nothing happened. 'It's supposed to perform a retinal scan. Somebody shut down the security system. The door is locked.'

'Woolman is trapping everybody inside,' Cassie said. 'Hector, use the—'

'Way ahead of you,' Hector said. 'Everyone, step back.'

He took the Devil's Fingernail out and began to cut. The door frame smoked as he sliced through the metal. When he finished, Hector took a step back and kicked the door. It fell inward with a heavy thud. He pressed his earpiece.

'Viv,' Hector said. 'Access tunnels might be locked on your end. You'll need to cut through them.'

'On it. The whole park is on fire. Please, baby, get the hell out of there.'

Mullins took half a dozen flares from a pouch on his jacket and ignited them. The red sparks burst forth, and he laid them in a row leading towards the now-open door. He then lit several more and tossed them into the pitch-black access tunnel.

'This way!' Cassie shouted. The crowd began to head towards the flares, cautious at first, but faster once they realized it was a sanctuary from the apocalypse around them.

Down the street, Cassie saw the ten-foot-tall statue of John Wayne Gacy dressed as Pogo the Clown engulfed in flames. Through the fire, she could still make out the garish purple smile and periwinkle blue triangles around its eyes, even as the paint began to peel off the monument like burning skin.

She saw a boy of no more than eight wearing a Past Crimes T-shirt, tears streaming down his cheeks as he clutched his mother's arm, while their father, clad in a T-shirt with the police sketch of the Zodiac Killer, recorded everything on his phone. Cassie ran to the mother and pointed her in the direction of the access tunnel. The boy looked back at her with a glimmer of recognition as they ran into the darkness.

Hundreds marched into the access tunnel, like some great migration to escape from a mythical hellscape. More and more ACMs filled the air. Cassie had no idea how many. Dozens? Hundreds? Water poured from the sky as though showerheads had suddenly turned on in the Utah sky. If Aly was suffering ill effects from the anesthetic, she wasn't showing it. She ran up to every person, every family she could see in the smoky haze, leading them towards safety. Cassie stopped for a moment and watched. Even though this girl was not her own, was not her family, she felt a swell of pride that nearly overcame her.

Helicopters hovered in the air, dropping stretchers and carrying away the injured and elderly. Cassie heard a boom and expected to see another wall of flame shoot into the air, but instead a police battering ram burst through the park wall, ambulances and fire engines following behind.

Through the haze, Cassie could see the Bundy Building looming in the distance. The lights in the tower were still on. She took out her binoculars and zoomed in on the windows. Just the other day, she had looked out over the park with a sense of awe and grandeur. The view had been spectacular. Now, it was horrifying.

She saw movement in one of the windows. She zoomed in. Her breath caught in her chest. Two men stood at the window: Stephen Woolman and Crispin Lake. They were side by side, watching the park burn. Lake looked so real. Then a figure appeared behind them. Maurice Wyatt.

Wyatt moved towards Woolman. Woolman turned around to face him. Wyatt said something. Woolman responded. Wyatt held a gun in one hand and handcuffs in the other. Woolman seemed to be unarmed. But he did not move. Wyatt moved closer, gesturing at Woolman's hands. Woolman did not move. Cassie got a bad feeling as she watched. Wyatt took another step towards Woolman. He aimed the gun at Woolman's head and held out the handcuffs.

And then, without warning, the top half of the Bundy Building exploded, the structure disappearing in a cloud of smoke and fire. Glass and metal and debris rained from the sky. Where Woolman, Lake and Wyatt had stood was now nothing but billowing black smoke and orange flame. The concussive blast blew through the park, knocking several people down, including Aly. Cassie helped her to her feet, then looked back up at the devastation.

'Wyatt . . .' Cassie said.

Hector grabbed Cassie's arm and said, 'We gotta move!'

'Wyatt and Woolman. They were in the Bundy Building.'

'Good riddance to Woolman,' Hector said, 'but we have to go.'

'Cassie, *come on*! Aly shouted.

Cassie took Aly's hand and they followed the crowed into the access tunnel. Cassie expected the tunnel to be pitch-black, nothing but darkness for miles. But when they got into the tunnel, they saw something astonishing.

Hundreds . . . no *thousands* of people were holding their phones out with their flashlights on. The entire tunnel was illuminated. People were carrying injured visitors and scared children towards the exit. People were calm. Orderly.

Cassie took a bottle from her bag and gave it to Aly. Aly took a large gulp, then handed it to a woman carrying a terrified little girl. The woman thanked her and helped her daughter drink. The girl looked at Aly and smiled. She squeezed Aly's hand.

'We're going to be OK,' Cassie said.

'I can't reach Vivian,' Hector said. 'I hope they've opened the far end and cleared the fences.'

'I have faith in her,' Cassie said.

'I do too.'

Suddenly, Aly fell to her knees. She began to cough. Cassie knelt beside her. Sweat poured down the girl's face. They'd pushed her too hard. She still hadn't recovered. Cassie took a towel from her bag and wiped Aly's forehead.

'She needs a doctor,' Cassie said.

'I got her,' Hector said. He picked Aly up, draping her legs across one arm and her back on the other. She rested her head on his shoulder.

'I'm OK,' she said wearily. 'Just tired.'

'You're the bravest kid I've ever met,' Cassie said. Aly managed a smile.

'You haven't met too many kids.'

'No, I haven't. But I bet it'd still be true if I met a million.'

They kept walking, slower now. Cassie could feel her head beginning to throb.

'You don't look so hot, Cassie,' Hector said. 'Not sure I can carry you both.'

'I'll be OK,' she said. 'Just a little further.'

She prayed that was true.

'Cassie,' Aly said weakly.

'What is it?'

Aly pointed behind them, into the tunnel where just they'd come from. 'Isn't that . . .'

Cassie turned around. Narrowed her eyes. There were hundreds of people marching through the tunnel.

'There,' Aly said, pointing to a man hunched over, walking slowly, a Past Crimes hat pulled low, shielding his face. 'Isn't that . . .'

Then the man's face came into view.

'It's him,' Cassie said. 'Woolman.'

Hector turned around. He saw Woolman. Hiding among the survivors of his own disaster.

'He killed Wyatt,' Cassie said, 'and was going to let me take the fall for all of this.'

'The hell he is,' Hector said. 'Take her.'

Hector gently put Aly in Cassie's arms, then marched off towards Woolman.

'Hey!' he shouted. 'Hey, you! Stop!'

Cassie followed him. 'Hector, be careful. You don't know what he—'

Before she could utter another word, Cassie saw a glint of light, a reflection off of a piece of metal. It happened so fast that Cassie couldn't even tell what had happened at first. Then she saw Hector fall to his knees, blood spurting from his neck.

'Hector!' she cried, running to the fallen man, Aly still in her arms. Hector held his hand to his flesh, red seeping from between his fingers. She put Aly on the ground and tore open Hector's backpack. She found a cloth and pressed it to the side of his neck. Within seconds, red had soaked through the fabric.

She pressed her earpiece. 'Vivian. *Vivian!* Goddamnit, it's jammed. Hector, can you hear me?'

He nodded, but his eyes were wide with pain and far. He whispered two words: 'Get. Woolman.'

Aly put her hand to Hector's neck, held the cloth in place, looked at Cassie and said, 'I got this.'

Hector put his hand on Aly's, trying to staunch the flow of blood. *Go*, he mouthed.

Cassie grabbed the backpack, stood up and swiveled around. There were so many people. She waded through the throng of survivors, examining faces, looking for Woolman. Then, about fifty feet away, she saw him. He walked slowly, shuffling along, trying not to draw attention to himself.

Cassie jogged toward him, slowly. She reached into the backpack and took out the EMP gun. As soon as she was five feet away, she raised it, preparing to swing, when she caught the flash of metal. She stumbled back as the knife passed through the air, and Cassie felt a searing heat on her abdomen. Immediately, a thin line of red began to seep through her shirt.

Woolman swung the knife again, but there was enough distance between them for Cassie to step backwards and let it sail through the air. She then brought the EMP gun down as hard as she could, cracking it squarely in the space between Woolman's ear and chin.

Woolman fell to his knees. Cassie raised the gun again for another swing. But before she could, Woolman sprang up and drove his shoulders into her midsection, hurling her backwards on to the hard floor of the tunnel and landing on top of her.

Cassie couldn't breathe. Her head spun. Everything seemed to be moving in slow motion. She blinked rapidly. Woolman kneeled above her. Blood seeped from a deep cut on his face. He held a knife in one hand and the EMP gun in the other. He was breathing heavily. Cassie looked to her right and saw her backpack splayed open. It was just close enough for her to reach.

She could hear voices surrounding them. *That's Cassandra West! And isn't that the guy who works with Crispin Lake? Oh my God, she's trying to kill him!*

Her hand fumbled inside the backpack, searching for what she prayed was still inside. Woolman brought the knife up, directly above Cassie's neck.

'You never should have come back,' Woolman said.

Cassie's hand closed around the device. She brought it up and placed it against Woolman's chest, right where she estimated his heart would be, and said, 'You never should have fucked with my husband.'

Then Cassie pressed the trigger.

Nothing happened. A terrifying fear swept through her. *He's an AP too. Both of them are.*

Then she felt it. Something on her face. She touched her cheek with her hand. It came away with specks of dirt. Woolman still hovered above her, but his eyes were wide, shocked. A trickle of blood leaked from his lips. Cassie shoved Woolman and he fell to the ground.

A wisp of smoke wafted up from a small hole in Woolman's

chest. Right where Cassie had pointed the Devil's Fingernail. Its beam had cut all the way through Woolman, all the way to the ceiling. He lay there, a perfect, neat, circular hole in his chest.

Cassie leaned in close. Woolman's breathing slowed. She waited until he took his last breath, and then she began to cry.

THIRTY-EIGHT

1:34 a.m.
One hour and thirty-four minutes post-launch

Medical teams poured into the tunnel. Cassie and Aly stayed with the unconscious Hector until EMTs found them and loaded him on to a gurney. When they got to the exit, Vivian was waiting for them. When she saw him, she cried out and ran to Hector's prone body.

'Babe, can you hear me? Hector, *please* say something!'

'He's lost a lot of blood, ma'am,' the EMT said. Spotlight drones hovered over the generator enclosure. Dozens of emergency vehicles had surrounded the flattened gates and were attending to survivors. A cacophony of tears and screams echoed in the night.

They loaded Hector on to a stretcher, which was then hoisted on to a waiting MediCopter, its blades kicking up dirt before flying out into the flame-tinged darkness. Vivian watched, tears streaming down her cheeks. Cassie took her hand.

'He's going to be OK,' she said. Vivian looked at her.

'How do you know?'

'Because I have hope. And somebody told me that hope is a compass.'

Vivian squeezed her hand and nodded. 'Are *you* OK?'

'Honestly? Not really.'

An EMT hooked Aly up to an IV. She winced as the needle found her vein. Cassie took a blanket and draped it over her shoulders.

'So what now?' Aly asked.

Cassie thought for a moment, then said, 'I don't know. But I promise you'll never set foot in the TAP Foundation again.'

Aly smiled and leaned her head against Cassie's arm. She shivered slightly. Cassie put her arm around Aly and rubbed her shoulders.

'Thanks,' Cassie said.

'For what?'

'Saving my life,' Cassie said.

Aly laughed. 'I think you have smoke inhalation. You're the one who got me out of that kid prison *and* the insane murder carnival that's currently on fire.'

'We'll call it even,' Cassie said.

Vivian came over to Cassie and Aly and sat down. She looked up at the sky, filled with smoke and ACMs and drones.

'So,' Vivian said, 'there never was a Crispin Lake.'

'No,' Cassie replied, 'there never was a Stephen Woolman.'

THIRTY-NINE

One month post-launch

Aly stirred in bed. Cassie had promised she would stop watching her sleep. Aly had woken up one night and informed Cassie that it was super weird. She was right. But it had been so long since Cassie cared about anyone's safety other than her own (and even that was modest care at best). It would take time for her to get used to it.

Earlier that night, Cassie and Aly had been firmly ensconced in a pretty awesome Earth+ game called 'Wretched Gargoyles' in which you played a wretched gargoyle (duh) whose job was to fly around over a whole bunch of eighteenth-century European villages, pillaging and looting while evading and/or chomping on villagers and evil clerics who wanted to possess you and use your wretched powers for their own nefarious purposes.

The sensation of flying around the dark-gray skies, while helpless souls fired piddly arrows at you, then swooping down and with your razor-sharp talons where you could choose between (a) biting their heads off with your wretched jaws or (b) picking them up and dropping them into a pile of red villager mush, which was far, *far* more entertaining than it had any right to be, was exhilarating.

When they finished their session – 'Not the entire game, there are like a thousand villages to scourge' Aly had said – they removed their visors and sat in silence for a moment. At first, the quiet moments between them were awkward. Tentative. Like they didn't know how to move forward given everything they'd lost. But over the last few weeks, they'd grown more comfortable with the quiet.

Cassie had never felt like she'd needed to protect Harris. He was willful, strong. She never really had a chance to protect anyone before – the opportunity had been wrenched from her ten years ago. Now, sitting next to Aly, looking at her bright, shy smile, Cassie felt like she'd been given a second chance.

'Play again tomorrow?' Cassie said. 'There's an English countryside full of unsuspecting villagers who would be a hell of a lot of fun to drop from the sky.'

Aly hesitated. Cassie felt a sinking feeling, like she was enjoying this time more than Aly was, that she was forcing Aly to placate her silly, delayed maternal instincts.

'Actually,' Aly said, 'do you mind if I play a little more tonight? Alone?'

'Alone?' Cassie said, curious. 'Do I really suck that much at being a gargoyle?'

'No, you're surprisingly good for an old person.'

'Gee. Thanks.'

'It's just . . . there's this girl. Her name is Talyn. That's not her real name, just her gargoyle name. Anyway, we started chatting last week during a multi-gargoyle siege of Rome, and she asked if I was free tonight to sack Paris with her.'

'So . . . you have a date. A gargoyle date.'

Aly's face turned bright red. 'It's just a siege.'

'That's how it starts,' Cassie said. 'One second you're laying siege to Paris, the next you're making each other mix tapes.'

'What's a mix tape?' Aly said.

'Maybe I am old. Do you know for sure this girl Talyn is who she says she is?' She had visions of Woolman flash through her mind. Aly nodded vigorously.

'She's sixteen and lives in Omaha,' Aly said. 'Her real name is Cristin Zhen. Trust me, I don't take any chances and we're both super careful. We shared user profiles and social media feeds, and everything checks out. I'm careful. She even sent me this.'

Aly pulled up a photo on her phone. It was of a teenage girl with blue and pink hair, holding up a handwritten sign that said: **Hey Aly, plunder and pillage with me? —Cristin (aka Talyn)**

The girl was smiling and adorable, and picturing her flying over the skies as a bloodthirsty gargoyle next to Aly made Cassie's heart soar.

'OK,' Cassie said. 'I do trust you. Just do me a favor and don't agree to meet in person until I've had a chance to check her out.'

'Deal, but we're just friends,' Aly said, unconvincingly.

'Tell me that after you've turned Versailles to rubble,' Cassie said. 'Just don't let your gargoyle stay up too late.'

'Cassie,' Aly said, 'don't make me say it. You're not my . . .'

'I know, I know.' Cassie paused. 'Are you OK here? I know it's not perfect, but—'

'It's great. You know you're actually a not-terrible gargoyle. For an old person.'

'That is a high compliment.'

The smile on Aly's face faded. She looked at Cassie and said, 'Can I ask you something?'

'Of course.'

'Do you ever stop missing them?'

Cassie thought for a moment, then replied, 'No. But you wouldn't want to.'

Aly nodded. 'Night, Cassie.'

'Night, Aly.'

Aly went into her room and closed the door.

Cassie could never replace what Aly had lost. All she could do was help Aly take the next, hard steps, wherever they might be. To find out what she wanted to do and who she wanted to be, to help her heal from the trauma of the last few months and, to put it simply, eviscerate anyone who stood in the way.

It was not exactly the scenario Cassie dreamed of when she and Harris met. She predicted a paved road, with stops along the way for marriage and children and life's other detours that, though difficult, made it worth living. The road she'd *actually* traveled was less like paved asphalt and more like a trough lined with cacti and burning hot coals. But at the end of it, here she was, sitting on a couch with a girl who, even though she was not by birth or blood, felt like family.

After the second Blight, dubbed 'The Murderland Inferno', which left thousands dead and reduced the Past Crimes park to rubble and ash, Cassie was finally able to say goodbye to Harris. His body was extracted from the R&D department and, ten years too late, given a proper Earth– burial.

Following testimony from Aly Miller and Salman Jalal about Stephen Woolman's role in the Blight and the fraud of Crispin Lake, Harris's name had been cleared. Mostly. There was still a contingent of conspiracy theorists who believed Cassie planned the whole thing from the start and killed both Stephen Woolman and Crispin Lake to cover her tracks. All it did was reinforce Cassie's belief that a man could commit the most heinous crimes imaginable, and there would always be those who found a way to blame a woman.

Maurice Wyatt's body was found in the wreckage of the Bundy Building. Salman Jalal gave the eulogy at his funeral. The EPP was under criminal investigation in twenty-six different countries, and the U.S. government had frozen nearly six billion dollars in Past Crimes accounts. Ten million dollars was disbursed to Cassie, the payment Crispin Lake had promised Harris. She debated taking the high road, refusing the money, but considering what had been taken from her, they were lucky she didn't go after more. She used a million of it to pay off Aly's debt from the TAP Foundation, negotiating Emmeline Procter down from one-point-five. If only Procter knew that Cassie would have paid every cent she had to get Aly out of there. Another half a million paid off her remaining Replenish debt. She had time to figure out what to do with the rest. Maybe start with a decent couch.

It took time to get used to having someone else around her small, cleaning-impaired apartment, but they were making it work. Aly spent every day from nine to three taking summer school classes in Earth+. She would be back at Westbury in the fall. At night, they ate a drone-delivered dinner and watched TV (Cassie had never been much of a cook, and this new setup required baby steps).

Aly would occasionally tell Cassie about her day, and Cassie would sit there, rapt, wishing she'd gotten to experience this kind of connection years ago. Then they would watch a movie or play an Earth+ game or just do their own thing. Aly got Cassie to appreciate old films, vintage pictures shot in lovely black and white, full of gangsters and dames, dangerous love and deadly desires, where white cigarette smoke wafted through the air like clouds. There was something peaceful about the monochrome, something simple. And then they would say goodnight and go to their separate rooms. Aly still had nightmares, and when she did, Cassie would sprint to her bed, take her hand, tell her the dreams were nothing more than realistic sims, sometimes frightening but never real.

And even though the complex in West Valley City had burned to the ground, Past Crimes lived on. Earth+ estimates placed the number of hours spent by visitors inside the Blight sim in its first month alone at over thirty-four *billion*, with twenty million new subscribers signing up. Upon using the sim, visitors found a Disclaimer, stating that the contents of the sim, specifically the West family's role in the Blights, could not be verified, and that the simulation should be considered entertainment rather than fact. Some listened. Many didn't.

The Found led an outspoken group of protestors demanding that Past Crimes servers be shut down, that the company's simulations be pulled from Earth+, with the company's billions in frozen assets disbursed among victims and charitable organizations. Their requests were uniformly dismissed by Past Crimes creditors. When there was that much money at stake, decency and philanthropy went out the window.

Cassie was about to fall asleep when her cell phone vibrated. A text from Salman Jalal.

Got a few minutes? It's important. – SJ

The message contained an Earth+ Lockbox code. Cassie put her visor back on and entered the code into her EPD.

She appeared in a small office. Salman Jalal sat on the other side of a desk. He smiled warmly when he saw her.

'How are you, Cassie?' he said.

'I'm OK,' she said. 'You look good. Or your Wrap does.'

'My Wrap has lost five pounds. Gotta keep up appearances now that I need more clients than just Crispin Lake.'

'So what's up?'

Jalal turned serious. 'I wanted you to hear it from me before the media picks it up. V.I.C.E. is planning to acquire all of Past Crimes' assets.'

'What does that mean?'

'They would own all sims and source codes, all unsold Theia inventory, all research and data, merchandise, unique Wrap configurations and all the land previously owned by Past Crimes.

Generators, server farms, warehouses, everything. Any research acquired would be limited to that which was obtained legally, of course. Anything they obtained from Harris or Aly or Drayden Downs is considered unlawful and is now property of the EPP.'

'The same EPP that's under investigation and stole my husband's body?' she said. 'That doesn't make me feel any better.'

'Nor me. But V.I.C.E. believes the Past Crimes brand is still very, very valuable. Past Crimes subscriptions skyrocketed after Murderland burned down.

'There's always money to be made off a catastrophe,' Cassie said. 'Lake proved that and then some with the Blight.'

'That was money,' Jalal said. 'This is *money*. My sources place the sale price at nine-point-six billion.'

'Jesus,' Cassie said. 'The bigger the catastrophe, the bigger the payout.'

'Not only that, but I've heard from insiders at V.I.C.E. that they've already begun reaching out to survivors of the second Blight. Lake, er, Woolman had begun preproduction on a new simulation. The second Blight. The Murderland Inferno. V.I.C.E. has already started licensing the thousands of recordings from inside the park that night. Obviously, you will *not* be the Vertex Ignis in this simulation, and if they make even the smallest insinuation, they'll be served with a lawsuit for more than the entire annual revenue of Earth+.'

'Let me guess. To debut on July nineteenth, 2057, the tenth anniversary of the *second* Blight.'

'You might have a future in marketing. V.I.C.E. has already submitted permits to build a new park in West Valley – with the technology capable of realizing Woolman's dream of merging Earth+ and Earth–, and populated by APs of the most famous criminals in history.

'Woolman couldn't do that in Murderland,' Cassie said. 'Everything inside was obsolete. He needed to start over.'

'Are you familiar with the concept of slash and burn?' Jalal asked.

'Something to do with farming, right?'

'That's where it originated. It's a technique where farmers cut down all the growth and vegetation in a given area – trees, shrubs, vegetation – then burn the detritus. The ash from the fires then creates nutrients which enrich the soil, allowing for the planting of new crops.'

'So the second Blight was Woolman's version of slash and burn.

Destroy the old complex, then build the most technologically advanced park in history on its ashes.'

'I think Woolman planned everything, except for his death.'

'There's just one problem,' Cassie said. 'Crispin Lake *was* Past Crimes. He was the frontman Woolman knew he needed but couldn't be himself. I don't see V.I.C.E. duplicating its success without him.'

'Crispin Lake was nothing but an exceedingly elaborate code. That code still exists. And soon V.I.C.E. will own it.'

'What are you saying?'

'Well, to put it bluntly,' Jalal said, 'who says they have to do it *without* Crispin Lake?'

'I want nothing to do with any of it,' Cassie said. 'I have my life back. Harris's name is his again. I just want to live.'

'Figured you'd say that. If anyone approaches me to get to you, I'll unleash the hounds. And by hounds, I mean my unparalleled legal prowess.'

'Thanks, Salman. I owe you.'

'You owe me nothing.'

'I still feel kind of bad about the whole "giving you an intramuscular injection causing you to lose all function and mobility in your limbs" thing.'

'And I will bring that up the next time I need a referral.'

'Deal.'

They both stood up. Jalal came around the desk. He reached out to shake her hand. Instead, she drew him in for a brief hug.

'Talk to you soon,' Jalal said. 'Stay well. Take care of the girl.'

'Doing my best.'

Cassie left the Lockbox and removed her visor. She sat there in her apartment. Silent. Unsure of what tomorrow would bring.

For ten years, Cassie had a single-minded goal. Clear Harris's name. Find the truth. She'd done both. For the first time in a decade, Cassie felt as though there could be a life out there for her. She didn't quite know what that was yet, but hope was a compass, and she was confident it wouldn't lead her astray.

She saw a soft blue light on her visor. A reminder. She smiled. Until she found her direction, at least she had a home.

Cassie placed the visor over her face and opened the Lockbox link.

The world faded to black. A melody surrounded her, cutting through the darkness. Cassie recognized it immediately. She sang along.

Amazing grace, How sweet the sound
That saved a wretch like me.
I once was lost, but now am found,
Was blind, but now I see.

When the verse ended, Cassie found herself standing in the now-familiar barn. Dozens of Wraps stood in a circle, holding hands. Young and old and everything in between, from every walk of life. When they saw her, they smiled and waved. She saw Hector Ruiz and Vivian Adair standing across the circle. They walked over to Cassie.

'May I?' Cassie asked. Vivian nodded. She touched the growing swell of Vivian's abdomen gently, marveling at how real it felt. 'I can't wait to meet her . . him?'

'We want to be surprised,' Hector said. He had duplicated the thick scar that ran nearly from his earlobe to his collarbone on his Wrap. They brought Cassie in for an embrace and held her tight.

Cassie looked around the circle. By this point, she recognized many of the Wraps. Several were new. And even though she did not know their names or their stories, she knew their sorrow. Several stepped into the center, just as she had. They told their names. Their stories. Their losses and their pain. And one by one they received an embrace, just as Cassie had.

When the introductions were finished, Vivian said, 'Now close your eyes. Listen to this moment. Together with your family but alone with your thoughts.'

Cassie did. She heard her own breathing, replicated inside the virtual world. For ten years, she had believed peace was not a possibility. Now she not only believed it but felt it.

Suddenly, Cassie heard a sound. Footsteps. She opened her eyes. Everyone else's were still closed. Had she been the only one to hear them?

Then Cassie saw movement. Outside of the circle, by the entrance to the barn. A figure stood just beyond the threshold, cloaked in shadow.

The figure had the build of a man, tall and lean, his face and features shrouded in the darkness. He had not been there just moments ago. He made no effort to move. No effort to join the group. He merely stood there. The man had somehow gotten into this Lockbox with the purpose of not only watching Cassie but making sure she knew she was being watched.

Her heart thumped in her chest. She let go of Hector and Vivian's hands and walked towards the entrance, trying to make out the man's face. She took another step. And another. She felt a chill at the nape of her neck. For a moment, she could have sworn the man smiled.

And then, just like that, he was gone.

ACKNOWLEDGMENTS

Every author has a moment in their career where they write a book that is both completely unlike anything they've ever written before, and so daunting in terms of its story and characters and what you want it to say that it feels like a mountain that climbs endlessly into the sky. This was that book for me, but thanks to the support of some incredible people I was not only able to climb that mountain, but for this book to coalesce better than I ever thought possible.

The first thanks must go to my agents, Amy Tannenbaum and Jessica Errera, who worked with me tirelessly on this book, read as many drafts and iterations as I did, and without whose invaluable advice and determination this book would not have been published.

My enduring thank you to the fantastic team at Severn House who saw the promise in this manuscript. Especially Rachel Slatter, my fantastic editor, and Martin Brown, both of whom championed this book since the moment it was acquired. I'm proud to be publishing this book with you.

Katherine Laidler, who did a pristine job copyediting this book (and who caught, among many other things, that I mistakenly had Cassie removing an IV from her arm . . . two paragraphs after the IV had already been removed from her arm). Copyeditors are the unsung heroes of publishing and we owe them all our thanks and a huge party in their honor.

To my family: Dana, Ava, and Lyla. Being outnumbered by a house full of amazing girls is the best thing to ever happen to me.

And to the readers and booksellers and librarians who have advocated for me and my books for years now, my gratitude is endless.

Lastly, this book is dedicated to the victims and their families whose tragedies have been spun into gold by others.